KAYLON BRUNER TRAN

Darkness and Light Intertwined

Book 3 of the Agent Orange Trilogy

To All Vietnam War-Era Veterans

Welcome Home

Preface

The stories of Chi, Linh, Augie, and Mark are works of fiction, but their stories were inspired by historical events as well as the autobiographies of those directly impacted by the American war in Vietnam. Although a direct relationship between Agent Orange/dioxin exposures and generational adverse health effects is difficult to definitively prove, the scenarios presented within these pages are supported by peer-reviewed scientific data. For more information, please explore the references listed within the appendix. I have made every attempt to maintain historical and scientific accuracy; however, any mistakes are mine alone and were unintentional.

Characters, Real/Historical Persons, Abbreviations

Major Characters *(Alphabetical by first name)*
  Alessi "Augie" Augustini (grandfather of Alessi Adams)
  Ashley England (girlfriend of Jeremy Dordi)
  Chi Anh Ong (mother of Linh; mother of Misty Borkowski)
  Dennis Dordi (U.S. Special Forces; father of Jeremy)
  Elizabeth Johnson/Higgins/Parker (Mark's mother)
  Jeremy Dordi, MD (son of Linh and Dennis Dordi)
  JB Borkowski (Chi's husband)
  Linh (daughter of Chi and unnamed French soldier)
  Mark "Junior" Higgins (son of Elizabeth; friend of Augie's)
  Melinda Tackett/Barker (Adopted daughter of Grace and John Tackett)
  Misty Borkowski (daughter of Chi and JB)

Real American Vietnam Veterans, included with permission:
  Ken Gamble (Founder of the Orange Heart Memorial Foundation)
  Bobby Tyner (Board member, Orange Heart Memorial Foundation)

Minor Characters appearing in multiple chapters *(Alphabetical by first or last name as used in text)*
  Alessi Adams (granddaughter of Augie; patient of Jeremy Dordi)
  Alex Barker (son of Melinda and Zach)
  Anthony Parker (USMC, ret; Second husband of Elizabeth)
  Bob England (Ashley's father)
  Charlie (derogatory nickname for VC or NVA soldiers)

Chris Barker (son of Melinda and Zach)

Eden Dordi (wife of Lucas Dordi)

Emily Martin (friend of Ashley's)

Eric (owns a construction company in San Francisco, often employs Dordi)

Evelyn England (Ashley's mother)

Grace Tacket (Melinda's adoptive mother)

James "Jimbo" Higgins (first husband of Elizabeth; Father of Mark)

Jerry (friend of Mark's)

John Tackett (Melinda's adoptive father)

Jonathan "JB" Borkowski (Chi's husband; Misty's father)

Juanita (Army nurse; friend of Linh's)

Julie Ryder (U.S. Air Force, friend of Chi)

Kevin (son of Loc Tin and Lucy)

Kim-Ly (friend of Linh's)

Lap (VC comrade of Chi)

Li Minh (prostitute at Yankee's Dream, friend of Linh's)

Lisa Pham (cousin of Emily)

Loc Tin "LT" Vong (ARVN veteran, friend of Dordi)

Lucas Dordi (Dennis and Linh Dordi's oldest son)

Lue Sien "Lucy" Vong (wife of Loc Tin, friend of Linh)

Mark Kennedy (fictitious Army Captain that betrayed Chi)

Major Collins (Augie's commanding officer)

Michelle Dordi (mother of Dennis Dordi)

Mr. Johnson (father of Elizabeth)

Mr. Ong (Nam Vinh Ong; Chi's uncle; brother to Viet; Owner of Yankee's Dream)

My-Le (friend of Linh's at Orphan Island)

Paul (Misty's boyfriend/husband)

Penny Augustini (wife of Augie Augustini; grandmother of Alessi Adams)

Risa (Cracker Barrel waitress)

Rob McMasters (Australian Army; friend of Chi)

Sara Augustini/Adams (daughter of Augie and Penny, mother of Alessi Adams)

Song #1 (Prostitute/homeless child that took Linh in)

Song #2 (Daughter of Linh; changed to Melinda after she was adopted)

Tam (Viet Cong, daughter of Trinh)

Teo (Linh's adopted son, Orphan Island)

Trinh (Viet Cong, friend of Chi)

Viet Thinh Ong (Chi's father; brother to Nam)

Vivian (friend and colleague of Jeremy; friend of Ashley's)

Zach Barker (husband of Melinda)

Historical Figures

Ngo Dinh Diem, President of South Vietnam, assassinated in 1963

Anne Frank, author of Diary of Anne Frank, murdered by Nazis in 1945

John F. Kennedy, President of the United States, assassinated in 1963

Ho Chi Minh, President of North Vietnam, 1945-1965 (died of natural causes in 1969)

Richard M. Nixon, President of the United States, 1969-1974

Franklin D. Roosevelt, President of the United States 1933-1945

Harry S Truman, President of the United States, 1945-1953

Abbreviations:

ARVN, Army of the Republic of Vietnam (South Vietnam)

CBI, California Bureau of Investigation

CICU, Cardiac Intensive Care Unit

DA, district attorney

DNA, Deoxyribonucleic acid (hereditary genetic material)

IED, Improvised Explosive Device

km, kilometer (1 km = 0.62 miles)

MSU, Mississippi State University

NVA, North Vietnamese Army

PCR, polymerase chain reaction (a method for copying DNA)

PTSD, Post Traumatic Stress Disorder

R&R, Rest and Relaxation

SFG, Special Forces Group (U.S.)

USMC, United States Marine Corps.

UCSD, University of California, San Diego

UCSF, University of California, San Francisco

WAFC, Women's Armed Forces Corps (South Vietnam)

VA, Veteran's Administration

VC, Viet Cong

VFW, Veterans of Foreign Wars

Chapter 1

Rural Vietnam, 1954
  Chi and Family

Chi Anh Ong was inconsolable. Her father, Viet, had left with her baby and would not be bringing her home. Chi's mother tried to comfort her. "Your father will leave Linh with an orphanage. They will love her and care for her. She'll be adopted and grow up healthy and happy." The woman sat on the bed beside her sobbing child and brushed the hair from her eyes. "We cannot keep her. You know that."

Chi was only 16 when she had fallen in love with a French soldier. He had promised to marry her and take her home with him, but he had lied. He quickly abandoned her when she told him she was pregnant. Chi's father had been furious. It was bad enough that she had gotten pregnant, but after the baby was born, it was obvious the child was not pure Vietnamese. The color of her skin was quite unusual. Not white, not black, not yellow.

Chi's father was horrified. "A *dark-skinned* Frenchman?" he yelled. "What were you thinking?"

"I loved him," Chi wailed. "I—I thought he loved me." She took a ragged breath. "He told me he loved me."

"This child has no future here," Viet told his daughter.

Chi knew her father was right. Mixed-race people had no rights in Vietnam. Only pure Vietnamese were allowed to attend school or hold a job. Chi didn't care. She told her parents, "I will protect her and take care of her."

For the next six months, Chi rarely left home. She and her mother doted on the baby, and Chi had begun to think her father had accepted Linh. She was wrong.

One night as Chi played on the floor with her daughter, her father told her, "It's time for Linh to go. She cannot stay here any longer."

Chi crossed her arms and looked up at him. "No," she said. Chi knew defying him was unacceptable, but what choice did she have? She would not give up her baby.

"I will take her to the orphanage in DaNang. They will find her another family."

Chi jumped up. "No!" she screamed.

Viet pointed at the baby and said sternly, "She will make your life extremely difficult."

"I don't care," Chi screamed again, making the baby cry. Chi picked up Linh and held her close. "I will never give her up!" She turned away from him and ran from the room.

Viet was shocked at Chi's outburst and defiance. He shook his head and told his wife, "Linh's presence is changing her. The baby must go. I will not let her destroy Chi's future."

Later that night when Chi and Linh were asleep, Viet gently took the child from her mother. He told his wife, "I'm taking the baby to the orphanage in DaNang." Chi's mother tried to dissuade him, but Viet's mind was made up. "The child is better off at an orphanage. They will find her a home."

Two hours later, Chi awoke and discovered Linh was missing. She knew immediately her father had taken her.

"She NEEDS me! She is just a baby!! MY baby!!" Chi pleaded with her mother to tell her where her father had taken Linh.

"I'm sorry, Chi, but this is how it has to be."

Viet Thinh Ong had every intention of leaving six-month-old Linh at an orphanage. He had ridden his motorbike, baby strapped to his chest, to DaNang and found Saint Mary's House of Hope Orphanage, but the door was locked and no one answered. He knew the nuns were there, but perhaps because it was the middle of the night, they ignored his banging. He had taken the child while Chi slept. Otherwise, she would again have tried to talk him out of it. He was not a heartless man, and he loved his daughter. However, he simply could not allow Chi to be saddled with this child who was destined to have a difficult life and, by extension, would make life hard for Chi. It was better this way, he told himself. But no one answered his knocking. Frustrated, he turned away and headed back to his bike. He decided he would wait until sunrise and then knock again. Viet had just settled in to wait when he noticed a teenage girl approaching him.

"Hey, mister, are you looking for a good time?" the girl asked. Although she smiled at him, there was no joy in it and her voice held no enthusiasm.

He looked at the girl. She was very thin and wore a dirty, ragged dress. Her feet were bare. She was a street child—no doubt abandoned by her family for being something other than pure Vietnamese. She was offering her body to him in exchange for money or food.

He shook his head and turned away. Then he had an idea. He turned back to her and asked, "Where do you live?"

She gave him another sad smile, thinking he had changed his mind. She pointed and said, "We have a camp just over there. I have my own tent. We will have privacy." She grabbed his hand and tried to pull him toward the camp where she and several dozen other orphans lived.

He removed his hand from hers. "No, thank you. But—uhm—I can bring you food and money if you will take my daughter's baby. Her name is Linh." He removed the sleeping child from the sling on his chest.

Without hesitation, the teen took the baby and held her close. "Where is her mother?"

"Dead," Chi's father lied. "She died in childbirth. My wife is sick, and we cannot take care of the baby any longer. I was trying to leave her with the orphanage," he said, waving his hand toward the building, "but they won't take her."

The girl frowned but nodded. "I will take care of her." She knew all too well the risks this little girl would face. Khanh had taken her in when she had been abandoned by her own family, and now she would take this child.

It was a vicious and seemingly never-ending cycle.

Viet gave her what little money he had with him and thanked her. He promised to return soon with rice and vegetables from his farm.

She nodded, doubtful that she would ever see the man again.

Chapter 2

Norfolk, Virginia, March 1954
  Elizabeth Johnson

It should have been a good day. It was her son Mark's second birthday, and Elizabeth had wanted to have a party. She didn't want anything too big. She just wanted to invite a couple of kids from the neighborhood and her parents, but her father said no. He always said no.

Three years ago when she had just finished her junior year of high school, she made a huge mistake. Elizabeth's boyfriend, Jimbo Higgins, had graduated a year early and would start college that August. He joined the Naval ROTC as a way to pay his tuition and planned to join the Navy when he graduated. The Korean War was only a year old, and although Jimbo had been too young to enlist or be drafted, he told Elizabeth they might call him up anyway since he would already be in the service. They were young and foolish, and she was terrified that Jimbo could be killed in the war. She thought she loved him. Elizabeth learned she was pregnant only a few weeks after Jimbo left for college. He proposed as soon as he found out, but her father refused to grant his permission. The day he came to ask for her hand, Mr. Johnson wouldn't even let Elizabeth see him. She heard everything, though, as she stood on the landing of the stairs just around the corner from the front door.

In 1951 America being an unwed mother was unthinkable and shameful. Jimbo did not want her to suffer such humiliation because of him. "Please let me do right by her," Jimbo begged. Elizabeth dared to peek around the corner. She saw Jimbo pleading with her father and she felt awful for him. He was so much shorter than her dad, and as he looked up at him, he looked like a child asking for permission to go out and play.

"No. How could you possibly provide for her? You have already demonstrated that you are irresponsible."

"You're wrong, sir," he had said in his most grown-up voice, but Mr. Johnson was unmoved and quickly ushered him out. Soon Elizabeth was forced to drop out of high school and rarely left their home until after Mark was born in March of 1952. Jimbo visited them in the hospital, but Mr. Johnson made it clear he was not welcome at their home. For that reason, whenever he could get away from school, they would meet in a park near the Johnson home. Every time he left Elizabeth and Mark, he promised he would never abandon them.

Elizabeth kept hoping her father would soften towards Jimbo and their son, but he hadn't. Last week when she asked to have a small birthday party for Mark with a few other children, he said no. When she asked if Jimbo could at least come to the house for a birthday dinner, he said no. Instead, she and Mark sat in her bedroom with her mother and tried to make the best of it. Her mother had presents and had baked a small cake, and she didn't care when Mark made a mess of it. Elizabeth was grateful for her mother, but the day was nothing like the one she had wanted to have for her son.

Chapter 3

DaNang, Vietnam, July 1954
   Viet Thinh Ong

A week after leaving Linh with the teenage girl, Viet returned to the orphanage where he had first tried to leave the baby. He wanted to find the homeless camp as well as the girl. He brought with him a large bag of rice, dried fish, and vegetables from his garden. Although he didn't know exactly where the homeless camp was, the girl had indicated it was to the north when they were standing in front of the orphanage. He parked his motorbike, gathered the bags of food he had brought, and headed in the direction she had indicated. About 100 feet or so from the orphanage, the trees became very dense, but he could easily make out the well-worn trail that wound its way through the woods. He followed the trail another 200 feet and found a large circular area that contained no trees or grass, just bare dirt beaten into hard earth from years of use by an unending sea of homeless children.

He stood on the edge of the clearing taking in the sight before him. There were a few tents haphazardly arranged along the perimeter of the clearing. Several lean-tos fashioned from canvas tarps discarded by or perhaps stolen from the French army were clustered together between two dead trees. In the center of the camp was a small firepit. Two girls in their early teens were tending a pot and stirring whatever was inside. Dozens of children of all ages occupied the camp. Some were sleeping on blankets out in the open, while many others were sitting around a massive pile of—something. It almost looked like garbage. The children were sifting through it, and occasionally one would squeal with delight at something they had found. As he watched, two teenage boys walked over to the pile and emptied the bags that they carried. Now he understood. The two older boys had been outside the camp scavenging whatever they could find. Those in the camp would sift through the boys' bounty for something useful. He heard a young girl cry out happily as she pulled out a pair of sandals and put them on her bare feet. They were too big, but she managed to keep them on as she pranced around the camp.

Chi's father looked more closely at the children. All were dirty and painfully thin. The weight of what he had done to his only grandchild suddenly hit him. Yes, Linh would have had a difficult life with Chi, but certainly it would have been better than this. He briefly considered taking the child back, but if he did, Chi would have no chance of finding a husband and having a normal life. No. Viet was certain he had done the right thing by his daughter. He would just need to check on Linh occasionally and make sure she had what she needed. He promised himself he would do that. He owed it to his daughter. Viet looked around for Linh and the girl, suddenly realizing he didn't even know her name. He walked into the camp and began searching for the two of them. Several of the younger children saw him, clearly wary of the stranger, but he didn't notice. He only wanted to find Linh and the girl. He remembered that she said she had a tent and walked to the one closest to him. A teenage boy sat on a wooden box in front of it—almost as though he were guarding the entrance. Viet spoke to him.

"I'm looking for a girl, maybe 16. She has a baby with her."

The boy was holding a stick and sharpening its end to a point with a knife. He looked up when the man spoke. "Lots of girls have babies."

Viet shook his head. "It isn't her baby. It's my grandchild. I asked the girl to take her last week." He held up the bags. "I brought food."

"Oh, you mean Song." The boy nodded. "She isn't here. I think she took the baby to the river for a bath. She'll be gone a while." He eyed the bags the man carried but didn't try to take them.

Viet frowned and looked around the camp. He wanted to give the food to the girl. He also wanted to see Linh. Tentatively, as though he was afraid of the answer, he asked the boy, "How is my grandchild?"

The boy shrugged. "Song will take care of her."

Viet started to speak again when suddenly the flap that served as the tent door was flung open and a man much older than himself stepped out looking flushed. He handed money to the boy, glanced at Viet, and quickly left. The boy closed the tent flap as he pocketed the money. He looked back at Chi's father. "I can give Song the food."

"I'd rather give her these myself. I want to make sure she gets them, and I need to know Linh is okay." He heard a girl's voice and turned toward it, hoping it was Song. It wasn't. At least now he knew her name, he thought. Finally, Viet turned back to the boy and held up the bags. "You'll make sure she gets the supplies?"

"I will," he said, grasping the handles of the bags, but the man didn't let go. The boy dropped his hands to his sides and shrugged. "Up to you, but Song won't be back for a few hours."

Viet sighed. He wanted to see Linh. He just needed to know the girl was taking care of her, but he couldn't wait around all day. Finally he nodded and said, "Please tell her they are from me. And thank her."

The boy smiled. "Sure thing, mister." He took the bags and watched as the man walked away. When he disappeared into the woods, the boy ducked his head into the tent. "Hey, Song. You had a visitor. Linh's grandpa brought food." He held up the bags.

Song was already dressed and had just picked up Linh. "I heard you talking to him. I was so afraid Linh would cry," she said, looking at the infant. "But she didn't." Song smiled at the baby and held her close. Then she said in a sing-song voice, "Who's a good baby?" and blew bubbles on her tummy making Linh giggle.

"Do you suppose he wanted the baby back?" he asked her.

Song sighed, "He probably feels guilty, but no. His daughter is dead and his wife is sick. What choice did he have? I just hope he will keep bringing us food."

Chapter 4

Norfolk, Virginia, May–October 1955
  Higgins Family

After Mr. Johnson rejected his initial proposal of marriage to Elizabeth, Jimbo was determined to prove he could take care of her and their child. Over the next four years, he worked hard and saved every dime he could. He finished college in May of 1955 and immediately enlisted in the Navy. By then the war in Korea was over, and Ensign Higgins was stationed at Joint Base Langley-Eustis only a few miles from Norfolk, Virginia, and the Johnson home. Langley-Eustis was a huge facility that housed multiple branches of the U.S. military, and Jimbo was ecstatic that he would start his training there. Mark had turned three in March, but, once again, Jimbo had missed his birthday. It pained him that his son was growing up without him. Now that he was so close and employed by the Navy, the time was right to propose again. When he was finally granted a few days leave, he put on his perfectly pressed dress uniform and planned what he would say to Mr. Johnson.

He looked at himself in the mirror and rehearsed the words. "Mr. Johnson, sir, I, Ensign Jimbo Higgins..." No. He shook his head and looked back at his reflection. He stared at himself for a moment. Then he stood up tall and said, "Mr. Johnson, sir, I, Ensign *James* Higgins, respectfully request your daughter's hand in marriage." Yes, that's better. It was time he dropped the childish nickname Jimbo. He looked in the mirror again. *James* would not take no for an answer.

It was a beautiful Sunday afternoon as James drove to the Johnson home. He parked in front and walked up to the door and started to knock, but then he put his hand back down. He took a deep breath and tried to calm his nerves. He had been told he was not welcome here, but he knew he had to confront Mr. Johnson in this place if he was ever to be with his family. Again, he silently rehearsed what he would say. When he finally knocked on the door, he only had to wait a moment before Mr. Johnson himself opened it. The two men stood eye to eye and, inwardly, James smiled to himself. He had grown quite a bit over the last four years and was now perhaps an inch taller than Elizabeth's father. It felt good. It felt *right*.

"Sir, I, Ensign James Higgins, have come to again request the honor of marrying your daughter." The words came out strong and confident—even better than when he had practiced. The inward smile grew wider.

The man looked him up and down. Then he turned away from him. "Elizabeth!" he barked.

A few months later, in October of 1955, James Higgins married Elizabeth Johnson in a small, private ceremony in the backyard of her parents' home. Their three-year-old son, Mark, was the ringbearer. Although James knew it wasn't the wedding Elizabeth had dreamed of as a child, he was determined to make her and Mark happy.

After the wedding, James had to return to the base while Elizabeth and Mark continued living with her parents. Although James never felt truly welcome at the Johnson home, at least now he was allowed to visit when his training allowed. The more time he spent at the Johnson home, the more anxious he became to make other arrangements for his family.

"I know your father thinks I am being ungrateful to him for letting you stay here, but he is too hard on Mark," James complained to Elizabeth.

"He has very high expectations of everyone."

"Expecting a toddler to be 'seen and not heard' is an impossible standard. I also don't like the way he constantly denigrates your mother. I don't want Mark learning that behavior."

Elizabeth nodded. "He's had a difficult life, but he does love us. He just has trouble showing it sometimes."

Chapter 5

Cam Ranh Bay, Vietnam, August–October 1955
  Ong brothers and Song

For more than a year Chi's father continued to take Song and Linh food and other supplies, but he was very distressed at the pitiful conditions of the homeless camp. He wanted to get Linh away from there. But how? He mulled the question over and over in his mind before he settled on an idea. His twin brother owned a bar in Cam Ranh Bay, the Frenchie's Dream. Cam Ranh Bay was a beautiful spot on the beaches of the South China Sea and was a favorite place for soldiers when they had a few days off for rest and relaxation, commonly known as R&R. Important to Viet's plan, the Frenchie's Dream was not just a bar but also a brothel. His brother, Nam Vinh Ong, prided himself with how well he took care of "his girls." They each had a small bedroom, and he gave them food and shelter in exchange for most of their earnings.

Cam Ranh Bay was a full day's drive from DaNang, but Viet was confident he could borrow his neighbor's car. His plan was to take Song and Linh to his brother's place. Song was a prostitute working out of a filthy tent. He felt the Frenchie's Dream would be a big step up for her. He also worried that Chi and Song would somehow cross paths. Moving her to Cam Ranh Bay would pretty much guarantee that would never happen. The more he thought about his plan, the more he liked it. Viet convinced himself that this arrangement would help both Song and Linh and it eased the guilt he felt over taking the child from Chi. He called his brother and asked if he had room for Song and Linh. As luck would have it, he had just kicked out one of his girls because she "got herself pregnant."

Viet felt a twinge of anxiety. What would happen to Linh if Song became pregnant? Still, being homeless in Cam Ranh Bay would probably be better than it was in DaNang. His brother readily agreed to accept Song but was reluctant to have a baby at his business. However, Linh was his brother's grandchild, and in the end Nam agreed.

Once the arrangements were made, Viet returned to the homeless camp and looked around. The camp was a miserable place to live any time of the year, but now that it was monsoon season it was far worse. The entire camp was muddy, and the firepit they used for cooking was filled with water. He found Song's tent and saw that it was completely saturated. All the better for his plan, he thought.

Viet stood outside the tent and called out, "Song? Hello. Are you in there?"

The flap opened and Song leaned out. "Yes. We're here. Come on in."

He crawled through the door of the tent and looked around for somewhere dry to sit. There was a wooden crate that Song had used for a crib when Linh was smaller, but now it had been flipped over and served as a chair. She offered it to him.

"Ah—no. I won't stay long." He told her of his plan to move her to Cam Ranh Bay.

"He'll take both of us? And give us a room? Inside a building?"

Viet nodded. As he had hoped, Song jumped at the chance to leave the camp and have a real home. He looked around the tent and felt wretched for putting Linh in this place. It was uncomfortably hot and stuffy, and the mold was spreading quickly because of the excessive humidity. The living conditions these children endured was far worse than anything he could have imagined. The Frenchie's Dream would be better. Moving *anywhere* would be better than this, Viet thought. He made Song promise not to tell anyone where she was going. He wanted there to be no chance that Chi would ever find Linh. The girl reluctantly agreed.

Less than a week later in October of 1955, Viet Ong drove Song and Linh to his brother's place in Cam Ranh Bay. When they arrived, he was surprised to see the name of the bar had changed from the Frenchie's Dream to the Yankee's Dream. He asked his brother why, and Nam explained, "The French are out. Now it's the Americans." He shrugged. "Better than having to call it the Commie's Dream."

Chapter 6

Norfolk, Virginia, March 1956
  Higgins Family

Six months after James and Elizabeth were married, he was finally able to secure family housing on the base. Although their new apartment was tiny compared to the spacious, two-story home Elizabeth had grown up in, he was determined to take care of his family without depending on Mr. Johnson.

"I promise it is temporary," he told Elizabeth after they had crammed their few belongings into the small, one-bedroom apartment. "It was the only one they had available. There's a park nearby. And we are on the waiting list for a bigger place."

"I know," she responded, forcing a smile. Although she was happy to be out from under her father's strict control, she was unsure about living on the base. Mark adored his grandmother, and he and Elizabeth would both miss her terribly. Elizabeth knew no one at Langley-Eustis and didn't have a car. She would be stuck in this tiny apartment with its outdated style and lack of windows. She knew it would be even worse when James was gone for long stretches of time because he was deployed. James was a good man and she loved him, but she often wondered what her life might have been like if she had not been so foolish before he left for college. Of course, she said none of this to James.

Chapter 7

DaNang, Vietnam, June 1956
   Chi and Trinh

Chi laid on the floor and stared at the ceiling. It had been nearly two years since her father had taken her baby away. Linh would be walking and talking by now, and Chi's heart ached. At first she had begged and pleaded with him to bring her baby home, but he had refused. She had fallen into a deep depression, and on Linh's first birthday she nearly took her own life. She had ridden her bicycle to the heart of DaNang and stood on the bridge that spanned the Han River. She hoped the fall would be enough to kill her, but she would let herself drown if it didn't. Just before she jumped, she closed her eyes. She had not wanted to see the water rushing up to meet her. However, in the moment before she jumped, her mind flashed images of Linh before her eyes, and she changed her mind. She would not give up. She would find her baby.

She grabbed her bike, which had been carelessly abandoned at the base of the bridge, and immediately began her quest. For nearly a year, as often as she could, she had ridden her bike to DaNang. Chi visited every orphanage she could find but always returned home disappointed and without Linh. Nevertheless, her mission to find her daughter renewed her spirit and gave her hope. Her parents saw her mood lift and her appetite return and mistakenly thought she had accepted the loss of Linh. They pretended everything was normal and never spoke of their grandchild. Chi's mother actively began trying to find her a husband. She seemed to think Chi would readily accept an arranged marriage, but she was wrong. She did not understand that Chi would never give up the search for Linh.

Everything changed when Chi met Trinh. She was an older woman selling fruits and vegetables at an open-air market in DaNang. Chi had just left the last orphanage in the city and was slowly walking her bike past the market. Although she had been gone all day and had forgotten to pack a lunch, she was not anxious to go home. Chi looked longingly at the woman's produce as she passed by. The woman called to her, smiling, and held up a mango.

Chi shook her head and responded, "No money."

The woman frowned and set the fruit down. She looked directly at Chi and seemed to make a decision. She waved Chi over. The woman offered her a small, slightly bruised apple, which she gratefully accepted. The woman chatted as Chi nibbled the apple. The woman introduced herself. Her name was Trinh, and she was a widow with two young children at home. Chi was surprised. The woman looked too old to have small children, but she didn't want to be rude, so she said nothing.

Trinh told Chi, "I've seen you riding your bike back and forth a lot the past few weeks. Do you work or go to school nearby?"

Chi explained what she was doing and why. She told Trinh that she had visited every orphanage that she could find without success. Next she had tried the Catholic churches thinking that maybe he had left her with one of them. "When I first started looking for her, my biggest fear was that when I found the right orphanage, they would tell me she had been adopted." Tears streamed down Chi's face and her voice quivered as she continued, "But no one has ever heard of her! I don't know where she is!" Chi wiped her eyes on her sleeve, took a deep breath, and tried somewhat successfully to hide her anger and fear. A little more calmly, she said, "I don't know what to do next. I can't give up."

Trinh responded with a suggestion. "There are several homeless camps in the city. Abandoned children tend to band together and will take in others that they find wandering the streets alone."

Chi shook her head. "Oh, no! My father promised me he took Linh to an orphanage!"

"What would he have done if the orphanage was full?"

Chi stared at her blankly. She had never considered that an orphanage would refuse to accept a child but now realized it must happen sometimes. Chi was horrified at the possibility that her beautiful baby girl was living in a dirty little tent city without the barest essentials like electricity or clean water. Would her father really have done that?

Over the next few weeks, Trinh led Chi to the homeless camps that she had seen in DaNang as well as a few just outside the city. Finally in a camp near one of the first orphanages that Chi had visited, she learned that a young girl had been approached by a man more than a year before. He told her his daughter had died and he was unable to care for her baby. For months the man brought her food and supplies, but then the girl and the baby disappeared. No one knew where she had gone. She didn't tell anyone she was leaving, but she had not been seen in a long time. The man who had given her the baby had also not returned. Everyone assumed they were together, but they didn't really know.

When a teenage boy told Chi that the baby's name was Linh, Chi was completely overcome by anger and frustration and began sobbing uncontrollably. She now felt as though she would never find her baby and the ache in her heart was so great she thought she would die from the pain. Trinh put an arm around her but knew there was little she could say that would bring her comfort.

As Chi slowly began to accept that she might never find Linh, she also began to fully comprehend the magnitude of her father's betrayal. He had not only betrayed her by taking Linh, but he had lied to her about where she was. He had assured her that she was in an orphanage run by Catholic nuns and that they were certain Linh would be adopted quickly. He told her that Linh would have a better life than what she could have in Vietnam and that Chi was selfish to try and prevent her from having that life. She had desperately wanted to believe her father was right and that Linh would be happy. Now she knew the truth, and she was angrier than ever. As they walked away from the homeless camp, she told Trinh, "I will never go home. I never want to see my father again."

The older woman took Chi by the hand. "Come home with me then, and you can decide what to do next." Trinh led her to a small village outside the bustling city of DaNang. A dozen tiny, primitive houses were clustered together amidst the trees. The houses were nothing like the modern, spacious home with its neat little yard where Chi had grown up, but she didn't care. Anywhere that her father wasn't was fine by her.

Trinh opened the door and motioned Chi inside. The dilapidated wooden structure that she called home had a thatched roof and only three rooms. Trinh made them tea, and they sat at her small kitchen table. Soon two young children who were perhaps six or seven years old appeared at Trinh's side. The woman gave them each an apple and told them to go outside. She then turned her attention back to Chi. Although she sincerely wanted to help the young woman, Trinh's interest in Chi was not purely as a friend. Trinh's goal was to recruit Chi for the resistance.

Chapter 8

Vietnam, Prelude to War
  Ho Chi Minh

Decades of French colonialism followed by Japanese occupation during World War II had devastating effects on the country of Vietnam and its citizenry. During the Japanese occupation, Ho Chi Minh formed the Indochinese Communist Party. He and his followers, known as the Viet Minh, had a singular focus of eliminating all occupying forces from Vietnam. During World War II, the U.S. military intelligence agency briefly formed an alliance with Ho Chi Minh because Franklin D. Roosevelt, the U.S. president, also backed the idea of an independent Vietnam. The U.S. provided much-needed aid to the effort, and, in exchange, the Viet Minh harassed Japanese troops and helped to rescue American pilots who had been shot down.

In 1945 after the war ended with Japan on the losing side, the French attempted to regain control of Vietnam, Laos, and Cambodia. This attempt was met by violent resistance from the Viet Minh. Although Ho Chi Minh had been trained in Moscow as a communist, his message to unify Vietnam and establish its sovereignty appealed to nearly all of the country's citizens, from peasants who were struggling under heavy taxes and poor economic conditions to wealthy, French-educated intellectuals. Ho Chi Minh traveled to France and spent months trying to negotiate Vietnam's independence. His efforts failed. Despite their previous opposition to a return of French rule in Vietnam, the United States began subsidizing the efforts of the French. The newly elected president of the U.S., President Truman, was convinced that defeating the Viet Minh was necessary to prevent the spread of communism in Southeast Asia. The failure of diplomacy quickly led to an all-out war between the U.S.-backed French in South Vietnam and the North Vietnamese who were supported by both China and the Soviet Union. However, despite the monetary assistance from the U.S., the French were defeated in 1954 bringing the first Indochina War to a close.

Ho Chi Minh's defeat of the French led to an agreement that would temporarily divide Vietnam into North and South along the geographical coordinate located at the 17th parallel. This agreement, known as the Geneva Accord, was largely designed to appease the U.S. and Soviet Union, each of whom continued to have a political interest in the future of Vietnam. Ho Chi Minh reluctantly accepted the agreement, which included a promise that an election would be held in 1956 that would unify the country under one leader. In the meantime, he and his Viet Minh guerrilla soldiers controlled North Vietnam, while South Vietnam was led by Ngo Dinh Diem. President Diem was initially supported by the Americans, as they mistakenly believed he would maintain democracy in Vietnam.

Chapter 9

Rural Vietnam, July 1956
  Trinh and Chi

After realizing that her father had lied to her and given Linh to a homeless teenager, Chi moved in with Trinh and gradually learned her story. During World War I, Trinh's father had been sent to the Western front to fight on behalf of the French. He was killed, leaving his wife and four children struggling to survive. As the oldest, Trinh had married at a young age to make it easier for her mother to care for the rest of her siblings. Trinh's difficult upbringing led her to despise the French, and she encouraged her husband to join the Viet Minh and fight against them for Vietnam's independence. Unfortunately, Trinh's husband had not lived to see the victory over France. He had died in 1951 in a battle in the Red River Delta.

Trinh's only child, a daughter named Tam, had also joined the resistance. At first she was simply a spy. As a young girl, she could easily go unnoticed while collecting information on French troop movements and activity. She fed this information to her father and his men. Eventually she married a man, also Viet Minh, whom her father had chosen for her. Marriage did not dissuade her from her undercover activities, and she learned from her husband how to shoot a variety of weaponry and set booby traps. Although Trinh was supportive of her daughter fighting with the Viet Minh, she encouraged Tam to come home after her second child was born. She did not. Ultimately she left her children for her mother to raise and would visit them whenever she could. Tam was determined her children would grow up in an independent Vietnam. Tam and Trinh's arrangement was not unusual. Over the course of the first and eventually second Indochina War, thousands of women would join the fight for Vietnam's independence often leaving their children to be cared for by others.

In 1954 after the country had been divided, Trinh found herself on the wrong side of the 17th parallel. She told Chi, "I agree with Ho Chi Minh. We need one Vietnam, not two. I don't trust President Diem."

Although Chi felt she and Trinh were becoming friends, it still surprised her when the woman openly admitted that she not only disliked Diem but that she supported Ho Chi Minh. Chi's parents were also concerned that President Diem was interested more in his own power than with the reunification of Vietnam; however, these were concerns to be expressed quietly at home and not to strangers. In January of 1956, six months before Chi and Trinh met, President Diem released Ordinance Number 6 which decreed that anyone expressing support for Ho Chi Minh would be imprisoned.

Trinh continued, "Your Frenchman—he wronged you in the worst way. The Americans will be no better. Ho Chi Minh will drive out these foreigners and reunite North and South Vietnam."

Chi wasn't sure what to say but did agree that she was tired of foreign occupation. The young woman shrugged. "What can we do?"

"For now, we wait. If the elections are held, Ho Chi Minh will win and the Americans will be forced to leave. If Diem does not live up to the Geneva agreement, then we will act. The Viet Minh will not stand idly by and let the Americans take over for the French." She slammed her hand on the table. "We will fight!"

The women talked long into the night, and Trinh painted a noble vision of Ho Chi Minh and his effort to rid Vietnam of occupiers and warmongers. She told Chi she could be part of the resistance and the reunification of Vietnam.

"How can I be of any use? I am just a young girl," Chi asked.

"We are the ones who buy and sell. You see me as a street vendor, but I have eyes and ears. I watch and I listen. The French soldiers ignored me and spoke freely. They thought I didn't understand their language, but I know enough. During the war, like Tam, I fed important information to the Viet Minh. If war with the Americans comes, I will do the same. You can too."

Now Chi lay on the bed that Trinh had prepared for her on the dirt floor thinking about everything that had happened and what the older woman had told her. Chi said aloud, "I will never go home, and I will never stop looking for Linh." She closed her eyes and wondered, "Will helping the Viet Minh help me find Linh?" Probably not, she decided. At least ridding Vietnam of foreign soldiers would prevent more young girls from falling victim to their lies and having mixed-race babies who would have no future. Chi fervently hoped that the elections would go forward. She was not a soldier and didn't want to become one. On the other hand, her anger with her parents and hatred of the French soldier she had once loved had hardened her, and she easily began to despise the Americans. She made up her mind to do whatever was necessary to save her country and the many Vietnamese women who might also be victimized by foreigners. Chi vowed that she would fight for Linh and others like her. She would do her part to finally unify Vietnam. That night for the first time since losing Linh, Chi slept soundly.

Chapter 10

Vietnam, 1956-1957
  The Final Prelude to War

As many had feared, the elections to reunify Vietnam were not held. Diem, the president of South Vietnam, had simply refused to participate. In response, the Soviet Union put forth a proposal to permanently divide the country into North and South Vietnam. The U.S. refused to recognize Ho Chi Minh's communist government and rejected the proposal. The impasse led the governments of both North and South Vietnam to begin a brutal crackdown of anyone suspected of working for or supporting the other side. In South Vietnam, President Diem began executing supporters of Ho Chi Minh. In response, Ho Chi Minh's guerrilla soldiers, known at the Viet Minh, initiated a widespread campaign of terror against Diem's government. Over the next two years, many were left imprisoned or dead on both sides of the 17th parallel.

Chapter 11

Norfolk, Virginia, 1957
   Higgins Family

James knew that Elizabeth was miserable on the base. He thought she would make friends with the other wives, but she really hadn't. He wanted her to be happy, and in 1957, after the pay raise that came with being promoted to lieutenant junior grade, they started looking at houses in the area. With the help of his parents, who were by no means well off, they were able to make the down payment on a house in an up-and-coming subdivision called Eagle's Nest. The split-level home was one of the smallest in Eagle's Nest, but it was theirs. James' hard work had paid off again. The subdivision, located in Norfolk, was near both of their parents' homes and was only a few miles from Joint Base Langley-Eustis. James knew he would often be deployed and would eventually be posted elsewhere. He wanted to buy a house in Eagle's Nest so his wife and son would have a permanent home close to their extended families.

Moving day was a family affair with James' brother, father, and even his father-in-law pitching in. They carried boxes and hand-me-down furniture into the house while Elizabeth tried to rein in Mark.

"Which room is mine, Mommy?" he asked as he ran circles on the porch. He held a toy plane high in the air as if it were flying.

"Your room is upstairs right next to ours," Elizabeth laughed and told him for the hundredth time. She asked him excitedly, "Do you want to go see it?" She took his hand and the two went inside.

"It's so big!!" he said as he began running circles in the empty room. Mark, now five, would have a space of his own for the first time in his young life.

Chapter 12

Vietnam, 1959-1962

War

Ho Chi Minh, North Vietnam's president, officially declared war on the South in March of 1959. The Second Indochina War, which in the U.S. would come to be known as the Vietnam War, had begun. In preparation for the coming battles, construction of Highway 559, later called the Ho Chi Minh Trail, began. The purpose of the road was to allow the North Vietnamese Army (NVA) to move troops, food, and supplies to the South. Over time the trail would become quite extensive and complex, but initially it was only a primitive footpath along Vietnam's western border through Laos and parts of Cambodia that connected Hanoi, the capital of North Vietnam, to areas in South Vietnam. Much of the trail ran through rugged mountains or dense jungle. Throughout the war, construction and maintenance of the trail was the responsibility of youth volunteers, many of them teenagers.

Meanwhile in South Vietnam President Diem's popularity, which was never good, was further eroded when he ignored concerns of his military leaders. They pointed to corruption within Diem's administration and his lack of popular support among the people. Instead of listening to his military advisors, he shut down opposition newspapers by arresting journalists and outspoken critics. In 1960 a failed coup against Diem led by South Vietnamese army officers resulted in a vicious response by the president. Thousands of people deemed "enemies of the state" were arrested, tortured, and executed.An equally large number of people who feared being arrested and killed fled to North Vietnam, many of whom would later return to the South as members of Ho Chi Minh's People's Liberation Armed Forces, more commonly known as the Viet Cong. These guerrilla soldiers, many of them women, eventually replaced the Viet Minh as the underground force fighting the U.S. and other Westerners on behalf of North Vietnam. Because many had been born in the South, which had slight cultural and language intonation differences than those in the North, they were easily able to blend in with the South Vietnamese.

Chapter 13

Cam Ranh Bay 1962

   Linh

Eight-year-old Linh was outside behind the Yankee's Dream washing sheets in a large tub of soapy water. She knelt on the hard earth and scrubbed the fabric trying to remove a stain. Linh had worked at the Yankee's Dream for as long as she could remember. As a toddler, it was her job to crawl on the floor of the bar after it closed looking for anything of value. On a typical day she would find a few half-burned cigarettes whose tobacco could be salvaged and some dropped coins. On rare occasions she had found paper money that had fallen from a drunk patron. She had a small bucket that Song would place around her neck, and she would deposit anything that looked promising into it as she crawled along. As she got a little older, she was relegated to the kitchen where she was taught to sort vegetables and wash dishes. When she was tall enough to reach the stove without standing on a box she began doing more of the cooking. These days she also did all the laundry. During business hours, she had to stay out of sight of the customers and was not allowed near the bar or the working girls like Song.

Mr. Ong was not kind to her. He told her, "I have no use for mixed-race trash if they can't entertain the paying customers."

Song was popular with the G.I.s, and so Mr. Ong treated her reasonably well. His attitude toward Linh was markedly different, and he never hid his distaste for the young girl. He complained about her constantly and frequently yelled at her. If she didn't do something exactly right, he would punish her severely. Linh grew to be fearful of the man and avoided him as much as possible.

Linh had finally gotten the courage to ask Song the question she had been thinking about for a while. She had begun to suspect that Song was not her real mother. Or maybe it was just a hope. If Song wasn't her mother, then maybe someday her real mom would come back for her. But after talking to Song last night, Linh knew now that would never happen.

Late the previous evening, after Song had finished working, they were snuggled together in bed. Instead of asking Song for a story, Linh had said, "I know you are not my mother."

"How do you know that?" Song asked, surprised. "I have always taken care of you," Song said matter-of-factly without any sign of anger.

"If you were my mother, I wouldn't call you by your first name."

Song laughed. "I guess that was a mistake on my part." She sat up and grew serious. "I suppose you are old enough now to know what happened. At least I can tell you what I know. It isn't much."

Now Linh sat up and looked at Song expectantly. Song took a deep breath and told her about the man on the motorbike. "He said your mom had died and that your grandmother was very sick. He knew he could not take care of you and tried to leave you at an orphanage. I don't know why, but they wouldn't take you. He didn't know what to do, so he gave you to me."

"My family didn't want me?" Linh asked softly.

"Oh, no! Your grandfather loved you very much. He just couldn't take care of you. I promised him that I would. At the time, I was living in a homeless camp with many other orphans. He moved us here because he thought it would be better for you."

"Mr. Ong is mean," Linh pouted.

"I don't think your grandfather knew that," Song said as she brushed the hair from Linh's face. She had often regretted moving them to Cam Ranh Bay but wasn't going to say that to Linh. "I know you don't like Mr. Ong, but it is better than being homeless."

Linh just nodded, disappointed that no one would ever come and take her away from Mr. Ong.

Chapter 14

DaNang, Vietnam, 1962-1964
   Chi

Living in DaNang, Trinh and Chi were in an ideal location to aid guerrilla soldiers traveling south. The Viet Cong preferred to travel at night, so occasionally they would hide them in their home during the day. Tam's children would play outside while Chi hung clothes to dry or tended the garden. If the Americans ever suspected the rundown wooden house that belonged to Widow Trinh was harboring enemy soldiers, they never investigated. Chi was glad they were doing something to help Ho Chi Minh and the reunification cause, but she wanted to do more. She began learning English, hoping she could be a spy like Trinh and Tam had been during the war with the French.

Chi was excited one evening when the VC guerrillas they were hiding were both female. They were on their way back North after carrying out a surprise attack on one of the American bases.

"Just the two of you?" Chi had asked, completely enthralled by these women.

"No. There were eight of us," one of the women had responded. "We don't travel together. Two women alone are not so suspicious."

"Oh," Chi nodded. She wanted to ask them more questions, but she was embarrassed. Finally she asked, "How did you become soldiers?"

The older girl shrugged. "It wasn't really a decision. My whole village was bombed by the Americans. My family was killed. I don't know how

I survived, but I did. When I crawled out of the rubble and saw there was nothing left of my home—my family...” Her voice trailed off and she looked away for a moment. The pain was evident on her face. Finally she looked back at Chi. “I picked up my father’s shotgun and joined Ho Chi Minh. I have been fighting ever since.”

The other girl nodded. “She’s a crack shot. We often put her on sniper duty. We will hole up somewhere just outside an American base, and she’ll take a couple of men out. While they scramble to figure out who is shooting, we set off the rockets. We slip out again before the smoke clears.”

Chi was fascinated by these women, both of whom were younger than she was. These women inspired her and made her determined to become part of Ho Chi Minh’s army. She was willing to do whatever was needed to rid Vietnam of its occupiers. Every time Trinh’s daughter, Tam, returned to DaNang to see her children, Chi would beg, “Please, let me go with you.”

Finally, Tam agreed.

Chapter 15

Cam Ranh Bay, Vietnam, 1964

   Linh

Linh, now 10 years old, didn't know what to do. Song was dead and she was no longer welcome at the Yankee's Dream. Linh knew there was a homeless camp near the farmer's market because sometimes Song would take them food, but she had never let Linh go with her. After Linh was forced to leave the Yankee's Dream, she had wandered the streets near the farmer's market hoping to find the camp. But after nearly two days with little water and no food, she still had not found the camp and was growing desperate.

She had spent the night under a bridge near the farmer's market trying to hide herself from whatever dangers there might be. She was too afraid to sleep and spent much of the night reliving the last few days in her mind. Song had been grievously injured when she had been hit by a Jeep driven by an American G.I. who had just left the Yankee's Dream. He was drunk and had forgotten to turn on the headlights. He had stopped to see what he hit and ran back into the bar to try and get help for Song, but she was dead by the time he returned with Mr. Ong. The G.I. apologized to Mr. Ong, but there were no repercussions for the soldier. For Linh, though, the consequences were severe. Mr. Ong let her stay the night in Song's room, but the next day she had to clean it and then leave. She was devastated. She had lost both her home and the only mother she had ever known.

Now the sun began to set on the second day after leaving the Yankee's Dream, and she still had nowhere to go. An exhausted Linh, grieving from the loss of Song and weak from hunger, slowly walked back toward the bridge.

Unknown to Linh, she was being followed. Bach had seen the girl before with the prostitute who sometimes visited the camp and brought him and the others food, although she had never brought the girl with her. Bach wondered where she was going and why she was by herself. Something seemed wrong. Finally he decided to just ask. "Hello?" he called from a distance. He added, "Aren't you a friend of Song's?" because he didn't want to frighten her, and he thought mentioning Song might put her at ease.

Startled, Linh turned toward the voice. She saw a thin teenage boy in a T-shirt and shorts standing just inside the tree line off the alleyway. "Hello?" she said, uncertainly.

He stepped into the alley a dozen feet from her. "I'm Bach. I live in the homeless camp on the other side of the creek. Song brings us food sometimes. Is she nearby?" He glanced around hopefully, though he was sure the girl was alone.

Linh burst into tears and covered her face with her hands. Between sobs she said, "She's dead."

Bach was not surprised. Prostitutes frequently died young or simply disappeared. "I'm sorry to hear that. Are you okay?"

Linh shook her head. "Mr. Ong made me leave. I have nowhere to go."

He nodded again. Even for Mr. Ong's brothel, this girl was too young. "You can stay with us." He approached her slowly and took her by the hand. "We have rice and beans. Have you eaten?"

She shook her head and allowed him to lead her across the bridge that she had slept under and into the woods. When they were a few yards away from the alley, she began to feel apprehensive. Song had constantly warned her about the many dangers that a girl could face in the city and that most men could not be trusted. Linh was about to turn and run when she saw a clearing in the woods and heard the unmistakable sound of children playing. As promised, Bach had brought her to the homeless camp Song had told her about. Linh sighed with relief but knew her life was about to get much more difficult than it had been at the Yankee's Dream.

Chapter 16

Vietnam, 1964
  Chi and Tam

Chi's first journey with Tam found her floating down a river in a sampan in the dark of night. The flat-bottom boat, powered only by the oars the women used, moved soundlessly through the water as they smuggled guns and ammunition to Viet Cong guerrillas farther south. If they were stopped by American patrols, they would pretend to be simple peasants trying to make their way home to their elderly and sickly mother. Although the munitions were reasonably well hidden in the false bottom that had been built into the vessel, a careful observer might realize the boat hung lower in the water than it should.

The true destination of the two women was one of the many tunnel systems that had been dug under South Vietnam during the French occupation. Now with the American War and their indiscriminate bombings, napalm attacks, and spraying of Agent Orange, the tunnel system was safer. Out of necessity, the system had also become far more expansive. Tunnels were used to store supplies, move individuals across the country undetected, and often as a hiding place from which to ambush U.S. soldiers. At a bend in the river that only Tam knew, they would leave the sampan and make their way to one of these tunnels, its entrance well hidden within the depths of the jungle.

Chapter 17

Norfolk, Virginia, 1965
  Mark Higgins

In 1965, when James had achieved the rank of captain, he was sent to Vietnam for his first tour. Mark, 13 at the time, missed his father more than he would admit. Throughout Mark's childhood, James was often deployed for long stretches of time. For this reason, whenever James was home, he tried to make up for his absences. He took Mark camping and taught him to fish. Mark was a pretty good baseball player, and James could easily be heard cheering from the stands whenever he was able to attend a game. Mark had said goodbye to his father more times than he could count, and it never got any easier.

Before he left, his father always said the same thing. "Take care of your mother for me."

"I will," Mark always promised.

Not surprisingly, Mark and his mother spent a great deal of time together and were very close. There was a small room, probably meant to be an office, just off the kitchen in their home. When Mark was very young, his toys filled the little room, and he would play while she cooked. He loved LEGOS, and his mother lavished praise on his elaborate creations, two of which she glued together and said she would keep forever. When he was older, the two of them would spend hours together in the little room off the kitchen putting puzzles together and talking. He could tell his mother anything, and, as far as he knew, she was always honest with him. He knew she had gotten pregnant in high school, and while he never once doubted that she loved him, he also knew his existence changed the course of her life.

She had wanted to be a teacher, but she had to drop out of high school when she became pregnant. Although she finally was able to get her General Education Diploma, college was out of the question. When he started school, she volunteered as a teacher's helper and seemed to really enjoy it. When he made the baseball team in middle school, she became the team mom and helped coordinate after-game snacks and rides to and from the games for kids whose parents couldn't be there. It seemed to him that his mother had been with him every day of his life. She was there for every event, big or small. He loved her with every fiber of his being, but it wasn't enough. He wanted his dad. He *needed* his dad. But his dad was a soldier, and the country needed him more.

As he said goodbye to his father yet again, 13-year-old Mark made a decision. He would enlist in the Navy when he turned 18. He would join his father's fleet, and they would serve their country together. Yes, he thought, that's exactly what I'll do. Then Mark remembered how his father always reminded him to take care of his mother. Well, I have friends. He decided he could ask one of them to check on her periodically and help her when she needed something. He nodded to himself, proud that he was thinking of everything. That night at dinner, he told his mother of his plans.

"I've been thinking about my future," he said after they finished the usual discussion about each other's day.

"Oh," his mother asked, trying to hide her amusement. She thought it was an odd thing to say for someone so young.

"I'd like to join the Navy after I graduate from high school. I can become an officer just like Dad. Maybe we could even be on the same ship together." Mark frowned. It sounded childish when he said it out loud.

But his mother nodded thoughtfully. Then she said, "I think you have to go to college to go in as an officer. At least that's how your dad did it."

"Oh," Mark replied, disappointed. "That's how many years after high school?"

"Most people take four years for college."

Mark quickly did the math in his head. "So it'll be nine years before I can join Dad?"

"I think so," she said, putting a hand on his shoulder. "But he'll be home again before you know it."

Mark just nodded and finished his dinner quickly so he could be excused.

Chapter 18

Cam Ranh Bay, Vietnam, 1965
   Linh and Teo

Linh had been living at the homeless camp for less than six months but had quickly come to love the freedom of coming and going as she pleased and of never having to deal with Mr. Ong. The kids had dubbed the makeshift camp "Orphan Island" because it was located on a strip of land between two creeks. They welcomed her and gladly shared what little they had. She was used to hard work and easily found things she could do to be helpful. Nevertheless, her transition from the relative comfort of the Yankee's Dream to Orphan Island wasn't without difficulty.

She still had a hard time eating from the garbage thrown out by the restaurants along the alley. Two of the boys at the camp were really good at stealing from the farmer's market, but she was too afraid of getting caught to try it. She hated begging for coins and tried to think of something else she could do. Another girl at the camp, My-Le, had a beautiful voice and could sing. Although she spoke no English, she had learned some of the songs the Americans liked. When Linh was younger and Song was still alive, she remembered seeing My-Le stand outside the Yankee's Dream and sing. The G.I.s would gather around and listen and throw her money. Mr. Ong chased her away. Now she knew that another business, the Coffee Café, invited her to sing inside. She was so popular, the Coffee Café started staying open at night. They began to serve beer and took customers away from Mr. Ong. Learning that My-Le had cut into Mr. Ong's profit made Linh happy. She had come to hate Mr. Ong.

Since Linh didn't have My-Le's talent, she tried to think of something else that she could do to help support Orphan Island. She walked along the alley, kicking a rock, thinking, and nibbling on the half-eaten apple she had found outside the Noodle Emporium, the restaurant that was next door to the Yankee's Dream. When she had finished the apple, she put the seeds and core in her pocket. She thought that she might plant them, and in a few years maybe some other orphan would have an apple tree. The thought made her smile.

She was still envisioning her apple tree when an unusual sound made her stop and look around. She heard the sound again. It was coming from the bushes along the tree line adjacent to the alley. It sounded like an injured animal, and she wasn't sure she wanted to investigate. How could she help it? What if whatever it was bit her? But the distressed cry came again, and she instinctively ran toward it. She reached the trees and looked around. "Hello?" she said, because she didn't know what else to say. Now the sound was a soft whimper, and she quickly located the source. It was coming from a large basket at the base of a tree.

Linh knelt beside the basket and slowly opened it, unsure of what she would find. Wrapped in a blue blanket inside, she found a baby. She had no idea how old the child was, but she guessed maybe six months. The little one smiled and flailed chubby arms at her. She picked the baby up, and the child clung to her and began sucking its thumb contentedly. She looked back in the basket, hoping to find a note with the baby's name. Although Linh couldn't read, there were others at the camp who could. Instead of a note, she found a small amount of fresh food, rice, and several large pieces of cotton fabric. She held the baby to her chest with one arm and picked up the basket with her other hand. She ran as quickly as possible back to camp and found My-Le in her tent.

Breathless, Linh collapsed on the canvas floor. "I found a baby!"

My-Le, who was nearly 16, looked up from her work. She was trying to patch a hole in the dress she preferred to wear while singing. "A baby?" she asked as she set her sewing down. She took the child from Linh. She wrinkled her nose. "A baby that needs a clean diaper."

"Will this work?" Linh pulled one of the cotton cloths from the basket and offered it to My-Le.

"Yes." My-Le carefully laid the baby down and pulled off the dirty diaper. She found a small scrap of fabric in her sewing basket and dipped it in the water she had been drinking. She cleaned the baby as best she could and showed Linh how to tie a fresh diaper around him. Linh told her how she had found him and both wondered how long he had been in the woods. "I don't think it could have been that long. He doesn't seem hungry," My-Le said. "No doubt he will be soon, though."

"Oh, what should we feed him?" Linh asked.

My-Le pulled rice and a mango from the basket. "We can make rice milk. The mango is soft. We can mash it up and see if he will eat it. He looks old enough." She looked back in the basket. "There are also several eggs. We can boil them and feed him the yolks mixed with rice."

Over the next few days, My-Le taught Linh how to take care of the baby. My-Le had lived in the homeless camp most of her life and had previously taken care of two other babies who had been left near Orphan Island. The first one didn't survive, but the second one did. He was now almost eight and an excellent forager.

"What have you decided to name him?" My-Le asked as she carefully watched Linh prepare rice milk.

"Teo," Linh said. "I think he looks like a Teo."

My-Le nodded and tickled the baby. "Welcome to Orphan Island, little Teo."

Chapter 19

Norfolk, Virginia, 1966-1969
  Mark Higgins

James first deployment to Vietnam lasted only a year. He came home in July of 1966, a few months after Mark turned 14. Mark's commitment to join the Navy had not waned in the previous year, and he eagerly told his father about his plan one night when his mother was out visiting her parents.

"I've been talking to one of my teachers at school. She thinks that if I take a couple of summer classes and load up during the school year, I can graduate a year early and join the Navy ROTC just like you did," he said in a rush. "After college, I can join the Navy and be an ensign and we can be stationed together." He was excited and was anxious for his father's approval. Remembering something else, he quickly added, "And I've talked to Jerry. You remember Jerry? He's going to join his dad's plumbing company after we graduate. He promised to come check on Mom. He'll help her out anytime." Finally Mark stopped talking and waited for his dad's response.

James, only recently back from the fiasco in Vietnam, was adamantly opposed to his son enlisting. He placed a hand on Mark's shoulder as he carefully considered his response. "I'm glad you are thinking about your future. While it's true that the Navy has been good to our family, it's also what has kept me away most of your life. Take your time. Enjoy school. The Navy will be there whenever you're ready, but there's no rush." He smiled at his son. "And I'm proud of you for remembering that your mother would be left by herself. Even though I'm sure Jerry is sincere, no one would take care of your mother the way you and I will."

"But I want to join the Navy," Mark said softly, trying to hide his disappointment.

"I know, Son, but for now just focus on your education. There's plenty of time for the Navy later."

It wasn't the response Mark had hoped for, but he didn't want to argue with his father. He changed the subject. "You'll be here this weekend, right? I've got a doubleheader on Saturday."

"Of course," his father replied as he squeezed his son's shoulder. "I'll be there for both games, and we can get pizza afterward."

True to his word, James was in the stands all afternoon, staying to the end even after the second game went into extra innings. After the games were over, the Higginses took Mark and two of his teammates to the Pizza Palace near the ballpark.

For nearly two full years, James was home almost every night and attended every game Mark played. When baseball season was over, James and Mark took a long weekend and went camping. It was the most time he had ever spent at home with his family, and Mark was elated.

James still had duties on the base, but whenever he was home he spent nearly every moment of his time with Mark. Although Elizabeth knew her son needed his father, she also needed her husband. It wasn't his fault that he had been gone so much of their marriage, but she still felt neglected. She had hoped they would finally be able to reconnect and renew the passion they'd had as teenagers, but it was not to be. In April of 1968, even though he was not yet 40 years old, James was promoted to Admiral. He would ship out immediately and once in Vietnam he would be given a fleet of Swift boats to command.

"When will you be back?" Mark asked his father the night he got the call from his own commanding officer.

"I'm not sure, Son. I'll be gone at least a year."

Mark just nodded. He tried hard to be stoic, but inside he was crying like he was five years old again.

April 1969 came and went with only the occasional letter from James. The war in Vietnam was escalating, and there was no end to it in sight. Early on plenty of men enlisted to fight in Southeast Asia, but as the war dragged on, the draft became the primary mechanism for the expansion of the American armed services.

The draft was supposed to be random, but everyone knew it skewed toward the poorer families. People complained, and, surprisingly, the government listened. Starting in 1969, the draft would be done by lottery. It was supposed to make the draft fairer so that the rich kids were drafted just as often as the poor kids. Birth dates would be randomly selected. If your birthday was picked early in the process, you were more likely to be drafted regardless of how much money your family had. While it was true that rich kids were more easily able to flee to Canada, anyone could get a college deferment. Of course, college wasn't always an option for the poor kids. In the end, the draft probably didn't have the intended effect of fairness.

Although his family was by no means wealthy, Mark knew college would be an option for him. His grades were good, and his mother was frugal. She had been saving for his college tuition for as long as he could remember. However, his parents had instilled in him the importance of doing your part. He felt it wouldn't be right to take the deferment. He decided that if he was drafted, he would willingly go. It was the right thing to do.

The night of the first lottery, December 29, 1969, Mark and a couple of his friends watched the live broadcast together in the Higgins' living room. Jerry, who didn't have the grades for college even if his parents had been able to afford it, was very worried about the draft. It wasn't a fear of being killed but concern for his dad's plumbing company. Jerry's parents were older, and his father's health was starting to deteriorate. Jerry was needed at home to help with the family business. Mark's other friend, Bruce, would take the deferment without hesitating. "I may be sick of school, but it beats the hell out of being shot at," he had said as they waited for the event to begin. Finally the man on TV finished his speech and introduced another man—the one who would pull the dates from the bowl. The boys sat on the couch and grew quiet. Elizabeth Higgins sat in her husband's chair off to the side anxiously watching the TV.

The man on the screen wore a dark suit and tie and looked very serious as he stuck his hand into an enormous, clear bowl filled with bright blue, plastic capsules. There were 366 of them—each bigger than a fat man's thumb. Inside each capsule was a piece of paper with a date written on it. There was one for each day of the year, including February 29th, leap day.

The first date that was called was September 14th.

Mark, Jerry, and Bruce stayed silent as each date was read and then posted to a large bulletin board behind a woman collecting the opened capsules. Of the three boys, Mark's birthday, March 17, was the first to be called. It was the 33rd date pulled out of the bowl, and everyone in the room knew Mark was likely to be drafted. Mark remained silent, but Elizabeth burst into tears. Mark stood and put an arm around her. "Don't worry, Mom. I'll be fine." She grabbed hold of him, and it was several minutes before she could let go.

Mark returned to his seat in time to hear Bruce's date, November 7, being called out. It was the 51st date on the list. According to Roger Mudd, the news anchor reporting from the scene, Bruce had about a 50/50 chance of being drafted. "Well," he said, rubbing his hands on his jeans, "looks like I'm going to college."

Jerry's eyes remained glued to the screen. With each date called, his risk of being drafted got lower and lower. After more than 100 dates had been called out without his being among them, he started breathing a little easier. Finally Jerry's birthday, February 6, was posted to the board. It was the 347th number drawn. Jerry was almost certain to be spared from the draft.

Mark got up and turned the TV off. His friends stood and stared at him awkwardly not knowing what to say. Bruce spoke first. "Take the deferment, dude. That's what I'm gonna do."

"Yeah," Jerry added. "Your parents will gladly send you to college. You're a smart guy. This war isn't worth your life."

"No. If I take the deferment, they'll just send someone else in my place. I'll go and do my part for our country. It's the right thing to do," Mark said. But then remembering Bruce's plan to go to college precisely to avoid the draft, he added, "I'm not really cut out for college the way Bruce is. I'd probably flunk out."

Bruce knew his friend was lying but appreciated him for saying it. He punched Mark in the shoulder and said, "Don't get killed. Okay?"

"That's the plan," Mark said with a grin. He wasn't worried. His dad was in Vietnam. Maybe he would see him? He didn't really know how it would all work, but he liked the idea of being in the country his father had spent so much time in these last few years. He imagined that years from now, he and his dad would sit together and tell each other stories from the war. They would both be veterans, and they would talk as equals. The thought made him happy, and he looked forward to his future.

After his friends left, Mark went looking for his mother. She had left the living room shortly after Mark's date had been called. He found her in the little room off the kitchen where the two of them had spent so much time together when he was younger. She was sitting in the leather chair his dad had bought her a few years before. She was looking at one of his sketch pads and crying.

"Hey! You'll get 'em all wet. I don't remember ever drawing a thunder-storm," he said, trying to make her laugh. He had been drawing for years and had filled dozens of sketch pads.

She closed the book and looked at him. "It doesn't seem right. They shouldn't be able to take a woman's husband AND her child."

"I haven't been drafted yet, Mom. And they won't make me go before I finish high school. The war could be over by then."

She dabbed her eyes with her handkerchief. "Maybe so. That would be good." She grabbed his hand. "It would be wonderful to have us all back together again."

Chapter 20

Vietnam, 1968-1969
  Chi

On her first journey with Tam, Chi was lost and frightened. But after nearly three years working side by side with her as a spy and weapons smuggler, 30-year-old Chi knew the jungle between Pleiku, South Vietnam, and Cambodia better than most. The two women had been in Hue in January of 1968 during the Tet Offensive, a massive nationwide attack on South Vietnam by the VC and North Vietnamese Army (NVA). Tam was part of a small crew manning an anti-aircraft gun, an S-60, that had their sights on an incoming helicopter. Tam had just reloaded the gun with a 36-pound 4 round clip when she and the rest of the crew had been gunned down by an American manning the Chinook's machine gun. After Tam fell, Chi and several others instantly took their place at the S-60 and fired at the helicopter, but it was out of range and they missed.

Late in 1968, many months after Tam's death, Chi found herself working with Brigade 559, the volunteer unit assigned to the Ho Chi Minh Trail. By then the trail had become far more complex compared to its primitive beginnings. Its length approached 1,500 miles and consisted of a complicated system of roads, waterways, and footpaths. In addition to the hundreds of miles of road, the trail now contained communications centers, ammunition dumps, and areas for troops to refuel and rest. Not surprisingly, the trail had also become a frequent target of U.S. bombing raids despite much of it being located in the supposedly neutral country of Cambodia. The young men and women who worked the trail were given S-60 guns, the same type of anti-aircraft weapons that Tam and Chi had used during the Tet Offensive. Chi was glad she could teach the others how to use the guns they had finally been provided. Despite their efforts defending against the bombings, the road was in constant need of repair. It was difficult and back-breaking work, but Chi and the others were determined to keep the road open. Injuries were common, but medical interventions were rudimentary at best and many died, either from the bombs that dropped on them or from diseases such as malaria. Food was scarce, and they learned, often by trial and fatal error, what could be eaten from the jungle.

In the spring of 1969, Chi was watching an NVA convoy pass by on the road when she heard and then saw a low-flying American plane. It was not a bomber, and she guessed the pilot was coming in for a strafing run. She dove into the jungle just as the plane's machine guns released a rain of bullets along the trail hitting many of the trucks carrying troops farther south. In the truck closest to her, she saw the driver slumped over the steering wheel. The truck, still in gear, slowly continued on. Without hesitation, Chi jumped in the cab, pushed the dead woman aside, and took control of the wheel. She had never before driven a truck but had watched others do it and quickly figured out enough to follow the vehicle in front of her. A few hours later the trucks came to a stop at an NVA camp in Southeastern Cambodia. The soldiers in the back of her truck clamored out and joined a hundred others. Some men had been injured by the machine gun fire and needed medical attention but most were unharmed. A dozen or so had died in the strafing run, including the original driver of Chi's truck. Their bodies were collected and would later be buried nearby.

Chi stood next to her truck and wondered what she should do. She saw the other drivers walking toward a large building and quickly fell in behind them. She got the attention of another woman, younger than herself, and asked, "Where's everyone going?"

The woman stopped, turned toward Chi, and pointed. "Headquarters. They will give us the next assignment. Probably driving back north." The woman scrutinized her. "You're new. I'm Yen."

Chi nodded. "I was with Brigade 559." She pointed to the truck she had just parked. "The driver was killed in that strafing run a few hours ago." She frowned. "I didn't know what else to do, so I took over."

Yen smiled at her. "That's how I ended up as a driver. It's definitely easier than filling in bomb craters." They walked side by side toward headquarters as Yen continued talking. "I keep volunteering for intelligence, but my accent gives me away as being from the north."

"I had a friend who was a spy. She sold vegetables at a market and gathered information that could be used against the French and then later the Americans. I worked with her for a while and then ended up smuggling guns with her daughter. Tam, the daughter, was killed during Tet. After that, I led a group of NVA through the jungle to Highway 559. That's how I ended up working on the trail. There was so much damage that our trucks couldn't get through." She shrugged. "I picked up a shovel."

Yen looked at her thoughtfully. "You could pass for South Vietnamese."

Chi laughed. "Because I am. I grew up in DaNang." Then she became serious. "My English could be better. Tam was teaching me. There was another girl in Brigade 559 who had learned English in school. She was teaching several of us words and phrases that we should listen for." She sighed. "I doubt I would make a very good spy without Tam."

Yen just nodded and the two women continued talking as they walked. Chi learned that they were less than 200 miles from Saigon.

As they entered the building, Yen pointed to a group of men. "Tell them what you've done. You have too much experience to work on the trail. Maybe they will send you to Saigon."

Indeed, less than a week later Chi was dressed as a prostitute walking a street on the outskirts of Saigon that was known for such things. She smiled and waved to the American soldiers. She feigned having even poorer English than she did and called out, "G.I., want boom-boom? Me give you good time!" Although the men she lured to her room with the promise of cheap sex quickly realized they had picked the wrong girl, they wouldn't live long enough to warn others of their mistake.

Chapter 21

Cam Ranh Bay, Vietnam, August 1969
Dennis Dordi and Linh

Teo had gone rogue again. Linh knew he was hungry. She had not been very successful lately in her begging. At 15, she was getting too old. The soldiers had always been kind and generous with her when she was younger, but now they looked at her with lust in their eyes. She shuddered. She did not want to become a prostitute like most of her friends. My-Le could sing, but Linh had not discovered a similar useful talent.

Linh left the homeless camp where she and more than two dozen other mixed-race and abandoned children eked out an existence. She followed the trail through the woods that led to the alleyway that served as an access to the back of the Yankee's Dream, the Noodle Emporium, and other businesses where Teo typically went to beg for food. Teo knew the Western soldiers frequented these establishments and would sometimes take pity on the child beggars, especially if the owner yelled at him or hit him. If begging was unsuccessful, he would see if there was anything edible in the trash behind the buildings.

Linh didn't dare go inside any of the businesses. Instead, she was careful to stay out of sight. She watched from a vantage point just inside the tree line adjacent to the alleyway. There was no sign of Teo behind the Yankee's Dream or the Noodle Emporium. However, Linh did see something that looked like a pile of clothes. Excitedly, she approached the pile thinking that Hung, the restaurant's owner, might have thrown out something useful.

Upon reaching what she thought was Hung's discarded clothing, she realized the "pile" was Hung himself. He was dead.

Linh frowned. She hated Hung and cared not that he was dead. But who did this? And where was Teo? Concerned for his safety, she ran back toward the tree line behind the restaurants. She stayed out of sight as she continued scanning the area around other businesses that Teo might have visited. Linh grew more and more concerned as she hurried along the path. She was debating turning around and searching in the other direction when she saw someone in the distance. Quickly, she tried to catch up to him. His back was to her, but she could tell he was carrying something. No—*someone*. A child! She tripped on a root and fell noisily to the ground.

The man in the alleyway looked behind him, but she was hidden in the trees and he couldn't see her. As he looked around for the source of the noise, she could see that the child he carried was Teo. He wasn't moving. My God, she thought. Did he kill Teo?

"I know you are there! Show yourself," the man said in something that resembled Vietnamese.

Linh debated what to do. She was afraid, but what if Teo was alive and hurt? She stayed out of sight, watching and waiting. Finally the man turned away and continued on down the alley. She stepped out of the trees just a little bit to try and get a better look at Teo. She watched the man carefully in case he turned around. Even though her eyes never left the man's back, he whipped around so quickly, he saw her as she dove for the tree line.

He yelled at her again. "Show yourself!"

Linh hesitated but knew it was no use to stay hidden. She slowly stepped into the alley.

The American soldier looked her over and Linh's skinned crawled. "Why are you following me?" he asked, again in barely understandable Vietnamese.

Linh took a deep breath and stood as tall as she could. In as strong and confident a voice as she could muster she said, "Where are you taking my brother?" She used the English word for "brother," but the rest of the sentence was in Vietnamese. The man seemed to understand.

He looked at Teo, surprised, as though he had forgotten about him. "He's hurt and I think he's hungry. I wanted to get him away from—from...," he looked back in the direction he had come as he searched for the right words in Vietnamese, "...people that wanted to hurt him."

Less afraid now, Linh stepped toward him holding out her arms. "I will take him."

"Where do you live?" the man asked.

She stepped back, distrustful again. "Around."

"Show me."

Linh shook her head. "Why?"

"Let me buy you and your brother something to eat."

She shook her head again and stepped back even further. "I am not for sale!" she said in perfect English. It was a phrase she had been taught by Song long ago.

"No, that's not what I meant." The man looked genuinely appalled. Linh was almost hurt. She knew most of the Westerners found her attractive, despite being shunned by the Vietnamese. No matter. She was not a prostitute. She crossed her arms and tried to look as though she didn't care what he thought of her. He continued, "I was going to buy the boy something to eat. He was kicked out of the bar I was in, and then I saw him going through the garbage. A man punched him, and I—I—dealt with him."

"You! You killed Hung?" Linh stepped toward him again. She couldn't be angry with the man who had killed Hung. She pulled Teo away from him. He was now conscious and confused and wrapped his arms around her neck. She hugged him tightly for a moment. She then looked back at the man. "I saw his dead body. Good riddance to him. A terrible man." Linh gently pried Teo's arms from her and set him down. He hid behind her and clung to her skirt.

"Let me buy you and your brother something to eat. Any restaurant you want."

She shook her head. "No restaurant will serve us."

"Even if you're with me? I have money."

Linh could tell he didn't understand, so she explained. "We are not pure

Vietnamese." She pointed to the boy. "His father was probably an American. I don't know who my father was, but he was definitely *not* Vietnamese."

The man looked at Linh again, scrutinizing her. She felt her face flush. He looked at her long, dark hair and almond-shaped eyes. His gaze lingered on the skin peeking out of her dress. Linh wondered if he was looking at her breasts or her oddly colored skin? Not white, not black, not yellow. She knew it was unusual, even for someone who was mixed. Finally the man's eyes turned to Teo, whose father had obviously been Black. He too would never be able to hide the fact that he was mixed. The man looked back at her and said, "Show me where you live. I will buy you food and bring it to you."

Linh crossed her arms again. "No. I am not a prostitute."

"Please, Linh. I am so hungry," Teo whimpered.

The man shook his head again. "I want nothing from you. I promise."

"Please, Linh," Teo cried.

Linh looked at the malnourished child that clung to her and then back at the man. "No sex?"

He shook his head. "No sex."

Linh took a deep breath and nodded. She didn't really trust him but took a chance because of Teo. He needed food, and she had not been able to provide much lately. She held Teo's hand, and they led the man to the farmer's market nearby. She and Teo stayed out of sight and watched until the man disappeared between the stalls. He quickly returned with fruit and vegetables. Best of all, he had bought dried fish!

Linh led the trio to the underside of the bridge where they could eat out of sight of the farmer's market or anyone passing by. It was the same spot where she had slept five years ago after Song was killed.

Teo and the man sat cross-legged on the dirt while Linh sat on a rock. She gave Teo some fish and bitter melon. She offered the same to the man, but he responded, "No. You eat."

She nodded and began to nibble on a piece of fruit. She wanted to make sure Teo had enough before she ate too much. She was aware of the man watching her. She looked at him. "You're American?" she asked in heavily accented English.

"Yes. With the 5th Special Forces Group." He could tell the words meant nothing to her and tried again. "Green Beret." She nodded, recognizing the famous moniker. He held out his hand. "I'm Dennis Dordi. My friends call me Dordi."

She hesitated, but his smile seemed genuine, so she shook his hand. "I'm Linh. This is Teo. I found him in a basket in the woods when he was only a few months old. We have been together ever since."

Dennis Dordi had four days of R&R and spent much of it with Linh and Teo. He was completely enchanted by this young girl who had nothing yet had carved out a life for her and the little boy she named Teo. He wanted to help her, and the next day he bought them more food, clothing, and shoes. She led him to their spot at the homeless camp. He saw that she and the other kids had created a small village of sorts using the discards of others. It had to be a difficult life, but somehow they managed to survive. At only 15, Linh was one of the oldest kids in the camp, and he wondered why.

Every evening of Dordi's R&R after Teo had eaten and fallen asleep, Dordi and Linh would talk long into the night. Dordi's Vietnamese was fair, as was Linh's English. They often laughed as words were mispronounced or incorrectly used and they had to figure out what the other one meant to say. Quickly, though, communication became easier, and they enjoyed each other's company. She was fascinated by his stories of the United States and his life growing up in Virginia. He told her all about California and how he hoped to live there after the war. He found a map and explained to her how to read it. He showed her where the United States was compared to Vietnam. He pointed out Saigon and Cam Ranh Bay as well as California and Virginia. She had no education at all, but Dordi could tell that her mind was very quick, and she possessed a keen sense of logic. Even though she couldn't read, she had no trouble understanding the concept of a map.

Linh also told Dordi about her own life. She told him she had never known her parents but was taken in by Song when she was a baby. She told him about the first ten years of her life at the Yankee's Dream and then of Song's death. Her face lit up when she told him about finding Teo. Dordi could tell she was a wonderful mother, despite being little more than a child herself.

She told him her biggest fear. "Most of the girls and also the boys—they become prostitutes at my age." She sighed heavily. "I know that's in my future. It is the only way I can support me and Teo." She smiled at him. "But the food you brought us—that will sustain us for a while longer. Thank you."

Dordi just nodded, unable to speak. Linh was so young. The thought of her being forced into prostitution and being used by men that would never know her—never love her—weighed heavily on him. But what could he do?

The last day of his R&R, Dordi brought Linh and Teo a tent.

"A tent!" Linh exclaimed as he surveyed their spot at the homeless camp. He found the most level area and cleared away the rocks to make it ready for the tent. When the ground was just right, he began setting it up.

"It isn't very big, but it will help," he said as he showed Teo how to secure it with stakes.

"Thank you, Dennis," Linh said, the gratitude evident in her voice. She put a hand on his shoulder as he knelt working on the tent. He smiled at her touch and liked that she was the only person, other than his mother, who called him Dennis. "Where did you get it?" she asked, positive she knew the answer.

Dordi stood and grinned at her. "Compliments of the U.S. Army," he said as he bowed, which made her laugh.

When darkness began to settle over the camp, Dordi said it was time for him to go back to his unit. He promised to return to Cam Ranh Bay whenever he got R&R again. He knelt down and let Teo hug him goodbye. Then he stood and embraced Linh. She was surprised that she hoped he would kiss her, but he didn't. True to his word, in the four days he had spent with them, Dennis had never made any sexual overtures toward her. Inexplicably, she was both pleased and disappointed.

Chapter 22

Highway 1, 1969
  Chi

Chi walked the streets of Saigon for only a week before she had to move on. There were plenty of men looking for "services" despite the widely known problem of sexually transmitted diseases among the working girls. It seemed that the promise of cheap, on-demand sex was irresistible for many soldiers far from home. Nevertheless, after her third victim was found, the American military police began asking questions, and Chi decided it was time to go.

Over the next few months, she rode the motorbike she had been given up Highway 1, which snaked along Vietnam's coastline adjacent to the South China Sea. She traveled from one place to another where Western soldiers might come looking for a good time. Her first stop was Phan Thiet, which she had been told was the home of an American outpost named LZ Betty. She parked her motorbike outside a woman's home that was known to be a VC sympathizer. Her job here would be the same as in Saigon. She would kill Western soldiers who came to her looking for "boom-boom," as it was often called. While Chi and the woman ate lunch and watched her children play, they discussed the logistics of her mission. The woman explained to Chi where she would work and how to dispose of the dead bodies.

Chi killed four men in Phan Thiet before heading north to Cam Ranh where she spent several days enjoying the spectacular views on the bay. Sitting on the beach looking out into the blue water, it was easy to pretend the war was over. But it wasn't and she knew she had work to do. After a few days of relaxation, she found the main street in the city and planned her strategy. Her Uncle Nam owned a legitimate bar and brothel there, and she purposely avoided it. She couldn't risk being seen by her father's brother. Instead, using intelligence she had been given before she left Saigon, she easily located the side street close to the American base that had gotten a reputation for cheap quickies. Three more men would die before Chi packed up her knife and continued north.

Over the next several months, Chi spent time in Nha Trang, Phu Cat, and Qui Nhon harbor. She lost count of the number of men she killed. More than 30. Maybe 35. She felt no remorse. They were uninvited occupiers and were preventing the unification of her country. They cared not one iota about her or the many other victims of the war. How many mixed-race children would wander the streets of Vietnam because of their lust? She was willing to kill all of them one by one if necessary. However, unlike some of her comrades, she never let them suffer. She saw no need to be cruel, though she also never gave them what they came for. She had enjoyed sex with her Frenchman, the only man she had ever been with, but now the thought of such intimacy was abhorrent to her. She killed her victims as soon as they were alone, when they had only one thing on their mind and had let their guard down. It was surprisingly easy.

Chapter 23

Cam Ranh Bay, Vietnam, November 1969
  Linh

Teo sat on his makeshift bed in the tent Dennis Dordi had given them a few months before and watched as Linh gathered up her few possessions. Mr. Ong, the owner of the Yankee's Dream, had an opening for a working girl, and Linh had decided the time had come. Teo knew she was upset, but she tried to pretend otherwise. "Li Minh says the money is good even though Mr. Ong keeps a lot of it. She says most of the soldiers are really young and the sex is over pretty quickly. It won't be so bad." She had told him this several times, and Teo wondered if she was trying to convince him or herself.

"You'll come visit me sometimes?" he asked her. He had just turned seven and was afraid of being on his own.

Linh sat beside him on the tattered blanket that served as Teo's bed. "I will come by so often you won't even know I am gone," she promised. She hugged him tightly and hoped it was a promise she could keep. She would give him any money she made so he could buy food. Although Teo was getting better at foraging through restaurant garbage without getting caught, there were a lot of kids competing for the same slim pickings. She had forbidden him to steal from the farmer's market, terrified he would be caught. If he had money, some of the farmers would let him buy the bruised fruit and wilted vegetables that they couldn't sell to their regular customers.

Finally, Linh left Orphan Island and made her way to the Yankee's Dream. She stood for a long moment staring at the door. She had not been inside the building since Song died and almost felt she were betraying her by returning to the place where she had been killed, but she knew Song would understand. Linh sighed heavily and reached for the door. Ignoring the "closed" sign she pulled it open and walked inside. The place was just as she remembered it. In the back of the room was the long bar where Mr. Ong served beer and little else. Two dozen wooden tables with mismatched chairs were scattered around, and the same jukebox with its cracked glass stood in the corner. A little boy of perhaps four was sweeping the floor, and it took her back to the days she had spent working here. Now she would have a different job.

She found the narrow hallway that led to the four bedrooms used by the working girls and quickly located the one belonging to Li Minh. She had started at The Yankee's Dream several months before Song died and over the years had helped Linh when she could. She was the one who told her that another girl had left. She had married a soldier from New Zealand and wasn't coming back. Li Minh pulled a box from under her bed and began rifling through the clothes trying to find something sexy for Linh to wear in the bar that night. She found a pink bikini top, white short-shorts, and a pair of white go-go boots. Smiling, she held them up. "These should fit you."

Linh took the clothes and the boots uncertainly. She took off her dirty dress and started to put on the new clothes, but Li Minh stopped her. "We need to clean you up a bit. Mr. Ong likes us to look fresh and neat." Li Minh took Linh—now almost naked—outside to a small, fenced area and sprayed her with a water hose. The water was cool and clean, and she was once again transported to her days as a child when Song would spray her with this same hose. The water felt good. Refreshing. After she had moved to the homeless camp, she was only able to wash in the muddy water of the small creek than ran along the road and divided the camp from the business district of Cam Ranh Bay. She had forgotten how good it felt to be really clean.

Li Minh gave her a towel and she dried off. She wrapped the towel around her small body and returned to Li Minh's bedroom. She put on the bikini top and short-shorts and then the boots, which were a little big. She looked at herself in the mirror. She could not imagine walking around in public with so much skin showing. She looked at Li Minh, her voice trembling. "I—I don't think I can do this."

Li Minh put her hands on her shoulders and looked at her friend. "Yes, you can. The first one is always the hardest. Just think about something pleasant, and it will be over before you know it." She gave Linh a small jar of Vaseline and told her to use it "down there."

"Why?" Linh asked, uncertainly.

"It will keep it from hurting, and the men are so stupid they will think you are excited to be with them. Win-Win."

"Oh. Okay," she said but was still unsure. She was grateful to Li Minh but wished Song were there.

Later that night, she watched Li Minh laugh and flirt with the men in the bar. Most were soldiers on R&R, but there were also a few civilians. Linh walked around nervously, uncomfortable in the high-heeled boots and completely unsure of what she should be doing. She saw Mr. Ong glaring at her, and, not knowing what else to do, she made her way over to where Li Minh was. Her friend sat on a table with her feet, clad in strappy heels, balanced lightly on a chair in front of her. She wore the pink bikini bottoms that matched the top Linh was wearing and a see-thru blouse with nothing under it. She leaned back on her hands, her breasts clearly visible through the thin fabric of her shirt, and looked at the men surrounding her. She said something and they all laughed. Li Minh caught sight of Linh, and she glided off the table and made her way to her. Li Minh put her arm around the younger girl's waist and said, "Boys, I would like you to meet Miss Linh. She is new here and needs someone kind and gentle to show her the ropes." Several men quickly volunteered, but Li Minh pushed them aside. She selected a thin blond American who looked to be only a little older than Linh herself. His face turned bright red as Li Minh took his hand and led the two of them back to Linh's room. As she was leaving, Li Minh whispered in her friend's ear, "Pleasant thoughts."

As the boy lay on top of Linh, she closed her eyes and tried not to cry. Remembering Li Minh's words, she tried to envision the beaches of California and could almost hear Dennis' voice describing them to her. As the boy grunted and finally climaxed, she heard Dennis say, "Compliments of the U.S. Army." In her mind's eye she could see Dennis bowing, but this time it didn't make her laugh.

Chapter 24

Norfolk, Virginia, February-June 1970
  Mark Higgins

Admiral James Higgins was injured in February 1970 when his ship was attacked by Viet Cong guerrillas along the Vietnam shoreline near DaNang. He spent more than a month at Walter Reed Hospital in Bethesda, Maryland, before being given three months of convalescent leave at home. Mark was ecstatic to have his father home for his high school graduation in May 1970 but deeply dismayed to learn he would be deployed again. Two weeks after Mark's graduation, he and his mother accompanied Admiral Higgins to the Langley-Eustis Base for yet another round of goodbyes.

Mark, now taller than his father, spoke first. "My number for the draft is pretty low. I expect I'll get called up before too long. Maybe I'll see you in Vietnam," Mark told his dad.

Admiral Higgins smiled at his son. "I hope not. I'd rather you stay here with your mom. She needs you."

"It's my duty to serve, Dad. You taught me that."

"I did indeed. And I am proud of you," James put a hand on his son's shoulder, "but I'd rather you stay here where it's safe. There is no shame in taking the college deferment."

"It's not up to you," Mark said simply. He knew it was foolish, but he liked the idea of serving his country alongside his father.

The older man nodded. "I know." James tried to convince his son to reconsider. He had seen firsthand the atrocities in Vietnam as well as the government mismanagement of the war. He wanted Mark to have no part of it, but his son would not be dissuaded. With a heavy heart, James hugged his son one last time and then he turned to his wife.

He held her hands in his, "When this war is over, we'll take that honeymoon we never got to have."

Elizabeth smiled. "I'd like that." She tried hard to mean it, but he had been gone more than he had been home, and she wasn't sure how she felt anymore. He had always provided for her and Mark, and part of her wanted to be the wife he deserved.

James embraced his wife and the two shared a passionless kiss. He said goodbye one more time and then he was gone. Again.

Chapter 25

Cam Ranh Bay, Vietnam, February 1970
  Dennis Dordi and Linh

In February of 1970, Dordi was again granted a few days of R&R. He procured a Jeep that someone had christened "Unfortunate Son." Dordi just nodded his head and smiled knowing the name was a reference to "Fortunate Son," the song by Creedence Clearwater Revival about the lucky rich kids who were able to avoid being sent to Vietnam.

He started the Jeep and a few hours later parked on the side of the alley near the bridge where Linh and Teo had eaten after the first time he had brought them food. He quickly crossed the bridge and found the path through the woods that led to the homeless camp. He stood outside their tent wondering if he should knock or somehow announce his presence. Before he decided what he should do, Teo spoke to him from behind. "Dordi!" The small boy ran and threw his arms around his friend.

"Hey, Teo," Dordi said, tousling his hair. "You've grown a few inches since I saw you last."

Teo let go and smiled up at him. Then he noticed the things Dordi had brought. "Are those for me?" he asked, eyes wide with excitement.

"Yes. You and Linh. Food and a couple of hammocks so you don't have to sleep on the ground anymore."

Teo frowned. "Linh doesn't live here anymore. She is at the Yankee's Dream. She works there now."

The news pierced Dordi, but he tried not to react. He said simply, "Well, then I guess these are for you." He handed the bag of food and the hammocks to Teo and asked, "Do you need me to set up the hammocks?"

Seven-year-old Teo had no idea how to set up a hammock, but he could tell Dordi wanted to find Linh. "Nah. I can do it." He knelt down and began unfolding one of the hammocks and tried to act like he knew what he was doing.

"Okay. If you don't need me, I'm going to check on Linh."

Teo nodded and said, "Thanks a lot, Dordi, for the food and everything." But Dordi was already hurrying away.

Dordi parked directly in front of the Yankee's Dream. He jumped from the Jeep and jerked the door to the bar open. He saw her as soon as he walked into the dimly lit room. Linh was scantily dressed and laughing at something the soldier on whose lap she was sitting had said. When she saw him in the doorway, her smile disappeared, and she turned away. He stood staring at her for a moment. Finally he tore his eyes away from her and walked over to Mr. Ong who was wiping the bar with a dirty cloth. Dordi spoke to the owner for a few minutes, and then he pulled out his wallet and gave the man several bills.

"Linh!" Mr. Ong yelled, and Linh jumped as though she had been slapped. "This man has bought your time for the next four days. Keep him happy."

The man on whose lap Linh was sitting was clearly disappointed and started to protest, but Dordi narrowed his eyes and gave him a look that made him reconsider. The unhappy soldier pushed Linh away and turned his attention to one of the other girls.

Linh was more embarrassed than she had ever been before and willed the floor to open up and swallow her. But it didn't. Dordi walked over to her and took her hand. "How are you, Linh?"

She turned away from him. Linh couldn't bring herself to meet his gaze. She had wanted him to come back the minute he had left, but she didn't want him to see her like this.

"Linh! You know what to do. Take him to your room!" Mr. Ong yelled at her again.

She wiped the tears from her eyes and led Dordi down the hallway. The door to her room was open, and he followed her inside and closed it. She stood in the middle of the small room with her head down.

He stood in front of her, and when she continued to look away from him, he said, "I don't want anything from you, Linh. I—I—just didn't like the way that man was looking at you. This isn't the life for you. You're better than this."

Now she looked up at him, her eyes filled with frustration. She said angrily, "What choice do I have? There are no other options for someone like me."

He frowned and rubbed a hand over his face. "I know, but for the next four days you can do whatever you want. You're free. I can take you back to the camp and you can see Teo."

The thought of Teo made her smile, and she surprised him by embracing him the same way the little boy had done earlier. Dordi was not a tall man, but he was nearly a foot taller than Linh. He looked down at the small girl who had her arms around his waist and desperately wished he could take her away from this place for good rather than for just a few days.

Chapter 26

DaNang, Vietnam, October 1970
  Augie

Eighteen-year-old Alessi Augustini—Augie to his buddies—had guard duty. He stood in the guardhouse at the perimeter of his base and stared into the blackness in front of him. He was supposed to be watching for Charlie, the derogatory name most Americans used for enemy soldiers. Instead, he was thinking about the conversation he'd had with his mother less than a year ago. He was thinking that he should have listened to her.

"You are going to graduate at the top of your class. You should go to college! Take the deferment!" she had begged him.

Augie had been adamant. He wanted to go to Vietnam. He told her he wanted to fight for his country. In truth, he wanted to emulate his father. Joseph Augustini had himself been only 18 when he and 150,000 others stormed the beaches of Normandy in June of 1944. He had been a first-generation Italian-American and eagerly enlisted to fight for his new country. Augie's father had survived the war and was awarded a Silver Star for bravery shown during D-Day and its aftermath. Although he always downplayed his actions, he was a true war hero to his son. Augie envisioned his own D-Day adventure and hoped to live up to his father's reputation. Instead, from his vantage point, this war seemed to have little opportunity for glory. He spent his days loading Agent Orange onto planes so that the herbicide could decimate the landscape of this beautiful country. Now as he stood guard watching for the enemy and hoping they wouldn't attack, he fantasized about saving his fellow countrymen if they did. In his mind's eye, he could see his father's pride as they pinned a medal on his chest.

The minutes ticked slowly by, and his thoughts turned back to his mother. They had finally agreed that he would not enlist, but he would also not request a college deferment. His fate was in the hands of the draft. He remembered the day he and his friends, all high school seniors, gathered at Sam's house to watch the lottery. A dozen of them crowded around the big, new color TV console. Sam's parents had bought it for the family for Christmas. That was why the boys were there—no one else had a color TV. Augie had never even seen a color TV. He sat on the floor, leaning against the leg of the couch. They watched as the man on TV reached into the gigantic bowl and pulled out the first capsule. He broke it open and read the date, "September 14th." He and his friends exchanged glances. No one had that birthday. One down, 365 to go.

He didn't remember the next few dates that were called out, but he remembered one of his classmates letting out a groan after the third or fourth birthday was read. His birthdate had been called, and he would be drafted. Most, although not all, draftees ended up in Vietnam. Augie had been jealous. He wanted his birthday to be called. He closed his eyes and may have even said a prayer. He opened his eyes just as the man read the date on the eighth slip of paper he pulled from the bowl. September 7th. His birthday. For the sake of those around him, he pretended to be disappointed and scared. In truth, he was elated. He was certain he would be a war hero like his dad. He desperately wanted to make the man proud.

In January, the conscription notices began to arrive in mailboxes all over the country. As expected, Augie and several of his classmates received their notices. Because they had not yet graduated high school, they were given temporary student deferments, a status known as 2-S. Almost before the ink was dry on their diplomas, their status changed to 1-A—meaning they were "ready to serve." As he had hoped, Augie was sent to Vietnam. He was inducted into the U.S. Air Force and would join the maintenance crew stationed at the air base in DaNang.

Now standing guard, Augie was frustrated. He had been in-country almost two months and had never even left the base. How could he be a hero if he never got to engage the enemy? He shifted the rifle on his shoulder and tried to focus on the darkness in front of him. He couldn't see shit. Charlie could be 3 feet in front of him and he wouldn't know it. He could be shot at any moment and would never even see it coming. He frowned. This wasn't at all what he had envisioned. He should have listened to his mother.

Chapter 27

DaNang, Vietnam, October-November 1970
   Chi

Chi eventually migrated from Saigon all the way to DaNang. She had not seen her parents in nearly 15 years and wondered if they were still there. Did they miss her? Sometimes she wished she could see her mother, but she never missed her father. Chi would never forgive him for his betrayal.

She hadn't been sure how she would feel returning to the city of her birth, but she found its familiarity comforting. Chi was tired of constantly being on the move and, working with other insurgents in the area, came up with a plan that would let her stay in business a bit longer. A farmer named Lap, also VC, owned a small shack on the banks of one of the waterways that fed into the Han River, eventually dumping into the South China Sea. He told Chi the home had previously belonged to his parents, who were dead. She could both live and work in the small home. She would walk the streets of DaNang offering Western soldiers "a good time." She would bring her clients back to the tin-roof home next to the waterway where she would kill them. Lap would then take the body away and dump it in the river. If their bodies were found, they would be far downstream from DaNang and no one would know who had killed them.

It was a good plan, and it worked well. Chi quickly grew comfortable in DaNang and even made friends with some of her neighbors. It had been a long time since she'd stayed in one place for more than a few days, and she found she liked having a place to call home.

Chapter 28

DaNang, Vietnam, November 1970
Augie and Mark "Junior" Higgins

A few months after Augie arrived in-country, another group of men fresh from basic training joined the U.S. Air Base in DaNang. Mark Higgins, the son of a Navy Admiral who commanded Swift boats along the coast of Vietnam, was among the cherries. Augie met him when he took the empty bunk in the enlisted men's hooch that was Augie's home away from home.

Augie was laying on his bunk rereading a letter from his girlfriend when the new guys walked in. He looked up and assessed the group. "Welcome to 'Nam where if Charlie doesn't get you, the snakes, bugs, or malaria will," he said without humor.

"Gee, that's not at all what the brochure said," Mark quipped, making Augie laugh. Mark threw his gear on an empty bunk and introduced himself.

Augie shook his hand. After learning Mark's father was a bigshot in the Navy, he was quickly nicknamed Junior. Augie introduced him to the others who were present in the room. He pointed to a huge Black man called Tiny and a guy from Atlanta, Georgia, who went by Einstein.

"We call him that because he nearly went on his first patrol without his rifle." Augie laughed. "He grabbed his book instead."

Einstein looked at the new guy and spoke in his own defense. "It's just that ever since I was a kid, I always want a book with me, just in case I have time to read. It's second nature for me to grab a book on my way out, but now I have to remember to grab my M-14 instead."

"Does anyone go by their actual name?" Mark, now Junior, asked.

Einstein replied, "Only the officers."

"And only to their faces," Augie added.

Junior noticed a small, handmade chart on the wall. He pointed to it and asked, "What's that?"

Augie stood and walked over to the chart. "This," he touched the paper gingerly, "is my short-timer calendar." He studied it a moment before he turned away and looked at Junior. He frowned and said, "Although I'm a long way from being short."

Junior studied the chart. The months of the year starting with September were listed across the top. Down the left side were the numbers 1 through 31. On each of the squares below the months was a number starting with 365 on September 1. The numbers counted down the days until August 30, which was labeled "Kiss my ass, Vietnam." About three months' worth of dates had been crossed out.

Junior looked at the calendar. "I guess I just have 364 and a half days left."

Tiny spoke for the first time. "At least it ain't a leap year."

Chapter 29

DaNang, Vietnam, December 1970
  Chi and Trinh

A couple of months after she got to DaNang, Chi rode her motorbike to Trinh's home. The woman was still there, but Tam's children were not. Trinh's grandson had died in the war, but her granddaughter was still alive. The last Trinh knew, the girl had volunteered for Brigade 559. Trinh made tea and she and the younger woman sat at the old wooden table in her kitchen and spent the afternoon catching up. Chi told her friend all about her adventures with Tam. Trinh knew her daughter had died, but Chi was able to tell her firsthand how it had happened.

"She was incredibly brave," Chi told Trinh.

Trinh just nodded. She had seen so much death that the details of Tam's demise seemed not to phase her, though Chi knew that it did.

Just as Chi decided it was time to go, Trinh matter-of-factly stated, "Your parents came here once."

"Here?" she asked, surprised. "Why?"

She shrugged. "They had been looking for you for a long time. They had been trying to find you ever since you ran away. At first, they thought they could just bring you home, but over the years, your mother just wanted to know if you were okay. Eventually, they talked to someone that told them you were living with me. But you had left with Tam by the time they came here."

"What did you tell them?"

"Oh, I told them we met. I told them that I had taken you to one of the homeless camps and you found out that Linh had been given to a girl there but then the two of them just disappeared. No one knew where they had gone. I told your father that you were so distraught you had killed yourself. I gave him graphic details of your gruesome end." Trinh sighed. "I have no regrets hurting him that way, but perhaps it was a mistake to give such details in front of your mother. She didn't take it well."

Chi wasn't sure how she felt. Her father deserved to think he had caused her death—and he very nearly had—but she hated that her mother also had to suffer. "Do you know if they are still here? In DaNang, I mean."

"I see your mother sometimes. She buys vegetables from me. She always wants to talk about you. I think it makes her happy to talk to the person who she thinks was the last to see you alive."

This made Chi sit up. "Does she come often?"

The woman thought for a moment as she refilled their teacups. "Maybe once every few months."

Chi wrapped her hands around the warm cup and thought about whether or not she wanted to see her mother. No, that wasn't the question. She definitely wanted to see her. The question was whether or not she should. She did not want her father to know she was alive, but she did not want her mother to suffer. On the other hand, Chi thought that the chances of her surviving the war were very low. Perhaps it was better to let her think she was already dead. Disappointed that she would not get to see her mother, she simply thanked Trinh and returned to the shack on the river that she now called home.

Chapter 30

DaNang, Vietnam, December 1970
 484th Maintenance Division

Augie, Junior, and the rest of the 484th Maintenance Division had spent the early morning hours pumping Agent Orange onto C-123 Providers, huge aircraft that would spray the deadly chemicals across acres and acres of the Vietnam landscape. First the 55-gallon black drums, each with an orange stripe, were loaded onto the back of a flatbed truck that would then be driven to the side of a plane. A two-inch hose was manually inserted into a barrel and a pump used to transfer the thick liquid into the 1,000 gallon tanks on the plane. If the soldiers had been properly trained, they would have diluted the syrupy Agent Orange with water or oil. However, that message never made it to Augie and his crew, and so they used the herbicide the way it came—at full strength. Once the planes were loaded and on their way, the men of the maintenance crew were left to clean the gunk out of the pumps and to dispose of the empty barrels. Disposal typically meant burying them around the perimeter of the base. Occasionally the barrels found a new use.

"Hey, Augie. What's today?" Tiny asked as he hefted a barrel over his head and tossed it into the pit they had dug the day before. Augie always knew the date because every morning he crossed the previous day off his short-timer calendar.

"December 22nd. Not that it feels like Christmas."

Tiny nodded. "What if we cut a couple of these barrels in half? We could make a grill and have a cookout for Christmas."

The other men nodded their agreement, and they quickly pulled three suitable barrels from the trash heap. They pried off the tops and peered inside. As was typical, about a half a gallon of Agent Orange clung to the inside of the barrel.

"No problem," said Augie. "We can just burn it off." The young men filled the barrels with wood and paper trash and set the barrels alight. Acrid smoke filled the air and burned their eyes and lungs. When the fires burned themselves out, they rinsed the barrels with water and declared them ready for cooking.

When the C-123s returned, some members of the maintenance crew would hand clean the sprayers, which were often clogged so badly the men had to use pipe cleaners to clear the nozzles. Other crew members used large hoses to rinse out the interior of the planes. More often than not, the men with the hoses—most of whom had not yet reached their 20th birthday—would turn cleaning the plane into a game. They would spray each other and slide head-first across the floor of the plane still slick with Agent Orange despite the water. By the day's end, all the men had been covered in Agent Orange or its wash multiple times. They breathed the fumes and swallowed contaminated water. On Christmas Day, they ate hamburgers that had been cooked on grills made from the black barrels with the orange stripe.

Chapter 31

Cam Ranh Bay, Vietnam, January 1971
  Linh

Seventeen-year-old Linh had been working as a prostitute at the Yankee's Dream for more than a year. The workday was over, and she lay in her bed trying to sleep, but every time she closed her eyes, she saw Dennis Dordi. Three times in the last year, Dennis had come to see her. Just like the first time, he always bought her time for however long he could, but he had never made any sexual advances toward her. Sometimes she wondered if he just saw her as a little sister, or, even worse, maybe he just wasn't attracted to her. She wanted there to be more to their relationship, and sometimes when they were together she thought perhaps he did as well. But then he would leave, and she would be back at work at the Yankee's Dream.

She turned over in her bed and looked toward the ceiling. It was too dark to see it, but she knew it well. Every stain, every crack was seared into her memory because that is what she focused on when she was working. She would lay in this bed and stare at the ceiling and try not to think about what was happening to her body. She closed her eyes, but it didn't help. She still saw the curved brown stain that had so many tiny little branches it almost looked like a feather. The feather teased her, reminding her that she was nothing more than a mix-raced prostitute with an adopted son. How could she possibly think Dennis or anyone else would love her or want to make a life with her?

She turned over again and buried her face in her pillow. She tried to empty her mind, but Dennis still occupied it. He would come to see her whenever he could slip away from the base, and he would always bring food and sometimes other supplies. Why would he do that if he didn't have feelings for her? She had hoped that when his tour ended, he would offer to take her and Teo with him, but he didn't. Instead, he extended his tour by six months. She had wondered—no—hoped that it was because of her. When she asked him, he just shook his head and said, "I'm a soldier. I don't know what else to do."

Chapter 32

DaNang, Vietnam, February 1971
  Augie and Junior

Augie and Junior had been given four days of R&R and were anxious to start their "vacation." Although technically their R&R would begin on Friday, they decided to drive the short distance to the city of DaNang as soon as they were dismissed on Thursday. Augie wanted to try the local food and get a beer. Junior wanted sex. The very vague plan was to spend the night in DaNang and go to Hue just a few miles farther north Friday morning. Other than the Tan Son Nhut airfield near Saigon where most Americans flew into the country, neither had seen much outside the DaNang Air Base. They had thought about venturing over to Dogpatch, the shanty town across from the base, but it was strictly off-limits because more than a few servicemen had met their end there. Too many VC amongst the civilians.

Around 4:00 P.M., they were just heading to the motor pool to get a Jeep when Junior said, "Wait. I forgot something."

Junior ran back to their hooch, pulled the footlocker from under his bed, and dug through clothes and other items until he found what he needed. He opened the box of condoms his mother had given him two years before. He knew his parents had been only 16 when she got pregnant and giving him condoms was her way of telling him to be careful. He had been hugely embarrassed at the time even though she had just left the box on his dresser without a discussion. Now he was glad he had them. He had never used one but was pretty sure he could figure it out. He stuffed several in his pocket and hurried to catch up with Augie.

Junior found his friend at the motor pool signing out a Jeep that someone had christened "War Eagle." They were told it was a reference to the unofficial mascot of Auburn University in Alabama. Augie, who was from Pennsylvania, had never heard of Auburn University, but he thought War Eagle was a good name for an American soldier's Jeep.

The two teenage soldiers drove the short distance to downtown DaNang and parked in front of a rundown, two-story building whose sign proclaimed "Beer and Perty Girls."

"What's a perty girl?" asked Junior.

Augie laughed. "No idea. Maybe it's supposed to say pretty or perky?"

"Well, I don't care. As long as she's a willing female, I won't be too picky," Junior said, straining to see inside the large window next to the door. He looked at Augie. "What about you?"

"Nah," Augie said. "I got a girl back home. Besides, I've heard a lot of the prostitutes have diseases."

"Yeah, I've heard that too. Isn't that why Doc keeps antibiotics on the base?"

"I suppose it is," Augie said as he took the keys from the ignition. Just as they got out of the Jeep, a Vietnamese woman that Augie guessed to be in her thirties appeared at Junior's side.

"Big, strong G.I., you want company?" She batted her eyes coquettishly. She wore a denim miniskirt and tie-dyed halter top that was too small for her surprisingly ample breasts.

Junior looked at Augie, unsure.

"Dude, you do what you want. I'm gettin' a beer."

The woman took Junior's hand and pulled him toward her. "Come with me. I show you good time. I make you real happy for real cheap."

Junior glanced back at Augie. "Meet you back here in—uh..." He turned and looked at the woman.

"One hour. Two dolla? Okay?"

Junior smiled. "Okay!" he said, without even a glance back at Augie.

Junior let the woman lead him down the dusty road and into a maze of small shacks and weathered buildings with tin roofs. They wove between the makeshift houses, many with laundry hanging to dry and all with barefoot children running everywhere. They passed something that looked like an open-air grocery store, and the woman holding Junior's hand nodded to the man behind the produce stand. Occasionally someone on a bicycle would fly past. Junior looked around, taking it all in, but then he began to get nervous. He realized he was completely lost and had no idea how to get back to the bar with the "perty girls."

"How much farther?" he asked.

"Here," she said, pointing to a shabby structure perched precariously on a bank overlooking a waterway. Mark guessed the creek was one of the many tributaries that fed into the South China Sea. The woman opened a small door that was so low, Mark had to duck his head as he went inside. The room was dim, but he was relieved to see it looked reasonably clean. An old canvas tarp covered with multiple large, brown stains lay on the floor like a rug.

Unsure of what he should do, he introduced himself. "My—my—name is Mark. Mark Higgins. Though the guys—they call me Junior." He smiled at her. He knew she was a lot older than he was, but she was pretty. The woman smiled at him and took off her top. Mark felt his face flush.

She smiled at him. "Go ahead, Mark," she said softly. "Touch me."

Mark licked his lips and nervously took a couple of steps toward her. His hands gently closed around her breasts, and just as he felt the soft orbs in his hands, he also felt a sharp stinging in his side. He jumped back as she pulled the enormous knife from his side. Instinctively, his hands clutched the gash that was now pouring blood onto the tarp. He looked at the woman and tried to understand, but before he could fully comprehend what was happening, she plunged the knife into his heart. As he fell to the floor, his last conscious thought was one of disappointment. He was going to die a virgin.

Back at the bar, Augie was growing impatient. Where was Junior? He looked at his watch. It had been more than two hours. Irritated and hungry, he ordered another beer and decided to try the soup he had seen a couple of the locals eating. By the time he finished his meal, it was almost 8:00 P.M., and there was still no sign of Junior. He was sick of waiting around and finally stood up and left the bar. He sat in the Jeep for a few minutes debating whether or not to drive around and look for his friend, but he had no idea where the woman might have taken him. They didn't really have a plan for where they would spend the night, but he knew Junior had hoped to spend it with a prostitute. Augie guessed the woman he had left with had agreed to keep him company for the rest of the day in exchange for whatever money Junior offered her.

"Screw it," Augie said as he started the Jeep. He decided to go back to the base for the night. He would return to DaNang tomorrow. If Junior was still missing, he would go to Hue without him.

Chapter 33

DaNang, Vietnam, February 1971

  Chi

Chi knelt beside the young man she had just killed. His name was Mark. He was the first soldier to ever tell her his name. He had been so nervous and embarrassed, and she wondered if he had ever been with a woman before. He was very young. Maybe 18. She thought about Mark's mother, who would soon learn of her son's death. Chi thought about Linh. She knew the pain of losing a child. It was a pain that never went away, and suddenly she knew she couldn't do this anymore. She was still a soldier. Still Viet Cong. Still dedicated to the reunification of Vietnam. But she didn't think she could kill them like this anymore. It was too personal. She didn't want to know their names. And she most certainly didn't want to think about their mothers.

Ten minutes later, Lap, the man she had nodded to at the open-air grocery, appeared at Chi's door. He quickly searched the dead teen's body for anything of value. In the young soldier's pants, he found a wallet with a small amount of cash in one pocket and several condoms in another. His shirt pocket held a small spiral-bound notebook the size of a deck of cards. The boy also had a nice watch with an inscription, though the English writing was meaningless to Chi and her accomplice. While Lap put the watch on his own wrist, Chi removed the dead soldier's boots. When nothing more of value could be taken, they rolled Mark's body up in the tarp and carried it outside. Although normally they would put the body in a boat for Lap to dump farther from the shoreline, tonight he had brought his horse-drawn wagon. He explained that the small sampan was needed elsewhere. They loaded Mark's body onto the wagon that earlier in the day had carried Lap's vegetables from his farm to the market nearby. They would leave the body in an alley near the bar where Chi had picked up the young soldier. Although they knew the dead man would likely be found the next morning, they were confident the locals would deny having seen anything—even if they had.

Chapter 34

DaNang, Vietnam, February 1971
Augie

At 7:00 A.M. the morning after Augie left Mark in DaNang, he was again in the motor pool. He was signing out a Jeep—this one named "Wolfman"—when Tiny found him.

"Junior's dead," the big man said without preamble. He was clearly shaken. "Damn. That's messed up. Who dies on R&R?"

Augie, still holding the clipboard and pen, just stared at Tiny. He couldn't make sense of what he was saying. "Dead? How can he be dead?"

"Couple of marines on R&R found him a few hours ago. He was dead in an alley behind some bar. He was stabbed and robbed. They took his wallet and his watch. They even took his boots. At least they didn't take his dog tags." Tiny rubbed his bald head. "Damn. He was a good kid."

Augie continued to stare at Tiny in disbelief. Finally he asked, "Are they sure the guy they found is Junior?" He shook his head. "He was fine when he left the bar. He went with some hooker. He was fine," he insisted. "Better than fine."

"Yeah, well, Major Collins wants to talk to you, see if you know anything."

Augie just shook his head and repeated, "Really, he was fine." He handed Tiny the clipboard and walked to the base's headquarters. Inside he found his commanding officer alone in his office. Augie said nervously, "You wanted to see me, sir?"

The man sat on the edge of his desk, arms crossed and looking serious.

"Airmen Augustini," he said, motioning him to step forward, "what can you tell me about Airman Higgins? The two of you were together yesterday?"

"Yes, sir. We were supposed to start R&R today. We were going to go to Hue, but—but we decided to leave last night after we were relieved for the day. We went to DaNang."

The major nodded. "And what did you do in DaNang?"

"Not much. As soon as we got there, he hooked up with a prostitute. I went in a bar for a beer. He was supposed to meet me back at the bar an hour later but never showed." Augie looked down at his feet and said, "I got impatient and left around 8:00. Came back to the base." He looked back up at Major Collins. "Is it my fault he's dead?"

Major Collins stood and put a hand on Augie's shoulder. "No, Son. The woman likely killed him and took his money. She probably killed him as soon as they were alone."

"Then I should have gone with him. Followed them," Augie said, clearly blaming himself.

"If you had, you'd likely be dead too. She probably had an accomplice." He motioned for Augie to sit. "Now, tell me everything you can about this woman. We need to find her so she doesn't kill any more of our guys."

Augie nodded and told him what little he knew.

Chapter 35

Highway 1, February 1971
  Chi

After helping Lap dump Mark's body in the alley behind the bar, Chi walked slowly back home. She had killed many men in the same way, but unlike all the others, his death weighed on her. When she got home, she saw the condoms and small notebook that Lap had found in Mark's pocket. They had been tossed aside as things that held no value. Chi gathered the condoms. There were four of them. She wondered if he planned to use one with her. Few soldiers did. They cared not about the girls they had sex with and likely never considered the consequences to her if she got pregnant. Certainly, her Frenchman hadn't cared, she thought bitterly. Mark had been different, but she had killed him.

Chi set the condoms aside and picked up the small notebook. Curious, she opened it and saw that Mark had used it as a sketchpad. She sat at the table where she sometimes ate and slowly looked at the pencil-drawn images. There were several small portraits of what Chi assumed were Mark's soldier friends. She was struck by how young they all were, and she surprised herself by hoping they would all survive the war and go home. There was one self-portrait. In the drawing, Mark sat on a bunk with a sketchpad propped on his knees and a pencil in his hand. He was looking up as though at his subject and smiling. Chi found herself smiling back at him as she stared at the handsome young face with the kind, round eyes, but then she frowned remembering that Mark was dead. She had killed him. She tried to shake away her uneasiness. She reminded herself that he was an American. The enemy. *She did her job.*

She slammed the notebook shut and stood planning to throw it in the trash. Instead she sat back down and opened it again. The notebook held two landscapes. One she recognized immediately. It was the Troung Son Mountains as viewed from the bridge at DaNang. She was amazed at the detail that Mark had achieved on such a tiny piece of paper. Next her eyes fell on the drawing of an older Caucasian woman, hair piled high on her head, looking out from the page. Chi looked at the woman's eyes. Why did they look familiar? There were two other drawings of this same woman, and Chi could not shake the feeling that they had met. Finally, she understood—the eye's belonged to Mark. The woman was his mother. Chi's heart ached for this woman who would soon learn that her son was dead. Dead because she had killed him.

The discovery of the notebook had been the last straw for Chi, and she decided to leave DaNang. She packed up what little she personally owned, including Mark's small sketchpad, and drove her motorbike to the market. She found Lap, thanked him for his help over the last few months, and told him she had a new assignment. Honestly, she had no idea what she would do next. A short while later she found herself once again driving on Highway 1. This time she was headed south, destination unknown.

Chapter 36

DaNang, Vietnam, February 1971
  Augie

Augie was still a little shaken after he left his commanding officer and returned to his hooch. Major Collins had asked him to gather Junior's belongings so they could be sent home to his family. When he got there, he found Tiny and Einstein sitting on the floor passing a joint between them. The two men were clearly stoned. As Augie walked by, Tiny held up the joint to him. Normally, Augie would pass. He always wanted to be at his mental best in case his hero opportunity presented itself. After months of seeing no action at all and now with Junior's death at the hands of a hooker, he didn't hesitate. He took the hand-rolled marijuana cigarette from the big man's hand and took a long drag on it. The smoke burned his lungs and he wanted to cough, but he willed his body not to respond. He exhaled slowly and then handed the joint back to Tiny.

He walked to Junior's bunk and sat on the edge. He was unhappy with the task he had been given and dreaded going through his friend's possessions. He still couldn't believe he was dead. He spent a minute watching Tiny and Einstein as they continued passing the joint back and forth. They were laughing. How could they laugh? Junior was dead.

Augie sighed and forced himself to get started. He pulled out the small, unlocked footlocker that was shoved under the bunk and hesitated only briefly before opening it. On top he saw an opened box of condoms and wondered if that was what Junior had forgotten and gone back to get. He hadn't thought he could feel any worse about Junior's death, but for some reason the condoms made it worse. He tossed them aside and looked back at the remaining contents of the locker. He found the usual. Spare T-shirts and skivvies, a dress uniform—which no one ever wore—and socks. Moving the clothes aside, he found a few letters from Junior's mother and a photograph. It looked like it might have been taken at his high school graduation. He wore a cap and gown and stood between two people Augie guessed were his parents. Junior looked like his father. His mother was tall and thin, but he couldn't see her face very well. She was looking up at Junior. He could tell she was smiling. She was clearly very proud of her son. Augie frowned as he carefully placed the letters and photo on the bed. Those should be returned to his mother.

Returning his attention to the footlocker, he found Junior's sketchpad and pencils. Junior would frequently sit on his bunk and draw, but he never wanted to show anyone his work. Junior said he wasn't very good, just liked to play around. Augie looked through the drawings. There were dozens of them. Augie was amazed by his friend's hidden talent. He had drawn scenes from everyday life on the base, but they were more than that. The drawings held emotion. One in particular caught his attention. It was all of the guys from the maintenance division goofing around with the water hoses. Grown men, more or less, playing and laughing like children. The drawing had movement. You could almost see the activity as it occurred. It was amazing. The next one surprised him. It was a drawing of Augie himself viewed from the side. He was standing guard, rifle on his shoulder looking out beyond the horizon. Augie thought he looked tough—like a real soldier. Like his father might have on D-Day. He looked at it for a long time, wanting to keep it but knowing he couldn't.

Reluctantly, Augie turned the page and his own image was replaced by one of Lia, the Vietnamese woman who worked for Major Collins. She was attractive, but fine lines had begun to form on her face revealing her to be closer to 40 than 20. Junior had drawn her three times side-by-side on one page. In the middle drawing, she looked exactly as Augie knew her. In the one on the left side of the page, Junior had drawn her younger. There were no fine wrinkles and no worry lines. She was just the beautiful young girl she likely had been 20 years before. In the third drawing, Lia was an old woman. The wrinkles were deeper and the skin sagged a little, but it was still clearly Lia. Augie was completely awestruck by Junior's talent, and the weight of his friend's death hit him again. His talent had been destroyed by a war that no one understood.

Less than 24 hours later, Augie was summoned back to the major's office for the second time in as many days.

"You wanted to see me, sir?" Augie asked Major Collins.

"Relax, Airman. Have a seat," the major said motioning him to a chair opposite his desk. Major Collins leaned back in his own chair and said, "Specialist Holmes from the Awards Division will be here tomorrow. He will ask questions about Airman Higgins' service and his death in order to determine if he should be awarded anything in addition to his campaign medal."

"Uhm. Okay," Augie stammered, unsure of what he was supposed to say.

The major leaned forward toward Augie and crossed his arms on the desk in front of him. "Is there anything you can think of—anything Higgins did while he was here that was remarkable?"

Augie frowned and thought for a moment, "Not really. We just load the planes with Agent Orange. He wasn't here very long. I don't even think he had been on patrol yet."

"I need something, Airman," the major said, growing frustrated. "The man died. We need to tell his family more than that."

Augie searched his memories for something useful. "Well, there was that rocket attack a couple of weeks ago. One of the rockets hit the petroleum storage area. Junior—I mean Airman Higgins was afraid the tanks would blow and ran to the hooches close by. He woke up a couple of the guys that had been on guard duty the night before. If the tanks had blown, they would've died if Junior hadn't gotten them out."

The major nodded. "Okay. That's good. Anything else?"

"Uhm, not that I can think of."

The major drummed his pen on the desk and thought out loud. "Airman Higgins will be awarded the Vietnam Service Medal because he served his country honorably. If he was killed in action, he also becomes eligible for the Republic of Vietnam Campaign medal."

"Yes, sir," said Augie, still unsure. "The hooker—she must have been VC. So technically he was killed by the enemy."

Major Collins stared at Augie for a moment then down at the form on his desk. "I'm going to write that he was given R&R due to his heroic actions during the rocket attack and that he was then killed by an enemy combatant en route to DaNang."

The two men exchanged a look. Finally Augie said, "Okay, sir. Do you need anything else?"

"No. That will be all," the major said as he began filling in the paper on his desk.

Chapter 37

Norfolk, Virginia, February 1971
  Elizabeth Higgins

Elizabeth Higgins, wife of Admiral Higgins and mother to Airman Higgins both currently serving in Vietnam, was in the kitchen preparing dinner. Anthony Parker, retired USMC and eight years her senior, would be joining her later. He was a neighbor in the Eagle's Nest subdivision where Elizabeth had lived for more than a decade. Anthony's wife, Margaret, and Elizabeth had been friendly but not especially close. The women had met at another neighbor's home who frequently hosted card games and book clubs. Over the years Margaret and Elizabeth had often crossed paths, and when the older woman died suddenly, the entire neighborhood rallied around her husband.

Within a year of Margaret's death, the other neighbors had drifted back to their own lives, but Elizabeth and Anthony had grown close. Very close. In truth, Elizabeth Higgins and her husband, James, had not been husband and wife in the biblical sense in a long time. Even before the war and his being sent to Vietnam, they had drifted apart emotionally. He was a good man and a good provider for her and their son, Mark. Elizabeth had never worked a day in her life outside their home, and although she had come to be disappointed in her marriage, she had never once considered divorce. Even after her relationship with Anthony became intimate, she wanted to keep her family together. She told herself that when the war was over and James and Mark came home, she would break it off with Anthony and try to rekindle the romance with her husband.

She looked at her watch when she heard the doorbell. She smiled, assuming it was Anthony. He was nearly an hour early. "I guess he can't wait to see me." She dried her hands on a kitchen towel and checked her hair in the hallway mirror. She opened the door with a big smile on her face expecting to see her lover—perhaps with a bouquet of flowers. Instead it was one of the chaplains from Langley-Eustis and a junior officer. Her eyes went from one man to the next and back again, her smile gone.

"Mrs. Higgins?" the chaplain asked.

She gave him a quizzical look. "Uhm—yes?"

"May we come in?" he asked gently.

Elizabeth stared at the man for a moment and suddenly understood why they were there. Either Mark or James was dead. She squeezed her eyes shut. Please don't let it be Mark, she thought. Please, please don't let it be Mark. By no means did she wish for her husband to be dead, but James himself would prefer his own death over that of their only child. Finally Elizabeth opened her eyes and choked out, "Come in," and led the men to the stylishly appointed living room. "Please sit down." As calmly as she could Elizabeth asked, "Is it my son or my husband?" The tears were already flowing, but she kept her gaze steady on the chaplain as she waited for the answer.

The chaplain pulled Elizabeth to the couch and sat beside her. He took her hand in his. "I am so very sorry, but your son Mark was killed in an ambush carried out by Viet Cong guerrillas a week ago."

"NO! NO!" Elizabeth shrieked. She grabbed onto the chaplain and began to sob. He held her until she finally pulled away from him and wiped her eyes with the handkerchief he offered her. She sat for a minute saying nothing, just aggressively fiddling with the cloth in her hands. Suddenly she stood, walked to the fireplace, and picked up a framed photograph from its mantel. She handed it to the chaplain. "That's Mark with his father and me at his high school graduation last May."

The chaplain looked at the smiling family with Mark in the center wearing his cap and gown. He was taller than his father but favored him in many ways. He handed the photo back to Mrs. Higgins and said again, "I am so very sorry."

She took the photo and stared at it for a long moment. She caressed the image of her son and then looked back at the chaplain and said, "He would have been 19 in March." She set the photo down and began to cry again. She held on to the mantel for support.

The younger man spoke for the first time. "Mrs. Higgins, is there someone we can call for you?"

She turned toward the voice and looked at the younger man as though she had forgotten he was there. After a moment she shook her head. "No—no. My friend is coming for dinner. He should be here soon. Although now, I..." Her voice trailed off and she collapsed on the couch with her head in her hands.

The chaplain took her hand and the two men waited. They would not leave until Mrs. Higgins' friend arrived. Twenty minutes later, Anthony Parker, flowers in hand, rang the doorbell. The young soldier opened the door and quickly explained the situation. Anthony tossed the flowers onto the entryway table and immediately took the chaplain's place on the couch. The chaplain and younger man took their leave closing the door quietly behind them.

Chapter 38

Grenada, Mississippi, March 1971
  John and Grace Tackett

John and Grace Tackett had wanted a baby for a long time, but for reasons that eluded the doctors, she was never able to get pregnant. The previous Christmas, Grace's nephew, just home from two tours in Vietnam, had told the family many stories from his time in-country. At first Grace wasn't all that interested but nodded politely as Gene spoke because she didn't want to be rude. However, when he told them about the hundreds of children who filled the orphanages and roamed the streets of Vietnam, she didn't have to pretend to be interested. He explained that many of the babies who were abandoned had been fathered by Western soldiers. Because the kids were not pure Vietnamese, they were often shunned by their families. He and his fellow soldiers would sometimes give food or candy to the street kids, and the VC would sometimes use them to lure Americans to an ambush.

Gene had been a medic in Vietnam and would occasionally visit the orphanages to provide the most basic of medical care to the kids. "The orphanages just have so little, and it seems the orphans never stop coming. Sometimes babies are left on the doorstep in the middle of the night. The older kids—the homeless ones—they are just treated so badly by the Vietnamese people. It was awful."

Of all the terrible things Gene had seen during the war, he seemed most troubled by the plight of the children left behind by American soldiers. "It's a problem we created. It's our responsibility to solve it," he said earnestly during Christmas dinner.

His mother, Grace's oldest sister, admonished him. "Enough of this talk. It's Christmas and you are home safe. We should celebrate." She raised her glass in a toast, and the talk quickly changed to more pleasant topics.

Although Grace said nothing, the information from Gene was a revelation. The thought of so many children needing homes weighed on her heart. She had never considered adoption before, but suddenly it made sense. Then and there she had decided to look into what it would take to adopt a baby from Vietnam.

Now three months later and armed with the pertinent information, she raised the issue with her husband one night after dinner.

"You know, John, I'll be 38 soon. The older I get, the less likely it is that I will get pregnant," she said as she sat next to him on the couch.

He looked up from the newspaper he was reading. "I know, but the doctors haven't found anything wrong with you. We just need to keep trying," he replied, turning his attention back to his paper. She had said this to him before, and normally this was where she would beg him to get tested. Perhaps the problem was with him, she would say. Maybe his sperm count was low or something. He would just shake his head irritably and say, "There's not a damn thing wrong with my sperm!"

Tonight, however, instead of suggesting he might be the reason they couldn't get pregnant, she took his hand in hers and said, "Remember Gene telling us that there were hundreds or maybe thousands of babies in Vietnam who are half American? Nobody wants them, and they end up in orphanages or" –she shuddered— "on the street trying to take care of themselves."

John looked at his wife sympathetically. "Yes, but what can we do about it?"

She smiled. "We can adopt from Vietnam! Maybe we can even find siblings. We could have the family we always wanted."

"You want an Asian baby? The kid wouldn't look anything like us. What would people think?"

"They would think we adopted. It doesn't matter that he or she wouldn't be like us. We would still be a family!"

John frowned, thinking it over. He loved Grace, and if he was honest, he had been terribly disappointed by their inability to have children. He had four siblings and always thought he would have a large family. But an Asian baby? Finally he nodded and said, "I suppose we could look into it. It could be very expensive."

"Actually, I have already made some inquiries. There's an adoption agency in Memphis that works with an orphanage in Saigon. The most expensive part is that we would have to fly over there and get the baby."

"Fly to Saigon? It's a war zone!"

"Not really. They say Saigon is very safe."

John frowned, still unsure. He looked at his wife. They weren't getting any younger, and he too had compassion for the orphans. He nodded, making a decision. Then he said, "Let me make some phone calls and get all the information and then we can decide."

Grace smiled at her husband. He didn't realize it, but she had won. In a couple of weeks, he would come back and tell her everything that she had told him tonight. The more they talked about it, the more he would think that the whole thing had been his idea. Eventually they would agree to move forward. He just needed to be the one who suggested it.

Chapter 39

Norfolk, Virginia, March 1971
Elizabeth Higgins

A few days after what would have been Mark's 19th birthday, Elizabeth received a small package from the U.S. Air Force. According to the official letter that came with it, the package contained all that was left from her son's life in Vietnam.

There wasn't much. The letters she had sent to him, along with a photo taken the same day as the one on her mantel. She found Mark's dog tags and clutched them in her hands so tightly the edges dug painfully into her skin. Without relaxing her grip on the dog tags, she closed her eyes and held them to her chest. She tried to imagine Mark was standing beside her, but it was no use. The emptiness and pain in her heart stubbornly reminded her that he was dead. She sighed heavily and opened her eyes. She had expected to be sent the gold watch with the leather strap she had given Mark for his 18th birthday, but it wasn't in the package. On the back of the watch, she had it inscribed with a quote from Benjamin Franklin, "You can do anything you set your mind to." She sighed again, remembering the day she had given it to him. He had worn it every day after he had gotten it, and she wondered why it hadn't been returned to her. She felt the tears gathering in her eyes but willed herself not to start crying again. "It's just a watch," she told herself.

The last thing she pulled from the package was a sketchpad. She smiled. Elizabeth knew exactly how talented Mark was with pencil and paper. He had not written many letters, but he had sent her numerous sketches, including two self-portraits. Now she opened the pad and took in the images he had not yet shared with her. As expected, they were stunning. Her eyes fell on the three-panel drawing of Lia, although Elizabeth did not know the woman's name. She smiled, remembering a similar set of drawings he had made of her a few years back. Her smile grew wider as she looked at the drawings Mark had made of his friends at the base. The young men were laughing as they sprayed water on each other. The next drawing was quite different, and her smile disappeared as she looked at four small children on the page in front of her. They were painfully thin, barefoot, and poorly dressed. The oldest, a girl of maybe seven, held the hand of a toddler. All the children were smiling and looking at a soldier. The man, wearing an apron over his messy uniform, held a tray in one hand while his other hand offered a bowl to one of the boys. The youngster held up both his palms ready to accept the dish. Despite the smiles on the children, the drawing was filled with sadness. Elizabeth didn't understand this picture at all. Clearly the children were on the base, but why? Why was this soldier feeding them? Where were their parents? Elizabeth had many questions but no one to ask.

Once she finished looking at all of the sketches, she looked through them again hoping she had missed one. She hadn't. There wasn't a single self-portrait in the sketchpad. She had all of the pictures of Mark she would ever have, and this time she didn't even try to hold back the tears.

Chapter 40

Cam Ranh Bay, Vietnam, April 1971
Dennis Dordi and Linh

Dordi's third tour in Vietnam was officially over, and he was in a Jeep—this one named "Ms. Wrong." He was supposed to be headed to the Tan Son Nhut airport in Saigon, but he had an important stop to make first.

He parked in front of the Yankee's Dream, threw the vehicle in park, and jumped out. Without hesitating, he opened the door and walked in. He saw Linh right away, and she smiled as soon as she saw him. She politely excused herself from the man she was talking to, a civilian Dordi guessed from the clothes and clean fingernails.

"Hi, Dennis." She gave him a brief hug and pulled him to a table to sit down. "R&R?" she asked, still smiling.

Now it was his turn to smile. "No. I'm done. No more extensions for me. I'm going home."

The smile left her face. "Oh," was all she said.

He took her hands in his. "Come with me."

"What?"

"Come home with me," he said again. He hesitated before finally continuing. "I know it may seem crazy, but I can't stand the thought of leaving you here. We'd have to get married so you could come with me, but we don't have to stay married. We can divorce as soon as we get to the States, but you can have a real life there. I'll help you. Or—or we could stay married. If you want. I love you, Linh. You probably know that."

She snatched her hands away from him. "You Americans are all the same," she said in a bitter tone he had never heard before. "I don't need to be rescued! I survived 15 years without you. I can do it again. Go back to America, Dennis Dordi. Vietnam is my home." She stood and left without looking back.

Dordi stared after her. They had never been lovers, but he loved her nonetheless. He thought she loved him. Even if she didn't, he could give her a far better life than what she had here. He had not been certain she would say yes, but it never occurred to him that she would be angry. He sat at the table for a long time. Finally he began to accept that she was not coming back. He stood and looked around. The bar wasn't crowded, and all eyes were on him. He looked at Li Minh hoping she might offer some explanation. He thought he saw a flicker of sympathy for him, but then she turned and left the same way Linh had. Slowly Dordi walked to the door and left the bar.

Li Minh knocked on Linh's door but entered without waiting for a response. Linh was lying on her bed sobbing. Li Minh sat beside her and stroked her hair. "Why didn't you tell him?"

"I just—couldn't," Linh said softly.

Li Minh nodded. Linh wasn't the first girl at the Yankee's Dream to get pregnant, and she certainly wouldn't be the last. Sometimes a girl would tell one of her customer's the baby was his. They knew which men were more likely to take responsibility and would help them or perhaps even marry them and take them home. "He loves you. He wouldn't care that the child wasn't his."

"No. I couldn't ask him to do that. It's too much."

"But you love him."

"I know. Now I will never see him again." Linh began to cry again.

Just then Mr. Ong stormed in. "What are you lazy girls doing? We have men that will pay for your company. Now get back out there." The two women stood, and Linh wiped her face with a rag. Mr. Ong stared at her. "You're getting fat, Linh. You better not be pregnant."

Chapter 41

Norfolk, Virginia, May 1971
  Elizabeth Higgins

Elizabeth sat at the antique writing desk in the little room off the kitchen. Pen and paper were in front of her, but she wasn't thinking about the letter she needed to write. She let her mind drift to happier times. When they bought the house years earlier, she told her husband that she didn't need an office. But to her surprise, the room had found many uses since the day they moved in. At first, before she had a desk, they set up a card table so that Mark could build his LEGO masterpieces without leaving a mess in the dining room. Later when Mark was older and the card table had been replaced by a lovely Queen Anne replica, the two of them would spend hours piecing puzzles together. When he was in middle school, she would sit in the recliner James had given her and read while Mark did his homework. It was also in this room when she first realized what a talented artist he was. She frowned, remembering how her father had made fun of his drawings. He never saw the value in them and told her she was wasting money buying him sketchpads. Before long Elizabeth was the only person Mark would allow to see his work.

When Mark started high school, he became less interested in spending time with his mother or even time in the little room off the kitchen. He preferred to be in his own room or occasionally had a bunch of his friends over. Those days she would take refuge in her little office to escape the rowdy boys and the inevitable mess they left in her normally spotless kitchen.

Although back then the noise and mess bothered her, now she would give anything to hear him and his friends ask, "Is there anything to eat?"

As she and James drifted apart, she found that she enjoyed having her own little nook of the house where she could read or write in her journal. But now every nook of the house was hers. Her son was dead and her husband was on the other side of the world. Now her office was a reminder that she didn't need a place of refuge. It had been nearly three months since Mark died, and she could no longer stand to be in this house. She could no longer be Mrs. Higgins. It was less about her husband and more about the constant reminder of the life she had lost.

Elizabeth bit her lip, looked down at the paper in front of her, and began to write. She tried to be kind because she truly did not intend to cause James pain. Merely she wanted to release him from his obligation to her. He had done right by her and kept his promise to make sure she and Mark had what they needed, but now, she told him, he was free to do whatever he wanted. He could keep his money and take up with another woman if that made him happy. She was leaving. She would sell the house if he wished and would put the money in an account for him to have when he returned. She wanted nothing but to be free, free of the house that her son had grown up in and free of the constant reminders that he would never return to it. Although she knew in her heart that leaving this house, leaving her husband, and even marrying another would not erase the pain of Mark's death, she didn't know what else to do. She simply had to leave, lest the grief crush her.

When the letter was finished and the envelope addressed, she placed it in her mailbox for the mailman to collect later that day. She had no way of knowing that Admiral James Higgins, in a war zone 9,000 miles away from their home in Virginia, would receive her letter just two days after learning their only child had died. The news of her divorcing him would pierce him far more than she could have imagined.

Chapter 42

Cam Ranh Bay, Vietnam, May–December 1971
   Linh

A month after Dordi left, Linh could no longer hide her pregnancy and Mr. Ong kicked her out. She returned to Orphan Island and moved back into the tent Dordi had given her and Teo. Five months later, she delivered a baby girl with the help of Li Minh and another young girl from the homeless camp. Linh named her Song.

As hard as Linh's life had been before, trying to take care of a newborn while living in the homeless camp was almost impossible. She had taken Teo in when he was six or seven months old and thought she was prepared to take care of Song, but the pregnancy and childbirth had left her weak and she didn't produce enough milk. Song was small and Linh knew she wasn't gaining weight as quickly as she should. She had to do something to try and save her baby. She went to the Yankee's Dream early one morning before they opened and found Li Minh.

"I have decided to take Song to one of the orphanages," Linh told her through tears. "She will die if I keep her."

The nearest orphanage was in Saigon and since Linh had no way to get there, Li Minh rode her bike to the nearby American army hospital to ask for help. Eventually she found a nurse named Juanita Becker. Juanita was being transferred to Saigon and would be leaving the following week. She promised Li Minh that she would find an orphanage that was willing to take Song.

All too quickly the day came for Linh to say goodbye to Song. Linh had no education and could not read or write, so she asked Juanita to write a note for her and give it to the nuns at the orphanage. She hoped someday Song would be able to read it. In English Juanita wrote, "My name is Song. I was born on November 5, 1971, in Cam Ranh Bay, Vietnam. My mother, Linh, loves me with all her heart and hopes that I will be adopted by a family that can give me everything that I deserve." Then Li Minh wrote the message again in Vietnamese.

Juanita held up a Polaroid camera. "Let me take a picture of you and Song."

Linh smiled and held Song close. Juanita took two pictures, and after they developed, she wrote their names and the date on the back of each and gave them to Linh.

Linh looked at the photos for a moment and then back at Juanita. "Thank you." Then she gently placed Song, one of the photos, and the notes Juanita and Li Minh had written in a box with a blanket. It was the same blanket that Teo had been swaddled in years before. She carefully set the box on the floor of the Jeep, wedging it in so it wouldn't move even if the road was rough. Linh kissed her daughter one more time. Juanita told her not to worry, though she knew it was a useless thing to say. She climbed in the Jeep and waved goodbye. Linh stood arm in arm with Li Minh as they watched Juanita drive away. Linh, who had never before asked God for anything, prayed that somehow, someday, she would see Song again.

Chapter 43

Grenada, Mississippi, October–December 1971
  John and Grace Tackett

The discussions between the Tacketts regarding the adoption of an orphan from Vietnam continued longer than Grace had anticipated. Initially John had not been comfortable with a baby that was a different race from them, but eventually he came around. He made his own inquiries into the cost and the process and then explained, unnecessarily, to Grace how it would work. After that, they agreed to move forward. The next step was the background check. If they passed, and they were confident that they would, then they would begin the process of finding their son or daughter.

Late in December of 1971, they got the news. They had been approved to adopt and could meet with an agency to find the child that was right for them. Grace was anxious to set up an appointment, but Christmas was always busy with family and church events. Sadly, she realized finding a baby would have to wait a bit longer.

Chapter 44

Philadelphia, Pennsylvania, August–December 1971
  Augie Augustini

Augie survived his one-year tour in Vietnam and returned home to Philadelphia. As planned before he was drafted, he joined his father's auto repair shop, "Augustini Auto Repair." He had worked in the shop for as long as he could remember, and his exceptional mechanical aptitude allowed him to learn quickly. Despite his talent diagnosing and repairing mechanical problems, before Vietnam most of the employees just saw him as the boss' son and didn't take his opinion seriously. However, only a year later he was a veteran just like many of them, and they treated him differently. Augie wasn't a war hero the way he had hoped, but he could see that his service to his country had earned him respect from the men at the auto shop. Most important to Augie, his father was proud of him.

By December of 1971, Augie had yet to fully transition to life after the war. He frequently thought about his time in Vietnam and often wondered about his friends, Tiny and Einstein, both of whom left Vietnam before he did. Einstein had been injured when his Jeep hit a landmine on his way back from driving Major Collins to the nearby ARVN base where South Vietnamese troops were stationed. The major had been killed, but Einstein survived and was sent home three months before his tour was to end due to the severity of his injuries. Tiny had gotten to Vietnam the month before Augie, and so he rotated out in July before Augie left the following August. After Mark had been killed and Einstein left, he and Tiny got pretty tight. It was only after

Tiny was on a plane back to the World that Augie thought about asking for the big man's address. Although Augie was genuinely interested in keeping up with his friend, he knew he probably wouldn't have written to him anyway.

That first Christmas home, Augie's father decided he would grill the steaks outside since the weather was unseasonably mild. His family complained about how it didn't feel like Christmas because, at 43 degrees Fahrenheit, it felt warm. Of course, it reminded Augie of his previous Christmas in Vietnam grilling hamburgers on the Agent Orange barrels in 75-degree weather. The heat from the grill, coupled with the humidity, made it feel even more oppressive than usual. As Augie sipped his beer and watched his family, he missed his buddies more than he thought he would. He didn't have the war stories that some men did, but he still had stories and he sometimes wanted to talk about his experiences. But no one seemed interested. If the subject of the war came up, someone, always a civilian, would just say, "Oh, I'm sure you don't want to talk about it," and they would change the subject. If they had ever just asked him, "Do you want to talk about your time in Vietnam?" he might have said yes.

He might have told them how Mark really died, rather than the official version of events. Augie still felt responsible for Mark's death, even though no one else blamed him. If anyone had asked, he might have told them about the time he and Tiny were part of a five-man scouting team after the air base was attacked. They were not that deep into the jungle when they ran into a group of what he would later learn were called "rock apes". Although Vietnam isn't supposed to have any apes, he and the men of the scouting team all saw them. They were short, very muscular, and covered in reddish hair. At first, Augie and the other men thought they were VC wearing some kind of weird disguise, but they had no weapons. Tiny raised his rifle to fire, and the apes all started throwing rocks with deadly precision. The scouting team got the hell out of there and all agreed not to mention it to anyone. It just sounded too bizarre. But later at a bar in Hue, he overheard other men telling a similar story. He and Tiny weren't the only ones who had seen the red rock apes.

And if anyone had asked him what was the worst thing he had seen in

Vietnam, the answer would have surprised them. It wasn't some grievous war injury of a comrade. He knew he was lucky that he hadn't seen anything like that. Nor would it have been the decimation of the Vietnam countryside by Agent Orange, which he most certainly had seen. No. The worst thing he saw in Vietnam was the children. The countless number of abandoned children of Western soldiers who wandered the streets begging for food. It was the barefoot and hungry children that haunted him most of all, but no one knew that because no one asked.

Chapter 45

Cambodia, January 1972

Chi

Chi followed Highway 1 all the way to Nha Trang. Although she made several stops along the way, she killed no one. Occasionally she was stopped and questioned by American military personnel. A woman traveling alone on a motorbike was not an uncommon sight, but some were still suspicious of her. Every time she was stopped, she would make up a different excuse as to where she was going and why she was traveling. The excuses were weak, and she wondered if somewhere in her psyche she wanted to be found out—that she was VC with nowhere to go. Mark's death still troubled her, and she expected the universe to punish her. Maybe she wanted it to.

When she reached Nha Trang, just north of Cam Ranh Bay, she stopped and debated where to go next. There was part of her that wanted to return to Cam Ranh and lay in the sand on the beach along the bay. There was another part of her that was afraid she would never leave if she did. It was such a beautiful, peaceful place. She desperately wanted the war to be over, and in Cam Ranh Bay she could pretend that it was. But the war wasn't over. Would it ever be? Frustrated, she restarted the bike and made her way west toward Ban Me Thout, a city not too far from Duc Lap and just inside Vietnam's border with Cambodia.

From Duc Lap, Chi made her way to Cambodia and rejoined Brigade 559 working on the Ho Chi Minh Trail. Although it was far more physically demanding than anything she had done in more than a year, it was a job in

"

which killing people face-to-face could be avoided. Just as before, she filled in bomb craters and helped to move debris from the road. In her absence from Brigade 559, it had been discovered straw could be woven into helmets to protect the workers from shrapnel. When someone first asked Chi if she wanted to help make the helmets, Chi thought they were joking. How could a straw hat protect anyone from shrapnel? But, indeed, the straw was woven so tightly and in layers that the helmets were reasonably effective against the flying rocks and debris that the bombs caused. And so at night, often by candlelight, Chi and many of her comrades would spend hours weaving the straw helmets together. As they worked, Binh, who had been educated abroad when he was younger, taught them English. Chi was already almost fluent in the language, but the lessons with Binh expanded her vocabulary considerably. Best of all, at least for a while she didn't have to kill anyone.

Chapter 46

Cam Ranh Bay, Vietnam, May 1972
Linh

A few months after Juanita left with Song, the nurse returned to Orphan Island with the good news that the baby had been adopted. She was anxious to tell Linh, but when she entered her tent at the homeless camp, she found a very sick Teo. Linh was trying to bring his temperature down using a bucket of water and a wet rag.

"What's going on?" Juanita asked, approaching the hammock which Teo occupied. She touched his forehead. "Geez. He's burning up." She looked at Linh. "My Jeep is at the bridge. Go get my medical bag."

Linh did as she was told and quickly returned. Juanita retrieved a thermometer and a stethoscope. "His temperature is dangerously high. We have to get it down." She grabbed Linh's bucket of water and dumped it on Teo's head, careful to hold him up so he didn't inhale the water. She asked Linh, "The stench in here tells me he has diarrhea. How long?"

"Three days. Also vomiting. He can't keep anything down," Linh told her, her voice shaking. "I think it was the fish."

"What fish?" Juanita asked as she put the stethoscope in her ears and listened to Teo's chest.

"The Noodle Emporium threw out a bunch of dead tilapia. I told him they were bad, but he didn't listen. He cooked them really well, but they still made him sick."

Juanita nodded. "Food poisoning. We need to get him to the hospital.

He's severely dehydrated." She picked Teo up and hurried to the Jeep. Linh followed carrying Juanita's medical bag. Twenty minutes later, Juanita rushed Teo into the enormous wooden building that served as the U.S. Army hospital. Unsure of what she should do, Linh waited outside near the door. The hospital was the largest building she had ever seen. It was two stories high with enormous windows that ran along the side. The windows held no glass but instead were covered by metal screens that allowed in the breeze and short tin canopies that she thought might keep out the rain.

As worried as she was for Teo, Linh could not help but be curious. It was the first time she had left the area where she had grown up. Her whole world had been the Yankee's Dream, the alley behind it, and Orphan Island. Careful to stay close to the hospital, she began to look around the army base. She wondered if this was what Dennis' base had looked like. There was a huge sign in front of the hospital that announced she was at the U.S. Army's 6th Convalescent Hospital. Although she could not read it, she recognized and understood the large red cross as well as the logo of the U.S. Army. Adjacent to the hospital were row upon row of smaller buildings. A few had signs written in English but most were unadorned. People in uniform were everywhere, most rushing to get somewhere but others walked more leisurely. She was surprised by the number of Vietnamese, both civilians and soldiers. There were also a fair number of children, and she wondered why they were there. Everyone ignored her.

Half an hour later Juanita still had not returned and Linh ventured through the open door of the hospital. Inside she found an impossibly large room with a countless number of beds. A few were empty but most were occupied. The majority held American soldiers, but she also saw Vietnamese soldiers as well as a few civilians. She didn't see Teo or Juanita. Off to the side she saw a female soldier sitting at a desk with a clipboard.

"Hello," Linh said, and the woman looked up.

"Hello," she responded, smiling. "Can I help you?"

Linh quickly explained why she was there and that she was anxious for news. The woman frowned and told her Teo had been taken to a room in the back, but she didn't know anything else. She pulled up a chair and told Linh she could wait with her.

A few minutes later Linh saw Juanita emerge from between the rows of beds. By the look on her face, Linh knew the news would not be good. She jumped up and rushed to the nurse. "What is it? Is Teo okay?"

Juanita pulled her to an unoccupied bed and made Linh sit down. Juanita sat beside her and held her hands. "He was feverish and extremely dehydrated. We hooked up an I.V. to give him fluids, but we were too late. I am so sorry, Linh. Teo is gone."

Juanita held Linh as she broke down. She sobbed—not just for Teo but for her baby she had given up, the loss of Dennis, and for the unending misery that seemed to follow her. Finally when she could cry no more, Juanita took her back to Orphan Island.

As they were leaving the base, Juanita grabbed a few supplies so she could help Linh clean the tent. It was an unpleasant and arduous task, but it had to be done. It also forced Linh to do something rather than just be overwhelmed by sorrow. When the tent had been scrubbed clean—or as clean as was possible—Juanita suggested Linh return to the army base with her for the night. "You can't sleep in the tent until it dries and the cleaning fumes dissipate." She looked at her watch. "If we hurry, we can get to the mess hall before they stop serving dinner."

Linh looked at her. "I don't really feel like eating."

Juanita touched her arm and looked at her sympathetically. "I know, but you need to eat and get a decent night's rest. Come with me."

Linh gave a nod and followed her back to the Jeep. They joined a few stragglers in the mess hall, and Juanita helped Linh make her selections. She was awed by the amount of food that was laid out in front of them. She looked at Juanita. "You said they would be closing soon. What happens to the leftovers?"

"Some gets thrown out, but most is taken to the civilian hospital a couple of miles away."

"Oh," Linh said. She was happy the food wasn't wasted, but disappointed she couldn't get it for Orphan Island. Thinking of the homeless camp made her think of Teo, and she willed herself not to break down again. She had known many children over the years who had died from malnourishment or disease. Last year two girls had gone into the woods looking for berries or nuts and never returned. They were presumed to be dead. She should be used to death by now, she told herself. But Teo was different. He was her family.

Juanita interrupted her thoughts by touching her arm. "Linh?"

Linh looked at her and tried to focus on the here and now. She knew that was all she could count on. She followed Juanita to one of the many long, wooden tables, and they sat on benches facing each other. Linh tried to eat but had no appetite.

"Eat, Linh. You did everything you could for Teo."

She shook her head. "But it wasn't enough." Tears welled in her eyes.

Juanita grabbed Linh's hand. "You gave him everything."

Linh shook her head again and covered her face with her hands. Then she pushed her tray back, put her head on the table, and wept. When it was clear Linh wasn't going to eat, Juanita put their trays away and then gently pulled Linh from the table. She led her to the nurses' quarters and found her an empty bunk. Juanita gave her something to help her sleep, and eventually she did.

The next morning Linh seemed a little better and Juanita wondered if she should tell Linh about Song. Perhaps it was too soon after Teo's death, but Juanita didn't know when she would be back in Cam Ranh Bay. She decided she had no choice. "I have some news for you," she said when she parked at the bridge near the homeless camp.

Linh looked at her, confusion written on her face. "News?" Linh forced herself to focus on the word. What news could Juanita have for her? She pushed aside her grief over losing Teo and suddenly realized it had to be about her daughter. Anxiously Linh asked, "Is Song okay?"

Juanita smiled. "Yes! She is wonderful. That's actually why I came yesterday—to tell you that she has been adopted by an American couple. She is already in the U.S. They picked her up last week." Juanita pulled out a photo. "One of the nuns gave me this."

The polaroid photo showed a smiling, well-dressed young white couple holding a baby—her baby. She stared at Song, who was sleeping and had clearly put on weight since Linh had last seen her. "She looks healthy." She blinked away the tears and tried to be happy. "They look like nice people." She turned the photo over and saw that someone had written on the back. She looked at Juanita, "What does it say?"

"It's just the date when they picked her up. May 10, 1972."

Linh bit her lip and looked at Juanita. "Do you know anything about the people that adopted her? Their names or where they live?" She thought about California and hoped Song lived there.

Juanita shook her head. "No. The orphanage can't tell you anything. They shouldn't even give you the photo, but Sister Chin wanted you to have it."

Linh's face cleared and she looked at Juanita hopefully. "I can keep the photo?"

"Yes."

Linh smiled and stared at the polaroid. Juanita was relieved, confident that the decision to tell her about Song had been the right one.

Chapter 47

Grenada, Mississippi, June 1972
  The Tackett Family

Song, now named Melinda, had been home with the Tacketts for just over a month. It had been a rocky start, but the new parents were figuring it out. A few months before at the adoption agency in Memphis, they had looked at dozens and dozens of photographs of children of all ages. Grace was saddened that there were so many toddlers without parents, but, she had her heart set on a baby. John looked at the older children whose features were more readily apparent than the tiny, wrinkled babies. "I thought most of the orphans were only half Vietnamese. Most of these kids are clearly Asian. Even the ones with a Black father have the almond-shaped eyes."

Grace cringed. She knew he only wanted to find a child that looked like them, but that wasn't how it sounded. Grace looked at the woman from the adoption agency who was helping them. "There aren't a lot of Asians in our little town. We just want our son or daughter to fit in."

The woman smiled a tight little smile and said, "I understand," although she really didn't. She thought they were being petty. Still, she wanted to find them a child they would accept because there were simply more orphans than there were parents willing to adopt. "Well, there is this one child, she is only a few months old..." She paused while she looked through her files. "Here. This one." She handed Grace a polaroid of a young woman holding a tiny baby wrapped in a blue blanket. On the back was written "Linh and Song, December 1971."

"The baby is a little girl named Song." She looked down at her folder. "She was born November 5, 1971. Her mother is only half Vietnamese and the baby's father is Australian."

Grace picked up the photo and looked closely at the baby. John looked at Linh. He said, "Well, her mother is quite pretty anyway." He looked back at the adoption agent. He rubbed his chin, thinking. "So the baby would be only 25% Asian and presumably 75% European. I suppose that's the best you can do?"

This time Grace did not hide her irritation. "We are not negotiating for a damn car!"

John was shocked to hear his wife curse. "I'm sorry. I just meant we aren't likely to go to Vietnam and find a blonde-haired, blue-eyed child."

The adoption agent gave him another tight smile. "No, you're not." She refrained from pointing out the obvious.

Grace, however, said what she and the other woman were both thinking. "John, you are aware that neither of us has blonde hair or blue eyes?"

John sighed again. He really wasn't as much of an ass as they thought he was. As a child, he had been picked on incessantly because he had a lisp. He had gotten to where he hardly spoke at school because the kids would scream with laughter no matter how hard he tried to control it. He eventually outgrew the speech impediment, but he knew firsthand how cruel kids could be to children who were different in any way. He didn't want that for his child. He didn't bother trying to explain. He just asked, "Is Song available for adoption?"

The meeting with the adoption agent was several months ago, and now the baby, whom they had named Melinda, was home with them. Grace was ecstatic to be a mother at last, but she worried incessantly about the note Linh had left for her daughter. "What if Melinda sees it when she's older and decides she wants to try to find her?"

"How would she even do that? The woman is in Vietnam," John replied, trying to reassure her.

"I don't know, but what if she does? Would it be terrible to just not give her the note? We can tell her that because her mother was so young, she couldn't take care of her." Grace frowned, "No. That's not enough."

"According to your nephew, mixed-race babies were mistreated in Vietnam. They weren't wanted."

"So we tell Melinda her birth mother didn't want her?"

John shrugged. "Maybe, but I don't really think we need to worry about it right now. It will be years before she is old enough to ask."

Grace nodded, but still worried that her little girl would grow up and reject her for the mother who had given her up. She put the notes and photograph in a small box with the blanket and took it to the attic. She would decide later what to do with them.

Although Melinda was too young to ask, Grace's friends were very curious. "Why would her mother give her up?" Grace was asked again and again. Initially she told her friends that Melinda's birth mother was very young and couldn't take care of her, but the excuse evolved multiple times over the years. For a while she told people that Melinda's birth mother was unable to take care of a mixed-race baby which later became "she didn't want a mixed-race child." Finally Grace simply said that Melinda's birth mother just didn't want her. Over time Grace herself probably forgot what the truth really was. The box in the attic began to gather dust and was eventually forgotten.

Chapter 48

Charlottesville, Virginia, Summer 1972
Dennis Dordi

Dordi had been back in Virginia for nearly a year but was not adjusting well to life in the real world. His brother, Phillip, had also recently returned to the States after two back-to-back tours in Vietnam and was having an equally difficult time. Their mother, Michelle, suggested they join a veteran's group, thinking it would be good for both of them.

"I don't need therapy, Mom," Dennis told her. "I'm just worried about my unit. I feel like I let my men down by leaving." In truth, he was still confused about Linh. Why not leave with him, even if she didn't feel the same about him? She had to know he would have helped her. He told himself a hundred times that it was stupid to carry a torch for a woman—no—a *girl* that clearly had no interest in him. Still, he thought about her constantly and couldn't shake the feelings he had for her.

His mother continued, "Well, your brother could use a good therapist. He won't go by himself. Go with him. At least get him to join that veteran's social group your father told you about. Anything is better than doing nothing."

Dordi sighed. He knew his mother was right. Phil had nightmares and seemed to constantly relive whatever had happened to him in-country. Where Dennis was simply distracted and preoccupied by Vietnam, more specifically Linh, Phil was reliving the war over and over in his head. Almost as bad, civilians were often hateful to returning Vietnam veterans, and while

Dordi had learned to ignore them, Phil took the unkind words to heart. He probably did need a therapist, but Dordi doubted he would ever seek that kind of help. Maybe getting to know other men just back from the war was a place to start. Finally he told his mother, "I guess it can't hurt."

A week later Dennis and Phil Dordi found themselves at the local chapter of the Veterans of Foreign Wars (VFW) playing poker with men who had spent time in Korea or Vietnam or both. Being with other men who had had similar experiences was good for the Dordi brothers even though the conversation rarely became serious. Soon both men looked forward to the Friday night poker games.

One of the regulars was a kid named Joey. He had been drafted and sent to Vietnam after dropping out of high school and had been stationed in Cam Ranh Bay. It was a relatively cushy assignment, and everyone in the group knew that Joey saw no real action. Nevertheless, he liked to embellish and pretend otherwise. Dennis and the other men who had been on the front lines frequently had to call "bullshit." Joey eventually realized that while he could stretch the truth to impress civilians, the men in this group saw through him.

"Man, I ain't got shit," Joey said one night, throwing his cards down. "I'm out," he added unnecessarily as he stood and pulled out a cigarette.

Dordi looked at his cards while two other men threw in chips and raised the stakes. He shook his head and tossed his cards on the table. "I'm out too." He stood and walked over to Joey, who was studying the huge map of Vietnam that had recently been added to the maps of Korea, Europe, and Japan.

Joey pointed to a spot on the map. "You ever make it to Cam Ranh Bay?"

Dordi nodded. "Some." The question made him think of Linh.

Joey liked to talk about his time in Vietnam but knew Dordi was a Green Beret and didn't bother trying to impress him with stories of seeing action. Instead he asked, "You ever been to the Yankee's Dream?"

Dordi nodded again. "A few times."

"Man, there was this one chick—Li Minh—she was one talented hooker," he said, smiling. Then he added, "I did 'em all, you know." He winked at

Dordi. "This other girl—what was her name? Linh. Yeah, that's right. Linh. Young, but a sweet piece of ass."

Somewhere in Dordi's mind he probably knew that Joey was just bullshitting him, but it didn't matter. Dordi threw the man against the wall and punched him in the jaw, knocking him to the floor. Dordi stood over him and was about to hit him again when his brother and another veteran grabbed each of his arms and pulled him off the younger man.

"What the hell did you do that for?" Joey said, rubbing his face and getting to his feet.

"Don't talk about Linh. Don't EVER speak her name again," Dordi said, turning away.

But Joey couldn't leave it alone. "Why? You got a thing for her? Wait...are you the one that knocked her up, took her out of action for the rest of us?"

Dordi stopped and whipped back around facing Joey. "What did you say?"

Joey, thinking he might get punched again, stepped back and changed his tune. "Nothing, man. It might not have been Linh. Maybe it was Li or Jun or who knows which one. I don't remember their names."

Dordi narrowed his eyes. "Was. Linh. Pregnant?" he asked, spitting out each word through gritted teeth.

"I don't know, man." He tried to back away, but Dordi stayed with him. Joey continued, "One of them was. Right before I rotated out. Yankee's Dream was down to just three girls because of it," Joey said, unsteadily. His hands were ready to protect his face if Dordi swung again.

Dordi pulled out his wallet and held up a photo of him with Linh and Teo. "Is this the girl?"

Joey looked at the photo and then back at Dordi. He knew that it was but was afraid to say it. He turned up his hands. "I don't know. Dude, they all look alike to me. Maybe it was her, maybe it wasn't."

Dordi stepped closer and grabbed the man's collar. "Think harder."

"Yeah, okay. That's her. She's the one that left."

"When was this?"

The man thought for a minute, afraid he would piss Dordi off even more. Finally he decided lying wouldn't help and said, "I guess it had to be May or

June last year because I rotated out in August. The last time I was in there, that dude who handled the money was yelling at her. I don't know what he was saying—never understood a word of that language. But she left right after. The older girl—I think her name was Li Minh or maybe Li Ming—told me she was pregnant and that was why she had to leave." Joey looked at Dordi, trying to gauge his reaction and fearing he would get hit again.

Dordi still held Joey by the collar, but he was no longer looking at him. He was just staring off in the distance. After several uncomfortable moments of silence, Dordi let him go. Joey scrambled away from him while Dordi just continued to stand in the same spot. Suddenly he turned and walked out of the building. His brother hurried off to join him, and the men at the VFW never saw the Dordis again.

Chapter 49

Philadelphia, Pennsylvania, Summer 1972
  Augie Augustini

At the end of the summer in 1972, Augie married Penny, his high school sweetheart. As he stood at the alter watching her bridesmaids walk down the aisle, arm in arm with the groomsmen, he thought about how they had become a couple.

They had first met in junior high school when Penny's family moved to Philadelphia from Pittsburgh. Unlike most of the girls in his school, Penny often spoke up in class. She wasn't afraid to ask a question, and she wasn't afraid to disagree with someone—even the teacher. Perhaps what was most remarkable to Augie was that she could disagree with people in such a way that it didn't seem argumentative. He watched her a lot that first year, hoping he could learn to "argue" the way she did. She could nearly always convert someone to her side. She did it so gently most people didn't even realize she was changing their mind, but he noticed.

Regardless of how interesting Augie found her, his attention toward Penny stopped there. Her face was quite plain, despite the dusting of freckles across her nose. She wore oversized cat-eye glasses, had braces, and wild red hair. Her clothes were far too big and looked like they belonged to someone else. Much later he would learn that the clothing *did* belong to someone else. They had belonged to Penny's older brother who had been killed in Vietnam in 1964, the year before Penny's family moved to Philly. Penny had adored her big brother and wearing his clothes was comforting to her.

By tenth grade, however, the braces and oversized clothes were gone. The red hair had been tamed and the goofy glasses replaced by stylish ones that enhanced, rather than hid, her blue eyes. The changes didn't happen overnight but bit by bit over two years. Nevertheless, the changes seemed to hit Augie all at once, and he became captivated by Penny in a way he had never expected. He asked her to the school dance their junior year, and she said yes. They had been together ever since.

His mother had asked him, "Why are you in such a hurry to get married? You only just got back from Vietnam. Live a little. You and Penny are still so young." But Augie was anxious to get married. He was a veteran. An adult. And he was ready to take on adult responsibilities.

Augie's reverie was interrupted when the music suddenly changed. The last bridesmaid and groomsman had taken their places beside the altar, and it was Penny's turn. Everyone stood and Augie watched his soon-to-be wife walk down the aisle with her father. She had written him nearly every day that he was in Vietnam, and he never doubted he would propose the minute he returned. He stood up as tall as he could and smiled as she walked toward him, eagerly anticipating the next phase of his life.

Chapter 50

Cam Ranh Bay, Vietnam, October 1972
  Dennis Dordi and Linh

After the incident with Joey, things finally started making sense to Dennis Dordi. He re-enlisted, and because it would be his fourth tour, his request to be stationed at Nha Trang, the Green Beret base nearest Cam Ranh Bay, was granted. He landed at the Tan Son Nhut Air Base in October 1972 and made an unauthorized stop at the Yankee's Dream before checking in with his commanding officer.

He saw Li Minh as soon as he walked in the bar, and she quickly hurried over to him. "You're back," she said, surprised.

"Where's Linh?"

Li Minh didn't hesitate. "Orphan Island."

He nodded a thank you and was out the door before she could reply. Li Minh smiled, genuinely happy for Linh.

Dordi parked the Jeep near the bridge and jumped out. He covered the distance to the camp in record time and found the tent he had given Linh several years before. It was a bit battered but still did the job. There was no sign of Linh or Teo. He found another boy, maybe nine, tending a fire nearby.

"Hello," Dordi said, trying to remember his Vietnamese. "I'm looking for Linh or Teo. Do you know them?"

The boy nodded. "Teo's dead," he said without emotion. "Linh is checking the traps in the woods." He pointed to an area north of the camp. Dordi didn't move for a moment. He was reeling from the news that Teo had died and knew it would have devastated Linh. He hated that he hadn't been there for her. He quickly regained his wits and took off in the direction the boy had pointed.

A few yards into the thickening woods, he saw her before she saw him. She was kneeling in the grass and looked to be resetting a trap. A dead rabbit lay by her side. "Since when did you learn to hunt?" he asked.

She was turned away from him, so he didn't see her smile. She responded matter-of-factly, "Since I gave up working at the Yankee's Dream." It took a tremendous amount of effort, but Linh purposely finished what she was doing before she stood and turned to face him. She tried to hide her elation at seeing him, not knowing for sure why he was back.

He looked at her. It had been 18 months and 12 days since he last saw her. She was the same but different. She had put on weight in all the right places, and she no longer looked like a child. They walked toward each other and embraced for a long moment.

Then, without breaking the embrace, she asked, "Why are you here?"

"I missed you," he said and held her even tighter.

After a few minutes, she broke away from him. She stepped back and looked at him—scrutinizing him. Finally she said, "Ask me again."

His face broke into a wide grin. "Come home with me."

"Okay," she said and stepped into his arms again. He leaned down and kissed her. In the moment that their lips finally met, he felt the demons that had been circling him for so long wither and die.

Chapter 51

Philadelphia, Pennsylvania, August–December 1972
  Augie Augustini

At the reception immediately after Augie and Penny's wedding, his father pulled him aside and told him, "You need to get life insurance."

Augie, who'd had a couple of beers already, responded with, "What?"

"Life insurance! You have a wife now. You'll probably have kids before long. You have to think about what would happen to them if something happened to you."

Augie had been solely focused on what would happen on the honeymoon but promised his father he would take care of it. Naturally, he forgot.

A few months later, when Penny announced that she was pregnant Augie suddenly remembered his father's advice and quickly took out a modest life insurance policy. He was surprised by Penny's reaction.

"I wish you had discussed it with me first," she had said.

Augie, who was still adjusting to married life, had no idea why she was upset and simply asked, "Why?"

"Because we are supposed to make these kinds of decisions together. It isn't a lot of money, but you still should have discussed it with me first."

Augie started to say his father, to his knowledge, had never discussed money issues with his mother, but he wisely didn't. Instead, he just agreed with her. "You're right, I should have. Do you want me to cancel it?"

She hesitated, "No, I guess not. It isn't a bad idea. It's just that you're young and healthy. It seems like a waste of money right now when we need to save as much as we can for the baby."

"It's just a few dollars a month. We'll be okay."

She nodded in agreement, but the look on her face told him she was still unhappy with him. Once again he realized that he should have listened to his mother. Maybe he wasn't as ready for marriage as he had thought.

Chapter 52

Vietnam, October–December 1972
Dennis Dordi and Linh

As Dordi watched Linh pack and say goodbye to her friends on Orphan Island and then at the Yankee's Dream, something occurred to him. Linh never mentioned a baby. He had been so focused on finding her that he had forgotten about her child. Where was her baby? Had Joey lied? Maybe the baby died? He could think of no other explanations. He decided not to mention it. She was coming with him, and that was the only thing he cared about.

A little more than an hour after Dordi found her in the woods, Linh climbed into the Jeep and left Orphan Island for the last time. As they drove down the familiar alley, much of her life flashed before her eyes. Good riddance, she thought. Linh knew he was taking her to Nha Trang, a city she had heard of but had never visited. Linh had never been anywhere and smiled at the possibilities that lay in front of her. First Nha Trang and then America. She breathed in the warm air and imagined finding Song again. Her daughter would be one in less than a month, and she wondered what Song was doing at that very moment.

Linh sighed heavily and looked at Dennis. She felt a pang of guilt and told herself that she had to tell him about Song. The fact that he came back for her proved that he loved her. Perhaps he loved her enough to not care that she'd had a baby with another man. Would he think less of her because she had given her daughter up? Then there was Teo. Teo *died*. Linh wiped away the tears that formed whenever she thought of Teo, and she wondered yet again why Dennis or any man would want to build a life with her if she couldn't take care of her children? She watched him as he drove. His eyes were on the road, and he didn't see the distress on her face. Out loud Linh said to him, "Before we go to America, I promise I will tell you my secret." But the words were whipped away by the wind and he heard nothing.

He drove her to the Nha Trang Air Base, which was used by both the U.S. Air Force and the Republic of Vietnam air force. As was common during the Vietnam War, South Vietnamese soldiers frequently brought their wives and families to the area where they were stationed. The rationale for having the families nearby was a practical one. So many men had been drafted that the mostly women and children left behind were particularly vulnerable to attack by bandits and enemy soldiers. Consequently, the civilian camps attached to ARVN bases were often much larger than the base itself. Dordi couldn't bring Linh to the American base, but he was certain he could make arrangements for her at the ARVN family camp.

Upon arriving at the civilian camp, Dordi quickly figured out who was in charge. Although it was not a military installation or even an official municipality, Dordi knew from experience that there was always a hierarchy. He discovered the wife of one of the ARVN commanding officers was clearly the leader. Linh stood back and watched Dordi negotiate with the older woman, who kept sneaking glances in her direction. After a heated discussion, the woman nodded and pointed to an unoccupied area, and Dordi began setting up the tent and hammock that he had procured for Linh.

"Where did you get these?" she asked. They laughed and answered in unison, "Compliments of the U.S. Army."

Then, her tone serious, Linh asked, "The woman you spoke with—she's okay with me being here?" Linh was very self-conscious. She knew that everyone could tell she was mixed-race. She didn't want any trouble.

Dordi stopped what he was doing and stood in front of her with his hands on her shoulders. "Yes. She assured me you will be treated just like everyone else. You'll be expected to be helpful to others, and they will be helpful to you."

"How did you convince her?"

Dordi smiled. "I can be very persuasive." Then his tone changed and the smile disappeared. He told her, "If they treat you badly—actually, if they treat you in any way *other* than really well, I want to hear about it."

She gave him an insecure smile, and he kissed her again—perhaps for the benefit of anyone watching. He was making a statement that she was important to him. When it was time for him to go, he held her close and whispered in her ear, "One year. That's all. I only have to survive one more tour, and then I will take you to the U.S. I promise I will give you a better life." She just nodded, knowing she couldn't leave with him unless she told him about Song, but she was so afraid that then he wouldn't want her anymore.

By the end of 1972 when Dordi reported for duty for the fourth time, the war was winding down for the Western forces. "Vietnamization," the name given to the process of ARVN taking over all aspects of the South's fight with the North, was well underway. Australia had already pulled out most of their soldiers, and the United States contingent was smaller than it had been in a decade. Although Dordi had a few missions that took him away from the base, he was able to spend much more time with Linh at the ARVN camp than either of them had expected. In fact, he spent far more nights at the ARVN camp than he did his own base. Although the hammock was not designed for lovers, they managed.

In the quiet moments late at night, they would lay awake and talk. He told her more about his parents and his brothers. Dordi also told Linh about his life in Vietnam, the missions, the fighting, the many covert operations, and the friendships. He told her about his closest friend, Loc Tin Vong. "I first met LT in—what was it? '63 or '64? It was my first tour, and as green as I was, he was even greener. But damn. He wanted to learn. I helped him learn English, and he tried to teach me Vietnamese. I ran into him again during my second tour. It was during the Tet Offensive. Fighting was intense and many of the men hadn't been in-country very long. Man, it was good to see him again. After that, I helped him train, and he eventually joined the Vietnamese Special Forces. We had a lot of missions together after that. We were lethal as a team. He's the one that taught me how to throw a knife. Damn. I miss LT." He paused, remembering his friend. "I think I would probably be dead by now if it weren't for him." Then he laughed and added, "And I KNOW he would be dead by now if it weren't for me." He grew quiet and hugged Linh tighter to his chest, knowing it was likely that LT had been killed since he last saw him.

Linh had far fewer adventures that she could share, but she told him more stories about growing up at the Yankee's Dream. She told him more about her adoptive mother, Song, and how she died. "That's when I ended up at Orphan Island. In some ways it was worse than being at the bar, but in other ways it was better. After I found Teo, I felt like I had a family." She grew quiet for a moment. "He was the reason I finally went to work for Mr. Ong. I needed the money to take care of him." She paused again and then continued. "I hated it. I hated every minute of it, but it was the only time I felt like I was really able to provide for Teo."

She wanted to tell Dennis about Song, but she was afraid. She just told him that she got fed up with Mr. Ong and finally left, but then she couldn't take care of Teo. "We were starving. I told him the fish was no good, but he was so hungry. He wouldn't listen." He held her close as she cried and remembered the child that she had found in the woods only for him to die a few years later. "He had just turned nine. His whole life was in that damn camp. He never got to see anything else." She grew quiet for a while. When she finally continued she told him, "After he died, I learned to set traps. I got pretty good at catching rabbits and other small animals. If I had learned sooner, Teo might still be alive."

They spent many nights talking and telling each other stories, but other nights they just enjoyed being together in silence. Less than two months after Linh moved to the ARVN camp, Dordi proposed. "I love you, Linh. I think I have since that first R&R."

He had a small, simple ring that he had bought in Virginia before he left. He tried to give it to her, but she shook her head and said, "No, I can't."

Dordi felt as though he had been punched in the gut. She loved him. He knew that she did. "I—I don't understand."

Linh offered no explanation. She just told him again, "No. I can't."

Dordi said nothing and just stared at her. She turned away from him so he wouldn't see the tears in her eyes. Without another word, he left the ARVN camp and didn't return.

Chapter 53

Saigon, Vietnam, December 1972
  Chi

Chi spent about six months on the Ho Chi Minh Trail before she decided she was ready to return to active duty with the VC. The near relentless bombing of the trail by the Americans had led to many deaths of young people working with Brigade 559, and it helped assuage the guilt she felt for killing the young soldier named Mark. She made her way south, eventually reaching the NVA headquarters in Cambodia just west of Saigon. Her assignment was simple, although dangerous. She would join one of several VC squads that routinely attacked the Tan Son Nhut air base during the day. The majority of personnel leaving Vietnam flew out of Tan Son Nhut. Since most American soldiers only spent a year in Vietnam, attacking as they were leaving accomplished at least two goals. First and foremost, killing the enemy was always a priority, even if their fight was over. Second, it was psychological warfare. Killing men who had laid down their weapons and were leaving demonstrated the resolve of the North Vietnamese and sent a message to their enemies—as long as you were on Vietnamese soil, you were within Charlie's reach.

Chapter 54

Nha Trang, Vietnam, December 1972
   Dennis Dordi and Linh

Linh knew she had made a mistake. She loved Dennis and he deserved an explanation. She borrowed a sleeveless, blue and white Western-style minidress from her neighbor at the camp. She put on a small amount of makeup and dabbed perfume behind her ears the way Li Minh had taught her. She wanted to look her best when she saw Dennis. Linh could have easily walked the short distance from the civilian camp to the headquarters of the 5th Special Forces Group, but she found a young ARVN soldier who was willing to drive her. She was grateful because she didn't want to get dusty or sidetracked by someone wanting to talk to her.

It was late afternoon when she was dropped off at the entrance to the American base adjacent to the ARVN encampment. She smiled at the guard, and he waved her through without even questioning her. She knew the Americans employed many Vietnamese women for various jobs and guessed the guard assumed that's why she was there. If security was as lax everywhere else, it was no wonder Dennis could acquire tents and such so easily.

She looked around the base and realized she had no idea where to look for Dennis. Just like the base at Cam Ranh Bay, there were several large buildings and row upon row of smaller buildings. Several signs were posted around the base, many in both English and Vietnamese, but she could read neither language and so the words on them meant nothing to her. She looked around for a moment, unsure of where to go. Then she saw two Vietnamese women walking toward one of the larger buildings and quickly approached them.

"Excuse me," Linh said in her native language, and the women stopped and looked at her. "I'm looking for a soldier."

"Plenty of them here," the taller woman said, frowning with distaste as she looked at Linh.

Linh self-consciously rubbed her arms. She knew her unusual skin color announced to the world that she was something other than pure Vietnamese. These women clearly thought less of her because of it. She tried to pretend that she didn't care what they thought and smiled as she said, "Well, one in particular. Dennis Dordi. He's a Green Beret."

"Oh. Well, if he's here, he'll be in a hooch on the third row toward the back."

"Thank you," Linh replied as the women quickly walked away from her. "Third row toward the back." She looked uncertainly at the many buildings. "That doesn't narrow it down very much."

Undeterred, she walked in the direction the woman indicated. She found the third row of buildings and made her way toward the ones furthest away. A few soldiers and civilians spoke or acknowledged her with a nod of the head but most ignored her. She got the impression that a woman in a short skirt walking among the barracks was not an uncommon sight. After passing more than a dozen hooches, she was excited to see a sign that meant something to her. Although she couldn't read the words, the logo on it matched the Green Beret patch on Dennis' uniform. There were only four buildings left. She approached the first one and knocked on the open door. A very dark-skinned and muscular American without a shirt appeared in front of her.

He removed the cigarette from his mouth and leaned on the door frame. "Well, hello there," he said, looking at her appreciatively. "How can I be of service?"

She smiled, "I'm looking for Dennis Dordi."

The man looked a little disappointed but nodded. "If he is here, he'll be in the canteen up front or the hooch next door." He jerked a thumb toward the next building and Linh thanked him. As she started to walk away, he called after her, "If you don't find him, I'll keep you company."

Outwardly, she ignored him, but inside she smiled. The Westerners weren't bothered by her uncertain heritage. She wished she could live on the American side of the complex and not the ARVN civilian camp where she was only accepted because of Dennis. She made her way to the next building and again found the door propped open to the occasional breeze. She stood outside ready to knock, but then was suddenly unsure of herself. From the doorway, she looked into the small room and saw that it had six sets of bunk beds all neatly made. Only one bed appeared to be occupied. A soldier lay on the bottom bunk hands folded across his chest. She saw it was Dennis, and her confidence returned. She thought he might be asleep, but he wasn't.

She was about to knock on the door when, without opening his eyes, Dordi said, "If you're looking for Peterson, he's in the mess hall." He could smell the perfume. Peterson always had a girl looking for him.

But it was Linh that replied. "No. I'm looking for you."

Dordi sat up so quickly he bumped his head on the bunk above him. "Linh," was all he said.

She walked over to him and sat beside him. "I'm sorry. You—you just surprised me."

He laughed. "Well, you showing up here sure surprised the hell out of me."

"Can we try again?" she asked.

He put his arm around her. "Whatever you want, Linh. Whatever you want."

Later that night when they were back in her tent and the lovemaking was over, she told him about Song. "That's the real reason I left the Yankee's Dream. I did hate it, but Mr. Ong gave me no choice when he found out I was pregnant. I thought I would go back after Song was born, but—but—I just couldn't put her through that. Growing up there was awful. I wanted a better life for her than that. Then I realized that I couldn't take care of her properly without the money from the Yankee's Dream. I knew she would die if I didn't go back, but Mr. Ong was just such a horrible man." She shuddered and took a ragged breath, willing herself not to cry. "In the end, giving Song up seemed like the best option for her. She was adopted and is in America now. It was my only choice to save her."

She said all this as they lay in the dark in the hammock with her head on his chest and his arms around her. Dordi stared into the darkness trying to think of what he should say to her. She *did* have a choice. If she had told him, he would have brought her home anyway when he asked her the first time. Hell, he'd have even brought Teo to the States if that's what she wanted. The thought made him smile and shake his head. Dennis Dordi, family man. He had always thought of himself as a tough guy. A badass Green Beret. But family man? Where the hell did that come from?

He didn't tell her he would have accepted Song. What good would that do now? It would just make her regret her choice even more. Then he began to wonder if Song was the real reason why Linh agreed to leave with him now. Is she secretly hoping she will find her child if she moves to the U.S.? Is that why she said no when he proposed, because she really *didn't* love him? Was she just using him now? Does she just want a ticket to the States? He told himself it didn't matter, but the thought gnawed at him and made him insecure in a way no woman ever had before.

Linh was lost in her own thoughts. There. It's done. I told him. Why doesn't he say anything? Does he still love me? Does he still want me? She wanted to ask him but was afraid of the answer, so she said nothing.

They lay in the dark each nursing their own insecurities. Finally the badass Green Beret who had once fearlessly picked up a live grenade and tossed it from his foxhole mustered the courage to once again ask the woman he loved, "Will you marry me?"

In the darkness he couldn't see her smile, but he heard her response. "Yes."

Chapter 55

Tan Son Nhut Air Base, Vietnam, March 1973
  Linh and Dordi
  Chi

Only three months after Dordi started his fourth tour, President Nixon signed the Peace Accord that ended U.S. involvement in Vietnam. By March of 1973, only six months into his year-long commitment, Dordi was released from service. Dordi, along with about 20 other Americans who had been stationed at Nha Trang, packed up and headed to the Tan Son Nhut Air Base near Saigon. Most of the men were U.S. Air Force but a couple of others were from the 5th Special Forces Group. Like Dordi, two other men had married Vietnamese women.

After reaching the airfield, most of the group began to disembark from the truck, but Dordi hung back and looked around. He knew they were not out of danger and a VC attack was always possible. When he saw nothing of concern, he jumped from the truck and scanned the area again. He was looking for anything suspicious, anything that didn't belong. Satisfied, he turned back and lifted Linh from the truck. He smiled at her as he gently set her on the ground. He leaned down, kissed her, and then wrapped a protective arm around her. Ever vigilant, Dordi continued to scan the area for any potential threats.

A hundred yards away, Chi and six other VC guerrillas hid in the brush just outside the fence that surrounded the base. Chi held the binoculars to her eyes and watched the Americans as they climbed out of the truck, grabbed their gear, and prepared to leave. The VC mission was to attack and perhaps kill a few men on their way back to the States. The VC frequently attacked the base. Although it was risky and the potential for being captured or killed themselves was quite high, it was important to keep the enemy on the defensive. For her part, Chi was to watch, determine the direction for the rocket launchers, and give the signal to attack.

They would attack when most of the men were out of the truck but still clustered around it. Chi raised her arm in preparation for giving the signal to launch the rockets, but she hesitated when she saw one of the soldiers help a Vietnamese woman out of the truck. The woman laughed as he placed her on the ground. Then he kissed her and hugged her close. He was also smiling. Despite herself, Chi found the scene touching, and she watched the couple for a moment. She looked more closely at the woman, studying her through the binoculars. She was young, maybe 20, and beautiful. She had the most unusual color of skin. Not white, not black, not yellow. Chi's heart rose up into her throat and she gasped. It was Linh. *Linh.* Her baby. After all these years, she had finally found her. But Linh loved an American and she was leaving with him. Chi had to stop her.

Chi tore her eyes away from her daughter and stepped back from the fence. What can she do? She must get to Linh. She looked at her very confused comrades. "It's no good. We may need to move. I'll do recon and report back." She dropped the binoculars and took off running before anyone could stop her or ask questions.

Chi's mind raced. She had to get to Linh. Fortunately, she and her comrades were not wearing the black pajamas that the VC so often wore. They had wanted to be able to blend in with the locals, if necessary, and for Chi, it was now *very* necessary. She made her way along the fence looking for any kind of opening or even a manned gate. She knew that many Vietnamese women worked on American bases. Could she simply pretend to be one of them? Her English was good, but she was dressed as a peasant. Women employed by the base dressed better. Chi had seen them coming and going many times and hated them for colluding with the enemy. No, she can't pretend to be one of them. However, the air base was home to not just American military but also the South Vietnamese air force. She decided that if she was questioned, she would pretend to be the wife of an airman.

She reached a side entrance to the base. The break in the chain-link fence contained a wooden structure with two openings, a large one for vehicles and a smaller one for pedestrians. Both openings were covered by a wooden roof. A small guardhouse stood in the middle between the two openings. Two Americans dressed in the uniform of the Military Police stood outside the small structure and were busy with clipboards as they appeared to check names off a list. A long line of men in clean and pressed uniforms stood patiently waiting to leave. Chi was on the opposite side away from the men on foot, including the two MPs. No Jeeps or other vehicles were waiting to pass through the gate. Keeping an eye on the MPs, Chi made her move when they were both preoccupied with their clipboards. She easily ducked under the mechanical arm that stood in the way of motorized traffic and entered the base unnoticed.

Chi was anxious to get out of the open and got away from the gate as quickly as possible. Numerous long low buildings were lined up in rows, and she darted between two of them. She wanted to run but knew that would look suspicious. She saw a woman squatting on the ground washing clothes in a metal tub. A small child stood nearby watching her as she walked past. Chi smiled at the little boy, and he smiled back. The woman barely glanced at her. Chi took a deep breath and tried to relax. Maybe she really would blend in. Now, where was Linh?

Chapter 56

Tan Son Nhut Air Base, Vietnam, March 1973
  Linh and Dordi

Linh and Dordi walked hand in hand toward the hangar where they would wait until it was their time to board a plane. This would be the fourth time Dordi left Vietnam, and he knew the drill well. The first leg of the journey would likely take them to Okinawa or perhaps mainland Japan. They would refuel and then spend the next 12 hours in the air before landing in the U.S. Maybe Alaska. Maybe California. He wouldn't know for sure until they had left Vietnam. All he knew was that in about 36 hours, he and Linh would be in Virginia having dinner with his parents. He looked at his wife of less than a week. "They are going to love you," he told her once again. He knew she was nervous about meeting his family.

"Are you sure? You don't think they will think badly about me because of—everything?"

"I told you to forget all that. I have. I've done things here I am not proud of. You did what you had to do to survive, just like every one of us here. They only need to know what you want them to know."

She nodded gratefully. Dennis had said this to her before, but she still worried about whether his family and his country would accept her. She squeezed his hand as they walked inside the hangar. As they took their seats, she took in the people around them. She saw another Vietnamese woman sitting across from her. Linh's eyes fell to the woman's hands. They were in her lap clutching the much larger, much darker hand of the handsome

G.I. who sat beside her. She scrutinized the couple. The woman was clearly pure Vietnamese, while her husband was a medium-skinned Black man. She continued studying the couple and wondered what their children would look like. She thought they might look like her—not white, not black, not yellow. The thought made her smile.

The group waited impatiently without much small talk. Everyone was nervous and anxious. Unlike every other time Dordi had left Vietnam, this time they didn't have to wait very long. Less than an hour after the truck had deposited them at the airport, Dennis and Linh Dordi, along with the others who had been stationed at the Nha Trang base, boarded a Flying Tiger DC 8. A short time later, the plane taxied down the runway and then lifted into the air. Linh had never before been on a plane and watched in amazement as the ground grew smaller and smaller below her. At first, she saw things she recognized, but soon they were too high up to make out anything more than the many rivers that snaked throughout her country. When they were over the ocean and she could see only water, she leaned back in her seat and looked at her husband. "I love you," she told him, resting her head on his shoulder. Dordi smiled and took her hand in his.

Chapter 57

Tan Son Nhut Air Base, Vietnam, March 1973
Chi

Less than ten minutes after Linh's plane took to the skies, Chi found the hangar she had seen from her hiding place along the fence. She had seen two different planes take off since entering through the gate, and she fervently hoped that Linh was still waiting. As she walked around the large room filled with soldiers, the only women she saw were American. She thought they looked like army nurses. She saw no Vietnamese civilians. Not wanting to give up hope, she circled the room again. Still no Linh. After making the round a third time, Chi began to accept that she was too late. She had lost her daughter again. She collapsed on an empty chair and tried to hold back the tears, but she couldn't. She cried for the first time in a decade—horrible wracking sobs that took her breath away. She felt as though she were a teenager again, waking up in the night to find her baby gone. She felt just as helpless and just as hopeless as she had that night. She thought the crushing grief would kill her, and she genuinely hoped that it would.

Chapter 58

Charlottesville, Virginia, March–April 1973
  Linh and Michelle Dordi

Dordi's parents lived about ten miles outside of Charlottesville, Virginia. Both were retired but still had rental property that brought them a pretty good income. After Dordi was released from the service, he and Linh briefly moved in with them while his mother planned a wedding. Although an army chaplain had married Linh and Dennis before they left Vietnam, that wasn't good enough for his mother, Michelle. They married for the second time in April of 1973 in a small ceremony attended only by his family and a few close friends. Before the wedding, Michelle took Linh dress shopping.

"You are even prettier than Dennis said in his letters," she said to Linh as she held up a dress for her to consider.

"Dennis told you about me?" Linh asked, surprised.

"Oh, yes. He didn't write me very often, but when he did, he was telling me about you. He told me all about the beautiful young girl he met in the alley behind some bar when he was on R&R."

"He said I was beautiful?"

Michelle smiled. "I believe his exact words were 'unique, exotic, and beautiful.'"

"What does that mean? Exotic?"

Michelle laughed. "It means he had never seen anyone like you before! He was completely taken by you. He also said you were very young, and he worried about you being on your own like you were. When he came home from his first tour—that was before he met you—he told me about all the homeless children in Vietnam. It really troubled him, but you were the only one he ever mentioned specifically. I knew immediately he thought you were special."

Linh's heart swelled. She had no idea what he had thought of her back then. "He was very kind to me and Teo, but he never…," she hesitated. "He never tried anything."

"Well, I should hope not! He was 25 and you were 15. But truth be told, he was completely taken by you from the moment the two of you met. He said you had skin the color of caramels, which he has loved since he was a child."

"What are cara…," she struggled with the unusual word. She hesitated then tried again, "Carma?"

"Caramels," Michelle repeated. "They are a delicious, sweet candy—and Dennis loves them."

Linh looked at herself in the mirror as she tried on the dress Michelle had found. She had always hated the color of her skin, but Dennis thought she was exotic. Unique. The color of candy. She smiled at the thought. She looked at Michelle, who was happily fussing over the dress Linh was wearing. She felt completely accepted, and she knew she finally had the family she had always wanted. She was happier than she had ever thought she could be. Then she thought about Song and her smile faded a little. She would be two and a half now, and, once again, Linh could only hope that she was happy and well loved.

Chapter 59

Tan Son Nhut Air Base, Vietnam, March–April 1973
   Chi

Chi's anguish did not go unnoticed by the people around her. One of the army nurses who was waiting for her plane to depart moved to sit next to the sobbing woman. She offered her a handkerchief and asked, "Is there anything I can do?"

Chi shook her head but gratefully accepted the handkerchief. She took a ragged breath and tried to speak, but no words came out. Suddenly she began crying again, and she buried her face in her hands.

Another woman, an airman stationed at the base, walked over and sat on the other side of Chi. "Miss, are you okay?" She repeated the question in what Chi thought was supposed to be Vietnamese.

Chi nodded. Haltingly, she finally managed to say in English, "I—I missed the plane." She wanted to tell them about Linh, but she just couldn't find her voice. She was too distraught.

The two women exchanged a knowing glance. They assumed some soldier had promised to take her home with him, but then backed out. They thought he might have purposefully given her the wrong information so that she missed the flight. It had happened before.

The airman, who introduced herself as Julie Ryder, convinced Chi to come with her. She led her away from the hangar to the mess hall and offered to get her something to eat. Chi shook her head, so Julie just brought her a glass of water. They sat at an empty table, and Julie tried to get the woman to talk to her. "Is it a man? Did he leave without you?"

Chi was finally regaining control of herself and thought about the woman's question. She quickly realized that having been abandoned by an American soldier might be a better story than the truth. Maybe they would help her go to America. In that moment, she didn't care about the war. She only wanted to follow Linh wherever she was going. She quickly made up a lie. "He said he loved me." She thought of the Frenchman who had betrayed her. "He said he would take me with him." She began to cry again and wasn't sure herself if she was acting or not. The pain she felt was very real.

"I am so very sorry," Julie said, squeezing her hand. "Did you travel far to come here?"

"I'm from—from Cu Chi," Chi responded. She didn't know what made her say that—she had never even been there. She knew it was a city northwest of Saigon and that there was an American army base there. There were also VC tunnels in that area.

The woman frowned, "Well, we probably can't get you home tonight. Tomorrow I can find someone to take you. For tonight, I will walk you over to the ARVN family camp and try to find you a place to stay."

Chi nodded but was thinking fast. She didn't want to leave the base unless it was to go to the States. "There really isn't anything for me at home anymore. My family—they are all gone," she said purposefully thinking about Linh so the tears would start again. "Can't I just stay here? Maybe...," she struggled to think of a name that sounded American. She thought of Mark, the young artist she had killed in DaNang. She still had his notebook and knew his death would haunt her for the rest of her life. It felt wrong to use his name, but she did anyway. She said to Julie, "Maybe Mark got the dates wrong?" She tried to sound hopeful. "Maybe he will come for me tomorrow?"

Julie looked at her sympathetically. "We can check the logbook. See if he was here or is expected soon." She hoped that Mark wasn't a jerk who had ditched this poor woman. Although Chi was pretty, she was clearly much older than most of the young soldiers. She was almost certain they would not find Mark's name on any manifest. Nevertheless, she asked, "What's his last name? Do you know his rank and branch of service?"

Chi picked answers randomly from her head, "Captain. He is a captain in the Army."

Julie bit her lip. An officer, she thought. Definitely not some draftee enchanted by a pretty peasant. More and more she felt like this poor woman had been duped. "And his last name?"

Chi had no idea. She racked her brain for a name—any name—that she knew could be American. Suddenly she remembered one. A good one. "Kennedy. Like the president." Chi watched Julie carefully as she said it and was relieved when the woman readily accepted the lie.

Julie nodded as she spoke. "Captain Mark Kennedy. I will try to track him down and see where he is," she said with determination. She found herself getting pissed off at a man she had never even met. Julie stood up, hands on hips, and looked around the mess hall as though she might see Captain Kennedy. Finally she looked back at Chi. "Let's find you a place to stay at the ARVN camp," she said as she began to walk. She motioned for Chi to follow her.

They walked by the American barracks, the officer's club, and the landing area for the helicopters. After passing the housing for ARVN airmen, they came to the civilian camp. It was immediately adjacent to the ARVN barracks, although it was outside the official footprint of the base.

Chi stuck to her story of waiting for Mark. Although Julie learned that there were two men with that name currently serving in Vietnam, neither, of course, was Chi's man. As far as Julie could determine, there was no U.S. Army captain named Mark Kennedy who had ever been in Vietnam. Julie eventually surmised that Mark Kennedy wasn't even his real name, and her animosity for him grew. She felt sorry for Chi and wanted to help her. Julie had her own history with men being less than honest and perhaps because of it felt an immediate kinship with Chi.

With Julie's help, Chi was quickly able to make herself useful around the air base. She was smart and her English was good enough that occasionally she stepped into the role of translator if none of the official translators were available. Chi's secret goal was to befriend a lonely soldier. She would pretend to love him and get him to take her to the States when he rotated out. But at 36 years old, none of the young men stationed at the base gave her more than a cursory glance. Even worse, most Americans had already left Vietnam, and the ones who remained were older, wiser, and married. Still, she stayed at the Tan Son Nhut Air Base and worked for the enemy because she knew Linh was in the U.S. She was determined to find a way to get there.

Chapter 60

San Francisco, California, April–June 1973
  Linh and Dordi

Shortly after the wedding, the newlyweds moved to California and Dordi quickly found a job with a construction company. Eric, the owner, was a veteran of the Korean War and, unlike so many businessmen at the time, was very happy to hire veterans of America's most recent conflict.

Linh enrolled in a free adult learning class offered by a nearby church. She wanted to improve her ability to speak English and was anxious to learn to read and write. However, Linh had no education at all. Even though the Vietnamese and English languages used the same alphabet, she had never learned it. It would take time, but she was determined.

Linh was not the only Vietnamese immigrant in the class. Two other students, a husband and wife, were also struggling to learn the language of their new country. Unlike in Vietnam, it seemed they did not look down on her for her racial mixture. Soon, the two women became good friends and Kim-Ly convinced Linh to take a part-time job working with her at a nearby nail salon. Linh loved it. She had a real job with real girlfriends, and she no longer cared what other people thought of her skin. She was *exotic*.

Despite their jobs, money was tight for the Dordis. They could only afford a small, one-bedroom apartment, but Linh, who had previously and only briefly had a tiny bedroom to call her own, felt like a queen in a huge castle. She was very happy shopping at thrift stores and secondhand shops and quickly made the small apartment cozy and welcoming.

Chapter 61

Tan Son Nhut Air Base, Vietnam, April–June 1973
  Chi and Rob

In early April of 1973, Chi was still at the Tan Son Nhut Air Base and was anxious to find a soldier willing to take her home with him. She thought she had met someone promising when she was asked to serve as a translator for an officer she had not previously met. Major Robert McMasters was stationed in Saigon but had some business at Tan Son Nhut Air Base. She knew he was attracted to her the moment she walked into the room. He had been casually leaning against a desk but stood up and moved to smooth out his uniform when he saw her. He walked toward her, smiled, and held out his hand. "Hello! You must be the translator. Thank you for coming. I'm Major Robert McMasters."

"Hello. I am Chi," she said as warmly as she could. She let him shake her hand, and she noticed he used both hands to envelop her proffered one.

"Just Chi?"

Chi smiled, "Yes, just Chi. How may I help you?" She batted her eyes the way she used to when she pretended to be a prostitute and tried to appear interested in him. He was tall and thin and, in Chi's opinion, rather plain looking. Important for her plan, he wasn't wearing a wedding ring, he was older than she was, and he seemed attracted to her. Perfect, she thought.

After their business was concluded, he invited her to the officer's club for a drink, and she readily accepted. A few days after their first meeting, the major was again in need of a translator, and Chi was summoned to help.

However, when she got to the interrogation room, only Major McMasters was there.

"I'm so sorry, but it looks like I won't be needing your help after all. Since I have wasted your time, let me make it up to you by taking you to lunch. We could even drive into Saigon if you don't have other plans." Of course, she didn't.

After their lunch date in Saigon, Major McMasters, who she called Rob, began visiting the base nearly every evening. He would take her to the officer's club for dinner, followed by long walks around the base. As quickly as she thought it was acceptable, Chi invited him back to her small, private space at the civilian tent city adjacent to the ARVN barracks. Her little corner of the camp was not very comfortable nor completely private since the walls were made of canvas, but Americans were leaving at an alarming rate, and she thought Rob might be her only chance to get to the States. Therefore, Chi pretended she was so crazy about him that she didn't care if anyone heard them. Rob, however, was a little less enthusiastic about Chi's accommodations, and less than three months after they met, he invited her to Saigon to spend the weekend with him. He told her he had his own little apartment on the base and that they could enjoy a romantic weekend together without anyone else around.

Chi was thrilled that things were going so well with Rob and was hopeful that he might even propose over the weekend. The war made many men needy and foolish and she hoped that Rob was one of them. She dressed in her prettiest dress and even wore a bit of makeup that Julie had given her. She waited out front near the gate and smiled broadly at him when he drove through it. For dinner, he took her to a lovely French restaurant in the heart of Saigon.

Chi was not happy about his choice in restaurants, but of course he didn't know about the Frenchman who had betrayed her. After they had ordered she simply said, "I'm surprised this French place is still in business given their disastrous defeat in 1954."

Rob, fork in hand, pointed to the bounty on the table in front of them. "But the food is still good, so I guess that the politics don't matter so much."

She smiled at him as she took a sip from her wine glass. Then she turned away from him so he wouldn't see the look of disgust that was no doubt on her face. Chi set her glass down, took a deep breath, and willed herself to focus. She turned back to Rob and asked him to tell her more about his childhood. They talked all through dinner, and Chi forced herself to smile and laugh at every little joke he told. She hoped she was being charming, but it was exhausting and her cheeks ached from the incessant smiling. She wondered how long she would have to keep up the act once he took her to the States. However, she needn't have worried.

After dinner, Rob drove her to the Australian embassy and parked in a spot right in front. Chi was confused. "Why are we at the Australian embassy?"

Rob laughed. "Because this is where I am stationed! Most of us Aussies left Vietnam back in January. Only those of us guarding the embassy are left." They were still sitting in the Jeep, and Rob reached over and took Chi's hand. "The rest of us will be leaving soon. I won't be in Vietnam much longer." He hesitated before continuing. He had a whole romantic thing planned, but what the hell, he thought. He couldn't wait. He blurted out, "I was hoping you'd come home with me." He leaned over to kiss her, but she pushed him away.

Chi tasted bile as her stomach twisted into a knot, and she thought she might vomit. He's Australian, she thought. She had him right where she wanted him but never bothered to ask him his nationality. "I'm such an idiot," she said out loud. "This explains why your uniform is different. I thought you were just in a different branch of the military. I didn't know you were Australian."

"Well, what difference does it make, love?" He took her hand again. "I'm crazy about you. And you're crazy about me. Right?"

"No, Rob, I am not. I want to go to America, not Australia." She pulled her hand from his and turned away from him. "Please take me back to Tan Son Nhut." He just stared at her as though he didn't understand what she was saying. When he didn't restart the Jeep, she said as kindly as she could, "I'm sorry, but I don't love you. I was just using you." She knew her words were hurtful, but she was hurting too. Tears of frustration began to form and she wiped her eyes.

Rob sat looking at her a little longer as he tried to process what she was saying. When it was clear to him that she meant what she said, he drove her back to the base. It was a short drive but seemed to take forever. Neither of them spoke. When he pulled up to the gate, she jumped out of the Jeep before it had come to a complete stop and left him without another word. He watched her walk away and was bitterly disappointed when she didn't even glance back. Finally he turned the Jeep around and drove away.

Chapter 62

Philadelphia, Pennsylvania, July–August 1973
  Augustini Family

Augie and Penny celebrated their one-year anniversary with an argument. The now very pregnant Penny was adamant that Augie stop smoking.

"You promised me you would stop. It isn't good for the baby."

Augie shook his head. "My mother smoked the whole time she was pregnant, and I'm fine. Besides, you don't smoke. You're the one that matters."

"But aren't they saying now that secondhand smoke is just as bad?"

Augie shook his head again and said irritably, "Well, *they* don't know everything." He picked up the newspaper and snapped it open attempting to emulate his father and signal to his wife that the discussion was over. Penny didn't get the message.

"But you promised," she said softly. He ignored her.

Augie's smoking was not discussed again until after Augie and Penny's daughter was born in August. By that time, Augie had developed a nagging cough. Penny used it to again encourage Augie to quit. "It's the smoking. It's damaging your lungs."

"It's just a cough. I'm fine."

Penny held the newborn up. "The doctor says the smoking isn't good for Sara. Please stop," she begged him.

Augie's first instinct was to argue with her. Although Sara had been born a month early and had spent two weeks in the hospital, he was certain that wasn't his fault. Besides, according to the doctor, she was healthy despite being underweight. In his mind that meant his smoking had not been a problem for Sara. On the other hand, he wasn't a doctor, and he couldn't be sure. He really didn't want to give in to Penny, but the cigarettes were expensive. They had a baby now, and he knew he should spend the money on other things. He took Sara from Penny's arms and held her close for a moment. Then he looked at his wife. "Okay. I'll quit."

"Promise? This time you have to mean it. Don't say it if you don't mean it."

He was about to say "I promise" when another coughing fit seized him causing Sara to cry. Penny took the baby as Augie tried to catch his breath. After several minutes the coughing eased and in a scratchy voice Augie managed to whisper, "I promise."

Chapter 63

San Francisco, California, May 1974–January 1975
  Linh and Dordi

In Vietnam, Dordi and Linh had always been diligent to use condoms. After they were married, they became a little careless. Only a year after they married, Linh announced that she was pregnant. Although she was ecstatic at the prospect of having another child, occasionally Linh would be overcome by sadness. Song was never far from her thoughts, and she sometimes felt guilty about having another baby after giving up her first. November 5, 1974, Song's third birthday, was especially difficult. Dordi came home from work to find his very pregnant wife curled up on the couch. Clearly, she had been crying.

"What if I can't take care of our baby? Song would have died if I kept her. Teo *did* die. What if I am just a terrible mother?"

Dordi did everything he could to reassure Linh. He told her all of the things that she already knew—that Teo had made his own choice and that she gave up Song because she loved her. Nothing could comfort her. Eventually he just held her until she was cried out.

Lily Marie Dordi was born on January 24, 1975. Despite all of her fears, Linh was a wonderful and attentive mother. In fact, it was Linh who first noticed some troubling signs and alerted Lily's pediatrician.

"Sometimes her skin looks a little blue. That's not normal. And shouldn't she have gained more weight by now?" Linh asked at Lily's one-month checkup. "She is just so tiny."

Initially, the doctor was unconcerned. "Well, Mrs. Dordi, you're not a very big person. Your daughter just takes after you." But then he too noticed that the skin around Lily's lips had a bluish cast suggesting she was not getting enough oxygen. He listened to her heart and didn't like what he heard. He ordered a few tests.

Lily was soon diagnosed with hypoplastic left heart syndrome, meaning that one-half of her heart was too small and could not meet the needs of her body. Her pediatrician explained to the Dordis that there was no treatment he could offer Lily and that most babies with the syndrome died within a few months of birth.

Linh and Dordi were devastated. Linh quit her job and dropped out of her English classes in order to stay home with Lily. She was determined to spend every moment with her and make whatever time she had as happy as possible.

Chapter 64

Tan Son Nhut Air Base, Vietnam, March 1975–April 1975
  Chi

After the disastrous relationship with Rob ended, Chi needed a new plan. She did everything she could to be helpful to the Americans, and she started paying much more attention to uniforms. But by March 1975, it was clear the end of the war was near. The NVA were steadily coming closer and closer to Saigon, and everyone knew the South was going to lose. American civilians had long since been evacuated, and now the Vietnamese working beside the Americans were offered the opportunity to leave as well. Chi didn't hesitate.

In early April 1975, Chi and many others boarded a chartered commercial flight that would eventually take them to the U.S. Unlike the thousands that would leave Vietnam later, Chi's trip was relatively calm and uneventful. The flight would make a stop in Manila to refuel and would then continue on to Los Angeles, California, where they would board buses to a refugee tent city adjacent to the U.S. Marine Corps base at Camp Pendleton. Of course, Chi didn't know all that as her plane taxied down the runway and lifted into the air. She only knew that soon she and Linh would once again be on the same continent. She looked out the window watching Vietnam disappear below her and wondered if she would ever see her country again.

Chapter 65

Philadelphia, Pennsylvania, March–April 1975
  Augie Augustini

Despite having quit smoking more than a year prior, Augie's cough had not improved. In fact, Penny felt it had gotten worse. She had read somewhere that green tea would help, but it didn't seem to make a difference. Plus, Augie hated it. Penny finally convinced him to see a doctor who diagnosed him with emphysema. Unfortunately, the treatments the VA doctor prescribed were not helpful, and Augie had to make several more trips to the VA to see two additional doctors. In early April of 1975, his diagnosis was changed to chronic obstructive pulmonary disease (COPD), a type of progressive lung disease.

Three weeks later, Augie reluctantly returned to the VA hospital for yet another appointment. This time he was to meet with a respiratory therapist who was going to teach him breathing exercises that were supposed to help improve his symptoms. Or maybe his lung capacity. He wasn't sure. As he waited in the lobby for the nurse to call his name, he watched the TV. The news was on and the images were from Vietnam. The war was very nearly lost, and it was becoming clear to all that Saigon would soon fall to the enemy. Over the next couple of hours, most activity in the hospital stopped as more and more people gathered around the TV. Marine helicopters were trying to evacuate as many people as possible. The scene unfolding in front of the men and women gathered around the small TV in the hospital lobby was becoming increasingly chaotic.

Augie grew more and more agitated as he watched the events half a world away at the American embassy in Saigon. He had been there—and for what? Junior had died. Thousands of half-blooded American orphans had been abandoned to survive on their own—and for what? What did they accomplish? Disgusted, Augie stood and walked out of the hospital. It would be a long time before he returned to the VA.

Chapter 66

Camp Pendleton Refugee Camp, California, April 1975
  Chi

After landing in Los Angeles, Chi and 200 other passengers from Vietnam boarded a dozen Greyhound buses for the last leg of their long journey. The bus slowed as it turned into Camp Pendleton, and Chi got a glimpse of where her new life would begin. They drove past rows and rows of barracks and numerous Quonset huts. Across from the huts was an enormous field where American soldiers, many shirtless, were erecting huge, dark green tents. Chi watched them, fascinated at how quickly they worked—seemingly in unison. Suddenly the bus came to a stop, and she looked away from the window toward the front of the vehicle. The doors opened and a dark-skinned American dressed in the uniform of a marine climbed aboard and stood at the front next to the driver. In the deepest voice Chi had ever heard he asked, "Welcome to Camp Pendleton. I'm Sergeant Clayton. By chance does anyone speak English?"

Chi and another passenger raised their hands.

The soldier's face broke into a relieved smile. "Would you mind serving as translators?" They both nodded, and he beckoned them to the front of the bus. He looked at Chi. "You're with me." Then he turned to the man. "Sir, go ahead and grab your things. You'll join another group." He pointed to a female soldier standing on the walkway in front of a building. "That's Corporal Kim. She can tell you where you are needed."

The man nodded but didn't move. "My family," he gestured to the woman and children around him. The marine started to speak, but Chi interrupted. "I'm alone. I can go. He can stay with his family and translate for you."

"That would be great. Thank you," he replied.

Chi turned and gathered her few belongings. The other refugee and his wife both thanked her. She smiled at them and then stepped off the bus onto the dusty road. She was surprised by how cold it was. She had been told California was always sunny and warm. She walked over to Cpl. Kim, a small Asian woman dressed in the same uniform as the man from her bus. "Hello. I am Chi. I can translate."

The woman looked up from her clipboard and smiled warmly at her. "Thank you. I am afraid none of us speak Vietnamese yet. She pointed to a bus. "They can use you there." She looked back at her clipboard. "You'll be with Sergeant Graves."

Chi hesitated a moment taking in the woman and her name. "You're Korean?"

Cpl. Kim smiled again. "I am American, but yes, first-generation. My parents were born in Korea."

Chi wanted to stay and talk to this woman. She wanted to ask her how her parents had come to be in the U.S. Had they been refugees like the Vietnamese or had they come for some other reason? Chi had been well educated in Vietnam, attending parochial school until she ran away. She tried to remember what she had been taught about the American war in Korea but nothing came to her. Reluctantly, she turned away from Cpl. Kim and hurried off toward her assignment. She was glad they had given her a job to do. It seemed to her that she was the only refugee without a family, and she was grateful to be needed.

Chi found Sergeant Graves, a tall, thin man who reminded her of the Australian she had ditched in Saigon. Rob had been a nice man, and she hoped he didn't hate her. She pushed the thoughts aside and turned her attention to the Sergeant. "How may I help?"

For much of the day Chi followed Sergeant Graves and translated as all of the new arrivals were given multiple vaccinations, health packets containing personal care items, and finally a standard-issue military jacket. There was only one size, and it was too large for nearly all of the Vietnamese, but it didn't matter. Vietnam, with its near tropical climate never dropped below 75 degrees Fahrenheit even at night. April in California could easily dip to 50 degrees. Add in the lack of humidity, and the Vietnamese now living in California felt as though they might freeze to death. They were grateful to have the oversized jackets.

Late in the day the 200 guests, as Sergeant Graves called them, were fed in the huge tent that served as a mess hall. The sun was beginning to set, and the men who had been working to erect the tents had gone elsewhere. Chi was amazed at how many tents there were. There had to be several hundred. How many refugees were they expecting?

Because she was among the first of the refugees to arrive, Chi was housed in a Quonset hut, a dome-like structure with wooden floors, windows, and real doors. The Vietnamese who would come later would live in the tents she had seen the soldiers erecting. Scattered among the many tents were dozens upon dozens of Port-a-Potties.

There were no TVs in the camp, but they did have several radios. On April 30th, as Saigon fell, the refugees crowded around the devices and strained to listen. Chi heard a woman's voice reading from a prepared report. "Saigon, the capital of South Vietnam, has fallen to the forces of North Vietnam and will now be known as Ho Chi Minh City after the famous leader who died in 1969. The new revolutionary government of Vietnam has vowed to return the city to normal as quickly as possible. Meanwhile in the U.S., the American government says that more than 65,000 Vietnamese have been evacuated from Saigon in the last 24 hours."

Chi turned away from the radio unsure of how she felt. Her side had won and North and South Vietnam were finally one, but she was here. She looked around at her fellow refugees. Many were crying, while others were angry or in shock. No one knew what to expect, either for their loved ones left behind or for themselves in a strange new country.

Chapter 67

San Francisco, California, April 1975
  Linh and Dordi

At the end of April 1975 when South Vietnam fell to the North and the American War in Vietnam came to its terrible end, Dennis Dordi could not tear himself from the TV. He watched in horror as the Tan Son Nhut Air Base was bombarded to the point planes could no longer take off. He watched his fellow soldiers try in vain to save as many civilians as they could. Before his eyes, the tanks of the North Vietnamese army rolled over the huge iron fences of the American embassy in Saigon. Several times Dordi stood and huddled close to the TV as the camera passed over South Vietnamese soldiers being rounded up by the NVA. He searched the faces desperately hoping that LT was not among them.

Unlike her husband, Linh refused to watch the news. She knew it would upset her, and she was determined to always be cheerful and happy for Lily. Linh knew her daughter's life would be short, and she would do everything in her power to make sure that every moment of Lily's life was the best that it could be. She would grieve for Vietnam after Lily was safely asleep in her crib.

Late in the evening, Linh found Dennis still sitting on the couch as the news replayed the major events of the day. She sat beside him and took his hand. "Are you okay?"

His head hung low and he rubbed his eyes. "How can I be? We failed."

"No. YOU didn't fail. You did everything that was asked of you."

"It wasn't enough."

Linh just squeezed his hand knowing there was nothing she could do to ease his pain.

Chapter 68

Philadelphia, Pennsylvania, October 1975
  Penny and Augie Augustini

In October of 1975, Penny learned she was pregnant again. She was not particularly happy about the prospect of another child because she was completely exhausted. Sara was nearly two and a half and was extremely active. She had already reached the "why?" phase and constantly demanded Penny explain everything to her. Although Sara was a little precocious verbally and could talk in short sentences, she also had a tendency to just break down in tears when she got frustrated. Whenever this happened—and it happened a lot—Penny would always say to her, "What's wrong, Sara? Use your words," hoping that as she grew older she would learn to express herself properly rather than simply cry.

It was a struggle for Penny to give Sara the attention she needed, take care of the house, do the shopping with a toddler in tow, keep up with all the laundry, and have dinner ready for Augie when he came home from work. Her own mother had raised three children and had a husband who did far less than Augie. How on earth had she done it she often wondered.

On top of everything else, Augie's cough continued to get worse, and he continued to ignore it. Penny knew he had started coughing up blood and begged him to go back to the doctor. On Sundays when they went to church, they had to get there early because it took so long for him to climb the 10 steps that led up to the sanctuary.

"Augie, this isn't normal," she finally said to him one Sunday as she and

Sara waited for him to reach the landing at the top of the stairs.

"I know it isn't normal," he responded. Because they were at church, he was careful not to sound angry, but she knew he was. Penny could see him tighten his grip on the railing. She knew his frustration was not with her but with himself. He didn't like being weak. He wasn't even 25 years old, but he must have felt 80.

He finally went back to the VA clinic when he began having difficulty at work. He would often have to stop in the middle of a job to catch his breath. He had started keeping a stool near whatever car he was working on in case he needed to sit down suddenly. He knew if his father hadn't owned the place, he would have already been fired.

At the VA, the respiratory therapist taught him to do the breathing exercises that he should have begun months before. She warned Augie that the disease had progressed significantly since his last visit and that it was likely that he would eventually need supplemental oxygen.

Chapter 69

Camp Pendleton Refugee Camp, California, June 1975–October 1975
  Chi and JB

By June of 1975, the tent city at Camp Pendleton housed several thousand Vietnamese refugees. Interestingly, Chi noticed that within the camp, former status had no bearing. The wealthy and well-educated were in the same boat as the uneducated peasants. The mixed-race and pure Vietnamese were now the same, and, at least from her experience, everyone assumed everyone else had politically and emotionally sided with South Vietnam. Although it was certainly in her best interest to tell no one of her previous VC activities and loyalty to the North, over time her hatred of the United States and its citizens dissipated. It had become clear to her that the vast majority of Americans seemed to genuinely want to help the Vietnamese who had traded one uncertain future for another.

Chi made herself valuable at the camp by working as a translator of both the language and the culture. When the USMC began offering classes in reading and writing English to refugees who already spoke the language, Chi and several others volunteered to teach those that didn't. Everyone was anxious to learn the language of their new country.

Early one evening in July of 1975, Chi was walking back from teaching one of her classes when she stopped to watch some of the children playing. The tent city backed up to a big hill, and the kids were using broken down boxes to slide down it. They were having a grand time sliding to the bottom, dragging the boxes back up, and sliding down again. Sometimes they crashed into each other or slid off the boxes and rolled down the hill instead. The kids would just scream with laughter. They were having fun and seemed to have no worries at all. Chi smiled. Although life in the refugee camp was far from ideal, these boys and girls were free to be children. She, like so many other Vietnamese, had never before lived in a country at peace. It felt good.

"It's good to see the kids happy, isn't it?" a man's voice said from behind her.

The voice startled her. Chi was surprised and dismayed that she hadn't even realized the man was there. That would *never* have happened in Vietnam because she was always sharply aware of her surroundings. Not being aware would get you killed. Was she losing her sixth sense already? The thought upset her, and so she was frowning when she turned to face the man who had spoken to her. She tried to remember what he had asked, but her mind drew a blank, so she said nothing.

Sensing her distress, the man assumed Chi didn't speak English. He knew very little Vietnamese but had been taught to say, "I'm an American photojournalist." He smiled as he spoke the familiar phrase and held up the camera that was hanging from his neck hoping to put her at ease.

She surprised him by responding in English, "Yes, I've seen you around." She smiled at him. "I'm Chi."

"You speak English!" he said, clearly surprised. "Hi Chi. I'm Jonathan Borkowski. My friends call me Johnny B or JB for short."

She continued to watch the children while JB took more pictures. He then turned his camera toward Chi. "May I?" he asked.

Chi frowned, "Why?"

He shrugged. "I'm here on assignment for *Our Life and Times* magazine in Los Angeles. You look like you are watching over the children. That's something that will resonate with our readers."

She nodded, understanding. The Americans were curious about them, and JB wanted to help build bridges. It made sense, and it made her want to like him. She looked back toward the children and smiled as he took a photo of her watching the scene in front of her.

After JB had taken his photos, he walked with her back to the Quonset hut she called home. As they walked, he told her that although he was now a civilian, he was a veteran of not only the Vietnam War but also the Korean War. "I enlisted right out of high school in 1952. They handed me a camera, and I spent the next year documenting the war over there. Then I volunteered to go to Vietnam, and I chronicled that war as well."

"When were you in Vietnam?" Chi asked.

"1965-66 and then again in 1970-71."

Chi nodded. She had been with Trinh and Tam during his first tour and was pretending to be a prostitute in DaNang for his second. Of course, she couldn't say that. She asked him, "Did you ever get to DaNang? That's where I grew up," she said, truthfully.

"Sure. They sent me all over, but I don't remember when I was there. I have a great photo that I took while standing on the bridge looking out to the sea."

"I would love to see it."

He smiled and they made plans to meet the next evening. "I have a whole portfolio from Vietnam that I can bring, if you want."

"Yes, I would like that."

The next night he met her at the picnic tables near her Quonset hut and showed her his photos. Most of them were of people doing ordinary things against the backdrop of war. Children playing in a bomb crater. Women hanging laundry beside a house that had been burned to the ground. A couple kissing under a tree while soldiers with rifles walked across the field behind them. "These are stunning," she said. "You've really captured what it was like for civilians trying to live a normal life and ignoring the war."

"Thank you. That was my goal." He pulled out a few more photos from a different folder. "These are the landscapes I took." He handed one to her. "This was taken from the bridge at DaNang."

"Oh," Chi said looking at it. "I'll be right back," she said, and she stood and hurried back inside. When she returned, she gave him the small, spiral notebook that had belonged to Mark. She sat down at the table and turned to one of the drawings. It was nearly identical to JB's photo.

JB was as mesmerized as she had been the first time she had looked at

Mark's drawings. Finally he looked up at her. "Did you draw these? They're amazing."

"Oh, no. I..." She hesitated realizing she couldn't tell the whole truth. "I saw a man drop the notebook. He was American. I tried to catch up to him to give it back, but the market was very crowded and I lost him," she lied. She looked away from JB. Why did it bother her that she had to lie to him?

"These are incredibly good," he said not noticing Chi's distress. "Look, here is another one that is nearly identical to one of mine." He held Mark's notebook in one hand and the matching photo in the other.

Chi reminded herself she had no choice but to lie. She forced a smile and turned back toward JB, focusing on his photo and Mark's drawing. The scene was one of her favorites. Her eyes lit up and her smile was suddenly genuine. "The Troung Son Mountains."

"I bet my newspaper would publish these. My photos next to the drawings. We could ask if anyone knows the artist. It would be great to find him. Maybe do an interview or something."

Chi looked away from him again and willed her voice to sound sincere. "Yes, that would be wonderful."

Over the next few weeks, Chi and JB spent more and more time together. When they first met, only some of what she told him was true. She told him about the Frenchman who had betrayed her, her daughter Linh, and of her father's betrayal.

"I ran away from home and tried to find Linh. I moved in with Trinh." Chi paused, thinking quickly. "She's a distant relative of my mother's," she lied. "She told me about the South Vietnam Women's Armed Forces Corps (WAFC), and I enlisted."

In truth, she had learned about the WAFC from one of the women at the refugee camp. Unlike women soldiers in the North Vietnamese army or the Viet Cong, women in the WAFC only held support roles and were not allowed in combat. Even so, women in the WAFC unit received weapons training and, according to her friend at the camp, a few had found themselves on the frontline actively engaged in the war. Armed with this information, Chi wove a story for JB that she had been in combat and had seen her share of death and destruction. She truthfully told him that there were many things she had done that she regretted, though she did not give him details. She told him that she had killed enemy soldiers and had seen others killed before her eyes.

When JB asked how she had escaped Vietnam, she told him that she met an army officer named Mark Kennedy, and that he too had betrayed her. "That's when I ended up working as a translator at Tan Son Nhut."

By now she had told the story of being abandoned by the American soldier so many times it almost felt like it had really happened. Even though she hated lying to JB, she felt she had no choice. She had vowed she would never tell anyone about her activities with the VC, which meant she would also not be able to tell him how she found Linh only to lose her again. And, of course, she never wanted to tell anyone the story of how she killed the young artist named Mark.

JB never once doubted Chi's version of her history. He had seen enough in Vietnam to understand how women had been drawn into the fight. He knew that the country had been a battlefield for more than a century with an endless series of occupiers brutalizing its citizens. It didn't surprise him that some of the women fought back. In wartime things can quickly spiral out of control, and good people would find themselves doing things they shouldn't—things that they would never normally do. JB had his own war stories that he had been too ashamed to share with anyone before Chi. He was grateful that she understood and never seemed to judge him.

One evening JB surprised Chi by taking her away from the camp to a restaurant in the nearby town of Oceanside. She had not left the camp since arriving months earlier and had enjoyed the evening immensely. After dinner he drove her through the town, and then they walked along the beach while the sun set over the ocean.

As they walked back to his car, Chi asked him, "Why didn't you ever get married?"

JB replied, "I guess I just never found a woman that understands. I was 18 when I went to Korea and then did two tours in Vietnam. You see things."

He paused choosing his words carefully. "You do things. You do things you are not proud of and that you never want anyone to know. They change you. They change your soul and make it hard to connect with someone that doesn't have those same demons." He frowned. "At least that is how it has been for me."

Chi stopped walking and took his hands in hers so that they were facing each other. She said nothing, but her meaning was clear. He leaned down and kissed her, and they both felt things that they had not felt in a very long time. She spent the night with him in his hotel room, and then he took her back to the camp the next morning.

In October of 1975, Camp Pendleton's refugee tent city closed after 50,426 Vietnamese refugees had passed through its canvas doors. All the refugees had been resettled elsewhere with most staying in California. Some had found relatives to stay with, but the majority of refugees had found a sponsor—usually a church—that would help them get on their feet. A few, like Chi, made other arrangements.

"Marry me," JB asked Chi one afternoon a month before the camp was scheduled to close. "You can move into my apartment in Los Angeles for now, but we'll get a bigger place as soon as we can."

They were walking arm in arm along the path that now circled the camp. It had been formed by the thousands of refugees with more time on their hands than they were accustomed to having. When Chi just kept walking and didn't respond to his proposal, JB stopped and looked at her. He said, "Did you hear me?"

Chi smiled at him, "I heard you. But no. I don't think we should get married. At least not yet."

JB wasn't hurt. They had talked about marriage more than once. He knew Chi loved him, but she had always told him that she wasn't sure she was the marrying kind. They continued walking along the path for a few minutes. Then JB asked another question. "Live with me in sin?"

Chi laughed, "Yes. I would like that very much."

Chapter 70

Norfolk, Virginia, December 1975
  Elizabeth Higgins Parker

Following the finalization of her divorce, Mark's mother Elizabeth had married Anthony Parker. Although he was nearly a decade her senior, the marriage had a joy and passion that her first marriage never did. In the rare moments that she could forget about Mark, she was truly happy for the first time in her life. She mourned her son's death every day but had eventually found a way to move forward.

A few days before Christmas when she was shopping for the holiday meal, she walked past a row of magazines. The latest issue of *Our Life and Times* magazine caught her eye. On the cover was a photo of some mountain range. Below it was a drawing of the same mountain range. The drawing was nearly identical to the photo, and she knew in an instant that it was one of Mark's. Forgetting about her cart full of groceries, she picked up the magazine and quickly found the cover story. There were several more photographs and multiple drawings. However, the centerpiece of the article was a drawing of the South China Sea, side by side with the matching photograph. The photos were taken by a journalist named Jonathan Borkowski, but the artist responsible for the drawings was unknown. According to the story, a notebook containing the drawings had been found in DaNang in 1971. The article concluded by asking the public for help finding the artist. There was a phone number to call.

As quickly as possible, Elizabeth paid for her groceries and went home.

Hands shaking, she dialed the number listed, and a woman's voice said, "Our Life and Times. How may I direct your call?" Elizabeth explained why she was calling, and the woman transferred her.

"This is Jonathan Borkowski. To whom am I speaking?"

"Hello. My name is Elizabeth Parker. The drawings—they are my son's. My son, Mark Higgins."

"Are you sure? Do you have a number where he can be reached?" JB asked without thinking. He held his breath hoping he hadn't been insensitive.

"He—he died in the war. 1971," she said trying not to cry. "I have other drawings from when he was there. The U.S. Air Force sent them with his things after—after he died."

"I'm very sorry for your loss."

"Thank you," she said. They spoke for several minutes, and Elizabeth told JB that one of the published drawings was a self-portrait of Mark himself. "It's the one where he has the sketchpad on his knees and he is smiling."

"Yes. We thought that might be the artist, but we couldn't know for sure."

Then she asked, "Would it be possible to get the originals, especially the self-portrait?"

"Of course. I'll have my assistant make the arrangements. What is the address?"

Elizabeth gave him the needed information and then asked, "Would you be interested in seeing his other drawings from the war?"

"Yes! We could do another story on Mark himself with photographs of him alongside his drawings. Perhaps I could come to Virginia and interview you?"

"Yes. I would like that very much."

JB promised to call her in the near future and make the arrangements.

Chapter 71

San Francisco, California, January–March 1976
  Dordi Family

Lily Dordi turned one in January of 1976, and Linh went all out. Although growing up she had never had a birthday party and had never even known anyone who had, she had been in the U.S. long enough to know that parties were the norm. Dordi said nothing as Linh spent more money than she should on cake, balloons, and a mountain of toys and books for the young Lily. Dordi's parents flew out to be part of the big event, and they brought even more toys for their grandchild. The day was a wonderful, happy event, and Lily clearly enjoyed every minute. She fell asleep early with both tiny hands clutched tightly around her new teddy bear with its pink bow.

Linh and Michelle cleaned the kitchen while Dordi and his dad tackled the disaster in the living room. Soon the four adults had returned the small apartment to its normal state and enjoyed a quiet moment before Lily's grandparents left for their hotel.

"Lily had a great day," Michelle said, squeezing Linh's hand. Then she laughed and said, "I think she enjoyed ripping the paper off all those gifts best of all."

Dordi's father laughed as well and, without thinking, said, "Maybe next year we should just give her a lot of wrapping paper instead of wasting money on toys."

The silence hung in the air for a moment before Linh broke it. "That's right. We should assume she will still be with us next year. It doesn't help her if we accept that the doctors are right."

Dordi's father was grateful for Linh's comment, but he knew as well as the others that it was unlikely they would be celebrating Lily's second birthday. Indeed, although Lily had beaten the odds by surviving more than a year, her luck would soon run out. Lily Dordi died on March 21, 1976.

As heartbroken as Dordi was, he was also well aware that this was now the third child that Linh had lost. His wife was strong, but was she strong enough to carry that burden? He didn't know.

Chapter 72

Los Angeles, California, 1976
  Chi and JB

Early in 1976, Chi realized that she was pregnant and wasn't sure what to do. She and JB were incredibly happy. She loved him, and she knew he loved her, but he didn't know the truth about her past, and it gnawed at her. After he asked her to move in with him, she began to hear a voice in her head that insisted she tell him everything. She knew it was just her subconscious trying to get her to do the right thing, but she refused to take its advice. On more than one occasion, she replied to the voice out loud, "He doesn't need to know. I'm not that person anymore."

After she left the refugee camp and moved into his small apartment in Los Angeles, he helped her get a job at a weekly newspaper that was owned by the same company as *Our Life and Times* magazine. Chi wrote a weekly article directed at helping new immigrants adjust to life in America since the Los Angeles area had recently had a large influx of refugees from Vietnam. The articles with titles like "So you want to drive in L.A.?" or "How to find relatives in the U.S." were published in both English and Vietnamese. Chi didn't make a lot of money, but she enjoyed staying busy and felt she was helping her countrymen. Best of all, Chi and JB were building a life together.

JB had proposed again the previous November, and again she had said no. That time, he was hurt, but she assured him, "It's me, not you. Can't we just be happy together without anything official?"

"Okay," he had finally said. "I won't ask again." Then to lighten the mood, he added jokingly, "If you change your mind and decide you do want to get married, you'll have to ask me. And you'll have to sweep me off my feet or I might say no."

Chi laughed, but inside she was hurting. She very much wanted to marry JB, but she had told him so many lies. How could she ever tell him the truth? In the beginning, she truly felt she had no choice. If she had told him she had been VC when they first met, he might have turned her in. She might have been sent back to Vietnam and lose any chance at all of finding Linh. The first time he proposed, Chi said no because she knew JB deserved to know the truth about her past, but she just couldn't bring herself to tell him. She was afraid. When she moved in with him after refusing his second proposal, the voice in her head became more insistent. *You have to tell him.* She responded, "I'll tell him if everything goes well." But it was easier to keep putting it off. Then he proposed a third time, and she said no a third time. The voice in her head warned her, "You have to tell him." But she had ignored her subconscious yet again.

Now she was pregnant, and she had no choice. She would tell him everything. Would he leave her? She didn't know.

"We need to talk," she told him as soon as he came home from work the day she had her pregnancy confirmed by a doctor.

"Is everything okay?" JB asked, clearly concerned by her demeanor.

"Well, that is for you to decide." Chi sat next to him on the couch and truly intended to tell him everything. She took a deep breath and said, "I wasn't completely honest with you before." He just looked at her without saying anything, and she continued. Chi told him that she had been VC and had worked on the Ho Chi Minh Trail. She told him she had been a weapons smuggler and a guide for the NVA. He already knew about her Frenchman's betrayal, her baby Linh, and then her father's actions. Now she explained. "I was just so angry and hurt, I needed to do *something*. Joining the resistance made sense to me at the time."

JB stood and began pacing in front of her clearly considering what she had said. In a voice that was almost too calm, he spoke without looking at her. "You told me before that you were with the South Vietnamese Women's

Armed Forces and had been in combat, that you had killed enemy soldiers." He turned and looked at her with a piercing gaze that was almost physically painful to her and asked, "Did you kill Americans?"

Chi struggled with herself. She wanted to come clean and tell him everything, but she could tell by his expression that he would reject her if she did. She shook her head vigorously and told him another lie. "No. I saw men killed, but, no, I never had to kill anyone. I, uhm—I just told you that because you felt guilt over some of the men you had killed. And I—I just wanted you to know that I understood how you felt. I'm so sorry, JB." She buried her face in her hands, hating herself for the lies.

JB didn't say anything for a long time. He paced around the room anxiously and then walked to the window and looked out on the street below. After a long, uncomfortable moment he turned back to Chi and asked, "If you were VC, how did you end up in the U.S.?"

"I told you that I dated an American. Mark Kennedy. Do you remember?"

"Yes. You said he told you to meet him at Tan Son Nhut Air Base and he would take you home with him, but he left without you."

She nodded, "Yes, that's what I told you and the people at the base, but that's not what happened. I *was* at the air base," Chi hesitated as the voice in her head screamed at her knowing she was about to tell him another lie. "My team was there doing reconnaissance. We were planning to steal weapons." Chi looked down at her hands and wondered if JB knew she was lying to him, but his face was unreadable. She hesitated a moment before continuing. "I saw Linh. She was with an American soldier. They were leaving together, and I knew if I ever wanted to see her again I had to come here. To the States. I abandoned my unit and tried to get to her, but I was too late."

JB knew the loss of Linh was a constant source of pain for Chi. Part of him wanted to go to her and embrace her, but another part of him was incredibly angry at having been lied to. The words he spoke were more accusatory than he meant for them to be. "And what about Mark Kennedy?"

Chi shook her head, grateful that she could at least be honest about something. "He didn't exist. I was just so distraught when I realized Linh had gotten on a plane and left before I could get to her." Chi started to cry, and JB softened a little. He sat beside her on the couch but resisted the urge to put his arm around her. She looked at him and then haltingly said, "There were two women, American air force—they asked me what was wrong, but I was so upset I couldn't speak. They asked if I had been left behind. I guess soldiers did that sometimes. Anyway, I—I…"

JB interrupted and finished her sentence, "You let them think you had an American boyfriend that dumped you so they would have pity on you."

"Yes."

"You only switched sides so you could come here."

"Initially, yes. I was desperate to find Linh, but the Americans were so kind to me. They were nothing like what I had been taught. They really wanted to help Vietnam. I could see that. I worked hard for them. Everything I told you that happened at the air base is true." She bit her lip realizing she had left out the part about the Australian officer. She easily convinced herself that he wasn't important. She looked at JB and tried to gauge his reaction, but his face was blank. Then he stood and walked away from her. "Say something," Chi begged him.

"Why are you telling me this now?"

She hesitated but finally said, "I'm pregnant."

JB was reeling. He loved Chi—or at least the person he thought he knew. An hour ago he would have been ecstatic to learn she was pregnant. But now? Now he didn't know what to think. He walked to the door and opened it. He clutched the doorknob so tightly his hand began to throb. He closed his eyes, still clutching the knob. After a moment JB turned and looked back at her. "I'm going to need some time with all this."

Alone in a hotel room, JB thought about everything Chi had told him. He was angry that she had lied to him but part of him understood. Certainly, learning she had been an enemy soldier was difficult for him, but many Americans had been opposed to the war. At least Chi had a reason to support Ho Chi Minh. Vietnam had been occupied by so many different armies, and he could understand how a young girl who had been betrayed by a foreign soldier would want to fight back.

He had been a photographer during the war and people often assumed that meant he had only been an observer and not a participant. That wasn't the case. He was a soldier first. He had to be. There were no bystanders in Vietnam. There were many things he had done in the war that he wished he could change, only some of which he had shared with Chi. How could he hold her to a standard he himself could not achieve? Still, she had been the *enemy*. He asked himself, can I forgive her? He did love her and wanted to be there for her and their child, but could he get past this? He wasn't sure.

Three days went by, and just as Chi began to accept that she would never see JB again, he came home. He sat beside her and told her he thought he could live with her past.

"You've told me everything?" JB asked.

"Yes," Chi lied. She would never tell him she had killed Mark or any other American. She reasoned he had probably left a few things out as well—things that maybe he was too ashamed to admit. At least that's what she told the voice in her head.

He nodded, "Good." He held her close, and a sense of relief washed over him. He loved this woman and wanted their life together to continue.

After a few minutes, Chi broke the embrace. "So—, " Chi said, "—will you marry me?"

JB looked at her for a moment, and she wasn't sure what he was thinking. Finally he responded, "When I said if you changed your mind you would have to sweep me off my feet, I didn't mean knock me down with a gut punch." Then he laughed and pulled her close to him again. "But, yes, let's get married."

Chapter 73

Philadelphia, Pennsylvania, May 1976
Penny and Augie

In May, Penny, who was only seven months pregnant, began bleeding and having labor-like contractions. Augie rushed her to the emergency room where she was immediately admitted to the hospital. The news was not good. The badly deformed baby had died in utero. After several hours in labor, the stillborn infant was delivered.

Months before, when Penny first learned that she was pregnant with her second child, she had been distraught. She was already completely exhausted and the thought of having two little ones to care for felt overwhelming. Slowly, she began to feel better. She realized Sara would be three by the time the new baby arrived and convinced herself that her daughter would be a good little helper. As the pregnancy progressed, she began to get excited and started marking off days on the calendar. Her due date was marked with a large, red heart. She and Augie had discussed names nearly every night at dinner and finally settled on Jason for a boy and Jennifer for a girl. Sara was thrilled that she would soon be a big sister and was nearly as anxious as her parents for the new baby's arrival.

Now nothing would be as they had planned. There would be no little brother for Sara. No new baby in the crib. For days, Penny could do little more than mourn the loss of her son. Her own mother, whose oldest child had been killed in Vietnam, knew there were no words of comfort that she could offer her daughter. She simply held her and let her cry. Sara, always nearby and always watching her mother climbed on the couch next to her and said, "Use your words, Mommy. Use your words."

Through her grief, her daughter's words made her laugh. Penny pulled Sara close and tried to take comfort in the fact that she at least was healthy.

Chapter 74

Los Angeles, California, May–November 1976
  Chi and JB

There were many rocky days that followed Chi's confession. Finally she and JB agreed to put the past completely behind them and never speak of the war again. Neither had ever expected to get married, let alone have a family, and they both wanted to focus on their future.

JB took his responsibility as husband and father seriously and knew he would make more money if he could write articles in addition to providing the photographs. He had received a tremendous amount of positive feedback from the article with Mark's drawings, and his editor agreed to let him take the lead on the follow-up story. It would be another opportunity to showcase his writing skills, but JB was anxious about the interview with Mark's mother, Elizabeth.

"Why don't you come with me?" JB asked Chi for the second time. "You can be my assistant, and the magazine will pay for your ticket."

"Oh, I would love to go, but the morning sickness…" She made a face and shook her head. "I think being on a plane would just be miserable for both of us," Chi replied. In truth, morning sickness or not, there was absolutely no way she was going to meet Mark's mother.

"Well, we haven't found a time that works for me to fly out there yet. You can always change your mind later if you feel better."

Chi just smiled and kissed her husband knowing she would *never* agree to meet Mark's mother.

Chi and JB welcomed a daughter, Misty Anh Borkowski, on September 4, 1976. At the time they were both considered "older" parents since Chi was 38 and JB was 41. However, despite the warnings and concerns raised by Chi's obstetrician regarding her age, all indications were that Misty was healthy. Mom and baby spent only two days in the hospital before JB was able to bring them home. By the time Misty was one month old, the new parents had largely adapted to the challenges that came with having a baby.

In late October, six weeks after Misty was born, JB flew to Virginia to meet with Mark's mother. The ensuing article was slated to appear in the December issue of *Our Life and Times*, a full year after the original article that had showcased Mark's drawings.

Although JB thought the interview went well and the drawings Mrs. Parker gave him were spectacular, he was struggling to say everything he wanted to say in the space his editor had given him.

"Can you read it and see what you think I should cut?" JB asked Chi after he had reworked the article yet again. "It's still nearly 300 words too long."

Chi put Misty in her crib, took the typewritten paper from JB, and sat on the couch with her feet tucked under her. JB sat next to her intending to watch her while she read it.

She looked at him annoyed. "You're hovering. Go make coffee or something," she told him.

"You want coffee?" He stood and walked toward the kitchen.

"No. I want you to let me read without you watching."

"Oh, okay," he said anxiously. He wanted the article to be good—really good. Good enough that he would get bigger, better assignments and, hopefully, a raise. He had not expected a baby to be so expensive. He grabbed his camera and said, "I'll just go for a walk."

He kissed Chi and checked on Misty one more time. On his way out the door he said, "Back in 30."

Chi was already engrossed in the article and just waved to him without looking up. She had not really wanted to read it. She didn't want to hear about Mark's mother's pain of losing her son. She didn't want to know more than she already did about the man she had killed, but JB needed her input, so she read it anyway.

The article began with Mrs. Parker explaining that Mark's father was in the U.S. Navy and had been gone a lot when her son was young. "When Mark was 13 years old, he told me he wanted to join the Navy so he could spend more time with his dad. He was very proud of his father and wanted to be just like him." According to JB, she had teared up as she said that. She also said Mark had been drawing most of his life. "From the moment he picked up a crayon, I knew he was an artist." Then she had laughed and added, "But his handwriting was atrocious. Barely legible. I never understood that." To prove the point, according to the notes JB had written off to the side, there would be a handwriting sample published with the article.

Chi was afraid reading about Mark's life would upset her, but she found the article surprisingly uplifting. Mrs. Parker was happy that Mark would be remembered and that his talent would be shared with the world. She had been afraid that his memory would die with her, but now she knew he would live on. "Almost like Anne Frank," she had said.

Chi frowned and considered Mrs. Parker's words. Chi had only recently read the diary of Anne Frank and, like millions of readers before her, had been heartbroken by the story of the young Jewish girl who died at the hands of the Nazis. She looked back at JB's article and read Mark's mother's words again. "Almost like Anne Frank."

No, Chi thought. Mark and his drawings were unlikely to have the same worldwide impact of Anne Frank, but she supposed there was no harm in his mother thinking that.

At the end of the article, JB provided information on Mark's service. He had been with the 484th maintenance crew stationed at the U.S. Air Base in DaNang from November 1970 until his death in February 1971. "He died when his Jeep was ambushed by Viet Cong guerrillas. Several others were injured, but only Mark died. They said he was a hero and died protecting others in his squadron." Next to the quote, JB had scribbled on the side of the paper, "Insert pic of Mrs. P with Mark's service medal and campaign medal."

Chi looked away from the article confused. Ambush? Medals? For a minute she thought maybe this wasn't the Mark she had killed, but then it made sense. The U.S. government couldn't tell a grieving family that their son had been killed by a prostitute. They would stretch the truth as much as possible so that his family could be proud of his service. "Well, damn," she said aloud. But she was glad. She was glad the air force lied to Mark's mother. He had been a good kid and he deserved to be remembered that way.

When JB returned, she told him, "It's perfect. Don't cut anything. I bet your editor will find the space for it just like it is."

As usual, Chi was right. The article ran just as he had written it with the photos and drawings that he selected. His editor had been very pleased. Although not pleased enough to give him a permanent bump in pay, his Christmas bonus was a little more generous that year.

Chapter 75

United States, November 1976
  Our Life and Times Magazine

The December issue of *Our Life and Times* magazine hit the stands in late November of 1976. Once again, one of Mark's drawings graced its cover. It was of a proud young soldier standing guard and ready to defend his countrymen.

As soon as the issue was published, JB sent Elizabeth a package by courier. After signing for the package, Elizabeth opened it and found two copies of the latest issue of *Our Life and Times* magazine along with the extra copy of the December issue from the previous year that she had requested. Elizabeth would keep one copy of the new issue for herself and would send the other two magazines to Mark's father. But first she poured herself a fresh cup of coffee and curled up on the couch. Although she had already read the story about Mark that JB had written after interviewing her and knew which drawings would be published alongside it, she was anxious to see it all in print. She sipped her coffee as she read Mark's story, which JB had titled *"Lost Talent: The Too Short Life of PFC Mark Higgins."* She was very pleased with how it looked and was ecstatic to see his name in print next to his drawings. There were also two photographs of Mark included with the article. One was the photo from her mantel that was taken the day of his high school graduation. Mark in his cap and gown stood between her and James. The other photo had been taken in Vietnam. Mark was standing next to a Jeep, shirtless and smiling. His dog tags around his neck glinted in the sun.

Although she had seen the photo before, she touched it gingerly and stared at it for a long time. Mark had sent it to her in the first letter she received from him after he was sent to Vietnam. It had given her much comfort at the time because it was proof that he was okay. Eventually Elizabeth tore her eyes away from the photo and flipped back to the beginning of the article.

After finishing Mark's story the second time, Elizabeth looked through the rest of the magazine. She was surprised to see two more of Mark's drawings accompanying other stories. One was the drawing of the children on the base being fed by a soldier. According to the article, there were thousands of orphans in Vietnam. Many were left to wander the streets and fend for themselves. Western soldiers often tried to help them by giving them food or medical attention. Elizabeth bit her lip and blinked away tears. Now the drawing made sense. Her heart ached at she looked at Mark's drawing of the orphans and she wondered if they had survived the war. The last story in the special issue on Vietnam was about Agent Orange and the suspected long-term effects of the chemical. Next to the article was Mark's drawing of his friends playing in the water when they were supposed to be cleaning the plane that had been used to spread the herbicide. The accompanying article included a list of presumptive effects of high-dose exposure to dioxin, which, according to the article, was a highly toxic contaminant of Agent Orange.

Three hundred miles away from Elizabeth's home in Norfolk, Virginia, Penny Augustini was out shopping with her mother-in-law in Philadelphia's Reading Market. Penny, who by then had physically recovered from Jason's birth and death, saw the magazine first. She picked it up. "It looks like Augie!" she exclaimed and handed it to the other woman.

Penny's mother-in-law looked at the magazine she had been given. "It IS Augie!" she replied, equally excited. The two women huddled together and began perusing the magazine. It was a special issue focused on "America's Longest War." The older woman quickly flipped to the first article and began reading aloud to Penny. It was just a brief recap of the war and included the number of men and women who had served over two decades, as well as the number killed, injured, or missing. They read the next article, the one about Mark, while standing in the aisle of the store. They bought several copies and gave Augie one as soon as they got home.

Augie recognized the drawing immediately. "My friend Junior—uh—his real name was Mark—he drew that picture of me. I didn't know he had drawn it until I found it after he died."

The three adults sat in the living room each reading their own copy of the magazine and examining the photos and drawings. Penny was horrified when she found the article about dioxin and Agent Orange and began reading out loud to the group. "Severe birth defects have been reported among the Vietnamese population living in heavily exposed areas," she paused and continued reading silently for a moment. Then she moved to the couch and sat beside Augie. She pointed to the magazine and said, "It says DaNang is a dioxin 'hot spot,' meaning it was heavily contaminated."

Penny turned back to the magazine and pulled it close to her eyes in order to read the small print below two of the photographs that accompanied the story. One showed a lush, green landscape filled with enormous trees while the second appeared to be of a desert since the vegetation was very sparse. On closer inspection, Penny noticed that the river that snaked through the photos was the same. Indeed, the small print stated that one photo was taken before Agent Orange had been sprayed while the other one was taken several weeks after the chemical exposure. The caption went on to state that the images were of a mangrove forest less than 100 km from DaNang. She looked at Augie, horrified. "You were in DaNang!"

Augie nodded. He leaned over her shoulder to see the magazine himself. "What else does it say?"

"Scientists report that lab animals exposed to high-dose dioxin develop a myriad of disorders, including diabetes, lung disease, and cancer. However, the U.S. government says these effects have not been demonstrated in humans."

Penny put the magazine down and looked at her husband. "Did Agent Orange kill Jason? Is that why you can't breathe?"

Augie just shook his head. "I don't know."

In Grenada, Mississippi, Grace Tackett was also out doing some last-minute shopping before the Thanksgiving holiday when she saw the new issue of *Our Life and Times* magazine. Unlike Penny, what caught her attention was not the young man standing guard on the cover, but rather one of the stories that the cover promised was inside. "Vietnam's Orphan Crisis."

Chapter 76

United States, 1976–1978
   Linh and Dordi

The week after Thanksgiving in December of 1976, Linh learned she was pregnant again. It had only been a little more than six months since Lily's death, and it was hard to be happy. She wanted another baby, but she was so very scared. Would her next baby die too? For the next two months, she wandered around their small apartment thinking about Lily and how they would soon bring a new baby home to the same place where she had died. Lily's crib was still set up in a corner of their bedroom because neither Linh nor Dordi had been able to bring themselves to remove it.

"It doesn't seem right," Linh said as she stood next to the crib with her hands resting on the rails.

"What doesn't?" asked Dordi.

"Nothing has changed since Lily died. Same crib, same bedding, same everything. It feels like we are just replacing her with a new baby. Like she never even existed," Linh replied as tears began spilling from her eyes.

"No one can replace Lily," Dordi said as he wrapped his arms around his wife. But he knew what she meant. He too had imagined bringing another child into the same space that Lily had occupied and was afraid the similarities would prevent them from enjoying being parents again. He wanted to move. A new apartment would give them a fresh start, and he thought it would help Linh focus on this baby without the constant reminders of Lily. Unfortunately, they really couldn't afford it. San

Francisco was just getting too expensive. Not knowing what else to do for Linh, he called his mother.

"Linh is just so conflicted. Anytime she begins to get excited about the baby, she feels guilty about being happy. I don't know what to do for her."

"She needs her mother."

"She's an orphan, Mom. You know that," Dordi said, slightly annoyed with her.

"She has me. Why don't you move back here? Let me take care of Linh," his mother immediately responded, and Dordi knew it was the best thing for his wife.

Although Dordi and Linh loved being in the San Francisco area, they really didn't have any strong ties to it. He was working with a construction company building an apartment complex, but the job would finish in the next few months and he wasn't guaranteed another.

Linh readily agreed to return to Virginia. This time they moved into one of his parents' rentals, a quaint two-bedroom house near the University of Charlottesville. Dordi worked with his father, and Linh spent most of her time with his mother. Michelle was just what Linh needed. In addition to helping Linh realize it was okay to be happy about the new baby, she also worked with Linh on her English and American history. Linh was anxious to become an American citizen. The requirements included not only being able to read and write in English, but she also had to understand the functioning of the American government. As Michelle and Linh prepared for the baby, the older woman quizzed Linh on the Founding Fathers and the three branches of government. The two women also spent many hours and a fair amount of money at a children's bookstore in downtown Charlottesville. Linh was determined to be able to read to her new son or daughter, and she would sit at the table and read children's books to Michelle as she prepared dinner each night.

To help her with her writing, Michelle suggested Linh keep a journal. Linh bought a spiral-bound notebook with a blue cover, and nearly every day she would write something. At first her entries were rather mundane, "Michelle and I went to the store." But as her writing skills improved, she began writing a bit more. She might relay a funny story from her day or something that happened that she thought was interesting. Occasionally she wrote about events that had happened long ago. Every November 5th, she would write something about Song. She might wonder where she was and what she was doing.

In 1977 at the end of July, she wrote about her new son. "Lucas Thomas Dordi, who his dad sometimes calls LT after his old army buddy, was born on July 8, 1977. The doctor said his heart is perfect." In the margin, she had drawn a small smiley face.

Six months later in January of 1978, Linh Dordi had fulfilled all of the requirements to become a U.S. citizen. Although being married to an American had shortened the length of time required for residing in the country, it did not change the other requirements. She had gotten her green card two years before and had now demonstrated good command of the English language. Linh Dordi took her oath of allegiance to the United States on January 23, 1978, in downtown Richmond along with 27 others from all over the world. Each new American was given a large U.S. flag. After a celebratory luncheon with her husband and in-laws, Linh came home and immediately hung the flag on the wall opposite Lucas' crib.

Dordi watched his wife as she pinned the flag to the wall and smiled. It was the happiest he had seen her in a long time.

Chapter 77

Los Angeles, California, 1978–1983
  Chi and Family

Misty turned two in September of 1978, a few months after her mother turned 40. Chi still wrote her column for the newspaper, which remained very popular with new immigrants. In fact, it was so popular that the paper had hired someone to translate her articles into Spanish in order to help Los Angeles' growing population of Mexican immigrants. Chi enjoyed her work but loved being a mother even more. As she watched Misty grow, she often wondered about Linh. On more than one occasion, she had accidentally called Misty by her older daughter's name.

After the December issue of *Our Life and Times* magazine won several prestigious awards, JB became more in demand as both a writer and photographer and began traveling a great deal. He loved it, and Chi didn't mind his absences too much. She had Misty. Because Chi was able to work at home and only part-time, nearly every afternoon she took Misty to the park a few blocks away. Chi became friends with many of the other parents, and they all watched over the children.

Over the next few years, her daughter made friends with some of the children at the park and would occasionally have playdates with them. After her first overnight playdate with Josey, another little girl who lived in the same building, six-year-old Misty asked Chi a question that surprised her.

"Am I adopted?" Misty asked as soon as Chi came to collect her the next morning.

Chi looked at her daughter as they walked to the elevator. "What? No, you are not adopted. Why would you ask that?"

"I heard Josey's dad ask Josey's mom if I was adopted."

Chi sighed. It was a common misperception. In 1978 mixed-race couples were still not all that common in the U.S. Misty was clearly part Asian and people assumed she was adopted if they didn't know Chi. Chi crossed her arms and asked, "And what did Josey's mother say?"

"She said no. That you were Asian but my dad is American."

Chi took her daughter's hand as she pushed the call button for the elevator. She tried to keep the annoyance out of her voice. "We are *all* American. You and your dad were born in the U.S., but I am a naturalized citizen."

"What does that mean?"

"It means I am just as American as Josey and her parents," Chi replied. She and Marilyn, Josey's mother, were good friends, and it upset her that she didn't realize she was a citizen. She knew she had an accent that gave her away as an immigrant, but it still bothered her. She turned her attention back to Misty and said cheerfully, "Any more questions?"

"Yes," she replied immediately. "Can I have a brother or sister? Josey has a brother AND a sister."

Chi sighed again. It wasn't the first time Misty had asked for a sibling. From the moment she could talk, she wanted a baby. She told her mother she would be the best big sister. Of course, Misty *had* a sister. An older sister. Linh would be 28 now, Chi thought. She realized she could be a grandmother and not even know it. She desperately wanted to know Linh was happy and loved, and it weighed on her heart to think that she might never know.

Initially when Chi and JB had unexpectedly found that they were pregnant, they thought they would never tell their child about Linh. But now, without really making a conscious decision, she looked at her young daughter and said, "You do have a sister, but she is much older than you."

Misty smiled excitedly. "I have a sister? What's her name? Where is she? Can we go see her?"

The questions came so fast Chi couldn't answer one before she asked another. She unlocked the door to their apartment and wondered what exactly she would tell Misty about Linh.

Chapter 78

Philadelphia, Pennsylvania, 1985-1988
  Augustini family

Despite the breathing exercises, Augie's lung disease had continued to worsen. By 1985 he needed supplemental oxygen, and the tank he had to wheel around with him made it impossible to work as a mechanic. His father moved him to the office where he sat at a desk and interacted with the customers rather than trying to work on cars. Augie was grateful to his father since managing the office allowed him to keep a job, but it wasn't the job he really wanted. He preferred working with his hands, but he didn't complain. He had a family to support.

Five years later at the age of 38, Augie was diagnosed with metastatic prostate cancer. Surgery to remove the prostate was recommended, but Augie refused. He had heard from other veterans about the common side effects of that procedure and had no interest in his sex life taking another hit. The oxygen tank was bad enough. Instead, he opted for aggressive chemotherapy. Although the drugs made him sick, they at least seemed to slow the progression of his cancer.

Unfortunately, Augie was not the only family member dealing with health issues. Several months before his daughter Sara turned 12, she started her periods. Her mother was very concerned and tried to talk to her husband about it.

"I was almost 14 when I first got the curse. My sister was even older," Penny told him one night as she got ready for bed.

"Well, I don't know anything about it. Take her to the doctor if you're worried," Augie replied clearly uncomfortable with the subject. He climbed into bed after adjusting his oxygen tank so he could lay down.

Penny rubbed lotion into her hands as she spoke. "It may be nothing. They say kids are developing earlier these days because of better nutrition. Maybe that's all it is." She pulled back the covers and got into bed next to Augie. He just nodded his agreement as he turned off the lamp next to the bed.

Penny lay back on her pillow and tried not to worry about her daughter, but she just couldn't shake the feeling that something was wrong. She told Augie, "I'll call the pediatrician tomorrow and make an appointment for her. It's probably nothing."

"Probably," Augie agreed.

Chapter 79

Grenada, Mississippi, 1988
Melinda Tackett

Melinda had known all her life that she had been adopted from Vietnam. Her parents loved to tell the story of being at the adoption agency in Memphis looking at pictures of babies. "We saw your picture and immediately knew you were meant to be ours." For a long time this story satisfied Melinda, and she was confident that she was well loved.

But as Melinda entered the awkward tween years, she, like most kids at that age, became insecure as she tried to figure out who she was and how she fit into the world. One day she asked her mother point-blank why her Vietnamese mother gave her up.

Grace, who had grown comfortable with the lie she had told her friends over the years, easily responded, "I'm afraid she just didn't want you. You were only part Vietnamese, and that was not acceptable to her." By then Grace had completely forgotten that Linh, Melinda's birth mother, was herself only half Vietnamese.

Melinda had been very hurt to learn she had been unwanted as a baby, and Grace regretted her blunt response. She quickly added quite truthfully, "I am so glad she gave you up because I can't imagine life without you." She hugged her child tightly to emphasize her point.

Although Melinda accepted her mother's explanation without question, she still wondered about the country of her birth. Melinda had been born halfway around the world in Vietnam but had no memory of any place other than the little town where she had grown up. She had never even been to Memphis, which was less than two hours away. She couldn't help but be curious. More than once when assigned some kind of paper or research project, she would choose a topic related to Vietnam. When she was in the 7th grade, she had to pick a country and make a topographical map using a homemade dough of flour and water. Of course, she chose Vietnam. In the 9th grade, her science teacher encouraged her to submit something to the science fair, and she presented evidence that Agent Orange was still causing birth defects in children in Vietnam even though spraying of the herbicide had ended more than two decades before.

Now as a senior in high school, she was writing her required English research paper on Operation Babylift in which thousands of orphans had been airlifted out of Vietnam at the end of the war. She read several books on the subject and knew that the majority of the children were mixed race and that their families had abandoned them because of it. The research she did for the paper confirmed what her mother had told her years before. She was given up for adoption because she wasn't pure Vietnamese. Although it made her sad that, like her, so many kids had to grow up without any knowledge of their original families, she also realized how lucky she was. Her adoptive parents were good people and they loved her, but she could not stop herself from wondering what her birth parents had been like. What might her life had been like if they had wanted her? Of course, she kept these thoughts to herself. She never wanted to upset her mom and dad. Still, she had an ache that never quite went away. It was almost as though she had a missing piece of her heart that she needed to find.

Chapter 80

Blue Ridge Mountains, September 1988
  Dordi and LT

When Dennis Dordi was growing up, his father would often rent a cabin in the Blue Ridge Mountains. Mr. Dordi and his three sons spent many long weekends in the woods of those mountains hiking, fishing, and swimming. When they were younger, Dordi and his brothers would build makeshift forts out of tree limbs or play hide and seek. As they got older, they would just run wild through the woods as fast as they could. They climbed every tree and dared each other to go higher and higher. Those were some of Dordi's favorite memories, and now he often brought his own family to the same mountains. Lucas, now 11, loved being in the woods as much as Dordi, and he had expected his son to come with him for the weekend. At the last minute, though, Lucas decided he would rather stay home with Linh. He wanted to help his mother paint the nursery for the new baby they were expecting. Honestly, Dordi wasn't that disappointed. He loved Linh and Lucas, but sometimes he missed being a bachelor.

Dordi had driven up the night before and rented one of the smaller cabins near the lake. He had just gotten back from collecting firewood and was about to start a fire when he heard the unmistakable sound of a Jeep. He was not expecting company. He grabbed the shotgun he always brought with him and waited until he heard footsteps coming up the stairs.

He yanked the door open, prepared for an intruder, but it was his old army buddy Loc Tin Vong. The two men had not seen each other since 1971, but it didn't matter. Dordi set the gun down and said, "You look like hell, LT."

"But still better than you, Dordi," retorted Loc Tin.

The old soldiers embraced briefly, and then Dordi stepped away from the door wordlessly inviting in his friend. They had first met in 1963 shortly after Loc Tin had been drafted into the South Vietnamese Army (ARVN). His unit's base had suffered extensive damage after being attacked overnight, and Dordi's unit, the 5th Special Forces Group, came to assist in its repair. At that early stage during the war, American Green Berets were officially in-country only to assist and train the South Vietnamese, but in reality they did much more. Over the next year, Dennis Dordi both inspired and trained the younger Loc Tin, who would eventually join the Special Forces of his own country. Several years later in 1968 the two men's paths crossed again. They had fought side-by-side during the deadliest year of the war and each credited the other with his own survival. After Dordi's third tour ended and he rotated home, the two soldiers lost touch. However, the bond they formed remained.

"How did you find me?" Dordi asked as he pulled two glasses from the cabinet. Loc Tin opened the whiskey he had brought.

"By accident," Loc Tin replied as he filled their glasses. "I stopped by the Feed Mill to pick up some supplies. I've owned a cabin up here for a couple of years and know Billy, the owner of the store, pretty well. He mentioned there was an old Vietnam veteran renting one of the cabins. I didn't think much about it until he told me that the guy could throw knives nearly as good as me. That's when I knew it was you. Even though your knife skills are not even close to being as good as mine."

"Well, if that's true, it's the fault of my teacher." The two men laughed and clinked their glasses together.

They took their drinks and the bottle of Jack Daniels out to the porch and sat in a couple of old rocking chairs that had come with the cabin.

Loc Tin asked, "How long have you been in Virginia?"

"Most of the last ten years, though we went back to California for a while. That's where my wife and I went back in '73 when I finally left the army for good. We settled in the Bay area and then came back here when Linh got pregnant again." Dordi paused for a moment and sipped his drink. Then he told LT about Lily.

"I'm really sorry, Dordi." Loc Tin knew what it was like to lose a child. He refilled their glasses and told Dordi about his life over the years. He told him how his first wife, Kim, had died at the end of the war. They had two children, but he had lost contact with them when he was captured by the North Vietnamese. "Eventually I learned they had been found wandering the streets. They were evacuated as part of Operation Babylift." He took a long drink and rubbed his eyes. Then he continued, "I don't know where they are. I was told they were brought to the States, but they could be anywhere. I just don't know. I just hope they survived and have had a good life."

After a few minutes of silence Dordi asked, "How did you get to the U.S.?"

Loc Tin stared into his empty glass for a moment and then looked at his friend. "I escaped from Vietnam on a small boat called the *California Dreamin'*." He stopped and pointed at Dordi, smiling. "I named it that because you always talked about going to California after the war." Dordi nodded and refilled their glasses yet again. "I met Lucy while I was getting the boat ready. She was the pilot. I'd never met a woman that could guide a boat before, but she was damn good. She brought us through a couple of bad storms, but finally the old boat couldn't take any more and fell apart during yet another storm. Most of the people we escaped with died, but she and I and a few others survived." Loc Tin paused again remembering the long-ago events. "We've been married a long time now. We have a good life. We have a son named Kevin." He sipped his whiskey.

They talked long into the night. Mostly reminiscing but also adding details of their lives since they last met. The good and the bad. Many of the stories started with "Remember that time..." They laughed a lot and at least for a while felt like young men again.

Chapter 81

Los Angeles, California, August 1990–August 1994
  Misty Borkowski

Misty started high school in August of 1990 and immediately hated it. She had been forced to change school districts after her parents bought a house over the summer and the family moved. She knew no one at the new school, and the few people she had met seemed shallow and uninteresting. Misty had zero interest in college and didn't see the point of most of the classes she was required to take. However, the school newspaper needed a photographer, and she had jumped at the opportunity. Being their photographer was the only thing she liked about school.

Misty's dad had given her his old Nikon F3 when she turned ten, and she wasted no time learning how to use it. JB said she had a good eye and once even used one of her photos for a story he wrote for *Our Life and Times* magazine. It had been thrilling to see her work and her name in print, and she decided then and there to become a photojournalist like her father. Now that she worked for the school, she hoped her parents would give her a new camera—or at least a newer used one—for her 14th birthday in September.

Indeed, her parents surprised her with a new Nikon F-601M. It wasn't the fanciest model, but Misty was ecstatic.

"Thank you! Thank you, both! I love it!" she told her parents as soon as she opened it. Her parents had given her several other gifts, mostly clothes, but it was the camera that kept her attention. Although she was adept at taking portraits and street scenes, her preference was to take photos of people when they weren't looking at the camera. She had several of her father as he perused his own photographs that he developed in his basement studio of their new home. She liked how the soft light of the darkroom played against the photographs that he hung to dry. Her favorite photo so far was one that she had taken of her mom. It had been taken the previous year when they still lived in the apartment in Glendale. Her mother had been sitting on the balcony overlooking the street drinking tea and watching the sunrise. Misty thought she looked serene and beautiful.

Now with her new camera, she was more confident than ever that she was prepared to chronicle the events around her. Indeed, she would soon have the opportunity to capture more than just the school news. Over the next two years, Los Angeles County would experience numerous riots and violent confrontations between the African-American community and the L.A. police. More than once, teenage Misty—camera always at the ready— managed to be in the wrong place at the right time. She photographed many events as they unfolded and helped bring the important story to the rest of the country. Her photos were often published in *Our Life and Times* magazine and several were picked up by newspapers across the country.

By the time Misty graduated high school, she had a national reputation as a photojournalist, and she was actively recruited by multiple colleges. Despite her previous opposition to higher education, she was intrigued by the opportunities at the University of Southern California. They offered her a small scholarship along with a paid position with the school newspaper. She accepted and matriculated in the Fall of 1994.

Chapter 82

Grenada, Mississippi, June 1995
  Melinda and Zach

Melinda Tackett married Zach Barker in a church wedding in the afternoon of June 10, 1995. The two had met three years before when they were both freshman pre-veterinary majors at Mississippi State University. They had numerous classes together, and Zach noticed the pretty, petite Melinda right away. She was one of the smartest students in the class and was always very serious and focused on her studies. Naturally, Zach made it his goal in life to make her laugh.

Zach had done a bit of improvisational comedy in high school and could turn just about any situation into a skit making everyone around him laugh until they cried. Once at the coffee bar in the university's student center, he adopted a British accent and convinced the poor barista behind the counter that he was an international coffee inspector. Zach was also a talented guitarist and possessed a unique singing voice. He had grown up in Nashville, the son of studio musicians, and had spent much of his youth around performers and was himself comfortable being on stage. After Melinda refused him the first time he asked her out, he began standing outside her second floor dorm room playing the guitar and singing ridiculous songs that he made up on the fly. She tried to ignore him, but she began to find his quirky pursuance of her endearing.

Even before Zach's antics to get her attention, Melinda had noticed him. He was handsome with broad shoulders and a perpetual 5 o'clock shadow that gave him a rugged look. Despite his good looks, Melinda tried to act uninterested. When she started college, she promised herself she would stay focused on her classes. Vet schools were highly selective, and she was determined to make sure she would be competitive. However, Zach was hard to ignore. Within six months of the start of their freshman year of college, they were dating. Within two years, they were engaged.

Chapter 83

Richmond, Virginia, 1990-1997
  The Vong and Dordi Families

It had been two years since Dordi and Loc Tin had reconnected in the mountains, and they soon introduced their wives. Both women had heard numerous stories of their husband's combat buddy and felt an immediate kinship. Neither Lucy nor Linh had ever had a sister, and, because of the war, both had been left without any family other than the ones they had created with their husbands.

After the Dordi's second son, Jeremy, was born, Dennis and Linh bought a three-bedroom house in a suburb of Richmond, Virginia. Two years later, Loc Tin and Lucy bought a fixer-upper in a neighborhood close by, and Dordi made good on his promise to help with needed repairs. Over the next few months, the Dordis and Vongs spent more time together than apart. Their boys, Kevin and Lucas, played well together despite the age difference. Lucas, the older of the two, was mildly autistic and had never been able to connect with kids his own age, but he and Kevin immediately bonded. Both of the older boys doted on little Jeremy. Because of the autism, Linh had always homeschooled Lucas and had not worked outside the home since her days at the salon in San Francisco. Lucy, who was part-owner of an upscale salon called the Pampered Lady Day Spa, easily convinced Linh to work there part-time.

Most of the women who worked at the salon were Vietnamese, and although they all spoke English, they typically spoke their native language to each other. Linh found she enjoyed conversing in Vietnamese, which she hadn't done in several years. She had tried hard to forget her life in Vietnam, but these women were good to her, and she quickly felt at home in the salon. Because Linh's English was among the best of the women at the Pampered Lady, she typically worked at the front desk. She answered the phone and greeted customers when they arrived. She would also make small talk with them while they waited their turn and then compliment them on their new hairstyle or their manicure. One day she noticed that a lady had changed her hair color. She had been a brunette when she had come into the salon, but two hours later she was a platinum blonde. Linh thought she was stunning, and she asked Lucy to bleach her hair the same way.

Lucy looked at her friend. "You want to go blonde?"

"Why not? She looks wonderful," Linh said, excited at the idea of completely changing her look. "I'll look American."

Lucy shrugged. "Why not. We are pretty slow today. If you don't like it, we can always dye it back, though that's hard on your hair."

"I think I will love it," Linh said as she sat in the chair and watched her friend work. "Maybe you could give me a new cut as well. I've never had bangs. Maybe I should try bangs?"

When she was finished, the change was dramatic. Linh looked at herself in the mirror tossing her hair this way and that way. Finally she smiled. "I like it. It's different."

Lucy laughed. "It is definitely different."

Chapter 84

Philadelphia, Pennsylvania, 1993-1997
  Augustini Family

In the summer of 1993, Sara Augustini, Augie and Penny's only child, married Jerry Adams at the church both families had attended for many years. Because of his oxygen tank, Augie did not want to walk his daughter down the aisle. Sara begged him to reconsider, and he eventually agreed. Penny found a medical supply company that was able to give Augie a small tank just for the day of the wedding. It was small enough that he could wear it on a strap around his neck almost hidden under his jacket. For the photos, he insisted on removing the tubes that fed oxygen to his nose.

Three years after their wedding, Sara and her husband announced that they were pregnant. Augie had been excited to learn he would soon become a grandfather, but, unfortunately, he died unexpectedly before the baby was born. He was only 44 years old.

Augie had been waiting for a subway train when, according to witnesses, his knees buckled, and he fell head-first into an oncoming train. He was killed instantly. It was a horrific event that made headlines in the paper for several days. Witnesses were understandably traumatized as was Augie's family. The investigation into his death surmised that Augie's tank might have run out of oxygen causing him to pass out and fall onto the tracks. This theory, though, couldn't be proven since the tank had been destroyed in the accident. His death was ultimately ruled an accident and neither foul play nor suicide was suspected.

Despite the official report, Penny had her doubts. Augie had grown increasingly despondent and had told her multiple times the family would be better off without him.

"How can I be a decent grandpa if I can't even take my grandchild camping or fishing?" he asked her again and again.

Penny loved Augie and tried hard to reassure him that he would be a wonderful grandfather despite his failing health. He would just shake his head and tell her that his life insurance would be of more use to them. He told her, "I'm pretty damn worthless to the family in the state I'm in." Penny had never imagined that Augie would take his own life, but now she wondered. The thought that he might have purposely fallen in front of the train had given her nightmares.

Two months after Augie's death, in May of 1997 his granddaughter was born. Sara, grieving from her father's recent passing, named her Alessi Augustini Adams after the grandfather she would never know.

Chapter 85

San Francisco, California, 1998–2000
  Dennis Dordi and Family

In 1998, shortly after Lucas Dordi turned 20, he was offered a job at a tech start-up in San Francisco. Despite being autistic, he had a natural aptitude with computers, and the job was perfect for him. Linh, of course, was afraid.

"He's never been on his own before. How will he manage?" she asked Dordi.

"He's a smart kid. He'll figure it out. This is a chance for him to have a normal life."

But Linh was adamant. She didn't want him to go.

Linh had lost three children and was understandably overprotective of both her sons but especially of Lucas. Dordi, however, was confident that the time was right for him to be on his own. As gently as he could he told Linh, "If we always take care of him, then he won't learn to take care of himself."

Linh was unmoved. The three of them discussed it over several days. Lucas insisted he would take the job, and Linh insisted he wouldn't. Linh was surprised that her husband was on Lucas' side. One night over dinner, she suggested a compromise. "What if we go with him? We can sell our house and move back to California. Lucas can get his own place. Maybe not at first, but after he's confident he likes the job. That way we will be nearby if he needs us. I promise I won't hover. I just need to know he is okay and that we can help him if anything happens that he can't handle."

Dordi and Lucas exchanged a look. They both knew the answer. Dordi never could say no to Linh. He nodded and said, "I'll call Eric and see if he is hiring."

Linh smiled and kissed her husband. "I'm certain he'll be happy to have you back."

Indeed, Eric was eager to have Dennis Dordi back on his construction crew. San Francisco was growing rapidly, and there were more construction projects than companies to run them. As expected, Lucas was quite successful at the new tech start-up. He fit in well with the team, many of whom, like him, were on the autism spectrum. Within six months of joining his new company, Lucas moved into a small apartment in the same complex as his parents and brother and was, more or less, living on his own. At first he joined his family for dinner nearly every night, but as he grew more confident and expanded his circle of friends, he spent less time with them.

Not quite two years after joining the tech company, Lucas surprised his parents by driving up in a new car.

"When did you buy a car?" Jeremy asked, looking wide-eyed at the shiny new Toyota RAV4.

"When did you learn to *drive?*" a completely stunned Dordi asked.

Lucas just smiled. "Andy from work. He said he was tired of driving me around and taught me. I got a good deal on the car because it is last year's model."

"You need insurance, Lucas," his mother told him sounding concerned.

"All taken care of, Mom. Hey, Jeremy, want me to take you to get ice cream?"

"Oh, yeah!" his younger brother responded as he climbed into the passenger side of the small SUV.

Linh just looked on in amazement as her two sons drove away. The transformation that she had seen in Lucas since he started working was nothing short of miraculous. She took Dennis' hand. "You were right. He needed to take that job to help him learn to take care of himself."

Dordi gently squeezed her hand in response. "And I am glad you insisted we move with him. Otherwise, we would have missed seeing him this way."

Chapter 86

Los Angeles, California, January-April 2000
   Chi and Family

For more than two decades, *Our Life and Times* magazine had regularly published articles covering various aspects of the war in Vietnam. More often than not, the stories focused on the American experience. Articles were written about young men who gladly joined the armed services, as well as those who avoided the draft by going to college or fleeing to Canada. They chronicled the experiences of a group of young, poor Black men who had been drafted just as they graduated from the same high school. Most had made it home, but some had not. The magazine won an award for an article detailing the heroics of a combat medic who refused to carry a gun but nevertheless put himself in harm's way in order to save the lives of his fellow soldiers. In 1975 they printed several stories about the rapid influx of Vietnamese refugees at the tent city that had been established for them at Camp Pendleton. In the two years following the fall of Saigon, several follow-up stories had been printed. However, by 1977 the editors felt their American readers had probably lost interest in the country that had dominated the news for so long. For many years thereafter whenever JB approached the leadership team with a story idea that included Vietnam, they said no. Despite the rejections, he kept trying. In January of 2000, when JB presented his editor with an idea for the 25th anniversary of the war's end, to his surprise his boss was intrigued.

"You want to go to Vietnam?" his editor had asked.

"Yes, sir. We fought the war to preserve democracy in Southeast Asia. We were told if Vietnam fell, the whole region would become communist—an arm of Russia. I think Americans would be interested in what happened after we left."

JB's boss nodded thoughtfully. "Maybe so. Don't you speak the language? I'm sure many of the government officials speak English, but it would be better if you can talk to regular citizens to get the real scoop."

JB shook his head. "I used to speak a little, but I doubt it would be much use anymore. Chi is still fluent. Perhaps I can take her with me?"

"Yeah, sure. That works," the man said as he walked to the window. He spoke as he looked out on the street below. "She might even be able to get more info than you. Not sure how people will feel about us Americans now." The man turned back toward JB, thinking out loud. "You know, maybe take your daughter as well. She can talk to the young people, and she has a unique eye with the camera." He looked directly at JB and wagged his finger at him. "But this isn't a family vacation. If the magazine is footing the bill, I want something that will really stand out, something worthy of being the cover story."

JB smiled. "You got it, sir. We won't let you down."

Less than two months later, the Borkowski family stepped off the plane at the civilian airport in Saigon. Misty was immediately hit by the oppressive heat. "Wow. Is it always like this? How do you breathe?"

Chi laughed. "Yes. It is always hot. When I first came to the U.S.—to San Diego—I thought I would freeze to death. We all did. But eventually we got used to it."

"I will *never* get used to this," Misty said as she used a napkin from the plane to wipe off the sweat that was already forming on her face.

The family spent nearly two weeks in Vietnam. The magazine had gotten them a large room at the Rex Hotel in Ho Chi Minh City, although to Chi and JB it would always be Saigon. They mostly stayed close to the city, although they did venture out to some of the nearby farms. Chi very much wanted to visit DaNang, but both time and money were short.

The first two days the family stayed together. They walked around Saigon showing Misty how to navigate the city. She was amazed by the traffic. Small cars, seemingly thousands of motorbikes, and bicycles flew by her without ever stopping. "How are you supposed to cross the road?" she asked. "There are no crosswalks."

Chi laughed and replied, "You just walk across wherever you want. The cars and motorbikes will go around you." Misty looked at her mother like she was crazy, and Chi responded, "I'll show you."

Misty was horrified when her mother stepped into oncoming traffic, but, just as she had said, all the vehicles glided around her and she made it to the other side without incident.

"This is crazy," she said to her dad.

"Welcome to Vietnam," he replied, smiling.

Eventually the family split up to cover more ground. Chi planned to talk to older people who would remember the war while Misty would try to interview the younger generation to get their thoughts on Vietnam's trajectory. Purposefully, only JB was registered with the local authorities as the official representative of the magazine since foreign journalists were required to be accompanied by a government agent. Although at the time Vietnam was developing a market economy, the communist government was still firmly in control. JB, in his capacity with the magazine, would be limited in where he could go and with whom he could speak. Since his wife and daughter were registered only as tourists, they would have fewer restrictions.

Together the Borkowskis learned that Vietnam had grown and largely thrived, despite the heavy-handed control of the communist government which many insisted was corrupt. Numerous American companies came to Vietnam after 1994 when the U.S. lifted its embargo. Foreign investment had brought jobs and development to the country and began to lift people from poverty. By 2000 Nike, famous for its athletic shoes, was one of Vietnam's largest employers and paid its workers far better than other more traditional means of employment. Of course, the influx of foreign companies also brought Western influence, which the government loathed. Although no one in authority would admit it, JB was convinced that the communist leaders worried that exposure of the Vietnamese people to Western ideas would make them less tolerant of those in power. Publicly, the government officials of Vietnam welcomed outside businesses, while behind the scenes red tape and bureaucracy often made it difficult for foreign companies to be profitable. Although some businesses, like Nike, managed to survive, many others would pull out after only a few years.

Misty agreed with her father's assessment. She could see that the younger generation of Vietnam was getting glimpses of Western culture and wanted to be part of it. By the year 2000, more than half of the population of Vietnam was under 25 years of age, and their collective voice was growing louder by the day. They were beginning to demand change. The young people of Vietnam wanted an end to government corruption and improved economic opportunities for all of the country's citizens. The article that the Borkowskis wrote for *Our Life and Times* ended with a prediction. Vietnam's youth would drive the political change that Vietnam desperately needed if it was to join the global community. If those in charge didn't listen, Vietnam would remain mired in the past.

JB's editor was pleased with the article, and their story marking the 25th anniversary of the fall of Saigon graced the cover of the April 2000 issue of *Our Life and Times* magazine.

Chapter 87

Starkville, Mississippi, May 2000
  Melinda and Zach Barker

In May 2000 Melinda and Zach Barker, along with their 75 classmates, graduated from Mississippi State University's College of Veterinary Medicine in Starkville, Mississippi. After the ceremony, the couple quickly located their family among the throngs of other students and families. Melinda and Zach had been married five years and would soon be moving to Gainesville where they would conduct specialty training at the University of Florida. Melinda had chosen to conduct her residency training in large animal medicine while Zach would specialize in large animal surgery. They both hoped to eventually return to Mississippi and practice veterinary medicine at a clinic dedicated to serving farmers.

At dinner after the graduation ceremony, both Zach and Melinda's mothers asked the familiar question, "When will it be time to start a family?"

Melinda and Zach exchanged a look. Then she responded, "I don't know, but not right now. Residency will be tough and stressful. Not a good time to have kids."

"And we barely have time for each other. I don't think it would be fair to a child," added Zach.

"Well, we could help out," Melinda's mother immediately responded. She looked at Zach's mother who nodded in agreement. Then she looked at Melinda and added, "You're not getting any younger, you know. You can't wait forever."

Melinda was about to say something she would regret when she felt Zach squeeze her knee under the table. She glanced at him, took a deep breath, and said, "Honestly, we're thinking we might adopt. There are so many kids that need homes. What would have happened to me if you and dad hadn't adopted me?" Her mother smiled at her and nodded. She started to say something, but Melinda quickly added, "But *after* we complete our residencies."

Chapter 88

Los Angeles, California, September 2001
  The Borkowski Family

Misty Borkowski turned 25 on Tuesday, September 4, 2001. The previous Saturday, she had celebrated with her friends and her new boyfriend Paul at one of the recently opened bars that offered live music. On Tuesday, her actual birthday, she and Paul joined her parents for dinner at one of her favorite local restaurants. Paul was a little nervous meeting Misty parents and was anxious to make a good impression.

Misty knew her dad had been asked to go to Boston for a few days but was trying to get out of it. After the waiter had taken their order and returned with bread and drinks, she asked, "What's the assignment? Anything interesting?"

He frowned. "Not at all. That's why I'd rather not go. The magazine wants to do a spread on the Big Dig. Some people are saying L.A. needs to do something like that."

"What's the Big Dig?" asked Paul, dipping bread into the seasoned olive oil the waiter had brought.

"It's a huge highway project in Boston. They are moving some of the roads that run through the city underground," answered Misty. She looked back at her dad. "I thought that was supposed to be done by now?"

"It was," he agreed. "But the whole project has been plagued by problems, mismanagement, and some say corruption. And of course it has cost much more than originally projected."

"Sounds exactly how L.A. would manage a project like that," Paul said with just a hint of sarcasm.

The conversation lagged and Paul tried to think of something he could say to Misty's parents. To fill the silence, he brought up their trip to Vietnam. "I read your article on the 25th anniversary of the fall of Saigon. It was really interesting, but Misty said you had difficulty meeting with some of the people you wanted to interview."

"Indeed," JB replied and spent the next several minutes telling Paul about how his government-assigned babysitter followed him everywhere and monitored who he could speak to. "They want to control the information that the West has about Vietnam." He motioned toward his wife and daughter. "But Misty and Chi were unrestricted, and they were able to talk to many of the people I couldn't. In the end, it worked out and we got the story."

When the conversation lagged yet again, Misty said, "Paul asked me where you had been stationed when you were covering the war, but I couldn't remember. I know you did two tours."

Misty's question led to a lengthy discussion between JB and Paul about the older man's wartime service. Misty listened intently. She had never heard her father talk about his time in Vietnam.

No one noticed Chi, who had become quiet. As she listened to the discussion, her thoughts drifted back to her own time during the war. She began to think about things she had long tried to suppress. Right after her confession that nearly tore her and JB apart, they had agreed to never again speak of the war. Of course, the memories were still there, and sometimes when she least expected it one would surface and the voice in her head would say, "I know who you really are, and I won't let you forget."

For a long time, only JB knew she had been VC. Occasionally someone would ask her how she had escaped Vietnam, but they were easily satisfied by the shortest version which was quite true. She had been evacuated before the end of the war because she worked with the Americans. Eventually, however, Misty had asked more difficult questions. When she was a teenager, Chi had told her what she had told JB. Her husband and daughter thought they knew everything about her past, but they didn't. Only Chi and that voice in her head knew everything.

Chi refilled her wine glass while JB and Paul continued to talk about Vietnam. She thought about Trinh and how the woman had convinced her that Ho Chi Minh's efforts were noble and that joining him would also be noble. And maybe in some ways it was. She fought to rid her homeland of foreign occupiers. Was that so awful? No, but the cost had been too high. She had killed so many young men who, like her, thought their actions were just. Noble. They were all naive and gullible. They had been deceived by those in power. Chi closed her eyes and saw Mark's face as he lay dead at her feet. It was her deepest regret. She reached for the wine bottle and refilled her glass yet again. It would be her third, which was two more than she normally drank.

She knew she was getting drunk, but she didn't care. JB and Paul were deep in a conversation about the war, and she heard her husband say something about Pleiku. Mention of that city reminded Chi of her first mission with Tam. They had carried weapons hidden in a sampan far downstream from DaNang toward Pleiku. Their mission was to transfer the weapons to an underground tunnel so that VC and North Vietnamese soldiers could be easily resupplied when needed. Chi shuddered as she remembered those tunnels. Dark and cramped. Tam pointed out the many hidden dangers inside the tunnels—booby traps designed to kill or maim, boxes that would release scorpions, trapdoors that would fall open and plunge you into a pit of poisonous snakes. Even though Tam was confident in her navigation, Chi was terrified of the tunnels. She shook her head in an effort to rid herself of the memories. She looked at her husband and forced herself to focus on his conversation with Paul.

She heard JB relay a story about photographing the entrance to one of the VC tunnels that his unit had found. "It was really ingenious how well they were hidden. I never went down in one, but some were really extensive and had hospitals and living quarters in addition to being supply depots."

Chi knew he was right, but she had never seen a tunnel hospital, only the heavily booby-trapped supply depots. She sipped her wine, envisioned the scorpions, and shuddered again.

Paul interjected, "I've heard the tunnels are open to the public now. Did you visit any when you were their last year?"

"Oh, God, no," Chi replied a little too loudly. "I spent enough time in those damn tunnels during the war. I never want to see them again."

"What?" Paul asked, completely surprised. "When were you in the tunnels?"

Chi looked at Paul and said more softly, "I had many jobs during the war. I smuggled weapons and resupplied the tunnels a few times."

Paul was still confused. "No." He hesitated before continuing. "That would mean you were Viet Cong." It wasn't a question.

Chi nodded and drank deeply from her wine glass.

Paul looked at Misty, and she took his hand. She whispered an explanation, "She was very young and wanted to support the reunification of Vietnam."

The table grew quiet, and Chi seemed to retreat back into her memories. Paul continued to stare at her with both amazement and more than a little fear. He knew how vicious the VC could be. He was having a hard time reconciling that this tiny woman could have been an enemy soldier. He looked at JB and wondered how an American soldier could marry a woman who had been Viet Cong.

JB seemed to read the other man's thoughts. He stared into his glass, turning it in his hands. Finally he said to Paul, "We all did things we regret." Then he gulped down the last of his bourbon.

"What things?" Paul asked without thinking.

JB shook his head. He obviously didn't want to go down that road. However, the voice in Chi's head was back and taunting her. It reminded her of Mark and then Mark's poor mother, who had convinced herself that her son would be remembered forever. Chi was arguing with the voice in her head and suddenly said in an angry voice, "I told you I regret killing Mark!"

Everyone at the table stared at Chi, and she realized she had spoken out loud. She lowered her head and fervently hoped no one understood what she had said.

But Misty immediately asked, "Who's Mark?"

"No one," Chi lied and reached for her wine glass. She stole a look at JB.

He stared at her for a very long moment. Then he asked, "Mark Higgins?" He desperately wanted to be wrong but feared he wasn't. "Is that how you ended up with his drawings?"

Chi was too drunk to think of a lie. Maybe part of her needed to confess. She had kept the secret so long. She nodded. "I was in DaNang walking the streets and pretending to be a prostitute. I took him home, and I stabbed him in the heart. He died in my arms. I—I can still see his face." Her voice trailed off and she looked away for a moment. Then she took a deep breath, looked down at her hands, and said softly, "We rolled him up in a tarp and dumped his body in an alley." Chi took another gulp of wine. She looked around the table at her horror-struck family. Her voice grew stronger as she said, "I'm glad the army lied to his mother. I'm glad they gave him a medal." She set her glass down and leaned back in her chair still thinking about Mark.

JB stared at Chi for a long moment considering what she had said. In a quiet but clearly angry voice he said, "You were a prostitute? You killed Mark? How many others?" He shook his head. "I don't know you at all, do I?"

JB stood and started to walk away. He hesitated and turned back. He looked at Misty. "See that your mother gets home. I'm going to Boston." He left without looking at Chi, but she jumped up and followed him out of the restaurant.

"JB, please wait." She grabbed his arm trying to stop him from leaving. "Let me explain."

He whipped around and glared at her. "What's to explain? I know all about the VC prostitutes. You lured men to your bed and killed them during sex." He shook with anger and had to suppress the urge to hit her. He had lost a buddy to a VC hooker.

"No, JB, it wasn't like that." She grabbed his arm again, but he jerked away from her.

"Save your lies. You've lied to me for 25 years. I've had enough."

"JB—please. Wait."

But he was already walking away from her. Chi stood on the sidewalk in front of the restaurant for a long time. Finally she turned and went back inside.

Chi sat at their table next to Misty. In her absence, the waiter had brought their dinner. Chi looked at her daughter but didn't speak. No one felt like eating.

Misty put her hand on her mother's. "What's going on? I don't understand. You—you were a prostitute? You killed Mark? Mark who? The one in dad's article from ages ago?"

Chi looked at her daughter. "Yes. That Mark. But I wasn't really a prostitute. It was just a way to lure men in. They didn't expect me to be armed. I—I—uhm." Chi closed her eyes and took a deep breath before continuing, "I killed several men that way. Mark was different. He was sweet and nervous. He told me his name like we were friends or something. Then—afterward—after I had killed him..." Chi looked down at her hands again not wanting to meet her daughter's eye. Then she said, "Afterward—that was when I found his drawings, and I—I just knew that he shouldn't have died."

Misty sat open-mouthed just looking at her mother. She had no idea what to say. She knew she needed comforting, but Misty was reeling with this new information. In a weak voice she managed to asked, "Why didn't you tell Dad? You should have told him when he wrote the article about Mark."

Chi began to cry. "I know! I wanted to. I tried to tell him everything before we got married, but I just couldn't bring myself to tell him that I had killed men—American men. And Mark. I just couldn't." She paused for a long moment, picked up her wine glass, but set it back down without drinking. She looked at Misty. "When JB interviewed Mark's mother, that was even worse. It was like we got to know him. He was a such good kid." Chi wiped the tears from her eyes as she began to choke up again. She managed to say, "I vowed I would never tell anyone. I couldn't forgive myself. How could I expect your dad to understand?" Chi looked toward the door of the restaurant. "Now it's even worse. He wouldn't let me explain."

Misty put her hand on her mother's shoulder and tried to find the right words. "You have to try to talk to Dad. Maybe you can make him understand." Misty embraced her mother. "You were very young. He knows that. Just talk to him."

Paul, who felt like an intruder watching such a private moment, finally knew the right thing to do. He stood and leaned down to whisper in Misty's ear, "I'll find the waiter and settle up. Then we can take your mom home." Misty nodded at him gratefully.

Thirty minutes later, Paul parked in Chi's driveway. JB's car wasn't there. Misty started to get out with her mom, but Chi told her no. "I just need to be alone."

Reluctantly, Misty nodded and watched as her mother walked up the steps to the door. The older woman fumbled a moment with her keys, then disappeared inside.

Chi could tell JB had hurriedly packed a bag. Clearly he wanted to be gone by the time she got there. She knew he would stay at a hotel for a day or two. She was certain he would take the Boston assignment. She was far less certain that he would come home to her afterward. She tried to call him, but he didn't answer. She lay on the couch and cried for a very long time.

The following Tuesday, JB had completed his assignment and was at Boston's Logan airport waiting to board his flight back to Los Angeles. As he waited in the terminal, he thought about calling Chi. He looked at his watch and realized it was only 3:00 A.M. at home, so he decided against it. Besides, he thought, it would be better to talk in person. Over the last few days, he had thought a lot about their life together and had come to the conclusion that they could get past this. He was hurt, but he also understood. He realized how hard it must have been for her to admit being VC. She couldn't know how he would react to that, let alone what he might have done if she had also told him she had killed Americans. She had been pregnant and scared but tried to do the right thing by telling him what she did. Maybe if he had been more understanding, she would have told him the whole truth then. Looking back on it, he could understand why she had lied about killing Mark.

Then there was the prostitution. Could he get past *that*? What would he have done if she had told him she had been a prostitute before they married? Certainly he would have rejected her immediately. However, he had been with prostitutes in both Korea and Vietnam. Was he so much different than her? He wished she would have told him sooner, but maybe even that he understood.

At some point he realized that she, like so many veterans, struggled with her past. When he was discharged from the army after Korea, he had issues. These days they call it Post-Traumatic Stress Disorder (PTSD), but it didn't have a name back then. Eighteen months in Korea and nearly two years in Vietnam left him with many demons. He had joined the VFW and had often talked to other veterans. It helped. Although the men rarely talked about the war, somehow being with others who had been there—who also had regrets or survivor's guilt—made a difference. Who did Chi have? No one. He realized it had been a mistake when he insisted they never speak of the war. Looking back over the years, he wondered how she was able to manage all that she had been through. He looked at his watch for the hundredth time. He was anxious to get home.

Finally he boarded American Airlines Flight 11 around 7:00 A.M. local time on September 11, 2001. JB took his seat just over the left wing of the plane and pulled out a book hoping to distract himself for the long flight. When the book couldn't hold his attention, he sat back and closed his eyes. He felt the plane taxi and then lift into the air. He thought about what he would say to his wife. Deep in thought with his eyes closed, he didn't notice the unusual activity taking place at the front of the aircraft. If he had, he might have realized sooner that his plane had been hijacked. Instead, it was only when he heard a woman near the front scream that he opened his eyes. The cockpit door was open, and when he stood, he saw that the pilot was lying on the floor. He appeared to be dead. A male passenger was barking orders and gesturing with his hands. He held a knife.

JB slowly sat back down and slid his credit card into the slot that would release the onboard phone embedded in the headrest in front of him. He called Chi, but she didn't answer. When their machine picked up, JB said as calmly as he could, "Babe, my plane's been hijacked. The pilot is dead and several men are threatening the flight attendants. I don't know what they want." Suddenly the plane banked hard to the left. "Looks like we are turning around. Maybe we are just going back to Boston." But when JB looked out the window, he saw the New York City skyline rapidly approaching. His heart sank into his stomach, and he knew he would never see his wife or daughter again. He said into the phone, "I love you, Chi. I am so sorry," just before the plane crashed into the North Tower of the World Trade Center. JB and 92 other people were on Flight 11. There were no survivors.

In LA, Misty's alarm signaled the start of a new day, and, as usual, she rolled over and turned on her bedside radio. As a journalist, she thought it was important to hear the latest headlines at the start of each day. Typically she would lie in bed with her eyes closed as she listened to the report. Instead, what she heard that morning made her jump out of bed and turn on the TV. The talking heads on the morning show out of New York were debating what kind of plane had hit the World Trade Center. It was assumed to be a terrible accident. Misty sat glued to the TV. The camera was focused on the smoke pouring from the North Tower of the iconic building when a large passenger jet crashed into the South Tower. "Oh, my God," Misty whispered. Immediately she and the rest of the nation realized that the plane crashes were deliberate. Hands shaking, she reached for the phone. She feared for her father and needed to call her mother. The phone rang just as she touched it. Misty jerked her hand back startled. She saw it was her parents' phone number and snatched it from its cradle. "Mom!" she blurted. Then more calmly asked, "Is Dad okay?"

"He called!" Chi wailed. "I was asleep! I—I didn't hear it ring."

The line went quiet for a moment, and Misty held her breathe still hoping her dad was okay. Maybe his flight was grounded or diverted. Finally Chi found her voice again and managed to choke out a few words. "He had to leave a message. He said—he said his plane was hijacked." Misty heard her mother sobbing on the other end of the line.

Misty reeled at the news. Her father was dead. She looked back at the TV and silently cried as she watched the chaos in New York City. Then she said into the phone, "I'm coming over."

A few minutes later Misty was dressed and out the door. As she drove, she thought about her father. When she was younger, she often worried that his plane would crash but eventually realized that he was far more likely to die driving in L.A. Now her childhood nightmare had come to pass. She thought about the last time she had seen him. She closed her eyes as the memories of that awful night at the restaurant came back to her. She had been sure her parents would make up, but now they never would. How would her mother cope?

Both Misty and Chi were completely devastated by JB's death, but Chi blamed herself. "He would never have been on that plane if it weren't for me."

Misty tried to comfort her mother. "No. This isn't your fault. His plane was hijacked. They are the ones who did this."

"But it is my fault JB was there. His death is my punishment for killing Mark."

Despite her own grief, Misty tried to be strong for her mother and tried to assuage the guilt she felt. "You know Dad. He would have gone to Boston anyway. His editor wanted him to go, and so he would have," Misty told her mother again and again.

"No. His death is my punishment for killing Mark," Chi said again. Nothing Misty said could ease her mother's pain.

U.S. government officials soon determined that Osama bin Laden was responsible for the attacks on 9/11 and quickly established an international coalition to remove his Taliban regime from power in Afghanistan. Less than one month after 9/11, Operation Enduring Freedom began with American and British bombing strikes against al-Qaeda and the Taliban forces in Afghanistan.

Misty begged her editor to let her go to Afghanistan to cover the war, but he refused.

"It's too dangerous. I have several other journalists with experience covering war zones. They can go," he had told her emphatically. More gently he added, "We've already lost one Borkowski. I won't be responsible for losing another."

Misty understood his reluctance, but she was determined. One day after work, Misty stopped by the local military services recruiting station intent on enlisting. The sergeant on duty explained that since she had a college degree, she could be commissioned as an officer. Furthermore, the U.S. Army would even allow her to choose her assignment. The recruiter explained that with her experience and degree in journalism she could become a U.S. Army Public Affairs Officer and work as a journalist for the military. Without hesitation, Misty Borkowski responded, "Where do I sign?"

Chapter 89

Gainesville, Florida, May 2000–July 2004
  Melinda and Zach Barker

Immediately after graduating with their doctorates in veterinary medicine, Melinda and Zach Barker moved to Gainesville, Florida, to begin their residency programs. Soon thereafter, they began the long process of adopting a child from the foster care system, which required a background check, a review of their finances, and a home inspection. Completing all the necessary steps took time, but in 2003, shortly after Dr. Melinda Barker completed her residency program, they were ready to welcome four-year-old twins, Chris and Alex, into their home. The boys had been in foster care for nearly two years after both of their parents had been killed in a meth lab explosion in East Tennessee. Although Melinda and Zach had always planned to adopt two children, they hadn't considered the possibility of adopting both at the same time. After meeting the boys and spending time with them, they didn't hesitate to take them both.

Although Melinda had completed her residency training, Zach's program would last another year. Melinda could have easily found full-time employment while her husband finished his training, but they opted for her to work only part-time so she could spend the majority of each day with the boys as they adjusted to their new life and new family. Money was a bit tight, but they were frugal and made it work. Still, the first few months were rough. The boys had been in three different foster homes since their parents had died, and they were understandably distrustful of their latest caregivers.

Slowly over time, Chris and Alex became comfortable with Melinda and eventually began to trust her. It was harder for them to bond with Zach since he was gone more than he was home. However, his goofy antics could always make them laugh, and they soon began to get excited whenever they heard his car drive up. By the time the boys turned five, an outsider looking in would not have known that Chris and Alex hadn't always been part of the Barker family.

Chapter 90

Baghdad, Iraq, June 2004
  Misty

Lt. Misty Borkowski was sitting on the passenger side of a Humvee watching the streets of Baghdad, the capital of Iraq, pass by her window. Once again, she tried to understand why she was there. After 9/11, she gladly signed up to defend her country against the terrorists in Afghanistan since they were responsible for the attacks that killed her dad. Instead, she had been sent to Iraq.

Many believed that the president of Iraq, Saddam Hussein, possessed weapons of mass destruction and was willing to use them against his enemies. If that was true, Misty supposed the war was probably justified. Still, he wasn't the one who attacked her homeland, killed her father, and made her want to join the army. She often resented being sent to Iraq instead of Afghanistan.

Misty picked up her camera and turned her attention back to the passing landscape. She saw al-Fardous Square where in April of 2003 the statue of Saddam Hussein had been torn down. Across from the square was the iconic Al Fidos Mosque. It was a beautiful structure with a colorfully tiled dome. She held her camera to her eye and snapped several photos before it disappeared from view. Silently, she hoped the building would not be destroyed like so many others had been. She sat back in her seat, camera at the ready, and continued to watch the city go by.

She had been in-country for more than a year and had seen a lot through the lens of her Nikon. One of her most recent shots was of a young soldier standing next to an open-air burn pit, an expansive ditch cut into the earth and used by the military to destroy any type of waste. The pits burned constantly and produced a thick, black smoke that snaked up into the bright blue sky. The soldier stood casually with his back to the camera watching the fire. Even from a distance, the smoke had burned Misty's eyes, and the stench assaulted her nostrils as she focused her lens and clicked the shutter. When Misty looked at the digital photo displayed on the camera's screen, she knew the army was unlikely to use it. Although artistically it was a good photo, it wasn't the right message for the Americans back home.

The U.S. Army preferred her to take photos of soldiers working or at ease on the base, but her camera frequently captured subjects other than American military personnel. She had photographed insurgents being taken to prison, starving children begging for food, and even Iraqi citizens waving American flags. As a woman, she was excluded from being assigned to a combat unit. However, in this war, like the one in Vietnam, the frontline was an ever-moving target. She had seen her fair share of death, both of soldiers and civilians. She hated photographing dead bodies but felt she had no choice. Death was an important part of the war and could not be ignored. When photographing them, she was careful to exclude the faces of the victims, preferring instead to capture the response of those around them.

Two days before climbing into the Humvee that would take her to Baghdad, Misty had been on a Blackhawk helicopter. She had been sent to document an aid mission just outside of Balad. The U.S. Army was bringing supplies to a civilian hospital that had been overwhelmed by casualties. As the Blackhawk had begun its descent, the wind turbulence caused by the rotors was so great it had blown down a small shack that served as a barn for a local farmer. The man's donkey had been killed when the rudimentary structure had collapsed. We paid him $400 in reparations. What troubled her, though, was that a month before the donkey's death, she had witnessed the negotiations for another collateral damage reparations payment. In that instance, a civilian's young daughter had been accidentally killed by U.S. Forces. At the time she had no way to judge whether or not $100 for the life of a child was an appropriate amount. Even considering that American money was worth far more than the local currency, the sum seemed paltry to Misty. Now she knew the donkey's life was far more valuable than the child's. It was a disturbing and sad commentary on the war, and sometimes she felt the images she captured with her camera were wholly inadequate. Like her father before her, Misty often wanted to write the articles that went with her photographs. A picture may be worth a thousand words, but sometimes words were also needed.

Today Misty was being transferred to Camp Victory, a component of the Victory Base Complex near the airport in Baghdad. The base had opened the previous year and housed multiple branches of the American military. In the middle of the complex was an enormous, stone-clad palace overlooking a small lake. It was one of nearly 100 palaces that had been built by Saddam Hussein during his reign in Iraq. The palace would eventually house III-Corps and be the command center of the base. Numerous grayish-white modular buildings had been set up by contractors working for the U.S. and were used for officer housing as well as administrative offices. Enlisted troops were housed in a massive tent city within the footprint of the complex. When Misty arrived in 2004, the base also contained recreation facilities which provided the troops access to commercial phones, internet, and a variety of indoor entertainment activities. It seemed an odd juxtaposition. War on the outside, fun and games on the inside.

Chapter 91

Mississippi, June–July 2004
  Melinda Barker and Family

Dr. Zach Barker completed his large animal surgical residency in June of 2004, and he and Melinda packed up the kids, left Florida, and returned to Mississippi. Both Drs. Barker had accepted positions with a new large animal veterinary practice in Jackson that specialized in serving a variety of farm animals including horses, cows, and goats. Although Zach joined the Farmer's Doctor Veterinary Clinic immediately, Melinda would stay home with the boys until August when Alex and Chris would start kindergarten. Melinda's parents still lived in Grenada and were thrilled that she and her family would be less than two hours away.

When they first returned to Mississippi, the original plan was to leave Alex and Chris with Melinda's parents for a few days while the Barkers looked for a place to rent in the suburbs around Jackson. Unfortunately, when Melinda and Zach tried to leave, the boys became hysterical. Their sons had been with the Barkers barely a year, and although they seemed to have adjusted well to their new life, it became clear that they didn't fully comprehend that Melinda and Zach were their forever family. Melinda realized that leaving them in a different home with new people likely led Chris and Alex to believe that she and Zach would never return for them. It had no doubt happened to them before.

Melinda's heart broke for her sons and all they had been through in their short lives. She told Zach, "You go. I will stay here with Chris and Alex."

Zach nodded. "Eventually they will understand. It just takes time."

"I know." Melinda sighed and then turned her attention back to the task at hand. "Madison is best because the schools are better, but I hear Gluckstadt is good too and a little less expensive. Maybe you should look there first," Melinda said, reminding Zach of the suburbs she thought would be the best as he was getting ready to leave.

"Yes, I know. I was there when we did the research." He laughed and squeezed her hand. "I promise I will call you before I sign anything."

Melinda smiled as Zach kissed her cheek. Both boys clung to her, fearful she would leave with Zach. She looked down at them. "I hope I'll be able to work once they start school." In Florida, she and Zach arranged their schedules so that one of them was always with them, but they couldn't do that forever.

Zach knelt down so he was eye level with the boys. "Y'all be good for your mom. Eat your vegetables and help your grandparents. I'll be back before you know it."

Chris and Alex let Zach hug them, but they never let go of Melinda. He tousled their hair, kissed his wife again, and waved one more time as he backed out of the Tacketts' driveway.

Less than a week later, the Barkers moved into a three-bedroom rental house with a wide porch in front and a big yard in back. It was located in Gluckstadt, one of the suburbs of Jackson that Melinda deemed had acceptable schools. The house was only a couple of miles from the elementary school and also only a short drive to the Farmer's Doctor, although in the opposite direction from the school. The day the family moved in, the neighbor who lived in the house next door came to greet them almost as soon as the Barkers arrived. She was an older lady who introduced herself as Mrs. Maddie Morris. She wore a white apron over a flowy, print dress and carried a plate of homemade chocolate chip cookies. Bo, her black cocker spaniel, followed her dutifully across the yard to the delight of Alex and Chris.

Mrs. Morris set the cookies on the wide rail that ran along the porch and spoke to Melinda who had been carrying a box up the porch stairs. Melinda set the box down and said, "Thank you, Mrs. Morris. That's very kind of you."

"Call me Maddie. This is just my way of saying welcome to our little slice of Gluckstadt! Y'all will just love it here. I've lived here since I retired from teaching over in Pearl four years ago." She stood on the porch next to Melinda, and they both watched the boys play fetch with Bo. She pointed to the dog and said, "He's 13, but he still loves to play." She looked back at Melinda. "I quit teaching after my husband died, and then I moved here to be closer to my daughter and her children. They're just a few streets over, and I keep my grandkids after school. They'll be excited to have your boys here. Where y'all from?"

"I'm originally from Grenada. My husband, Zach, grew up just outside of Nashville. We met in college at Mississippi State."

"Oh," Mrs. Morris said frowning. "My daughter's husband went to Ole Miss and my daughter works at their medical school in Jackson." She paused and then smiled at Melinda. She touched her arm and said, "But I guess we won't hold it against you that you went to the wrong school."

Melinda smiled politely. She didn't want to be rude, but they needed to get the U-Haul unloaded. Just then another neighbor brought over a pitcher of lemonade. She handed the pitcher to Melinda but spoke to Mrs. Morris. "Are you talking this poor lady's ear off already, Maddie?" She looked at Melinda. "I'm Harriet and live in the blue house across the street. You just holler if you need anything. My husband knows everything about weeds and grass and such, and I'm pretty handy with a toolbox." She turned to the older woman. "Come on Maddie. Let these people do what they need to do. You can gossip with her later." Harriet took Maddie by the hand and practically drug her off the porch. Melinda was grateful and made a mental note to thank her later.

Chapter 92

San Francisco, California, 2004-2006
  Dennis Dordi and Family

Jeremy, the Dordi's youngest son, had been very unhappy to leave Virginia in 1998. It was the only place the 11-year-old had ever lived. However, by the time he graduated from high school in 2004, he felt as though he were a native Californian and had no desire to leave. His grades were excellent, and he had been accepted into every college to which he had applied, including his first choice, the University of California in San Diego. Unfortunately, it was located on the southern tip of the state many miles from his family, and it would be expensive. Jeremy knew the small scholarship he had received would not go very far and that his parents were not in a position to help pay his tuition. Jeremy didn't want to take out student loans and reluctantly opted to enroll in a small school less than an hour away from home. It was less expensive than his first choice, and the generous scholarship would cover all of his tuition and even part of his housing expenses. Although the school was much less prestigious than UCSD, it had a well-respected pre-med program and a good reputation with medical schools in California.

In August 2004, Dordi and Linh moved Jeremy into his dorm.

"I'm so proud of you," Linh told her youngest child more than once. She beamed as she added, "Finishing high school a year early and you still graduated near the top of the class!"

After getting Jeremy unpacked in his dorm, he politely declined joining his parents for lunch. Reluctantly, Linh let Dordi lead her away. "He'll be fine," he said.

"It's like he's anxious for us to leave."

"Of course he is. He's ready to be on his own. And he needs to be," Dordi said taking her hand in his as they walked to the car. Linh looked back toward the dorm trying to see if she could pick out Jeremy's window, but she couldn't be sure.

As they drove home, Linh took Dennis' hand. "It will be strange having the apartment to ourselves. No one to take care of or worry about."

Dordi laughed and kissed his wife's hand as he drove. "You will never stop worrying about our boys." He checked the side mirror and changed lanes. "But it will be good to be alone together again."

"Yes," she said looking at him. She thought about the days so long ago when she was 8 years old and Song told her that her mother was dead. She had thought she would be stuck with the horrible Mr. Ong forever, but Dennis had come into her life and everything changed. It hadn't always been easy, but it was a good life, and she was grateful.

A few months after Jeremy started college, Lucas introduced his family to Eden. They had met at work and had been dating for more than a year.

"I thought it was time for you to meet her. We've decided to get married," Lucas told them at dinner the first time he brought her over to his parent's apartment.

"Married?" Dordi and Linh said in unison.

A couple of months later, Linh met with Eden's mother and the two women began planning a spring wedding.

Chapter 93

Iraq, 2006
  Misty

Misty had been in Iraq for nearly four years and would be leaving the country for good in less than three months. During her time in-country, she had taken thousands of photographs. Although many were of fellow American soldiers doing soldierly things such as jumping from helicopters or conducting artillery missions, she preferred to photograph them in the quieter moments when they were cleaning their rifle at the end of an operation, reading a letter from home, or taking a nap despite the obvious chaos nearby. Today, however, she was on assignment. She was to photograph a ramp ceremony. It was a solemn event in which fallen soldiers began the first leg of their long journey home.

At the airfield in Baghdad, Misty, now a captain, stood back and watched respectfully as the flag-draped coffins were carefully carried toward the large C-130 transport plane. Each casket was carried by eight soldiers dressed in military battle fatigues. Hundreds of other soldiers lined the airstrip forming a corridor for the procession. On this day there were seven caskets. She watched the procession through the lens of her camera. No one spoke. The only sound was the quiet marching of the pallbearers and their escorts.

Misty had previously attended and photographed two such ceremonies, but this one was different. This time she knew one of the men who lay in a casket. She had been there less than 24 hours before when he had been killed by an IED, an improvised explosive device. They had been on patrol east of Karbala when someone, she wasn't sure who, noticed footprints leading away from the main path. They were in a marshy area of the country surrounded by rivers and streams. On her first patrol in-country, she had been surprised by the amount of vegetation as she had always envisioned Iraq as being nothing but desert and rock. She knew better now. Yesterday, not for the first time, she had found herself trudging through the wet grass. She held her camera at the ready and captured their progress as they followed footprints left by another. Whether by friend or by foe was unknown.

The tracks ended at the edge of the lake. Misty took photos of her comrades standing by the water which was illuminated by the sun hanging low in the sky. The fading light glinted off the lake and silhouetted the soldiers against the sky. Misty wasn't listening to the discussion. Her job was to take the photos. She was lining up another shot when Lt. Peters suddenly dove into the lake. The unexpected action took her by surprise, and she lowered her camera to pay attention. The other men stood staring at the water where Peters had disappeared. Their hands were on their weapons which were always at the ready. Peters was gone a long time—too long to be underwater Misty thought. The patrol leader must have agreed because he was barking orders for another soldier to dive into the lake and find him. The man had just handed his rifle to another when suddenly Peters popped up out of the water.

"Weapons cache!" he shouted toward the bank where the rest of the patrol stood watch.

It was a common practice. A large storage tank would be lowered into the water, its door on the bottom. The air within the tank would prevent water from rising into it when the door was opened underwater thereby allowing the interior to be used to hide weapons and other supplies. The communications officer called in the coordinates so that the cache could be destroyed. Misty and her team turned and headed back toward the main road. They were feeling good at their success. But the feeling was short-lived. It was destroyed by the unexpected explosion that also ripped Peters apart. The two men next to him were injured but would survive. The group would later learn that the IED had been activated by Peters stepping on the device hidden beneath the foliage. It had been filled with nails to cause maximum damage to those around it. Misty had been further back taking photos of her team as they made their way back to the Humvee. After the explosion, she didn't hesitate. She jumped into action to offer any aid that she could. No more photos for a while.

Now she watched as the casket that held the remains of Lt. Peters was carried to the plane. His father, a lieutenant colonel, had also been stationed in Iraq. Today he served as the lead escort for his son's coffin. He would stay with the casket for the long flight home and would be there when it and the six other fallen soldiers were carried off the plane in Dover, Delaware. Misty lifted the camera to her eye intending to take a photo of Lt. Colonel Peters as he saluted his son's casket. She hoped to capture the emotion in his eyes that belied his stoic outward demeanor, but just as she was about to activate the shutter, she hesitated. It didn't feel right. This was a private moment between father and son, and she let it pass undisturbed by the clicking of her camera.

Chapter 94

San Diego, California, 2008-2013
  Jeremy Dordi

The University of California at San Diego (UCSD) had been Jeremy's first choice for his undergraduate education, but it had been out of reach financially. Four years later, in August of 2008, Jeremy matriculated into their medical school. He, like most of his classmates, would have substantial student loans when he graduated, but it was a sacrifice he was willing to make. For as long as he could remember, his goal had been to become a doctor so he could help prevent birth defects like the one that had led to Lily's death or perhaps prevent disorders like the autism that had often made Lucas' life difficult. Unfortunately, Jeremy soon realized that medical school largely focused on diagnosis and treatment of disease rather than prevention. For Jeremy, he felt a strong need to be able to offer his patients more than just a diagnosis and a prescription. By the time he finished medical school in 2012, he knew he wanted to become a physician-scientist and do research into the causes of disease. If you understand why diseases occur, perhaps you can discover how to prevent them.

After medical school, he stayed at UCSD for his residency training in Obstetrics and Gynecology. The UCSD program had been his first choice because it came with a six-month research requirement. He would spend his research rotation working with Beverly Jansen, PhD, a scientist studying dioxin, the chemical contaminant in Agent Orange that made it so toxic. The goal of her research was to not only understand how dioxin caused disease but also to prevent those diseases from being transmitted to future generations. Jeremy was convinced that his parents' exposure to Agent Orange during the war was the cause of Lily's heart defect and Lucas' autism, and he was excited to join her lab. By the time he began his research rotation during the first half of his second year of residency, he had read most of the papers published by Dr. Jansen's lab and had become familiar with many of her team members' names.

The first day of his research rotation, he found Dr. Jansen in her office. The casually dressed woman looked up from her computer when he knocked on the open door. She frowned and Jeremy had the impression that she was surprised to see him.

"Jeremy, I forgot you were starting today. I've got a grant due in a few days, but you can work with one of my graduate students, Vivian. She can help get you started."

She stood and walked past him into the lab. The large room consisted of four long benches arranged in parallel. On either side of each bench were multiple workstations. Some stations held various pieces of scientific equipment while others were clearly work areas used for isolating protein or DNA from tissues or for conducting other types of hands-on work. Multiple full-sized, residential-style refrigerators were lined up along one wall opposite huge sinks that were attached to the ends of the workspace benches. Several people, some wearing lab coats and some not, were working at the benches or staring at computer screens.

Dr. Jansen walked to one of the middle benches where a young woman sat in front of a computer attached to a microscope. The bench next to her held multiple plastic boxes filled with glass slides. Vivian wore a lab coat over shorts and a T-shirt and was staring at the screen in front of her. It held a magnified image of a section of tissue, which Jeremy immediately recognized as endometriosis embedded within a section of intestine. He frowned knowing that the patient from whom the sample originated had likely suffered significant G.I. issues because of her disease.

"Vivian, this is Jeremy Dordi," Dr. Janson told the younger woman.

Vivian turned from the computer and stood as she held out her hand to him. Jeremy was struck by how pretty she was. Vivian had a dazzling smile, was very tan, and had long blonde hair. She was taller than she had looked when she was seated. For a second he forgot why he was there but quickly regained his composure, shook her hand, and said, "Hi, Vivian. It's good to put a face with the name. I've read one of your papers. Your work is very interesting."

She smiled. "My ONLY paper, but thank you. I have another one that's being reviewed. Hopefully it won't get rejected." She looked back at Dr. Jansen. "I'll give him the grand tour and get him started. You'll have that figure you asked me for in less than an hour."

The older woman nodded and then left Vivian and Jeremy without another word.

"So," Jeremy said, "is she always so..." He searched for the right word, but Vivian interjected.

"Cold and businesslike? Yes. But she's brilliant and dedicated. You'll learn a lot from her."

Indeed, the six months Jeremy spent with Dr. J, as everyone called her, solidified his desire to conduct medical research in addition to seeing patients. Jeremy knew he had found what he had been looking for and would continue working with the Jansen lab long after his rotation had ended.

Chapter 95

Los Angeles, California, 2013
  Chi and Misty

Chi Borkowski turned 75 in 2013 and her family and friends surprised her with a party. Although she had retired from the company that owned the newspaper and magazine, she still kept in touch with many of the friends she had made there. Misty, by now an acclaimed photojournalist, was perhaps *Our Life and Times* most sought-after reporter. At the time of Chi's party, she had just returned from her second trip covering the war in Afghanistan as a civilian.

Chi's neighbor, the elderly Mrs. Warren, was confused. "I thought you went to Iraq?"

Misty nodded. "Yes. I spent four years in the Army after 9/11. Most of that time I was stationed in Iraq as a photojournalist. I came home in 2006."

Mrs. Warren sat on the couch next to Misty and sipped her drink. "But I heard you say something about Afghanistan."

Misty nodded again and patiently explained, "Yes. After I left the army, I went back to work for *Our Life and Times*. They asked if I would be willing to go to the Middle East for them. I agreed and went for a few weeks in 2010 and again this year. Both times I went to Afghanistan."

"My husband was in Korea," the woman told her, and Misty sighed knowing Mrs. Warren would now begin telling her the same stories she had heard before, but she listened anyway. She knew Mr. Warren had died long ago and that their two children were far away. The old woman was lonely, and Misty felt sorry for her.

After the party and the guests had left, Misty and Chi sat on the same couch that she and Mrs. Warren had occupied earlier.

Misty took her mother's hand. "I have one more gift for you."

"Oh, Misty. You do too much for me. The party and the book are more than enough." Misty had compiled more than 100 of her and her father's family photos taken over the years and had a local company print them on glossy paper and bind them into a book.

Misty ignored her mother's protests and handed her a small box wrapped in brightly colored paper. Chi took the present and opened it carefully in case she wanted to reuse the paper for something else later. She set the wrapping paper aside then turned her attention back to small box it had held. It was a *MyDNA* kit.

"What is it?" Chi asked.

"You've seen their commercials. *MyDNA* will analyze your DNA and tell you what part of the world your ancestors came from."

Chi gave Misty a confused look. "I know where my ancestors came from."

"Yes, but it can also tell you who you are related to. Linh must wonder about her parents. If she had her DNA analyzed, the company will email you and tell you that they have found a relative. They will tell you how to contact them."

Chi sat up and looked more closely at the small box in her hand and then looked back at Misty. "You think this will help me find Linh?"

Misty nodded. "It's possible."

Chi hugged her youngest daughter. "Thank you, Misty."

After her mother's apartment was tidied up, Misty said goodnight to her. In her car driving to her own home a few miles away, Misty thought about Mrs. Warren. Was she herself destined to become a sad, lonely old woman telling the same tired stories to anyone who would listen? Misty and Paul had gotten married a couple of years after she came home from Iraq, but it hadn't worked out. He wanted children, but she wasn't sure. She had seen so many kids in Iraq suffering because of the war. She had seen young men and women die or be horribly injured. It made her afraid. She didn't want to bring a child into the world only for them to suffer. Her husband didn't understand her fears, and eventually he left.

Now at 37 Misty had only her elderly mother to call family. She had given Chi the DNA kit because she knew her mother had spent most of her life worrying and wondering about her lost daughter. Misty sincerely wanted her mom and Linh to be reunited, but, if she was honest, she wanted to find her sister nearly as much as her mother did. If she found Linh, Misty would still have family even after her mother was gone.

Chapter 96

Richmond, Virginia, 2015-2016
  The Dordi Family

Dennis Dordi's 98-year-old father died in March of 2015. He had been married to Dordi's mother, Michelle, for nearly 70 years, and he had no idea how she would manage on her own. Dordi immediately suggested to Linh that they should move back to Virginia. By then Lucas and Eden had a 7-year-old daughter and a 3-year-old son. Linh was torn. She knew her mother-in-law needed her and wanted to be there for her, but she hated the thought of moving away from her grandchildren.

"We can fly back a couple of times a year, and you can video chat with them every day if you like," Dordi told her.

Linh didn't really like either of those ideas and wanted to stay in California. Linh knew she could convince her husband to agree if she tried; he never could say no to her. Instead, she kept quiet. Dennis needed to go home, and she would go with him.

In June of the following year, Jeremy finished his residency and accepted a fellowship position at University of California in San Francisco (UCSF). His time would be divided between the clinic and the research laboratory. He would share a university-supported lab manager with another fellow. A good lab manager was essential and could run the lab on a day-to-day basis even if he was in the clinic. Still, he knew he needed to secure external funding if he was to continue research after his fellowship ended. His intent was to build on his work with Dr. J and submit a grant to the Veterans Administration looking at the health effects associated with burn pit exposures of veterans of Iraq and Afghanistan. Vivian, whom he had worked with when he was a resident, would be an important collaborator.

Shortly after Jeremy submitted his first grant application, his mother Linh was diagnosed with advanced breast cancer. Jeremy flew home as soon as he could get away for a few days.

"It's the dioxin from the Agent Orange. It has to be," an anxious and agitated Jeremy told his dad on the way home from the airport.

"Does it matter? Your mother is very sick. I just want to know what to do for her now."

Jeremy knew his father was right, of course. The only thing that mattered now was his mom and doing whatever they could for her to help her beat this disease. Jeremy knew he couldn't change the fact that his mother had cancer, but he was determined for his research to prevent someone else's disease and said as much to his dad.

Dordi responded, "That's important work, Jeremy. I'm proud of you. But this weekend, just spend time with your mom. You can solve world problems later."

Jeremy nodded as they pulled the car into the driveway of his parents' home. Jeremy jumped out as soon as it stopped and didn't bother collecting his bags. He just took the porch steps two at a time anxious to see his mother.

Chapter 97

Gluckstadt, Mississippi, 2016
  Melinda and Family

Alex and Chris Barker had just celebrated their 16th birthdays, and Zach and Melinda surprised them with a car. It wasn't anything fancy—just a dark blue 2008 Nissan Altima that they had bought secondhand from a friend. It had over 100,000 miles on it and a dent in the rear bumper, but the boys were ecstatic.

"No more school bus!" Alex told his brother.

"Or having to bum a ride from Tony after practice," responded Chris. Both boys played on the baseball team which practiced right after school. Then Chris had another thought and asked, "Can we take it to the away games?"

"I thought Coach liked for the team to ride the bus together?" Melinda asked.

"He does, but if the freshmen have a game too, he lets the older kids drive themselves. There's not enough room on the bus for everyone."

Melinda didn't like the idea but didn't want to dampen the boys' excitement. She smiled and said, "I guess it depends on where it is. I don't want you driving in Jackson during rush hour."

The answer seemed to satisfy the boys for the moment, and they quickly moved on to fighting over who would get to drive first. Melinda heard Chris say, "I'm the oldest, so it should be me," as she walked out of the room. Chris was all of seven minutes older than his twin brother and never let Alex forget it. Melinda knew the teasing was good-natured and that her boys got along better with each other than many of her friends' children. Whether it was because they were twins or because of the two years they had spent in foster care, she didn't know. She sometimes envied their relationship. She would have given anything to have a brother or sister when she was growing up.

A few months later Melinda's mother called her at work, and she immediately knew something was wrong.

"It's your dad," Melinda's mother said as soon as she picked up the phone. "They think he's had a heart attack. He has to have surgery."

"When?" Melinda asked.

"They're prepping him now."

"Where? Grenada?"

"No. They transferred him to Oxford."

"Okay. I'll be there as soon as I can," Melinda said thinking about the patients she would need to get someone to cover for her.

"Don't be in a hurry. Just be safe."

Despite her worry, Melinda couldn't help but smile. Her mother had been telling her that same thing since the day she got her driver's license. Now she said it to Chris and Alex every time they left the house in their own car.

It was nearly four hours later by the time Melinda finally pulled into the hospital parking lot in Oxford, Mississippi. She found her mother in the waiting room of the cardiac unit. Two empty coffee cups and a tattered magazine sat on the small table beside her.

"Any news?" she said as she took the seat next to her mother.

"The nurse came out a little while ago. He has four blockages. They are doing something to fix it."

Melinda nodded at the news. It wasn't good. Coupled with her father's excess weight and diabetes, she wasn't optimistic about his prognosis. She and her mother had tried for years to get him to get his weight under control, but he was unconcerned. Now she knew it might be too late.

Indeed, although John Tackett survived the surgery and returned home after more than a week in the CICU at Oxford, he suffered a fatal heart attack only a few months later. The Christmas after her father died, Melinda asked her mom to move in with her family. Several years before, she and Zach had bought the blue house across the street from their rental. Their neighbors, Harriet and her husband, sold it to the Barkers at a great price. The older couple had decided to buy a camper and were determined to visit every state in the continental U.S. Although the blue house wasn't much bigger than their rental home, it had a much larger yard and was theirs to update however they wanted.

Zach and Melinda had ripped out the old carpet and found that the hardwood floors underneath were in surprisingly good shape. They painted all the rooms themselves and let the boys choose the colors for each of their rooms. Eventually Melinda hoped to have the money to renovate the kitchen and often walked around the room thinking about the possibilities. A couple of months after her father died, she was looking at her kitchen and dining room and realized how easy it would be to add a room onto the back of the house.

Melinda told her mother, "We could sell your house and build an addition on to ours. Then you'd have your own room."

Her mother shook her head. "I'm not moving."

"But you don't need this big house just for you. If we sell it, we can renovate ours and you can have whatever you want. You could even have your own bathroom."

"I have my own bathroom here. You can sell my house when I'm dead. Then you can renovate," her mother stubbornly replied.

Melinda was hurt. "This isn't about renovating my house," she said softly. "I just didn't want you to be alone."

Grace sighed. "I'm sorry, dear. I didn't mean it like that. It's just that I like my house, and I like my routine. My friends and my church are in Grenada. I miss your father, of course, but I'm happy here."

Melinda was surprised. She thought her mother would jump at the chance to spend more time with her grandchildren. Melinda had never really thought about her mother having a life outside the family, but why wouldn't she? Now Melinda was a little disappointed in herself for not paying more attention to her parents' lives and wondered what else she might have missed. She said to her mother, "Okay. Whatever you want."

"Thank you. I want to stay home. At least for now. Maybe in a couple of years I will change my mind. Maybe we could sell my house when the boys graduate and go to college. I could move into one of their rooms and we could put the money toward tuition."

"Well, that's very generous of you, but we have been saving money for college for years," Melinda replied. "You keep your house as long as you want it," she said as she hugged her mother.

Chapter 98

Blue Ridge Mountains, 2017

Linh

It was a cool fall morning and Linh sat in a rocking chair on the porch of the rented cabin. She drank her coffee and watched as the light from the sun began to filter through the trees. Despite the cancer diagnosis, she was content. She breathed in the morning air and listened to the sounds of the forest waking up. She wondered how many more days she had, but she was not sad. She reflected on her life and had few regrets. Every day of course, she thought about Song. But, somehow, in her heart, she knew her first child was healthy and happy. While she would always mourn the loss of Lily, Lucas and Jeremy had filled her world with joy.

Her thoughts turned to Dennis, whom she loved more than she had once thought it was possible to love anyone. He had not only rescued her from the terrible life she had in Vietnam but had also given her a family. Not just Jeremy and Lucas but also parents. She mourned the loss of Dennis' mom and dad as deeply as any of their biological children. Even now, when something weighed heavily on Linh, she would sometimes talk to Michelle, and her mind would easily respond with words of advice as though the woman were still with her.

Dennis had also given her a best friend. These mountains had brought LT back into her husband's life—and his wife into hers. In many ways, she and Lucy were so different. Lucy longed to return to Vietnam where Linh had tried to forget the land of her birth. Linh had worked hard to learn

English and had not spoken Vietnamese in years when she met Lucy. After she started working at the salon, she was surprised at how easily she slipped back into speaking her native tongue. Lucy and LT also typically spoke Vietnamese when Dennis wasn't around, and Linh realized she no longer minded. She had finally made peace with her past.

When she was diagnosed with cancer, she had refused the aggressive treatments. Although chemo and radiation might prolong her life, she knew they might also take the living out of it. She took another deep breath and thought about Lily. She would finally see her again and that made her smile. Her sons had both built lives for themselves and would be fine without her. She was disappointed she wouldn't live to see Jeremy marry and have children, but he was a good man and that made her happy. Her biggest worry was Dennis. They had been together so long, she wasn't sure they knew how to be apart. She had seen what Dennis' father's death had done to his mother. She sank into a depression that ultimately took her own life. Dennis was strong, but was he stronger than Michelle? She took a sip of coffee, but it had grown cold and she set it aside.

She thought about Song again. She knew she had done the right thing in putting her up for adoption, but she had held out hope that someday they would find each other. She had recently started a journal of sorts—letters to her daughter. Unlike the tattered old notebook she had used to help her learn to write, the one for Song was special. It was made of a beautiful, soft leather and had thick, cream-colored pages. Although she now knew she would never see her first child again, it made her happy to write the letters and tell her daughter things she would have said if she could. Before she died, she thought, I'll give the journal to Dennis and ask him to give it to Song. The old Green Beret needed a new mission. Maybe it would be enough to see him through after her death.

Just then the door to the cabin opened and Dennis appeared at her side. He had a blanket and a fresh cup of coffee for her. "Do you need anything?" he asked as he leaned down and kissed her.

She took his hand and pulled him to the chair beside her. "Only you."

Chapter 99

Grenada, Mississippi, 2018
  Melinda Barker

Two years ago, Melinda's father died at the age of 80. Six weeks ago, her 81-year-old mother died. Last weekend, Melinda had driven to Grenada to watch as the living room and dining room furniture were removed from her childhood home. She had donated it to a local charity her mom had been involved with for years. Today she, Zach, and their sons left home early in the morning and would spend the day in Grenada to continue cleaning out her parents' home. Melinda expected she would spend the next several weekends getting it ready to sell. When her mother first suggested she use the money from the house to pay tuition, Melinda really didn't think they would need it. She and Zach had been saving for their education since the boys started kindergarten, but college was more expensive than they had anticipated and having two in school at the same time would strain them financially.

Alex had his heart set on Mississippi State. He planned to follow in his parents' footsteps and become a veterinarian although he planned to treat cats and dogs instead of farm animals. Chris, on the other hand, wanted to design video games. It was a burgeoning field and only a few colleges offered a degree in it. He had found High Point University in North Carolina and fell in love with the beautiful campus. It was a long way from home and more expensive than MSU, but the generous scholarship Chris received would help. More importantly, he seemed to have found his niche and was finally excited about college. Melinda hoped that between the money she and Zach had saved, along with the money from her parents' home, it would be enough for their boys to graduate from college without the student loans she and Zach had needed.

Melinda thought about her mother and wondered, not for the first time, if that was why she had refused to leave her house two years ago. If they had sold it after her father died and renovated Melinda's home, they would likely have had to borrow money for the boys to finish college. Did her mother know that? Did she stay in Grenada by herself so that she could help her grandsons? Melinda would never know for sure, but she strongly suspected it had been her mother's plan all along. It made her miss her even more.

They pulled into the driveway early on Saturday morning and Melinda made assignments. She told her sons to start in the garage while Zach began in the kitchen. Melinda wanted to start in her parents' bedroom. Everyone had four large boxes marked keep, toss, sell, or donate. Extra boxes were in the living room which was now empty of furniture.

Working in the bedroom, Melinda first stripped the bed, putting the sheets and any towels she could find in to wash. She folded the quilt—an ancient thing that her grandmother had made by hand—and put it in the keep box. Most of the books would be donated to the school or library, and she placed them in the appropriate box. She quickly cleaned out the dresser which held mostly clothes. They went into the donate or toss box, depending on condition. Her mother's half-used bottles of perfume sat on a decorative mirror on the dresser, and, for the first time, Melinda had difficulty maintaining her focus. She had spent the last two years grieving for her father and had come to grips with the inevitable loss of her mother. But are you ever fully prepared to lose someone you love? Catching the scent of her mother's favorite perfume was a painful reminder that she was gone.

Melinda decided to deal with the perfume later and turned her attention to her parents' large walk-in closet. Again, she quickly went through the clothes and put them in the appropriate boxes. The donate box was the first to be filled, and she went to the living room for another. She was surprised to find Chris adding her father's handheld toolbox to a very large array of miscellaneous items in the living room.

"What's this?" she asked, pointing to the pile.

"Oh. Well, some things we weren't sure which box they should go in. So we started an 'ask Mom' pile."

Melinda looked at the huge assortment of her parents' things. From the number of kitchen items she saw, it was clear to her that Zach was also using it. She rubbed her temples to try and prevent the headache that was beginning to form. It's times like these that make me wish I had a sister, she thought. Aloud she just said, "Okay. I will look through it later." She grabbed a box and headed back to the bedroom closet.

Over the next few weekends, Melinda worked with whoever was available to finish the major task of cleaning out the house. Two months after her mother's death, Melinda's sons and her close friend Maria came with her to tackle the attic. She expected most of it would be thrown into the big trash bin they had gotten from the local waste company, but some things she wanted to look at first. Chris and Alex were tasked with bringing everything downstairs. Maria would determine what needed to go to Melinda before being thrown out. Boxes full of paper always went to Melinda—and there were a lot of them. Many were full of old bills and bank statements and would need to be shredded just to be safe.

Maria coughed as she opened a dusty box. She caught her breath and said, "Melinda, you'll really want to look at this one. It's full of stuff from when you were little."

Melinda looked up from the floor where she was sitting and took the large box Maria held out. She set it in front of her and pushed the box she had been going through aside. Maria sat on the floor next to her watching curiously as Melinda pulled out a variety of things. Childish crayon drawings, handmade Christmas ornaments, her christening gown, and dozens of other items from the first 10 or 12 years of her life. She pulled out a stack of yellowed cards bound together with a rubber band that had become brittle. "These are all my old report cards from elementary school," she said handing them to her friend. Melinda turned back to the box. At the bottom, she found a large shoe box that might have once been white but was now gray. Curious, she set the smaller box on her lap and lifted the lid. Inside she found a blanket she had never seen before. It was pale blue and as far as she could tell, there was nothing special about it. She wondered why her mother had kept it. When she unfolded the blanket to look at it more closely, two handwritten notes and photograph fell out of it.

Maria picked up the photo. "I think this is you!" she exclaimed and handed it to Melinda.

Melinda slowly took the old polaroid and gazed at it for a long moment. The faded photo was of a young Asian girl holding a tiny baby wrapped in a blanket that might have been blue. She flipped it over. On the back was written "Linh and Song, December 1971." She handed the photo to Maria then picked up the two small pieces of paper. She looked from one to the other and told Maria, "One is written in English and the other is probably Vietnamese." She returned the Vietnamese note to the box and read the note written in English aloud. "My name is Song. I was born on November 5, 1971, in Cam Ranh Bay, Vietnam." Melinda bit her lip and looked at Maria.

"That's your birthday! This IS you! Your name was Song," Maria said excitedly.

Melinda nodded and continued reading. "My mother, Linh, loves me with all her heart..." Melinda stopped, choking back tears. Finally she started again. "My mother, Linh, loves me with all her heart and hopes that I will be adopted by a family that can give me everything that I deserve." Melinda was overcome with emotion. She had been told all her life that her biological mother was ashamed of her because she was mixed race. She thought she was unloved and unwanted, but this note said otherwise. Her mother *had* loved her. Clearly she gave her up in the hopes she would have a better life.

Maria put an arm around her friend and took the note from her. She looked at it wondering why Melinda's mother had never shown it to her. She looked back at Melinda, who was wiping her eyes on her sleeve. "I guess this young girl is your birth mother."

Melinda took the photo from her and looked at it. "Yes, I think so."

"Song," Maria said, looking at her friend. "It suits you."

Chapter 100

Blue Ridge Mountains, February 2019
Dennis and Jeremy Dordi

After his mother had been diagnosed with breast cancer, Jeremy visited as often as he could. Now that she had died, he realized it hadn't been enough and he was determined to spend more time with his dad. It had not even been a year since they lost his mother, but Jeremy could already see the change in the man. His father was lost without anyone that needed him.

To make matters worse, Lucy, the wife of Dennis Dordi's closest friend, had died a few months before Linh. LT had long ago bought a cabin in the Blue Ridge Mountains, and after both their wives died, he and Dordi spent more and more time there. It seemed to bring them peace. Jeremy didn't have a lot of money, but he managed getting through medical school without amassing as much debt as many of his peers. When he found out that the small cabin his dad always rented when he was by himself was for sale, Jeremy immediately called Lucas. The brothers were in agreement, and Jeremy made the arrangements.

"I have a surprise for you," Jeremy said when his dad picked him up at the airport. He had flown to Richmond for a quick visit. Jeremy had told his dad that he had rented a cabin in the mountains for them, but when they got there, he explained that the cabin was his.

"You can come whenever you want. Or you can live here full time if you prefer."

Dordi was overwhelmed with his son's generosity. He knew he still had student loans and had only just started making decent money. Dordi didn't want his son taking on debt for him. "I don't know what to say, Jeremy. It's too much."

"It's not just from me, Dad. It's from Lucas and Eden too. We want you to have it."

Dordi knew Lucas and his wife were well paid for their computer expertise, but they also had two children. "Are you certain you want to do this? I don't want to be a burden."

"We're sure, Dad. We think you'll be happy here."

Dordi walked around the familiar cabin. Every inch was wood, worn smooth from the years. The floors creaked, the bathroom sink dripped, and some of the windows were hard to open, but he loved it anyway. There wasn't a piece of drywall or even a single painted surface in the entire cabin. He knew every inch of it. He laid a hand on the leather recliner that had sat in front of the small Magnavox TV for as long as he could remember. Then he looked at Jeremy and asked, "The furniture comes with the cabin?"

"Yes. He sold it as is. It needs some work, but I figured you could handle just about anything."

Dordi smiled. Now he understood. His wife had given him a mission while his sons found him projects to fill his day. His wife and children were trying to take care of him the way he had always tried to take care of them. He put a hand on his son's shoulder and said, "Thank you, Jeremy."

Chapter 101

Gluckstadt, Mississippi, March–August 2019
  Melinda Barker

A few months after her mother died, Melinda used a *DNAStory* kit to have her DNA analyzed. She very much wanted to find Linh, her birth mother. Her parents had said she was put up for adoption because her Vietnamese mother did not want her—didn't love her—because she was not pure Vietnamese. Through the years she had read enough about the history of Vietnam to know that that could have been true, but the note she had found in her parents' attic suggested otherwise. A month after submitting her sample, she received her results. "Wow. This is crazy," she told her husband as she looked at her phone. They were on their way home from work, and she checked her email while he drove.

"What's crazy?" Zach asked.

"I'm like the human version of a mutt." She read from the information on the screen. "According to this, I am a mix of Vietnamese, Northern European, French, Chinese, German, and Melanesian."

"What's Melanesian?"

Melinda shrugged. "No idea."

Zach and Melinda continued to discuss her results for several days making guesses about her parents and how they might have met. For weeks Melinda incessantly checked her email hoping for a message from *DNAStory* that they had found a relative. But after several months went by, her hope began to wane.

Chapter 102

San Diego, California, November 2020
  Ashley

Ashley England was a petite, 28-year-old with a master's in molecular biology. She was a whiz at DNA analysis, and she knew every member of her lab depended on her. Nevertheless, today she was going to quit her job. She was both excited and sick to her stomach as she stared at the computer screen. The resignation letter she had written the night before was open and Ashley kept rereading it. She was very ready to leave but dreaded telling her boss. She had joined Dr. Beverly Jansen's lab nearly five years ago as a research assistant. Two years ago, she had been promoted to lab manager. It came with a nice raise but also a lot more responsibility. It was a salaried position, meaning no matter how many hours she worked, she did not get paid overtime. Nearly every week, she worked more than 40 hours. She was tired of it.

Ashley knew she was good at her job and had often been told she was a technical genius. She truly loved the work, and she knew it was important. Unfortunately, she also had to manage people and she didn't enjoy that at all. Dr. Jansen had several graduate students who Ashley had to train and supervise. Even though she had far more experience than they did, they often treated her as though she were inferior. It irked her. On the other hand, the lab also had two post-doctoral fellows, Vivian and Emily. They had become her closest friends and kept Ashley sane. They knew she was unhappy and that she had been looking for a job. At lunch today, Ashley would tell them that she had found one.

After lunch, she planned to turn in her resignation letter to Dr. J. Thinking about that conversation made Ashley's stomach lurch, and she wondered if she should skip lunch. She wasn't afraid of Dr. Jansen so much as she just didn't know how to explain to her why she was unhappy. Dr. J had no life outside the lab and was singularly focused on the research. She was brilliant, but the concept of work–life balance eluded her. The hours that Ashley was expected to work left little time for a personal life. She loved the research that they did but felt there should be more to life than just work. How would she explain that to Dr. Jansen?

Ashley reread the resignation letter for the hundredth time and tried to decide if it was adequate. Her thoughts were interrupted by Emily. "Viv is just grabbing her purse and will meet us at the elevators. You ready?"

Ashley nodded and closed her laptop as she stood. She pulled her purse from the drawer next to her desk, and the two women walked out of the lab and down the hall to the elevators. Vivian was already there and pressed the call button when she saw them.

Vivian looked at Ashley quizzically. "You okay? You've been awfully quiet today."

Ashley looked around the small space to see if anyone else was around. The elevator lobby was empty other than her and her friends, but she decided not to say anything yet. "I'm okay. Just a lot on my mind. I'll tell you when we get outside."

"That sounds ominous," Emily replied just as the elevator dinged and the doors opened.

Outside, the three women walked the short distance to a small Greek restaurant that had been started by two UCSD students a decade before. It was a great place to have a quick lunch but was even better for drinks on Friday night at its outside bar.

Ashley and Emily both ordered chicken gyros, and Vivian order the steak shawarma platter which was huge.

Ashley and Emily both looked at their friend. "You're going to eat all *that*?"

Ashley asked.

"What? I missed breakfast," Vivian replied. "I'm starving."

Emily shook her head. "How you can eat so much and stay so thin is beyond me."

They took their food and found a table outside.

As soon as they were seated, Vivian said to Ashley, "Okay. Spill it."

Ashley bit her lip and looked at her friends. "I've accepted that job in Sacramento."

Vivian was excited for her. "The one with the CBI?" She knew Ashley had recently interviewed with the California Bureau of Investigation's DNA analysis division and was hoping to get it because she wanted to learn forensic genealogy. The CBI had become somewhat famous in recent years because they had caught the Green River Killer using genetic material he left at a crime scene by comparing it to DNA sequences stored in databases like *DNAStory* and *MyDNA*. Ashley had extensive experience working with DNA and was fascinated by the work the CBI was doing with it.

"Yes, that's the one," Ashley nodded. She hesitated and then continued, "I have to tell Dr. J today."

"Does she even know you are looking?"

Ashley frowned and her stomach turned over again. She couldn't eat and just pushed the food around on her plate. "No."

Vivian sucked in her breath. "She is NOT going to be happy."

"I almost told her after the interview. It went really well, and I had a good feeling about it." She sighed before she continued. "Then I decided I didn't want her to know I was looking in case I didn't get the job."

Emily, who had tried multiple times to talk Ashley out of leaving, finally spoke. "When do you leave?" she asked softly.

"I start February 15th, but I'm turning in my notice today. I'm going to offer to work til the middle of January. That will give Dr. Jansen some time to find a replacement."

Vivian and Emily exchanged a look. "You can't be replaced," Vivian said.

"Everyone can be replaced," Ashley responded, sipping her drink.

"No. I joined Dr. J's lab as a student back in 2011. It was a mess," Vivian said emphatically. "It took me nearly six years to graduate because I ended up being her research assistant as well as doing my dissertation project. I'd probably STILL be a student if you hadn't joined the lab. Two other research assistants *and* a lab manager burned out before you got there."

Ashley smiled. She knew it was true. Dr. J might be brilliant scientifically, but her people skills were lacking. She was also incredibly disorganized. Ashley wasn't offended by Dr. J's brusqueness and, without waiting to be told, had cleaned and reorganized the lab to make it more efficient.

"The lab will fall apart without you."

"No, it won't," Ashley disagreed. "Besides," she looked at Emily, "your post-doc won't last forever. You'll eventually leave whether I stay or not."

"I need to move on too," Vivian lamented. "It isn't good to post-doc in the same lab you did your graduate work in."

"Well, you had special circumstances," Ashley said and Emily quickly agreed.

After Vivian had graduated with her PhD, she left Dr. Jansen's team and joined a different lab at UCSD. Because Vivian had family in the area, she wanted to stay in Southern California. Unfortunately, her new lab was shut down after the principal investigator had to retract four papers because the data had been faked. He also had to return nearly 2 million dollars in government grants. Vivian had only been in the lab six months and none of the retracted publications were hers, but the scandal tainted her nonetheless. After that, Dr. J had been the only person at UCSD who was willing to give her a job.

The three women ate their lunch and continued to talk. Emily still tried to convince Ashley to stay, but she had made up her mind. She would rather assist law enforcement catching criminals and solving crimes than researching the connection between dioxin and endometriosis. "I'll leave it to you two to solve the mysteries of human disease," she told them.

After lunch, Ashley printed and signed her resignation letter. She carried it to Dr. J's office and peeked in the open door. She was almost disappointed to see the woman sitting at her desk. She took a deep breath and knocked. Dr. Jansen looked up and smiled at her, no doubt expecting she had new data to show her. "Come on in. Do you have something interesting for me?"

Ashley sighed as she stepped into the office and closed the door.

Chapter 103

Los Angeles, California, 2020
  Chi and Misty

Misty had to face it. Her mother was getting old. At the age of 82, Chi was mentally as sharp as always, but physically she was struggling. She was moving much slower these days and was beginning to have difficulty navigating the stairs in the house her parents had bought so many years before. After Misty graduated from college, she moved to an apartment in downtown L.A. It was a great place to be when she was in her twenties— lots of excitement and cool restaurants. Living downtown was expensive, though, and these days she was spending far too much time driving to her parents' house to check on her mom. She knew it was time for a change.

"Hey, Mom," she said as she walked into the front door of her childhood home, arms laden with take-out from her mom's favorite restaurant.

"Hey, yourself," Chi responded, slowly getting up from the recliner her father had always used.

Chi went to the kitchen to get plates from the cabinet—she hated eating out of take-out containers—while Misty unpacked the bags.

"I've been thinking about buying a house," Misty said. "I've been looking online, and there are some affordable places in La Puente and Carson. Both are convenient to downtown and Carson is close to the airport."

Chi frowned. "Farther from me, though."

"Well, Mom, I was thinking you could move in with me." She gestured to the house around her, "You don't really need this much space, and the house needs work. I don't think you want to put money into fixing it up."

Chi sat at the table and looked around her home. She knew it was time to go, but it was also the last place that she had shared with JB. She missed him every day. She supposed that wouldn't change no matter where she lived.

When Chi didn't respond, Misty continued, "Will you at least think about it?"

Chi smiled at her daughter. "I don't need to. It's a good idea. We can sell this old place and put the money toward a new one."

Six months later, Misty and Chi had settled into a quaint, two-bedroom bungalow in Carson, California. It was on a quiet street with limited traffic. Most of their neighbors had small children, and Chi quickly found she enjoyed sitting on their new porch in the afternoons watching the kids play. Jordan, one of the little girls in the neighborhood, looked like she might be part Asian, and whenever Chi saw her she thought of Linh. Her oldest daughter would now be in her sixties. She had been so optimistic that she would find her after Misty had given her the DNA kit, but that had been years ago and nothing had ever come of it. Now as she watched Jordan, she wondered again if Linh was happy. In her mind, she replayed the scene she had witnessed at the Tan Son Nhut Air Base so many years ago. She hoped that Linh and the American were still together and that he hadn't deserted her the way her Frenchman had abandoned her. She turned her attention back to Jordan who was playing hopscotch with several other children. Chi smiled and imagined it was 1960 and that the young girl was Linh, healthy and happy and without a care in the world.

Chapter 104

Springfield, Tennessee, November 11, 2020
  Ken Gamble and Bobby Tyner

Ken Gamble took his coffee out to the patio, sat on the well-worn Adirondack chair he always used, and watched as the sun began to rise. Rain had been predicted, but the sky was clear. Good, he thought.

He sipped his coffee and thought about the day ahead. Today they would dedicate the Agent Orange Memorial. He and his friend and fellow Vietnam veteran Bobby Tyner had spent the last several years making the project a reality. It had taken a tremendous amount of effort to secure a location, raise money to pay for it, and, of course, battle government red tape for the approvals needed. It hadn't been easy, but they had done it.

Ken had been 17 years old when he enlisted in 1962. Two years later, he was sent to Vietnam where he did two tours with the Brown Water Navy. More than once he and his crew had been in the path of the C-123s as they sprayed Agent Orange along the banks of the rivers that they traversed. The herbicide effectively destroyed the ground cover and made the waterways safer for their patrols, but the long-term price of short-term safety would be far greater than any of them could ever have anticipated.

Like Ken, Bobby felt it was his duty to fight for his country and defend the freedoms so many took for granted. He purposefully dropped out of high school in 1964 expecting he would be drafted. When he wasn't, he volunteered. After completing his combat training, he was shipped off to Vietnam. Although he spent only a year in-country, he remained on active duty in the U.S. Army for nearly a decade. He was released from service as the war came to a close though the memories and the remnants of the days spent in Vietnam would never leave him.

Although Ken and Bobby's paths never crossed in Vietnam, their past service brought them together for a new mission back in the U.S. Today at 3:00 P.M., the two veterans would unveil the Agent Orange Memorial. The cenotaph was designed to honor all Americans who had served in the U.S. Armed Forces in Southeast Asia between November 1, 1955, and May 15, 1975. The day of its dedication, the memorial consisted of two slabs of black granite etched with the names of 480 individuals who had served during the war, some still living and some who had passed on. An orange heart had been engraved beside nearly every name and marked those who had died or continued to suffer due to the effects of Agent Orange. A triangular wooden box with a glass cover was set on top of the granite, straddling the two slabs. Inside the box was a carefully folded American flag.

Long before the Agent Orange Memorial was constructed, Ken had designed the Orange Heart Medal. He felt strongly that exposure to Agent Orange should be recognized with a Purple Heart. "It's an injury like any other," he had often argued. The VA disagreed and Ken had taken it upon himself to rectify the problem. In 2018 he began awarding Vietnam veterans an Orange Heart Medal instead. He awarded 300 medals that first year, and his intent was to give one to every veteran who had been exposed to the deadly chemical mixture that came to be known as Agent Orange. Although the cost of having a name etched on the cenotaph had to be borne by the veteran or their family, the medals were distributed at no cost to those who served. Raising money for both projects and distributing the medals was a full-time job and ultimately led Ken to partner with Bobby. By the end of 2020 when the memorial was dedicated, Ken and Bobby had awarded nearly 8,000 medals.

It is estimated that 2.7 million American men and women served in Vietnam during the war, and Ken hoped to eventually have every single name on the cenotaph. A veteran or veteran's family had to request his or her name be added, but not everyone knew of the memorial. Ken and Bobby were working to change that.

Several hours later, Ken met Bobby at the site of the memorial. They walked the grounds and spoke quietly as they watched people arrive. More often than not, the veterans sported clothing that contained an American flag, often with a "Vietnam Veteran" baseball cap. A few minutes before 3:00 P.M., Ken and Bobby stood together near the Agent Orange Memorial and looked at the crowd. Men and women from all over the country had come to witness its dedication. Bobby clapped a hand on Ken's back, "It's time."

Ken nodded and stepped up to the podium as the crowd fell silent. A thousand people stood solemnly with their hand over their heart as the colors were presented and the national anthem was sung. Speeches were made and music was played. Finally all 480 names etched on the memorial were read aloud. By 5:00 P.M. the service was over, but the crowd remained. It was an emotional event with many friendships formed or rekindled.

Three hours later, the crowd finally began to dwindle. When everyone else had left and only Bobby and Ken remained, Bobby looked at his friend. "Mission accomplished."

Ken shook his head and pointed to the memorial. "Not yet. Not until all 2.7 million names are on that wall."

Bobby took off his hat and scratched his head, nodding. "Well, then I guess it's back to work."

Chapter 105

San Francisco, California, December 2020
  Dr. Jeremy Dordi and Alessi Adams

Dr. Jeremy Dordi was in his clinic seeing patients. Most had been to see him before, but one was a new referral from a gastroenterologist named Dr. Walker. Jeremy took Alessi Adam's chart from his nurse and knocked on the door she indicated.

"Come in," a woman's voice responded, and he pushed the door open.

Jeremy walked into the small exam room and greeted his new patient. "Good morning, Ms. Adams. How are you feeling today?"

"I'm okay. Thank you for seeing me."

Jeremy turned to the young woman in a short white coat standing next to him. "This is Amanda, a medical student. She is here to observe, if that is ok with you."

Alessi just nodded as Jeremy sat down on the wheeled stool near the small sink and reviewed her medical chart.

Alessi Adams was 23-years old and had experienced a multitude of gynecological issues and gastrointestinal symptoms over the years. In 2013 she had been diagnosed with irritable bowel syndrome (IBS) and had been somewhat successful managing her symptoms by altering her diet. Unfortunately, her symptoms had worsened in the last few months, and she had sought help from Dr. Walker. Although Dr. Walker initially agreed with the IBS diagnosis, she began to suspect that Alessi had endometriosis and referred her to Dr. Dordi.

Jeremy looked up from the folder at his patient. Alessi, wearing a paper gown and sitting on the exam table, looked very uncomfortable. Jeremy tried to put her at ease by engaging her in conversation.

"You're from Philly? What brought you to California?"

The young woman in front of him perked up at the question and became animated. "I'm doing a clinical dietician internship. After I was diagnosed with IBS, I got really interested in how food can impact health. Paying attention to my diet really helped me and I thought getting certified as a clinical dietician would allow me to do the same for others." Alessi bit her lip and grew silent for a moment. Dejected, she said, "But now nothing is working anymore. I don't know what to do."

"That's why Dr. Walker referred you to me. Endometriosis can cause many of the G.I. symptoms you have experienced."

"What exactly is endometriosis? Dr. Walker was pretty vague. I looked it up online, but it was kind of confusing."

"Probably because everyone's disease is a little different. We also think that there is more than one cause. Stated most simply, endometriosis is a reproductive disease that women can develop. Tissue that looks like the endometrium—the lining of the uterus—grows outside the uterus and causes problems. Some studies, including data from my lab, suggest that the disease is systemic, meaning it effects the entire body, not just the reproductive system."

"And you think that may be what's causing my G.I. symptoms and not IBS?"

"Yes. Your symptoms are not completely consistent with IBS, but if you have endometriosis, it could easily affect your G.I. tract. Based on some of your other symptoms—," he glanced back at her chart, "—painful inter-course, heavy menstrual bleeding, migraines, and abdominal cramping—I think it is likely." Still looking at the chart, he pointed to something. "This is interesting. You've complained of sharp, shooting pains down your right leg." He looked back up at Alessi.

She nodded and then said, "It doesn't happen all that often. Maybe a couple of times a week. But when it happens, I can't walk for a minute. I have to hold on to someone or something to keep from falling." She looked down at her hands which held on tightly to her paper gown. Without looking at Jeremy, she continued, "When I was in high school, I had to quit soccer because of it. I loved soccer."

Jeremy could see Alessi was upset and on the verge of tears, but before he could say anything, Alessi, suddenly angry, said, "I've had most of these issues for ten years. I've seen *dozens* of doctors. Not one has ever mentioned endometriosis. Why?"

Jeremy needed Alessi to relax and spoke calmly, "It can be difficult to diagnose. Unfortunately, not all physicians are aware of the problems that the disease can cause."

"Well, then medical schools need to do a better job!"

"Yes," Jeremy agreed and then changed the subject in an effort to distract her. "Alessi. That's an unusual name."

The young woman nodded as she wiped her eyes on the sleeve of her gown. "It's Italian. I'm named after my grandfather. His father was first-generation Italian."

"Are you and he close?"

"Me and my grandfather?" she asked. Alessi shook her head. "No. He died a few months before I was born."

"I'm very sorry to hear that," Jeremy said sincerely. He returned to her medical chart. "You were born preterm."

"Just a little. Thirty-five weeks. I stayed in the NICU for 12 days, but that was mostly because I was so small. They said I was the size of a 32-week-old baby."

Jeremy looked back at the chart and did some mental math. Finally he asked her, "Do you know how old your grandfather would be if he were still alive?"

Alessi shrugged. "I'm not sure. My grandmother will be 70 next year. We're planning a big surprise party for her. Anyway, I know they graduated high school at the same time. They got married after my grandfather got back from Vietnam."

That's exactly what Jeremy had wanted to know. "Do you know anything about his time there?"

"Not much. He was in the air force but wasn't a pilot or anything." She frowned. "Why do you want to know about my grandfather?" Alessi was frustrated. She was the patient, not her dead grandfather.

"Well, Alessi, there are some studies that suggest endometriosis can be caused by exposure to dioxin. That's a highly toxic compound that was present in Agent Orange, an herbicide that was used extensively during the Vietnam War."

"Oh, I know all about Agent Orange. My grandmother insists that's what killed my grandfather."

"Really?" Jeremy asked.

"Well, that's what my grandmother says. He actually died when he fell onto a subway track and got hit by a train."

"Oh," Jeremy said, clearly horrified. "That's—that's awful." Alessi nodded without commenting and Jeremy continued. "I'm confused then. If he was hit by a train, why does she think Agent Orange killed him?"

"According to my grandmother, he was depressed. He had a lot of health issues. My grandmother thinks it was suicide, and she blames it on his exposure during the war. There's actually an Agent Orange memorial somewhere in Tennessee I think. My grandmother is going to have his name added to it."

"There's an Agent Orange memorial?"

"Yes. They have a website. I don't remember what it is, but you can look it up online."

"I'll do that," Jeremy said. He took a notebook out of his pocket and wrote himself a reminder.

Alessi was growing impatient. "I don't understand. How could my grandfather's exposure to Agent Orange possibly affect me? I wasn't even born yet."

Jeremy turned his attention back to his patient and explained, "Dioxin can alter a man's sperm and can sometimes cause changes that can be passed down multiple generations." Jeremy let the information sink in and then asked, "Was he your maternal or paternal grandfather?"

"Maternal," Alessi responded. Before Jeremy could ask his next question, she continued, "My mother has a lot of the same problems that I have, but she was never diagnosed with anything."

Jeremy set her medical records beside him and stood. He walked over to where she sat on the exam table and said, "Well, we haven't diagnosed you with anything yet, but I can promise you we will find out if you have endometriosis or not."

"And if I do? Can you help me?"

Jeremy sighed. The answer, truthfully, was that there were very few good treatments for endometriosis, especially if Alessi wanted to have children someday. Of course he didn't say that to his patient. Instead, he said simply, "I promise I will try."

Chapter 106

Sacramento, California, February 2021

   Ashley

Ashley sat in her car in the parking lot of the massive CBI building where she had worked for two weeks. She *hated* it. She was bored out of her mind. She did the same two techniques over and over again and wondered why they didn't simply replace her with a robot. Seriously, they could. She knew companies like *DNAStory* that did excessive amounts of DNA analysis used robots. She thought she would be involved in the actual crime-solving. She thought she would be using her brain, but a trained monkey could do what she did. "No," she said out loud, "a trained monkey would be bored out of his mind!" She banged her fists on the steering wheel in frustration.

In Dr. J's lab, she wasn't just a technician. She was also involved in the analytical discussions, understanding what the data meant and making changes to experiments as needed. The new lab didn't do anything like that. They weren't trying to understand what caused disease. Instead, her lab simply amplified DNA from a crime scene and handed it over to someone else. It was akin to making copies of documents without ever getting to read them. Maybe they were interesting, maybe they weren't. How would she know if she couldn't read them?

Ashley leaned her head on her steering wheel and willed herself to go inside. How long could she force herself to do this job? She had always thought when she took a position she should work at least two years before she quit. Less than that seemed unfair to her employer. Could she really do this for two whole years? She tried to focus on the positive. The pay was good. The hours were regular. Lance, her boss, wasn't the slavedriver that Dr. J had been. "It isn't that bad," Ashley said aloud trying to convince herself. "The people are nice. The equipment is top-notch." And, she supposed, having worked at the CBI would look good on her resume when she started looking for the next job. "Okay. I can do this. It's only two years. I can do anything for two years."

She turned off the car, opened the door, and stepped out into the sunshine. As she walked to the door of the CBI building, she calculated how many days it would be before she could quit. Counting holidays and weekends, she estimated it was 716 days. "Okay. Just 716 days. I can do this." She stood in front of the door for a moment and then said again, "I can do this." She took a deep breath, pushed the door open, and went inside.

Chapter 107

Philadelphia, Pennsylvania, February 2021
  Penny Augustini

Augie's widow, Penny Augustini, looked at her watch and realized the mail should have been delivered. She slowly got up from her chair and walked outside and down the short path to her mailbox. She remembered the day long ago when her daughter, Sara, was first learning to drive and backed over it. Augie hadn't gotten upset. He simply made Sara help him repair it. The memory made her smile, but the happy moment passed quickly. Augie had died nearly 25 years ago, but she still hadn't gotten used to him being gone. She supposed she never would. She had been 45 when he died, and many of her friends encouraged her to remarry, but she knew she wouldn't. What she and Augie had couldn't be replicated, and she had never even wanted to try.

Penny opened the mailbox hopeful that perhaps today something interesting would be waiting for her. Maybe, she thought, I will find a card from my granddaughter. Alessi had been good to write since she had been away in California doing her internship. Sometimes she would send a postcard with a beautiful photo of the ocean or maybe the California coastline at sunset. Penny reached into the box and pulled out a stack of envelopes. Mostly junk. Nothing interesting. She sighed and then bent down to get a closer look to make sure she hadn't missed anything. The postcards could easily be overlooked if they were leaning against the side of the mailbox. When she peered inside, Penny was surprised to see she had indeed missed something.

Shoved all the way to the back was a small package.

She pulled out the brown paper-wrapped package and looked at the return address. It was from the Orange Heart Medal Foundation. She hurried back inside and stood at her counter as she opened the package. Inside she found a brief letter and a medal. The letter explained that, as she had requested, her husband, Alessi "Augie" Augustini, would have his name listed on Phase II of the Agent Orange Memorial that had recently been erected in Springfield, Tennessee. She was invited to attend the ceremony, which would be held on March 29, 2022. Additionally, Augie had been awarded the Orange Heart Medal to recognize him for his suffering due to his exposure to Agent Orange during the war. The heart-shaped medal hung on an orange ribbon. The face of the gold medal was painted orange and outlined in green. Inside the heart was a small, dark green relief map of Vietnam. Penny clutched the medal in her hand and held it close. Nothing could replace Augie, but somehow this recognition that while he may not have died during the war but still died because of it gave her a measure of comfort.

Chapter 108

Vietnam, February 2021

Jeremy Dordi, MD

Jeremy had first learned about Doctors Without Borders when he was in college. He volunteered with them one summer and helped build a clinic in Central America. During his fellowship with Dr. Jansen, she had let him take two weeks off to go to Vietnam with the same organization. He spent most of the time in a rural clinic and treated patients with everything from infected wounds to malaria. He also visited several orphanages where he vaccinated children against a wide range of diseases. It had been both a heartbreaking and invigorating trip. He had grown up hearing about the plight of the thousands of children who had been born to Western servicemen and knew his mother had been one of them. On his first trip, he had been shocked that so many years after the war ended, the number of abandoned children was still a major problem. Extreme poverty was common in some parts of Vietnam and led many mothers to give up their children because they were unable to care for them. As a result, the orphanages were always full, and the street kids seemed to be everywhere.

It had been nearly seven years since his last trip to Vietnam, and he had finally been able to get the time to return. The ten members of Jeremy's group would spend two weeks in Vietnam. Most of the time would be spent in the Central Highlands where medical facilities were scarce. They would set up a small clinic where they could treat patients and perform minor surgical procedures. During the two-week period, each member of the group would also spend a day at an orphanage in either DaNang or Saigon.

As before, the days he spent at the clinic were incredibly busy. He set broken bones, managed infections, and even amputated a farmer's gangrenous arm. He saw patients with malaria and syphilis. He delivered two babies and vaccinated dozens of children. Two Vietnamese women who looked to be in their mid-twenties came to the clinic from a nearby village every day to help. They translated for the doctors, learned how to properly clean wounds, place and remove stiches, and assist mothers in childbirth. With this training, these young women would be able to provide some basic first aid after Doctors Without Borders left. The non-profit group would continue to send supplies, and in six months another medical team would return and provide more advanced medical care. He worked 14 hours a day for 12 days. It was exhausting but also gratifying. He knew he was making a difference.

The day before Jeremy's group was to leave Vietnam, he visited St. Mary's House of Hope orphanage in DaNang. His driver parked beside a two-story white brick building with large windows. Jeremy, medical bag in hand, opened the windowless door and found himself in a small office area. A woman dressed in a traditional nun's habit was speaking to a small group of well-dressed Westerners. For a moment he wondered if he was in the wrong place, he thought he would be the only volunteer today. However, the others looked more like business people, and he decided they might be there to adopt one of the children. He hoped that was the case. He waited patiently for the nun, whom he assumed was Sister Sun. After several minutes she broke away from the others and walked to him.

"You must be Dr. Dordi." When he nodded, she continued, "I'm Sister Sun. I have a room ready for you. Give me just a few moments and I will get you set up."

"Terrific. Thank you." The nun left with four of the five people who had been in the crowded little office when he arrived. He spoke to the only other person left in the room, a woman about his own age dressed in a light-gray pantsuit. "Hi, I am Jeremy Dordi. I'm here with Doctors Without Borders." He held out his hand, which she shook.

"I'm Lisa Pham, an adoption attorney from Sydney," she said. "You're American?"

"Yes. I'm from San Francisco."

"Oh. I have a cousin in San Diego. She's doing a fellowship or something. She's a scientist."

"No kidding? I did a fellowship at UCSD and know quite a few people there. I might know her or her mentor."

"I don't remember who she works with, but my cousin is Emily Martin. She studies endometriosis."

Jeremy laughed. "I've met her! She's a friend of a friend and works with Beverly Jansen. I did an internship with Dr. J as well."

"Wow. It really is a small world."

The two continued to speak for a few minutes and learned they were both staying in the same hotel. They agreed to meet for dinner later in the day. Soon, Sister Sun returned to the office and led Jeremy to a small room with an exam table. He spent the next several hours seeing dozens of children. Thankfully, most were healthy and just needed routine vaccinations.

As agreed, at 7:00 P.M. that evening, Lisa and Jeremy met in the lobby of the Avatar Hotel. Lisa, who had been in DaNang multiple times, knew of a funky new bar and bistro not far from where they were both staying. As they walked, she pointed out different places he should visit.

"Unfortunately, this is just a working trip. No time to really sightsee. Maybe someday."

"It's an incredibly beautiful country. You should try to spend some time here."

Over dinner Lisa explained that her grandmother had been born in Vietnam and married an Australian. "She and her sister were orphaned when they were 12." She screwed up her face trying to remember. "Or maybe she was 13? I don't remember. Anyway, too old for most orphanages. They were lucky though. Because they spoke English, one of the orphanages took them in. My grandmother and her sister helped translate to facilitate adoptions. I guess I'm carrying on the tradition."

Jeremy nodded. "They *were* lucky. My mom was only half Vietnamese and was abandoned. She grew up in a homeless camp near Cam Ranh Bay."

"Oh, that's awful," Lisa said. "I can't imagine what that must have been like."

"She never talked about it. But she eventually met my dad, and he brought her to the States. Most of the homeless kids end up turning to prostitution to survive. Thank God she never had to do that." He got quiet for a moment and then continued. "She died of breast cancer a few years ago."

Lisa nodded sympathetically. "I'm so sorry for your loss. There's a lot of cancer in Vietnam and in veterans."

"Yeah. Agent Orange. The gift that keeps on giving," he said in a voice heavy with sarcasm. He sipped his beer.

"Is that why you joined Dr. Jansen's group? That's why Emily went to the States. She wanted to study Agent Orange and endometriosis. Her sister, my cousin, was diagnosed with it a few years ago. Emily is convinced it's because of their grandmother's exposure to Agent Orange and is hell-bent on proving it."

"Yes." He smiled. "That's exactly how we met. We were both hoping we would discover something that would make a difference to patients..." His voice trailed off as he thought about Alessi Adams. His expression changed and he added, "Not sure we have made much progress on that front though."

Chapter 109

Springfield, Tennessee, March 2021
  Ken Gamble

Ken rubbed his eyes and yawned, anxious to go to bed. Instead he sat at his computer looking through his email. It had been a busy day, and he hadn't had time until now. He wasn't necessarily expecting anything important, but he liked to respond quickly if someone contacted him about receiving an Orange Heart Medal or having a name added to the memorial.

He had a dozen new emails, five of which he deleted without opening. He clicked through the remaining messages, most of which didn't require a response. However, one was particularly intriguing. It was from Dr. Jeremy Dordi in San Francisco. He had recently learned about the Agent Orange Memorial and wanted his father's name added to it. He also mentioned that he conducted research on dioxin/Agent Orange and if there was ever anything he could do to be helpful to please reach out. Ken sat back in his chair suddenly energized. California, he thought.

In recent years, Ken and Bobby, on behalf of all Vietnam veterans, had been working to have laws passed to recognize the victims of Agent Orange exposure. His home state of Tennessee had been first, adopting the resolution in February of 2019. Shortly thereafter, Bobby had spearheaded the effort to get the law passed in South Carolina. To date, a total of six states had passed similar resolutions while an equal number were considering their own version of the law. The goal was to eventually have all 50 states adopt an Agent Orange recognition bill, but they had not yet begun the process in

California because Ken didn't know anyone there. They needed a Vietnam veteran that was a California resident to be the point man and find a state representative to sponsor the bill. Ken stared at the email and wondered if this Dr. Dordi could help.

Ken clicked the "reply" button and smiled as he composed an email to Dr. Dordi accepting his offer of assistance.

Chapter 110

Sacramento, California, July 2021
  Ashley

The CBI cafeteria was huge, and tucked in a corner was a small area made to look like a coffee shop. Ashley was there waiting on a vanilla latte when her phone rang. She pulled it out of her pocket and smiled as she glanced at the screen. "Emily! What's up?" Just as she answered her phone, the barista called her name. Ashley nodded to the lady behind the coffee counter and mouthed "thank you" as she took the proffered cup. She walked to an empty table nearby and sat down.

"What are you doing the third weekend in August?" Emily asked.

"Uhm, I don't know. Let me check my calendar," Ashley said. She sipped her coffee and without looking at her schedule, she added, "Oh, look, my date with a wealthy tech mogul just got canceled, so it looks like I'm free."

Emily laughed, "Can you meet us in San Francisco? Vivian and I will be there for the Endocrine Disruptor Conference. It ends at noon on Saturday, but we could meet for dinner Friday night and then spend Saturday afternoon and all day Sunday touring the city. I've never been to San Francisco, and Vivian promised to show me around. We have an extra room because one of the grad students can't go. Please say you'll come! We miss you."

"Yes! I would love that. I haven't been to San Francisco in ages."

"Yay! I'll email you the details and the hotel where we're staying."

"The last time I was there, we went to this little sushi place in Haight-Ashbury. It looks like a dump, but it was *sooo* good," Ashley told her, genuinely excited at the thought of seeing her friends.

"You'll get to meet Jeremy. Vivian's friend. He's attending the same conference."

"Is he the one she works with who has a VA grant? He gave me contact information that my boss needed for his sister."

"Yes, that's him. You'll like Jeremy. He's a great guy."

The two friends talked for a few more minutes, and then Emily said, "Gotta run. Check your email!"

"Bye," Ashley said as the line went dead. She continued to sit at the table while she drank her coffee. No food or drinks were allowed in the lab. She looked around the cafeteria and thought about the last few months. Her job was definitely getting better. After she had helped Lance's sister, he had given her a low priority cold case since he knew she wanted to learn more about forensic genealogy.

It was an interesting case. Back in the early nineties, a man named John Michael Jacobs had been arrested for killing multiple women. Although the police and prosecutors were convinced they had the right man, the judge ruled the DNA evidence—evidence that irrefutably linked Jacobs to the crimes—inadmissible. At the time Jacobs went on trial, the use of DNA to identify criminals was still new and the judge didn't trust it. As a result, Jacobs walked. A few months later Jacobs was found dead in his apartment. Although it was clear he had been murdered, no one really cared if the case was solved and it quickly went cold.

Ashley had been very helpful to Lance's sister who had multiple health issues that were likely linked to their father's exposure to Agent Orange. Lance himself had been born with spina bifida and was missing one of his lower legs. Before he met Ashley, he had no idea that he and his sister's issues could have been due to their dad's service during the war. Ashley also told him that his sister might be eligible for health benefits because of their father's exposure. Ashley suspected that was why Lance decided to give her a shot at solving the Jacobs murder. He wasn't optimistic that she would but thought it would at least be an opportunity for her to learn.

Lance had given her a bloody glove that had been found in the parking lot near the murder scene a few days after the crime. The glove might or might not have anything to do with the Jacobs murder, but he had asked her to try and get DNA from it. If the blood belonged to whoever murdered Jacobs, they might be able to identify him. However, the investigators on the scene had clearly not been trained in how to properly handle DNA evidence. Ashley's analysis revealed that the glove contained DNA from multiple people *and a dog*, making it useless for solving the case. Nevertheless, Lance had been impressed with her ability to identify all seven genetic samples.

Ashley thought that it was her success analyzing the blood from the glove that led Lance to put her on the team working on the Vigilante Virginian case. For more than four decades, someone in the Virginia area had been murdering notorious criminals. Although many people thought he was a hero, the new Virginia District Attorney disagreed. She wanted him thrown in prison and had asked the CBI to help identify him. Ashley wasn't sure how helpful she had been so far, but she was determined to contribute any way she could. Ashley stood, downed the last of her coffee, tossed the cup in the trash, and headed back upstairs to her lab. As she stood waiting for the elevator to arrive, she remembered how earlier in the year she mentally ticked-off the days until she could quit. She hadn't done that in a while and vaguely wondered how many days she now had left before the two-year mark. She smiled realizing that she didn't care anymore. The elevator dinged its arrival, and she stepped into the car. She was still smiling as she pressed the button that would take her to the lab.

Chapter 111

San Francisco, California, August 2021
Jeremy and Dennis Dordi
Ashley

It was late in the evening when Jeremy got home from the Endocrine Disruptor convention. He parked in front of his apartment, grabbed his bag, and took the stairs two at a time. He was anxious to talk to his dad. At the convention, he had met a friend of Vivian and Emily. Her name was Ashley, and they had immediately hit it off. The three women had originally planned to go sightseeing on Sunday, but Ashley and Jeremy ended up spending the day together when Emily and Vivian were too hungover to go. Jeremy opened the door to his apartment, threw his bag on the floor, and dialed his father's number. He sat on the couch with his feet on the coffee table. After four rings, Jeremy was about to hang up when his dad answered.

"This is Dordi."

"Hey, Dad." Jeremy imagined his dad sitting in one of the rocking chairs on the porch of the cabin. "You got a minute?"

"I've got nothing but time. Everything okay?"

"I met a friend of a friend this weekend. She is a DNA analyst with the CBI—the California Bureau of Investigation."

"What does that mean?"

"Well, that's not really important, but she works with the CBI to solve crimes. Her name's Ashley. Ashley England. Anyway, she and I were talking about Mom and how she didn't know who her parents were. Ashley suggested you and I get our DNA analyzed, and then we could at least get an idea of where Mom came from." Jeremy heard ice clinking as his dad took a sip of something. Probably bourbon. When his father said nothing, Jeremy continued, "I've already ordered kits for us. You'll get it in the mail in a couple of days."

"How does my DNA help with finding out about Linh?"

"Well, Ashley said it's helpful to know what you are so we can know which half of me came from her."

"I guess that makes sense. So where did you meet this girl again? Ashley?"

"There was a medical conference in town, and my colleagues from San Diego were here. Ashley used to work with them, so she came to San Francisco for the weekend, and they introduced us."

"And she just immediately talks you into getting your DNA analyzed?"

"Well, no. It wasn't like that. We were just talking. She knows all about dioxin and Agent Orange, and when Vivian mentioned I had just been in Vietnam, Ashley wanted to hear about that. I guess I said something about Mom being an orphan and not knowing her parents. That's when she suggested getting the *DNAStory* kits."

"You like her."

"What?"

"I can hear it in your voice. You like Ashley."

Jeremy knew his dad was right, but he had only just met her. He said, "Yeah, maybe, but I don't know her very well."

"Sometimes you just know."

Uncomfortable with the subject, Jeremy tried to refocus his father's attention. "The DNA kit. What do you think? Will you do it? I really want to see what Mom is." He frowned and then corrected himself. "Was. What Mom was." It had been three years, but he still had trouble believing she was gone.

"I'll think about it."

I'll think about it, Jeremy thought. In other words, no. But he just said, "Okay. Well, let me know. I gotta run. I'll talk to you later."

"Tell Ashley I said hello," his father teased him. They both said goodbye and hung up.

Two weeks later, Jeremy received his results and immediately called Ashley. They had spoken several times since they'd met at the conference.

"Hey. What's up?" Ashley said when she answered the phone.

"I got my DNA results back. I wanted to call you first since it was your idea," Jeremy replied.

"That was fast!"

"Fifteen days exactly. Not that I have been watching my inbox or anything."

Ashley laughed. "So spill it. What are you made of?"

Jeremy said, "Well, it's a crazy mixture. Biggest contributions are from Vietnam and Northern Europe, but also a hefty chunk of Chinese and French and a small amount of Irish and Melanesian."

"Wow! Throw in some dog DNA and you could be the bloody glove," she said.

"What?" he asked.

Ashley hesitated as though she had said something wrong. "It's an inside joke. Sorry. What is mela—melaninin?"

"Melanesian. I didn't know either and had to look it up. It refers to someone from Melanesia," he replied.

"Well, that clears things up."

He laughed. "It's a group of islands off the coast of Australia. I think that must be from my mother's side because they are a darker-skinned people."

"Ooh—I really wish we could analyze her. She would be so interesting," Ashley said genuinely curious. "What about your dad? Did you ask him?"

"I asked. He said he would think about it, which when I was growing up was another way of saying 'no, but I don't have a legitimate reason to say no.' Or at least that's what it seemed to me. I sent him a kit, but I am not optimistic."

"Call him with your data. It may make him curious," she suggested.

"Maybe," he responded.

They talked for several more minutes. While they were at the conference,

Ashley had mentioned she would be traveling to Australia soon to be a bridesmaid in Emily's wedding. Now he learned that Ashley's flight to Australia left from San Francisco. He invited her to have lunch with him before she left, and she agreed. She also accepted his offer to drive her to the airport and pick her up when she got back. He was smiling when they finally hung up happy that he would see her again soon.

Chapter 112

Tennessee and South Carolina, September 2021
  Ken Gamble and Bobby Tyner

It was late in the evening when Ken hung up the phone. He had been talking with Pete Markum, the Vietnam veteran in California that Dr. Jeremy Dordi had identified. Pete had been in the 5th Special Forces Group alongside Dennis Dordi, Jeremy's father. Pete had been very willing to spearhead the effort in California, and he and Dr. Dordi had together approached multiple state legislators until they found one willing to sponsor their resolution recognizing the suffering of veterans due to Agent Orange exposure. Unfortunately, their bill had failed to make it out of committee.

Ken sat at his desk for a minute after getting the disappointing news from Pete. Then he picked up the phone again and hit the button labeled "Thorn," because Bobby had been a thorn in Ken's side ever since they met. Anytime Ken got frustrated with the system, there was Bobby needling him on.

Bobby picked up after the second ring. "Isn't it past your bedtime, old man?"

"You're one to talk." The two veterans continued to insult each other for a few minutes before Ken got to the point. "Our California resolution is stuck in committee. Doesn't look like it's going to go forward anytime soon."

"Well, that was just the first try. The more states we get on board, the harder it will be for California to ignore it. If everything goes as expected, we'll have at least seven states with our law on the books by the end of the year."

"And another five considering it."

"Exactly," Bobby said. "California will come around sooner or later."

"Yeah, I hope you're right."

"All 50 states. That's the goal."

"I know, *Thorn*," Ken said with mock irritation. "It was my idea to begin with."

"Yeah, but without me you'd still be trying to write the first draft."

After a few more good-hearted insults, the two men said goodnight and hung up.

Chapter 113

Jackson, Mississippi, September 2021
   Melinda Barker

Drs. Melinda and Zach Barker had just helped a farmer with a pregnant heifer in distress. The first-time mother was having a difficult delivery, but the Barkers came quickly and helped ease the calf into the world. After making sure both mother and baby were doing well, the Barkers said goodbye to the farmer and climbed back into their truck. Just as she clicked her seatbelt into place, Melinda's phone dinged.

Melinda pulled her phone from her pocket and looked at the new email. It was from *DNAStory*. Nearly three years had passed since she had submitted her sample, and she had all but forgotten about it. Excitedly she read the email to her husband. "*DNAStory* has found that you share significant DNA with another *DNAStory* member. Based on our analysis, this person is a probable grandparent, grandchild, or half-sibling. Click here for more information and instructions on how to connect with your relative." She read it again and then looked at Zach. "I was really hoping it was my mother."

Zach reached for his wife's hand. "But any relative is huge."

"Not necessarily. A sibling could also have been put up for adoption. They may not know any more than I do."

"True, but still good to know you have a blood relative."

She nodded and clicked on the "more info" button. She read aloud to Zach as he drove home. "His name is Jeremy Dordi and he lives in

California. He is mostly Vietnamese and Northern European. He also has some Chinese and French but also Irish, and—" she paused for dramatic effect "—Melanesian!"

"Okay. Y'all are both mutts." He laughed. Then he turned more serious. "Hopefully, you can get in touch with him."

"Yes. I am emailing him right now," she said as she typed out a message on her phone.

Chapter 114

San Francisco, California, September 2021
 Jeremy and Ashley

It was nearly 9:00 P.M. on Friday night and Jeremy was driving home from the hospital. It had been a good day, albeit busy. He reached his apartment and immediately went to the kitchen to find something to eat. He pulled out his phone and checked his email while leftovers warmed in the microwave. He saw that he had an email from *DNAStory*. The email told him that he had a DNA match that was most likely a grandparent, grandchild, or half-sibling.

The microwaved beeped, but Jeremy didn't hear it. He walked to the living room and sat on his couch. He debated clicking on the "more info" button but wasn't sure he wanted to see the other person's DNA results. It had to be a sibling, he thought. Finally he clicked the button and saw that his relative was mostly Vietnamese and European. He felt sick and closed the email before he could read any more. Without making a conscious decision, he found Ashley's info and hit the video call button. She was in Australia for Emily's wedding. For reasons he didn't completely understand, a phone call would be expensive, but they could video chat for free.

Ashley was smiling when she answered. "Hey, Jeremy! What's going on?"

"Oh," Jeremy said, looking at Ashley's image on his phone's screen. Although he found Ashley attractive, she wasn't a girly girl. He had always seen her in jeans with only a little make-up, but today she looked different. "You look great. You're all dressed up."

"Emily and Tom's wedding. It starts soon."

"Really?" he asked. "I thought that was tomorrow."

Ashley laughed. "I'm in Australia. It *is* tomorrow."

"Oh, right. I forgot. I'm sorry to bother you then. I can call you later."

"No. Now is fine. I have a few minutes. What's going on?" she assured him. He could tell she was walking and realized she had entered another room.

"Oh, well, if you are sure. Uhm—you remember I got my DNA results?" He said, sounding uncharacteristically uncertain.

"Yes, of course."

"Well, it turns out I have a sibling. Well, a half-sibling. Mix of Vietnamese and European. I had no idea."

"Wow. That's amazing news! Are you excited? Do you think you'll try to meet them?"

"I don't know. I just now got the email. I haven't responded. I'm still just trying to comprehend it."

Ashley frowned. "What's wrong? You sound worried."

"Not worried. Well, maybe worried. Uhm—it's just my dad. He talked a lot about the orphans in Vietnam. It really pissed him off that so many soldiers were careless and fathered children with Vietnamese women and then abandoned them. That's how so many ended up on the street, just like my mom. I think he would be really devastated to know he left a child behind like that. So I'm not sure what I'm going to do."

"Oh. Yeah. I guess I can understand that would be a really awkward position to be in. I am so sorry, Jeremy. That really is a tough situation. I don't know what to say," she replied.

"Look. I know you're busy. I just needed to tell someone. I don't expect you to have all the answers," he said trying to sound more upbeat than he was. "I'll let you go. I'll see you at the airport in a few days."

"Hey, I'll buy you dinner when I get in and we can talk. Okay?"

"That'd be great. Thanks, Ashley."

Jeremy hung up the phone feeling no better for having called her. What did he expect? He just dumped this on her and couldn't imagine that she would know what to do any more than he did. He just needed to think this through.

The microwave beeped again, and he went to his kitchen and opened it. The day-old spaghetti had lost its appeal. He stared at it a moment, dumped the food in the trash, and went to bed.

Chapter 115

Jackson, Mississippi, September 2021
  Melinda and Zach

Zach put an arm around his wife. "Still nothing?" Melinda was once again staring at her email no doubt hoping for a response from Jeremy.

She shook her head. "Nothing."

"It's only been a few days. Give it time."

She looked at him, annoyed. "I've given it *three years*. I've been patient. Why did he have his DNA analyzed if he didn't want to connect with a relative?"

"I don't know," Zach responded but tried to think of an excuse. "Maybe he's on safari in Africa and doesn't have internet." She rolled her eyes at him, and he continued, "He could be an astronaut who left for the International Space Station right before you emailed. Or—" he paused dramatically "—maybe he's that serial killer we heard about on the news. What do they call him? The Vigilante Virginian? What if THAT'S your brother, and he can't email you because they caught him!"

That made her laugh. "That would be just my luck. I find a blood relative only to discover he's a serial killer."

Zach said seriously, "Hopefully not, but I'm sure there is a reason. Just try to be patient."

She sighed and looked at her phone again. "I don't really have a choice, do I?"

"Not really. You sent a message. It's up to him now."

Chapter 116

San Francisco, California, September 2021
  Ashley and Jeremy

Ashley kept her eyes on the "fasten seat belt" light and released the restraint the instant the captain turned it off. She stood and stretched, glad to finally be home. Well, almost. She lived in Sacramento but had left from San Francisco because the flight was cheaper. She smiled knowing that Jeremy would pick her up. She was looking forward to seeing him again. She was grateful Emily had given her melatonin for the flight back. She had actually slept and felt far better now than when she had arrived in Sydney two weeks before. Eighteen hours on a plane was not her idea of a good time.

She grabbed her carry-on and waited impatiently for her turn to deplane. Finally she was in the terminal and made her way to baggage claim. She quickly found the carousel that promised to bring her luggage and saw that Jeremy was already there. He smiled broadly when he saw her, and she was suddenly aware that she must look wretched. She also needed to brush her teeth. She gave Jeremy a brief hug and thanked him for coming.

"No problem at all." He helped her get her bags, and they made their way to his car. As they left the airport, Jeremy said, "Do you still feel up to going out to eat? I know you must be exhausted."

Ashley knew Jeremy was anxious to discuss his DNA results and his half-sibling. She suppressed a yawn and said, "I'm okay. More hungry than tired, so dinner would be nice. As long as you are still up for it?"

Jeremy drove to a family-owned place not too far from his apartment. It was the middle of the week, and the place wasn't crowded despite being dinnertime. They were seated quickly and within 30 minutes of arriving were enjoying wine and an appetizer of fried calamari.

"Tell me about your half-sibling. What do you know?" she asked as she dipped a piece of squid into the spicy tomato sauce and popped it into her mouth.

He shook his head. "I know nothing really. I printed out the file but haven't looked at it. I'm not sure I want to." He hesitated. "Dad will just be so angry with himself. He and my mom were married for — what? — 40 years? He rescued her from living on the streets in Vietnam and knew how hard her life had been growing up that way. It would devastate him to learn he fathered a child in Vietnam. I'm not sure it is worth it."

She nodded. "I get it. The mixed-race orphans were treated so badly. He would probably beat himself up knowing he had abandoned one to that life. You don't have to tell him, you know. But it is still worth knowing he or she is out there. At least look at the information first. Then you can decide what to do."

"I suppose," he said handing her the pages he had printed. "You look at it. Tell me what it says."

She took the papers from him and looked them over carefully. Something she read clearly surprised her. He sat up and leaned forward. "What? What is it? What do you see?"

She sat the papers down and picked up her wine glass to give herself time to think. She had no idea how to tell him what she now knew.

"Just tell me. Whatever it is. It can't be any worse than what I already know."

Oh, yes, it can, Ashley thought. She sat her glass down without drinking and looked at him. As gently as she could she said, "Your half-sibling is not your father's child. She is your mother's child."

Jeremy shook his head. "That's not possible. My mom was only 19 when they got married. When would she have had a baby?"

"I don't know," she said as she took his hand. "But your half-sibling is also part Melanesian. She has to be your mother's child."

He took the papers from her and read it for himself. His sister was 8 percent Melanesian. He was 6 percent. The percentages of Chinese and Vietnamese were identical. He was a bit more French than his sister. However, the remaining European ancestries were very different between them. Jeremy had small amounts of Irish and Italian but his sister did not. She was nearly 20 percent German; Jeremy had none. Ashley was right. The half-sibling was from his mother. She was born three years before Lily—meaning his mother had had a baby before she and his father married. "I—I—don't understand." Jeremy looked at Ashley.

"Maybe you should talk to your dad," Ashley said gently.

He looked up at her clearly confused. "She would have been only 16 when this woman was born. That was three years before my parents were married. I just never thought—never thought..." His voice trailed off, and he contemplated the meaning of this new information.

Jeremy knew from his travels to Vietnam that most of the homeless children, both boys and girls, turned to prostitution to survive. He suddenly realized how naïve he had been. He had always assumed his mother had somehow escaped that life. Now he wondered. Is that how his parents met? Was his dad a client? The thought made him sick to his stomach.

Their food came, and Jeremy tried to eat. He knew Ashley was famished and didn't want to make her uncomfortable by not eating, but his stomach churned and he could only pick at his food.

Ashley watched Jeremy struggling with what he had just learned and tried to think of something to say that would make him feel better. She said again, "Talk to your dad."

"Do you think he knows?"

She shrugged but then thought about it. "They were married a long time. I think she would have told him."

Jeremy nodded. "Mom hated her past—hated her life in Vietnam. She never talked about it. Maybe this is why." He picked up the papers again. He read aloud the little bit of information that *DNAStory* had provided about his relative. "Her name is Melinda Barker. She is 49 years old and lives near Jackson, Mississippi."

Ashley nodded. She had read that info as well. "You know, my parents live in Crystal Springs. That's only about 30 miles from Jackson. If you want to try and meet her, I'll go with you and we can stay with them."

Jeremy looked at her blankly. "Meet her?"

"Why not? Meeting her won't change the past. It won't change whatever happened to your mom. But Melinda is your sister. *Your sister.* Right this very minute she's probably wondering about you. That may be why she did the DNA thing. She probably wants to know more about where she came from. Your mom grew up on the street. She must have taken Melinda to an orphanage so she would have a chance at a better life than the one she could give her." Ashley leaned forward and took Jeremy's hand again. "She did the right thing by her child. She saved her from a life on the street. And Melinda must have been adopted, otherwise she wouldn't be in the States."

Jeremy shook his head. "No. I—I'm not sure. I don't know if I want to meet her or not. My dad—I just don't know."

"What would your mom want?"

Jeremy looked at her uncertainly. "What do you mean?"

"If your mom was here at this table and she saw this information about her daughter—her first child—what would she do?"

Jeremy responded without hesitation, "She would be on the first plane to Mississippi." He leaned back in his seat and sighed heavily.

Ashley said gently, "I don't think the circumstances of how that child came to be would matter. Your mother loved her enough to give her up, but I imagine she would have spent her life wondering and worrying about her."

Jeremy nodded. "She would want to know that she was okay."

Ashley agreed. "I think so."

A week later, Ashley was sitting at her desk writing in her lab notebook when her phone rang. She looked at the screen and smiled as she answered, "Hey, Jeremy! What's up?"

"Remember how I was debating on what to say in an email to Melinda?"

"Yes. Did you figure it out?"

"No, but she emailed me. She actually emailed me a couple of weeks ago, but it went to my spam folder. I just happened to check it today because I was expecting another email that I didn't get."

"Oh, that's terrible. She probably thinks you don't want to meet."

"Well, I'm not sure I do. I still need to talk to Dad."

"So what did her email say?"

"She's looking for her biological mother. She was adopted from Vietnam when she was a baby. She knows her mother's name was Linh, and her birth name was Song."

Chapter 117

San Francisco, California, October 2021
Jeremy and Dennis Dordi

Jeremy would have preferred to talk to his dad in person, but Ashley had convinced him the conversation couldn't wait. He had promised her that he would call him over the weekend when he wasn't rushed or tired. Truthfully, he was just delaying. He had no idea what he would say. Now it was Saturday morning, and he knew he had to make the call. He poured himself a cup of coffee and walked to his small living room. He opened the blinds to let in a bit of light and then sat on the couch and stared at his phone. He looked back at the window and decided that now there was too much light. He stood up and adjusted the blinds again.

"Okay. You're just stalling," he said aloud trying to convince himself to make the call. He sat back down on the couch and picked up his phone again. He stared at it a moment and then finally clicked on his dad's number.

"This is Dordi," he heard his father's familiar response.

"Hey, Dad."

"Jeremy. Good to hear from you. Everything ok?"

"Yes. No. Well, I don't know…"

"What is it? What's wrong?"

Jeremy tried to think of the best approach but finally just said it. "Remember I did the DNA analysis? I was hoping to find out what Mom was."

"Yes. Did you find out anything?"

"Well, yes. But more than just that." He paused. He nervously drummed his fingers on the couch as he tried to figure out what to say.

"Spit it out, Jeremy. What did you find?" Dordi asked, but suddenly he knew. "Did you find Song?" The question hung in the air for so long that Dordi thought they had been disconnected. "Jeremy? Are you still there?" After a few more seconds of silence, he asked again, "Jeremy?"

"I'm here," Jeremy responded. He hesitated a moment and then asked, "You knew about Song?"

"Yes, of course. Your mother and I—we had no secrets." Dordi rubbed his face, not wanting to have this discussion over the phone. "Why don't I fly out there? I could see Lucas and the kids too."

"No, Dad. You don't have to do that. I just—I just don't understand."

Dordi sighed, "Your mother grew up on the street. She had a very difficult life."

"I know that."

"Well, there are things you *don't* know," Dordi said a bit more forcefully than he intended. He didn't feel right telling Jeremy things that he and Linh had agreed never to discuss with their children.

"So tell me."

Dordi had begun pacing the floor of his cabin but now stopped and leaned against an old table. He picked up a photo of him and Linh taken at their wedding in Virginia. He looked at the photo for a long moment and then turned his attention back to the phone. "You better sit down."

Jeremy and Lucas had been told long ago that their mother had been abandoned as a baby and that she had grown up in a homeless camp called Orphan Island in Cam Ranh Bay, but they had never been told about Song, the Yankee's Dream, or even Teo.

Now Dordi told his son much more than he ever thought he would. He explained how Linh had found the baby Teo and took him in. She turned to prostitution to try and support him. Dordi told him that she had become pregnant and then gave up Song because she didn't want her growing up the way she had. "About the same time she learned that Song had been adopted, Teo died."

Jeremy sucked in his breath then said in a rush, "That's why Mom was always so overprotective. I always thought it was just because Lily had died, but she lost three children." Jeremy paused, the enormity of what his mother had dealt with at such a young age was hard to fathom. Things made more sense now. He said to his father, "That's why you gave into her when she wanted to go back to California after Lucas got that job."

"Yes."

Jeremy fell silent trying to process all that he had just learned. Dordi patiently waited knowing how overwhelming it must be for him.

Finally Jeremy's thoughts returned to the Yankee's Dream. "So is that how you really met? Because mom was a prostitute?"

The question came out as an accusation, but Dordi knew his son was just upset. "No. Your mom was still at Orphan Island when we met. She was only 15. I had been at the Yankee's Dream when Teo was thrown out of the bar. I followed him because I wanted to help him. It was right after that that I met your mom." Dordi continued to talk with Jeremy occasionally interrupting with questions.

Finally when Dordi grew quiet, Jeremy asked, "Should I contact Song? Her name is Melinda now."

Dordi didn't hesitate. "Yes. Linh would want us to, and I have something for her—something Linh asked me to give her."

"You do?"

"Yes. Linh always hoped she would somehow find Song. When she was diagnosed with cancer, she began writing letters to her. She hoped maybe I could give them to her. I would very much like to do that."

Chapter 118

Gluckstadt, Mississippi, October 2021
Melinda

"Zach!"

Zach was just stepping out of the shower when he heard his wife yell his name. He grabbed a towel and stepped into their bedroom. Melinda was sitting on the bed staring at her phone. He smiled. "Jeremy emailed?"

She looked up at him tears in her eyes. "Yes."

Zach sat beside her, and she read the email to him. "Hi, Melinda. I'm sorry I didn't email you sooner. Your message went to my spam folder. I probably should have emailed you as soon as *DNAStory* told me about you, but I was just so shocked to learn I had a sister. My parents never told us about you. I'm sorry to tell you that our mother died of breast cancer a couple of years ago. When I received the email telling me I had a sister, it took me awhile to ask my dad. You were born before my parents got married, and I didn't know if he knew about you. I didn't want to hurt him. But he *did* know, and he has something for you from Mom. He said she never forgot about you and had always hoped she would find you someday." At the bottom of the email was Jeremy's phone number.

Zach hugged his wife, who was now sobbing. "That explains a lot, " he said. Melinda just nodded trying to get her emotions in check. Zach added, "And now you know he isn't a serial killer."

Melinda smiled at the joke as she wiped her eyes on her sleeve and dialed Jeremy's number.

Chapter 119

San Francisco, California, November 2021
  Jeremy and Ashley

The plan was set. Jeremy and Ashley each managed to get a long weekend off, and early Friday morning the two of them would fly to Jackson, Mississippi, by way of Atlanta. Dennis Dordi would fly from Richmond to Atlanta and then take the same connecting flight to Jackson. Ashley's dad would meet them at the Jackson airport and take them to her parents' home in Crystal Springs, a small town less than an hour from where the Barkers lived. On Saturday Jeremy, his father, and Ashley would drive her mom's car to meet Melinda and her husband.

Ashley left work a couple of hours early on Thursday and drove to San Francisco. She would spend the night at Jeremy's. They had known each other less than four months, but they had clicked right away. After her trip to Australia, they had spoken on the phone nearly every day. At first it was because of Melinda and the DNA results, but pretty soon they called each other just to talk. Twice since then, Jeremy had driven to Sacramento on a Saturday so they could spend the day together. Both times he had left after dinner. Although they had shared several kisses, neither of them had been ready to take that next step. Ashley had a feeling this weekend would be different. At least, she thought, she was ready. She was pretty sure that Jeremy was the right guy for her.

She parked her car in front of his apartment building and grabbed her bags. He opened the door before she had a chance to knock. He took her suitcase from her, pulled her inside, and gave her a kiss.

"It's good to see you," he said and squeezed her hand. He continued talking as he walked into the kitchen, still holding Ashley's hand. "I'll put the steaks on the grill if you'll open the wine," he said and handed Ashley a corkscrew. "Salads are ready and waiting in the fridge. The baked potatoes are in the oven, but they should be ready."

"I didn't mean for you to go to so much trouble. We could have just gotten pizza."

He shrugged, smiling. "I thought it would be a nice change."

She smiled back and thought yep, he's ready too.

After dinner they took their wine glasses to the living room and sat close together on the couch.

Ashley asked him, "Anything interesting at work?"

Jeremy took a sip from his glass. "Actually, yes. Do you remember me telling you about my endometriosis patient, the one originally diagnosed with IBS?"

Ashley thought for a moment. "The nutritionist? Is she the one you gave all those articles on diet and endometriosis? Then the day of her surgery you asked if she had any questions, and all she wanted to talk about were the papers you had given her?"

"That's the one," Jeremy said with a laugh. "Anyway, she emailed me. She is doing really well. She finished her internship and has joined her pediatrician's practice. She'll do nutrition counseling for his patients. He was the one that first diagnosed her with IBS when she was in high school."

"Hmm. I would have thought she would want to focus on reproductive health. She could have joined your practice," Ashley suggested.

"I actually thought about that. Some of my patients would really benefit from nutritional counseling, but she wanted to go back to Philadelphia and be close to her family. She asked me to refer her to an endometriosis specialist in Philly"

"Did she say how she was feeling?"

"Yes. She said she still feels good even though it's been nearly seven months since her surgery. She knows she may eventually need surgery again, but for now she said she has very little pain and her G.I. symptoms are much better."

"That's wonderful," she said, drinking the last of her wine. "I really hope it works out with the pediatrician's office."

Jeremy nodded. "I have a feeling it will. She's really motivated to help others. And it sounded like the pediatrician was really excited to have her work with him." He refilled their wine glasses and asked, "What about your work? Anything new on the Vigilante front?"

She made a face. "Ugh. Not really. We're getting pretty frustrated, but we aren't giving up." She sipped her wine. "Any word on the renewal of your grant?"

"Still waiting on the official notice of award, but my program officer says it should come any day." He looked at Ashley. "Maybe after you catch that vigilante guy you could move to San Francisco and be my lab manager." Ashley looked at him thoughtfully. She wasn't sure what she thought about that idea. He added, "You know Vivian is a co-investigator and is negotiating a position at UCSF, so you'd be working with both of us."

Ashley looked away for a moment considering what he had said. Then she turned back to him and replied, "Return to academic research? I don't know. The lead investigator I worked with previously was pretty demanding."

"Well, the lead investigator on the VA grant really likes you, and you could probably negotiate just about anything you wanted."

Ashley laughed and kissed him. "Okay. If we ever catch the vigilante, I promise that I will seriously think about it."

They talked for another hour before Jeremy looked at her and said, "Our flight's pretty early. I guess we should go to bed." He hesitated but then added, "There's the guestroom on the right. Or..."

She pulled him to her and kissed him again. Neither of them made it to the bedroom.

Chapter 120

Georgia and Mississippi, November 2021
  Ashley, Jeremy, and Dordi

Jeremy and Ashley's flight landed nearly an hour before his father's flight, and they waited at the gate where he was expected. Ashley was nervous. She was now officially Jeremy's girlfriend and would soon meet his dad. Of course, he would be meeting *both* of her parents.

"There he is," Jeremy stood and waved when he saw Dordi step through the door of the jetway.

Dordi walked over to his son. They embraced briefly, and then the older man turned to Ashley. "You must be Ashley. Jeremy has told me all about you. People just call me Dordi."

"Hi," Ashley said suddenly at a loss for anything to say. She looked at Dordi and tried to see Jeremy in him. He wasn't as tall as his son but had the same dark hair. Dordi's eyes were a vivid blue, where Jeremy's were brown. Despite his age, Dordi was more muscular than his son, but the jawline was the same as was the arch of their eyebrows. Both men were handsome, though Jeremy's father had a more rugged look to him.

Jeremy asked his dad, "Are you hungry? Ash and I haven't eaten, and we still have a couple of hours before the Jackson flight."

The trio found an amazing, full-service restaurant that made them feel like they were in downtown Atlanta rather than inside an airport. The only thing that gave it away was the huge monitor on the wall that announced arrival and departure times of the various flights.

Ashley already knew everything Dordi had previously told Jeremy about Linh and Song. During the meal, Dordi elaborated as much as he could about Linh's life before the two of them had married. Jeremy asked lots of questions, and mostly Ashley just listened.

"I wish we had thought about DNA testing when she was alive," Jeremy said. "Maybe we could have found Song before."

Ashley touched his arm. "But she'd be so happy to know you found her now. And think how much it will mean to Song—I mean Melinda—to have the letters from your mom."

Several hours later, Ashley's dad found them in baggage claim at the Jackson, Mississippi, airport.

"Hi, Daddy," Ashley said giving her father a big hug. She turned to the two men with her. "This is Jeremy Dordi and his father, Dennis Dordi."

"Nice to meet you, sir," Jeremy said holding out his hand.

"Bob England," Ashley's father said shaking Jeremy's hand. Then he turned to Jeremy's father, "Good to meet you, Dennis. You're the Green Beret. Thank you for your service," he said sincerely as he shook Dordi's hand.

"Thank you. Most people just call me Dordi."

"I'd love to hear about your experience in the war. If you want to talk about it. My dad was killed in '68. During Tet. I barely remember him."

The two fathers walked ahead carrying most of the luggage. Jeremy took Ashley's hand. "You never mentioned your grandfather was in Vietnam."

She smiled and tilted her head coyly. "There are *lots* of things you don't know about me, Jeremy Dordi."

He smiled. "Well, I look forward to learning everything there is to know."

Chapter 121

Mississippi, November 2021
  Melinda, Zach, Jeremy, Dordi, and Ashley

Early the next morning, Jeremy, Ashley, and Dordi were getting ready to leave her parents' house. In less than an hour, they would meet Melinda and Zach for breakfast at a Cracker Barrel restaurant just off I-55 in Jackson. "Are you sure you don't want a little something to eat before you leave?" Ashley's mother, Evelyn, asked the group.

"We're fine, Mom," she laughed. "We'll eat when we get there," she said and gave her a hug. The trio climbed into Evelyn's Oldsmobile sedan, and Ashley adjusted the seat and mirrors before starting the ignition. She waved to her parents as she backed out of the driveway.

"I've never been to Cracker Barrel before," said Jeremy.

"There's one in Sacramento, but it isn't quite the same experience that you get in the South," Ashley replied.

They continued making small talk for the 45-minute drive. Despite being 15 minutes early, when they pulled into the parking lot, Jeremy saw Melinda and Zach were already there. He recognized them from the photos that Melinda had sent. She and Zach were sitting in two of the many rocking chairs that were arranged side by side along the porch that ran across the front of the restaurant. As always, the place was packed.

Ashley parked and they all climbed out of the car. Ashley hung back letting Jeremy and his dad meet Melinda first. She watched from maybe 10 feet away as Jeremy walked up to Melinda. She was looking at her husband and didn't notice Jeremy before he spoke. The woman turned toward Jeremy, and Ashley saw her cover her face with her hands for a moment clearly overcome by emotion. Her husband stood and pulled his wife from her rocker. She was a small woman, short and thin with long, medium brown hair. Ashley knew she was 50 years old, but appeared to be younger. Her husband had to be a foot taller than she was, but he was not as tall as Jeremy. Both Melinda and Zach wore jeans and cowboy boots. Melinda was talking animatedly with her hands. Ashley was content to watch the newly formed family from afar, but suddenly Jeremy realized she wasn't next to him. He looked around and waved her over.

She walked up to the group and held out her hand to Melinda. "Hi. I'm Ashley."

But the woman ignored her hand and embraced her instead. When she let go, she said, "Jeremy tells me you're the reason we're all here, that you talked him into the DNA kit and then encouraged him to talk to his father. I can't thank you enough." Then she embraced her again before Ashley could reply.

Finally the group went inside the restaurant. Its lobby looked like an old-fashioned general store filled to capacity with a random assortment of gifts, books, and candy. Jeremy was looking around trying to take it all in when Melinda said, "It's nearly an hour wait for a table, but Zach and I got here early and put our name down, so it won't be long now."

Indeed, less than 15 minutes later, they were seated at a table. A pretty, young waitress with a long ponytail and a strong Southern accent greeted them. "How y'all doin' today? My name's Risa, and I'll be takin' care of y'all." She poured them all coffee and then scurried off after promising them she would be right back to take their order.

After Risa left, an awkward silence fell over the table. Melinda had so many questions she wanted to ask, but she wanted to be polite. Her first few questions were to ask about their flight and how Ashley and Jeremy had met.

After Melinda's third or fourth icebreaker question, Ashley shook her head. "I'm sure you have many other questions you'd rather know the answers to right now."

Melinda bit her lip and gave Ashley a grateful nod. "I want to know everything. I just don't know where to begin to even ask."

Ashley touched Dordi's arm and said softly, "Tell her how you and Linh met."

Dordi silently gathered his thoughts then he leaned forward, elbows on the table. Just as he started to speak, Risa returned and asked, "Y'all know watcha want?"

The group quickly gave Risa their orders and then all eyes turned to Dordi. Risa was still writing in her order book as Dordi began. He started with seeing Teo get kicked out of the Yankee's Dream. He told them how he had followed the young boy and saw the altercation behind the Noodle Emporium. Without thinking, he told them how he had killed the man who had punched the child and knocked him unconscious. Dordi didn't notice the exchange of concerned glances from everyone at his table, including Risa. Her pen had gone still and hung in the air above her order pad.

Dordi sipped his coffee, and Ashley looked at Risa. "Is everything ok?" she asked the waitress.

"Oh! Yes! Sorry! I'll get these orders to the kitchen." Risa hurried off and the group turned back to Dordi.

Dordi rubbed his chin. "I realized the man was dead. I didn't think I hit him that hard, but I was pretty pissed off. The boy was just so small. I picked him up and started walking. I had no idea where I was going. I heard something behind me. It was Linh. She—" Dordi's eyes teared up and he looked away suddenly aware of Risa refilling everyone's coffee cup. Dordi cleared his throat and continued, "She was the most beautiful woman I had ever seen. Long dark hair and skin that was almost luminous. It was the color of milk caramel. I couldn't take my eyes off her. But I knew she was very young..." His voice trailed off and Dordi retreated into his own private thoughts for a moment.

Just then another waiter brought out a tray of food and set it on a stand next to their table. Risa smiled at him. "Thanks, Billy!" Very slowly, she began to distribute their food. Dordi nodded a thank you to her as she put a plate in front of him. He picked up a fork but didn't eat. He just continued talking about Linh. Once everyone had their food, Risa topped off everyone's coffee as an excuse to keep listening. No one noticed because everyone was completely engrossed in Dordi's story. He added many details that he had not had a chance to share with Jeremy. He choked up when he told them about asking her to leave with him the first time—the time she said no.

All eyes were on Dordi, but Ashley noticed a movement to her left. When she looked up, she saw Risa standing next to the table, coffee pot in hand.

Ashley looked at the waitress. "I don't think we need anything right now, Risa."

"Oh, no! I wasn't checking on y'all," Risa replied waving a hand at Ashley. Then she added, "Honey, I was about to ask if I could pull up a chair and listen in. I wanna know what happens next too." She put a hand on Dordi's shoulder. "Did you convince Linh to change her mind?"

"Eventually," he said, "but it was a couple of years later."

"Oh, that's good. I was worried," the waitress replied and continued to stand next to the table.

Ashley said, "We should be ready to go soon, so maybe you could leave the check now."

Risa frowned. "Oh, okay." She set the coffee pot down, slowly pulled their check from her pad and set it on the table. Then she stood for a minute watching Dordi. When he didn't continue with his story, she reluctantly picked up the coffee pot and turned away to attend to her other tables.

After everyone had finished their breakfast, Melinda and Zach suggested they follow them to their house. "It's not far and we'll be more comfortable."

At the Barker home, Dordi explained why Linh had refused his offer to take her back home with him. "She told me 'Vietnam is my home,' and told me to leave. She was angry and I didn't understand why. But after I was back home I found out completely by accident that she was pregnant. We had never been lovers, so the baby..." He hesitated, looking at Melinda. "You—ah—you weren't my child. She told me later she didn't feel she could leave with me knowing that." He paused and toyed with the coffee cup in his hand. "But I loved her. I would have accepted you. But she didn't know that."

Dordi talked for a long time, his love for Linh evident. He told them what Linh had been told. Her mother had died in childbirth, and her grandfather had given Linh to a homeless girl named Song when she wasn't even a year old. "Song died when she was ten," Dordi told the group. Then he turned to Melinda. "She named you after her."

Dordi had brought numerous pictures of Linh, including one that Juanita had taken of Linh and Song. It was nearly identical to the one Melinda had found in her adoptive mother's attic. She showed it to the group and said, "They must have been taken at the same time."

When he was finished telling Linh's story, Dordi turned to Ashley and held out his hand. She knew he wanted the journal with Linh's letters to Melinda. Dordi had shown it to Ashley and Jeremy the night before, and she put it in her purse for safekeeping. Now she handed it to Dordi. He held it in his hands for a long moment. Part of him didn't want to let it go, but he knew that he had to. It was what Linh wanted and he always did what Linh wanted.

Slowly he pushed the leather bound book across the table. "Linh always hoped that somehow she would find you. When she was diagnosed with cancer, she realized she probably wouldn't. She began writing letters to you. They are here," he said, tapping the book.

Melinda gingerly picked up the book and held it in her own hands. Trembling, she started to open it.

Ashley looked around the table at the three men staring at Melinda. Then she turned back to her and said, "It's okay if you want privacy. We don't mind."

Melinda looked at Ashley and smiled. "Yes, I think I would like a minute to myself. Thank you." She stood and took the journal to her room.

After she had left, the others just sat in silence for a moment. Then Zach decided he should tell them about Melinda. "Her parents told her that her birth mother didn't want her because she was mixed. By the time I met her, she had read enough about Vietnamese culture to understand that was probably true. She had accepted it. She had a good life and loved her parents. It was only after they died and she found that picture and the note that Linh had left her that she realized the truth. She wasn't angry with her parents but became anxious to know more. I'm so grateful to y'all."

Late in the afternoon, Ashley, Jeremy, and Dordi left the Barkers after promising to return the next day. Over dinner with her parents, Ashley, Jeremy, and Dordi relayed the day's events.

Evelyn said, "It's just all so fascinating how y'all found each other using DNA." She took a bite of her dinner and then said absently, "Maybe she'll find her dad now too."

"Oh, I hadn't even thought about him," Jeremy said. He looked at his own father. "Uh, do you know anything about him?"

Dordi shook his head. "No. Linh wasn't certain. She thought he was Australian, though she said he could have been American."

Jeremy shuddered thinking of what his mother had been through. Ashley put a hand on his shoulder and then said, "She should upload her DNA to GEDMatch."

"What's GEDMatch?" asked Bob.

Ashley looked at her dad and explained, "It's an international database. It helps relatives that use different companies or that live in different countries find each other. If Melinda's father is in the U.S., he might have used a *MyDNA* kit instead of one from *DNAStory*. If he isn't in the States—and it sounds like that's a distinct possibility—then GEDMatch is the only chance she has of finding him, at least using DNA."

Chapter 122

Carson, California, December 2021
 Chi and Misty

"Mom!"

Chi heard her daughter call her from the living room. "What is it, Misty? Is everything ok?" Chi was in the kitchen and dried her hands on a towel as she walked into the living room where her daughter was watching the news.

"Did you see the news?!" Misty pointed at the TV, which by then was showing a commercial.

"Well, I don't know. Which story?"

"That vigilante guy. The serial killer. They caught him!" Misty replied, breathless.

"That's wonderful. And why should I care? Was he coming after me next?" Chi teased.

Misty took a deep breath and when she spoke again, she was a little calmer. "They used DNA to find him. Both his sons, who had never met each other, had used DNA kits. But one of the sons was in the U.S. and the other was in Australia, so they didn't get connected at first. After they both uploaded their samples to a third company, called GEDMatch, they found each other. One of the brothers had been adopted and was looking for his birth family. Anyway, using GEDMatch, he found his brother. Even though their father had never given his DNA to GEDMatch, he had left blood at a crime scene. Once the brothers DNA was made available, the CBI was able to show they were related to the Vigilante Virginian. That's how they caught him."

Chi still didn't understand but thought this might have something to do with her trying to find Linh. She asked, "What is that? Ged what?"

"GEDMatch." Rather than explain again, Misty simply told her mother, "If Linh is looking for you, she probably thinks you're still in Vietnam. We need to send your data to GEDMatch!"

Chi smiled. "Yes. Yes, let's do that. Thank you, Misty." Chi turned back toward the kitchen where she had been washing dishes. She still had no idea how GEDMatch might help, but she was willing to try anything. She could tell Misty was excited, and she tried not to get her hopes up too, but it was useless. Maybe, she thought, just maybe I will finally find Linh.

Chapter 123

Carson, California, December 2021
  Chi and Misty

Two days after Christmas, Chi received an email from GEDMatch. "GED-Match has identified a likely relative. Based on our analysis, Melinda Barker of Jackson, Mississippi, is your grandchild, grandparent, or half-sibling."

Chi looked up from the computer. "Misty!"

Misty was in the laundry room sorting clothes. She stuck her head out and called back to her mom, "Yes?"

"Come here! We got an email!"

Misty frowned. Her mother knew how to check her email. Why did she need her? Unhurriedly, she started the washer, moved the next load of clothes out of the way, and walked to the desk where her mother sat.

Misty laughed, "What's with the goofy smile?"

Her mother pointed at the screen. "I have a grandchild."

Chapter 124

Carson, California, February 2022
  Everyone

Chi had, of course, been heartbroken to learn that Linh had died, but she also learned her life had been happy and filled with love. She and Dordi had spoken on the phone numerous times in the last six weeks, and he had told her everything that he could about her daughter. Ashley and Misty had also talked. They had been making arrangements for everyone to meet. It had taken more than a month to coordinate, but finally Chi would meet not only her daughter's husband and their children but also her great-grandchildren.

Everyone had come. Dordi had flown in from Virginia, bringing more photos and Linh's old spiral notebook she had used to improve her writing. Melinda came with her family and even Lucas, who normally hated large gatherings, came with Eden and their children. Ashley and Jeremy were also there, of course. The group was far too big for Misty's small house, so the event took place in a hotel nearby. The group gathered on a large balcony overlooking the pool. Misty leaned back on the railing and just enjoyed watching the group for a few minutes. She was incredibly happy both for her mom and for herself. For so long it had only been the two of them. Now they had a dozen relatives. Although Misty would never get to meet her sister, she now had her sister's family—and it was huge! Her mom was laughing and telling stories in a way she had not seen since her father had died.

Chi and Dordi were the center of attention. They both told stories from the war. Chi confessed to the group that she had been VC. She put a hand on Dordi's knee and spoke directly to him. "I saw you and Linh at Tan Son Nhut in 1971. I would have killed you that day if you hadn't been with Linh."

Ashley was completely captivated by what she heard and wanted to spend much more time with Chi. She told Jeremy, "Maybe I could even write a book about her. I think it would be fascinating!"

"A scientist turned author?" Jeremy mused. "Maybe don't quit your day job." But then realizing Ashley was serious, he added, "Sure. Why not?"

Later when Ashley asked Chi how she would feel about having a book written about her, she answered by giving her Linh's battered notebook, its cover nearly gone. "Maybe tell her story too."

Ashley hugged the old woman and promised that she would.

Epilogue

Over the years after Melinda, Jeremy, Chi, and Dordi met, they stayed close. Ashley wrote and published her book (*Lost and Found: The life and times of two Vietnamese refugees*). She took a copy to Cracker Barrel, and, although Risa no longer worked there, the manager promised to get it to her. The book sold well, but not nearly enough for Ashley to quit working. She did, however, leave her job at CBI so she could take the lab manager position working with Jeremy. The two would eventually marry and both wanted to adopt when the time came.

Although Ken, Bobby, and Jeremy had not been successful in their initial attempt to have California pass the Agent Orange Resolution, they had garnered the support of a number of members of the state legislature and had no intention of giving up. The men were confident that they would eventually get the law passed in all 50 states.

When Chi died at the age of 90, Dordi buried her next to Linh in the grave that would have been his own. He said it just seemed like the right thing to do. After the ceremony, Misty stood at the foot of her sister's grave and looked at the freshly turned earth of her mother's. A thought crossed her mind that made her smile. Mother and daughter—reunited at last.

The Agent Orange Memorial Foundation

Although *Darkness and Light Intertwined* is a work of fiction, non-fiction elements and real people have been woven in with the fictional characters and events. Among these, Ken Gamble and Bobby Tyner, both Vietnam veterans, should be recognized for their tireless efforts on behalf of all veterans of the American War in Vietnam.

Ken Gamble established the Orange Heart Medal Project in January 2018 using his own funds to design the Orange Heart Medal, which is now patented and Trademarked. The Orange Heart Medal Project has been designated a 501c3 organization. Bobby Tyner joined the board of the Orange Heart Foundation in August of 2020.

As of late August 2022, Ken and Bobby have awarded 9382 Agent Orange Medals. Currently, medals are awarded to eligible service members or their surviving family at no charge. At this writing, bill H.R. 4982, to recognize the Agent Orange medal, is under consideration by the Armed Services Committee. This effort is being spearheaded by Mr. Van Drew, a congressman from New Jersey. To make a request, please visit their website. http://www.orangeheartmedal.org/

Ken Gamble also established of the Agent Orange Memorial in Springfield, Tennessee which currently lists 660 names with more individuals to be added in Phase III. The goal is to eventually have all 2.7 million names of those who served in the U.S. Armed Forces in Southeast Asia between November 1, 1955, and May 15, 1975. Applications for a request for a name to be added can also be found on the Orange Heart website.

The Orange Heart Medal Foundation was recently successful in designated a portion of Hwy 41 (Robertson County, Tennessee) as the Orange heart memorial Parkway and a second segment designated the Gold Star Family Highway.

As stated within *Darkness and Light Intertwined*, the foundation is also actively working to have all U.S. states recognize Agent Orange exposure as a war injury. As of August 2022, seven states have passed resolutions on behalf of veterans with Agent Orange exposure. These states are Tennessee, South Carolina, Ohio, Indiana, Alabama, Mississippi, and Texas. Similar laws are currently under consideration by the legislatures of several other states.

End Notes

Multiple people contributed to *Darkness and Light Intertwined,* and I owe debts of gratitude to them all.

The Soldiers:

Mr. Robert Longhauser. Bob spent a year in Vietnam with the U.S. Army 1st Infantry Division and was essential to the crafting of *Lives Intertwined* (Book 2 of the trilogy). As I began to write *Darkness and Light,* he kindly continued to answer questions and provide additional guidance regarding certain fictitious events that are written into the final book of the trilogy.

Anonymous. I had several extensive conversations with a friend I've known since grade school. He joined the Army out of college and spent time in both Afghanistan and Iraq during U.S. military operations in those countries. He prefers not to be named here, but please know that he spent two decades in the Army, was awarded numerous commendations, and retired as a Lt. Colonel a few years ago. Now that he has retired, he spends his days in the Mississippi Delta raising cattle and enjoying his grandchildren. He gave me more information than I could possibly include within the pages of *Darkness and Light Intertwined,* and I've encouraged him to write his memoir. His stories and experiences need to be shared with others.

Paula Austin, USMC, retired. Paula, a close friend for a number of years, has been invaluable to the development of multiple concepts of all three books within the Agent Orange trilogy. Additionally, for *Darkness and Light,* she was able to provide needed insight from the perspective of a female soldier.

Ken Gamble and Bobby Tyner. A very special recognition and my immense thanks go to these men. Their efforts on behalf of Vietnam veterans cannot be understated, and I am grateful they allowed me to write them and their current mission into *Darkness and Light Intertwined.*

Ken Gamble enlisted in the Navy in 1962 and was sent to Vietnam two years later. For his service in-country, he was awarded the Vietnam Service Medal with three battle stars, Vietnam Expedition Medal, Meritorious Service Medal with palm leaf, National Defense Medal, Good Conduct Medal, and the Vietnam Civil Action Medal.

Bobby Tyner enlisted in the U.S. Army in 1965 and spent a year in Vietnam (1966-1967). Sgt. Tyner was discharged from the Army just prior to the end of the war in Vietnam and was awarded the 2 Bronze Star. He currently resides in South Carolina and was instrumental in that state passing the Agent Orange resolution.

The Civilians:

Keri Wiginton. Keri is a health and wellness writer who has written extensively about her continuing journey with endometriosis. Not only did she spend several hours with me on a Zoom call detailing her personal experience with the disease, she also read relevant parts of the book and made important suggestions to keep the story real. Keri is an advocate for women with endometriosis and is especially interested in sharing her experience using nutrition as an adjuvant therapy to manage her symptoms. In large measure, Keri was the inspiration for Alessi's story. A link to her website and several of her writings can be found in the appendix.

Christina Meza. Christina is one of those friends who will tell you like it is even when you don't want to hear it. Her honesty has, without a doubt, made all of the books within the Agent Orange trilogy immensely better. She was the first person who I told when I decided to start writing novels and was the first person with whom I shared draft chapters. Without her early encouragement, feedback, and support, I would never have finished the first book, let alone three. She has been an amazing proofreader and editor, and the reader should know that any mistakes that remain are mine. Much to her dismay, I occasionally rewrite as I make her corrections.

Kevin Osteen, PhD. Kevin has been my friend and research partner for more than three decades. He has also been incredibly supportive of my novel writing and has willingly tolerated my using him as a sounding board for story development. Many years ago, he told me his own experience of watching the draft lottery with his friends. His story was a tremendous help to me as I crafted the lottery experiences of Augie and Mark, and I hope their stories will resonate with others who came of age in those difficult times.

My Family:

Leana Bruner England. Leana is my big sister—19 months older and half an inch taller. Like Christina, she has read numerous draft versions of the trilogy as well as many fledgling chapters. Her willingness to read each of the books while under development, provide early feedback, and *then read them again and again* has been critical as I learn how to write fiction. I cannot express enough how much I love, respect, and appreciate her.

David England. David, my friend as well as brother-in-law, may be my most important beta reader. Like Christina, he won't sugarcoat his opinion if he doesn't like something. Each of the books are better because of his input. Equally important, positive feedback from him is all the more encouraging because he won't say something that isn't heartfelt.

Kristin Burris. Kristin is my first cousin and seems to be in competition with Leana for the moniker of "Kaylon's biggest cheerleader." Because of her tireless efforts on my behalf and her voracious love of reading, she has become my newest beta reader. I am forever grateful for her love and support in all my endeavors.

Cover Design: Miblart.com.

Photo credits: Audrey Noe, back cover author photo; Christina Meza, inside author photo.

Appendix

The following books and websites were valuable to me as I wrote *Darkness and Light Intertwined*:

Agent Orange and Burn Pits
Websites and online articles:
History of Agent Orange (video):
https://www.facebook.com/406812189768330/videos/432093384066889
https://burnpits360.org/about-us/
https://look.substack.com/p/when-the-full-truth-emerged-it-was
https://www.u-s-history.com/pages/h1860.html
https://www.vietnamfulldisclosure.org/children-agent-orange/
https://www.va.gov/disability/dependency-indemnity-compensation/
https://theconversation.com/agent-orange-exposed-how-u-s-chemical-warfare-in-vietnam-unleashed-a-slow-moving-disaster-84572
https://www.acq.osd.mil/eie/Downloads/Congress/Open%20Burn%20Pit%20Report-2019.pdf
https://www.theguardian.com/us-news/2016/feb/16/us-military-burn-pits-chemical-weapons-cancer-illness-iraq-afghanistan-veterans
https://truthout.org/articles/us-military-defoliants-on-okinawa-agent-orange/

Scientific Publications:
Bruner-Tran KL, Mokshagundam S, Barlow A, Ding T, Osteen KG (2019) Paternal Environmental Exposures and Risk of Adverse Pregnancy Outcomes *Journal of Current Obstetrics and Gynecology Reports* 1-11. doi: 10.1007/s13669-

019-00265-w).

Eskenazi B, Ames J, Rauch S, Signorini S, Brambilla P, Mocarelli P, Siracusa C, Holland N, Warner M (2021) Dioxin exposure associated with fecundability and infertility in mothers and daughters of Seveso, Italy. *Human Reproduction.* Feb 18;36(3):794-807. doi: 10.1093/humrep/deaa324.

Ngo AD, Taylor R, Roberts CL, Nguyen TV. Association between Agent Orange and birth defects: systematic review and meta-analysis. Int J Epidemiol. 2006 Oct;35(5):1220-30. doi: 10.1093/ije/dyl038. Epub 2006 Mar 16.

Rier SE, Martin DC, Bowman RE, Dmowski WP, Becker JL (1993) Endometriosis in rhesus monkeys (Macaca mulatta) following chronic exposure to 2,3,7,8-tetrachlorodibenzo-p-dioxin. *Fundamentals of Applied Toxicology.* 1993 Nov;21(4):433-41. doi: 10.1006/faat.1993.1119.

Rumph JT, Stephens VR, Archibong AE, Osteen KG, Bruner-Tran KL (2020) Environmental Endocrine Disruptors and Endometriosis. *Advances in Anatomy Embryology and Cell Biology.* 232:57-78. doi: 10.1007/978-3-030-51856-1_4.

Combat photography

https://www.pbs.org/newshour/nation/pentagon-releases-military-photographers-stunning-photo-last-moments

https://contrastly.com/what-its-like-to-be-a-photographer-for-the-military/

https://www.newsweek.com/exhibit-war-photos-iraq-and-afghanistan-89767

https://www.pbs.org/newshour/show/female-photojournalists-discuss-their-work-in-iraq

Draft Lottery, 1969

https://www.youtube.com/watch?v=OkJH6sapQMA

https://youtu.be/25cmARmo5qs

Endometriosis:

https://www.gynecologiconcologyinstitute.org/endometriosis/endometriosis-gastrointestinal-symptoms/

Endometriosis Association https://endometriosisassn.org/

World Endometriosis Research Foundation https://endometriosisfoundation.org/

Endometriosis and Suicide by Rachel Cohen: https://adenofighters.wordpress.com/2016/10/12/endometriosis-and-suicide-an-excellent-article-by-rachel-cohen/

Endometriosis and Risk of Suicide by Phillipa Brdge-Cook: https://www.hormonesmatter.com/endometriosis-risk-suicide/

Keri Wiginton, health writer and endometriosis advocate. Her info and writing can be found at www.keriwiginton.com and/or keriwiginton.contently.com,

Below the Belt, a documentary directed by Shannon Cohn. https://www.belowthebelt.film/

First Indochina War

https://sites.tufts.edu/atrocityendings/2015/08/07/indochina-1st-indochina-war/

Info on Veteran suicide/PTSD:

U.S. Department of Veterans Affairs: https://www.ptsd.va.gov/

Suicide Awareness Voices of Education: https://save.org/

LA Riots

https://www.history.com/topics/1990s/the-los-angeles-riots

Marijuana use during the Vietnam War

https://wayofleaf.com/blog/marijuana-during-the-vietnam-war

https://www.history.com/news/drug-use-in-vietnam

Operation Babylift:

War Cradle: The Untold Story of Operation Babylift, by Shirley Peck-

Barnes

Personal Stories:

https://cherrieswriter.com/2012/03/08/vietnam-freedom-bird-why-cant-i-remember-the-ride/

https://pbase.com/rcalmes/image/53407815 (short-timer calendar)

https://archive.ec47.com/dnangpic.htm (photos of DaNang AB, 1970, Ed Bennigfield)

Rock Apes and other weirdness https://mysteriousuniverse.org/2017/01/bizarre-encounters-with-the-weird-in-the-vietnam-war

Refugee Camp

https://graphics.latimes.com/tent-city/

https://www.cbs8.com/article/news/local/zevely-zone/san-diego-vietnam-refugees-camp-pendletons-tent-city-45-years-later/509-c957a545-9862-4b4f-aa8c-2482db6d7f87

Vietnam War Medals

https://www.medalsofamerica.com/blog/vietnam-war-medals-meanings/

Vietnam after the war

https://money.cnn.com/magazines/fortune/fortune_archive/2000/05/01/278967/index.htm

https://www.youtube.com/watch?v=abdI0dK7sMk

Vietnamese Women in the war

Websites:

https://www.indiewire.com/2017/09/the-vietnam-war-ken-burns-lynn-novick-mai-elliott-women-truck-drivers-pbs-1201880165/

https://rarehistoricalphotos.com/female-viet-cong-guerrila-1972/

https://www.scmp.com/news/asia/southeast-asia/article/2130573/behind-enemy-lines-vietnams-female-spies-who-helped-change

https://www.girlmuseum.org/girls-undercover-women-spies-of-the-viet-cong/

Opinion | South Vietnam's 'Daredevil Girls' - The New York Times (nytimes.com)

https://www.bbc.com/news/in-pictures-37986986

Books:

Even the Women Must Fight: Memories of War from North Vietnam by Karen Gottschang Turner with Phan Thanh Hao

Viet Cong Tunnels:

https://medium.com/@willrussell_46069/life-of-a-tunnel-rat-in-vietnam-ab1fe5394232 (warning: graphic descriptions)

https://www.wearethemighty.com/popular/viet-cong-vietnam-war-tunnels/

Viet Minh/Viet Cong:

https://classroom.synonym.com/difference-between-viet-cong-and-viet-minh-12083891.html

https://alphahistory.com/vietnamwar/viet-minh/

https://politicandthevietnamwar.weebly.com/geneva-conference-1954.html

https://www.historyplace.com/unitedstates/vietnam/index-1945.html

About the Author

Kaylon Bruner Tran holds a PhD in reproductive pathology and is passionate about understanding how diet and environmental exposures interact to impact human health across generations. She has always loved writing and storytelling. Long ago, she began writing personal essays to help her remember special or funny events in her own life. When her sons were very little, she was annoyed that so many cartoons included an evil scientist. In response, she began making up stories about good scientists to tell them at bedtime. Now she is weaving the personal and professional struggles of good scientists into novels for adults.

If you enjoyed *Darkness and Light Intertwined*, please consider leaving a review on Amazon, Good Reads, or your favorite book review website. Kaylon reads every one and is very grateful for the feed back.

If interested, you can follow Kaylon on Facebook (Kaylon Bruner Tran, PhD) or visit her website at www.kaylonbrunertran.com.

Also by Kaylon Bruner Tran

Time Intertwined: Book 1 of the Agent Orange Trilogy

Time Intertwined weaves neglected aspects of the Vietnam War into solving a modern-day genealogical mystery.

Lives Intertwined: Book 2 of the Agent Orange Trilogy

Lives Intertwined follows the use of DNA analysis in the hunt for a serial killer. However, the results reveal far more than what was intended and has ripple effects across two continents and multiple lives.

Edge of Justice

Edge of Justice is a slightly spicy psychological thriller that follows Maggie Dalrymple's online dating nightmare. It will leave you asking, "How do you define justice?"

Deadly Deceit

Dr. Jeffrey Stanton fell for Leslie the moment she smiled at him, but he never expected his obsession with her would put his freedom—and even his life—in jeopardy. *Deadly Deceit* will make you wonder, "How well do I really know my spouse?"